His ...
but ...
One look at Lexi and he knew
she belonged to him.
She was created for him.
And he'd never
let her go...

Praise

Sea Haven novels

"A new cast of characters as heartwarmingly interesting as those in her Drake Sisters novels and as steamy as those in her Dark novels." —Fresh Fiction

"The Queen of paranormal romance." —USA Today

"Ms. Feehan is at the top of her game with this magical romance." —The Romance Readers Connection

"Suspenseful, engaging—fraught with magic, action and romance . . . I HAVE to read the next one in the series." —Smexy Books

"An action-packed and romantic tale. Awesome as always!" —RT Book Reviews

"Avid readers of Ms. Feehan's work should dive in." —Fiction Vixen

"Once again, Christine Feehan brings a sizzling story of seduction and sorcery to her readers. Fans of previous Feehan novels, particularly the Drake Sisters series, will be enchanted by her new series." —Examiner.com

"Stunning, vivid, lushly visual . . . It's the perfect way to escape." —Romance Books Forum

"A wonderful love story . . . Truly original." —Penelope's Romance Reviews

CH

Earth Bound

CHRISTINE FEEHAN

JOVE BOOKS, NEW YORK

JOVE

An imprint of Penguin Random House LLC
375 Hudson Street, New York, New York 10014

EARTH BOUND

A Jove Book / published by arrangement with the author

ISBN: 978-0-515-15557-0

PUBLISHING HISTORY
Jove mass-market edition / July 2015

PRINTED IN THE UNITED STATES OF AMERICA

10 9 8 7 6 5 4 3 2 1

Cover illustration by Dan O'Leary.
Cover design by George Long.
Cover handlettering by Ron Zinn.

Penguin
Random
House

For Charlotte, with love

Be sure to go to christinefeehan.com/members/ to sign up for my PRIVATE book announcement list and download the FREE ebook of *Dark Desserts*. Join my community and get firsthand news, enter the book discussions, ask your questions and chat with me. Please feel free to email me at Christine@ christinefeehan.com. I would love to hear from you. Each year, the last weekend of February, I would love for you to join me at my annual FAN event, an exclusive weekend with an intimate number of readers for lots of fun, fabulous gifts and a wonderful time. Look for more information at fanconvention.net.

ACKNOWLEDGMENTS

No book can be written without a little help along the way somewhere. I would like to thank my wonderful power hour sisters, C. L. Wilson, Kathie Firzlaff, Susan Edwards and Karen Rose! And thank you to Brian, of course. As always, Domini, thank you for your help when I need that extra research done *right now*, and to Brian Feehan for brainstorming to activate the brain cells in a crunch. You all are the best!

1

PAIN was a strange entity. It could live and breathe, existing in every cell in one's body. It could cripple, rob one of breath, of dignity, of quality of life. Pain could be the first thing one felt when waking and the last thing one felt when falling asleep. It was an insidious enemy. Silent. Unseen. Deadly. Gavriil Prakenskii had decided some time ago to make pain his friend.

If he was going to survive, if it was even possible with pain as his companion, he would come to terms with it—and he had. Until this moment. Until pain wasn't about the physical or the mental, but all about the emotional. That was an entirely different kind of pain, and one he was completely unprepared for.

His life was one of absolute discipline and control. He planned his every move, and his contingency plans had backup contingency plans. There was never a moment that he wasn't ready for. There was never a time when anything shocked or surprised him. He stayed alive that way. He had no friends, and he thought of everyone he encountered as an enemy. The few people he had ever allowed himself to feel even a drop of friendship with had eventually betrayed him, and he simply counted those painful moments as important lessons to be learned.

He was used to deceit and betrayal. To blood, torture, pain and death. He was used to being alone. He was most comfortable in that world because he understood it. He was thirty-seven years old and he'd been in that world since he'd been a child. He knew more ways to kill or torture a human being than he could count. It was instinctive, automatic and a natural part of him. He carried death with him the way others might carry their identities, because he *was* death. If he came out of the shadows, even for a moment, it was to deliver that killing blow.

Few ever saw him. He lived in a shadowy world, and moved through it like a phantom, a ghost in the night, leaving dead bodies in his wake. He wasn't real, was nothing more than a shadow someone might catch a glimpse of. Insubstantial. Without substance. He hadn't been human in years. Yet here he stood in the early morning, dawn streaking long rays of light through the velvet black of night with his well-ordered world crumbling around him so that he felt the earth actually move under him.

His palm itched. Not a small nagging itch, but a full-blown do-something-this-minute-to-alleviate-it itch. Gavriil pressed his hand tightly into his thigh and held it there, his heart suddenly beating hard in his chest. Life sometimes threw curves at the most unexpected times—yet he should have known this might happen.

He had walked into a place of power. Energy rippled in the air and came up through the ground. It was in the wind and in the very water he felt flowing beneath the ground. This place, this farm he had come to, was dangerous and yet he hadn't heeded the warnings—hadn't expected the danger would be to him or what form it would take. He had come, and now someone would pay the price.

A young woman came toward him through a field of corn, the stalks taller than she was. She moved with grace, a fluid easy manner, occasionally stopping to pull one of the ears down and inspect it.

He couldn't take his eyes from her or the way the plants leaned toward her, as if *she* were the sun, not that bright ball beginning its climb into the sky. She was dressed in vintage blue jeans, frayed, full of holes and faded light from many washings, and a carelessly buttoned dark blue plaid shirt. He knew she'd buttoned it carelessly because the top and bottom buttons were undone, and he had a ridiculous urge to slip them into the closures for her—or maybe open all the rest.

Her auburn hair was very long, probably past her waist, and very thick, but she had it pulled back away from her face in a careless ponytail. Her face was oval and rather pale, but her eyes, as they surveyed the cornstalks, were a striking cool, forest green. Even in the dim early morning light, he could see her intriguing eyes, surrounded by long dark lashes. Her mouth was full and luscious, her teeth white and small.

Even dressed in her working clothes, there was no hiding her figure. Full breasts and a small tucked-in waist emphasized the flaring of her hips. She was a pixie, ethereal, just as unreal as he was, and she was so beautiful it hurt.

He knew her. He had always known her. He'd known she was somewhere in the world waiting, and the itch in his palm and the pain paralyzing his mind told him this woman belonged to him and only him. How completely unexpected and unacceptable was that?

He'd come to the small town of Sea Haven off the northern California coast to warn his youngest brother, Ilya, that he was on the same hit list as the rest of the family and to see his other three brothers who had settled there. Seven brothers, stepping-stones, their parents had called them, torn apart when they were children. They'd been forced to watch the murder of their parents, and then they'd been taken and kept separated in the hopes that they would forget all about one another. Now, all seven were on a hit list.

Gavriil had known it was coming, he just wished they'd had more time to prepare.

He watched the woman as she continued toward him. He was deep in the shadows and utterly still so that there was no chance of drawing her gaze. She had just changed his entire plans. His entire existence. As she stepped out of the cornfield and the light bathed her face, he could see her flawless skin, the curve of her cheek and high cheekbones.

She looked far too young for a man like him. It had nothing to do with age and everything to do with who and what he was. Still. His palm itched, and that sealed her fate. He wasn't about to throw away the only thing in the world he could truly call his own. He didn't have much to offer her. He was hard and callous and damned cynical when it came to the world around him. He could be ruthless and merciless as well and he would be, he knew, if anyone tried to stand between this young woman and him.

He didn't even care in that moment, with the dawn breaking, spilling a fire of red into all that glorious hair, that he didn't deserve her. Or that he didn't even know her or she him . . . He didn't care that he was far older and as lethal as hell and had no business with a woman like her or that his body was in pieces and he looked like a rag doll sewn together. None of it mattered to him.

She belonged to him, this woman. She was created for him. She was the one woman he could bind to him. Gavriil pressed his thumb into the center of his palm. He was broken, and there was no fixing him. He was a killer, and there was no taking that back either. He didn't get a do-over— and that emotional insight, that pain, was far worse of a burden than the physical one he bore.

She was the youngest woman on the farm where his brothers lived. Lexi, they called her. She turned her head abruptly toward the back of the property and just as suddenly switched direction.

The moment he'd stepped onto the property, the large farm with his brothers and the six women living on it, he'd felt the ripples of power and knew the farm was protected, not only by his brothers, who were dangerous, but by elements. Earth. Air. Water. Fire. He even felt spirit.

Had he been less powerful in his own right, without his own gifts, he would have been far more cautious about following her through the thick foliage along a broken path. Nothing could deter him from his chosen course. He was stalking his prey, moving like the ghost he was through the heavy foliage as she made her way toward some secret destination.

Gavriil knew she was going somewhere important to her, and that she didn't want anyone to know. She moved stealthily and occasionally darted little glances around her, as if she suspected someone watched her. He knew he wouldn't set off her radar. He didn't give off enough energy to do that, not even when he was slipping up on his prey and about to deliver the killing blow.

He glided rather than stepped. He had learned to walk softly in his school as a young boy, but pain was an even better teacher. Taking heavier steps jarred his body. She was moving faster now, heading straight for a vehicle, a small open wagon, and she'd gone quite pale.

Something was wrong. He glanced around him, looking for wildlife, a bird, a squirrel, anything at all. The skies were suspiciously empty. He didn't trust it when a forest was silent in the early morning hours. Even the insects had ceased their continuous racket. Something was terribly wrong. He felt it with every step he took. He could tell she felt it as well, but she didn't believe.

Lexi Thompson hurried along the faint path leading to the back of the property where she'd left the little trail wagon parked. She wanted to take another look at the adjoining property that was up for sale—now in escrow. Thomas and Levi had put a bid on it, and the owners had sold quickly without negotiating too long. She was very excited about the possibilities the acreage represented.

The farm was doing so well. The new greenhouse was

already producing far more than she expected the first year out. The orchards were yielding large crops, and the fruit was fantastic. Her lettuce field had been ruined by a helicopter landing right in the middle of it when some men had come to kidnap her sister Airiana, but she still had managed to save some of the crop and Max had managed to save Airiana.

The bottom line was Lexi needed more space—and someone to help. All the other women had jobs away from the farm. In the beginning those other businesses had been necessary to support the farm, but this year they'd gone from running in the red to being comfortably in the black, and she intended it to stay that way. She worked hard every single day, from sunrise to sunset and sometimes more. She poured herself into the farm, and at times it was frustrating, backbreaking work. There was only one of her and she needed help if the farm was to continue to sustain them.

She sighed softly. The problem was her sisters loved living on the farm and eating the food, but each of them had their own business—ones they loved—outside the farm. She wasn't certain how to approach the others to tell them she needed more full-time help.

Lexi stuck her thumbnail in her mouth and bit down on it repeatedly, a long leftover habit she continually vowed she'd quit. When she realized what she was doing, she snatched her thumbnail from between her teeth and rubbed her palm down the side of her jeans.

She was suddenly uneasy, and she stopped and took a careful look around. She spent most nights sitting on her porch swing, apprehension growing in her. She knew she was paranoid, especially ever since her sister of the heart Airiana and her fiancé, Max, brought home four very traumatized children.

The children's parents and a sister had been murdered and the children abducted by a human trafficking ring. Had not Airiana and Max rescued them, they would have been killed.

Knowing children were on the farm, that they were vulnerable and at any moment something terrible could happen to them, had made her more paranoid than ever. She realized her thumbnail was between her teeth again and she blew out her breath in total exasperation.

She detested being the weak link on the farm with her panic attacks and paranoia. She tried to make up for her failings by working long hours and making a success of their family business. She couldn't sleep in her house, or bed. She'd tried, and she just couldn't do it.

To her everlasting shame, when she was so exhausted she knew she had to sleep, she would sleep in the porch swing, or in the sleeping bag she had stashed in the corner of the porch, out of sight. Sometimes she even slept on the roof. She knew it was silly, but the house didn't feel safe to her. Nothing felt safe.

Fortunately, she lived alone, so nobody knew how truly paranoid she was. There were weapons stashed all over her house, taped under tables and down the cushions of the furniture, so many she was afraid to have the children visit her home—but she wasn't actually certain she could harm another human being. Well—she had—but it had made her sick.

She lived on the farm with warriors, yet she, the most paranoid of all, felt powerless to harm others. She could barely kill a snail eating her precious crops. She felt weak beside the others, the weak link they all had to rally around and protect. Things were tense on the farm and it seemed as if they needed warriors more than breadwinners.

The trail wagon was right where she'd left it when she took her early morning walk through the gardens and various crops, the keys still in the ignition. She slipped inside the open vehicle and paused with her hand on the keys to take another long look around her. She was even more uneasy than usual.

Dread filled her. She could feel the emotion as if it was an actual being, pouring inside her like an insidious monster, robbing her of her ability to breathe, to think, to do anything but sit still, her mouth dry and her heart pounding

too fast. She jammed her fist into her mouth for a moment—
the absolute wrong thing to do.

When she was in a full-blown panic attack she couldn't
even move. She was frozen to the spot, useless to her family. A liability. She worked out every single day. She went
religiously to self-defense training. She could shoot a gun
and throw a knife accurately at any target—even moving
targets. What was wrong with her that she couldn't be like
her sisters?

She swallowed a sob and forced her mind to work properly. *Nothing* was wrong. Nothing. No one could get on the
farm with their warning system. Each of her sisters of the
heart was bound to an element, and the three men residing
with them were just as gifted. Should anyone wishing them
harm come to the farm, Air would call to Max and Airiana.
Earth would tell her. Water would summon Rikki. Judith,
bound to spirit, would feel any disruption at all. Fire called
to Lissa. And Blythe just knew.

*No one could possibly slip through the power rippling
throughout the farm, not with the men, Judith and Blythe
amplifying it,* she reminded herself.

She forced air through her lungs, always grateful her
family rarely witnessed these moments of weakness. She'd
been certain the addition of the men to their family farm as
well as all the self-defense and weapons training would
help her through the panic attacks, maybe even make them
stop altogether. It hadn't happened.

"What's wrong with you?" she murmured aloud, and
started the ignition. "You're such a freakin' baby."

Straightening her shoulders, she drove determinedly toward the back entrance, the gate that led to the road that
came into their property virtually through a forest. She felt
as if the towering trees were guardians watching over those
living on the farm. She loved that they were surrounded on
three sides by forest. Some of their acreage remained part
of a mixed forest, but behind them the trees were thick and
untouched. She drove down the road to the entrance to the

next property. She coveted that acreage—she had from the moment it had come up for sale.

Lexi turned off the engine and sat for a moment just drinking in the sight of all that beautiful soil, untouched. No one had ever lived on or worked the property, and she'd often pushed her hands deep into the dirt and felt the rich loam just waiting to grow something beautiful.

Usually when she came to this spot, any residual feelings of fear vanished, but it didn't seem to be happening now. She still felt as if she couldn't quite breathe, as if air was just out of reach. Her lungs burned and her stomach churned. She slipped from the trail wagon and walked to the gate of the property bordering hers, crouching down to push her hands into the rich soil—another trick that helped when her mind refused to calm.

The moment the soil closed around her hands the peace she so desperately needed slipped into her. She knelt there beside the gate, pushing her hands deep, feeling a connection to the earth that set her heart soaring free. She felt the ebb and flow of the water running beneath the ground, the heartbeat of the earth, the very sap flowing in the trees. The connection was strong—deep—and she knew it would always be her saving grace.

The ground around her hands shivered, and her eyes flew open in sudden alarm. She moistened her lips and looked down at the soil where she'd buried her hands. Her heart skipped a beat and her mouth went dry. She could see the boot prints stamped into the soft ground. Worse, on the gate was a symbol. She'd seen the symbol hundreds of times. It was burned into the wood, a brand, a sheaf of wheat tied with a cord. The same symbol was burned into her upper left thigh.

Bile rose and she fought it down. She would not lose it, not now when everything she had fought for was at stake. Levi, Rikki's husband, had told her not to leave the farm—that it wasn't safe yet. Her sister Airiana had a madman after her, so the farm was virtually on lockdown. Their combined gifts protected the farm itself, but not them if they went off the property.

"Did you think I wouldn't find you, Alexia?"

Her body froze. The air rushed out of her lungs. She closed her eyes briefly. She knew that voice—she would never get it out of her head. Sometimes when she rocked on her front porch swing in the middle of the night, wide awake, she would hear his voice—that hated, horrible, holier-than-thou voice commanding her to her knees. Commanding her to pray for forgiveness, commanding her to perform unspeakable acts to atone for her sins and then flogging the skin off her while demanding she thank him for saving her from her corrupt, disgusting body.

She lifted her head slowly, keeping her hands buried in the soil, trying to find her breath, her resolve. She'd trained for this moment, and yet now that it was here, just his voice alone had her body solidly frozen. Her mind refused to compute beyond terror.

"While you're there on your knees, you might consider begging forgiveness."

She closed her eyes briefly, terrified to look up, but knowing she had to. A thousand plans were formulated and then discarded. Duncan Caine. He always made her feel so powerless. His punishments were the worst. He was enforcer to one of the branches of the cult the Reverend RJ had started. The Reverend, who had started the cult, and Caine were cousins and cut from the same depraved, sick cloth.

She swallowed hard, desperate not to give him the satisfaction of her being sick all over his polished boots. She was not going back with him. She'd told the police all along to look for Caine, that he was still alive, but they assured her he was killed in a shoot-out when they'd raided the farm and arrested several key members of the cult.

This man had crawled through her bedroom window in the middle of the night with her parents right down the hall. He'd held a knife to her little sister's throat and told her he'd kill her sister if she didn't come with him. She'd gone, and she was grateful she didn't struggle. Caine's men surrounded her home, ready to murder her parents, older brothers and her little sister. She'd gone quietly with him to protect her family.

She'd been eight years old, and her life had changed forever. She'd been beaten, starved and raped, forced to "marry" Caine and become his "wife." The one saving grace had been the farm. He'd forced her to work from sunup to sunset, and she'd loved every second of her hands in the soil, coaxing the plants to grow. She could forget her life and pretend she was a girl on a farm with no endless nights of hell to worry about.

Caine and the other cult members had learned that with her working the farm, they prospered. That didn't stop the beatings or the cruelty; if anything, Caine wanted her cowered and completely under his thumb. He'd dug a hole in the ground and forced her into it several times after beating her senseless. The problem with the punishment, he found, was that she healed fast and didn't seem to mind being in the ground with the soil all around her, so he'd found a metal box and when he was especially drunk and feeling mean, would force her into it.

"Did you really think anyone could keep you from me? Your betrayal has brought God's wrath down on you and you will be punished. I've searched for you, a cheating, betraying wife. Jezebel. God sent me to save you in spite of yourself."

He reached down and grabbed her ponytail, yanking her head up so that her eyes were forced to meet his. He wore his beard bushy to cover his weak chin and his eyes blazed fire like a madman's. He'd been the demon in every one of her nightmares. He was the devil, evil incarnate.

He leaned close to her, pressing his foul-smelling mouth next to her ear. "I killed them all, one by one. I told them you wanted them dead in order to be with me. I knew that's where I made my mistake. You didn't cleave to your husband as you should have because the sins of your former life were too great for you to overcome as long as those sinners lived. You had to be shown the way. You had to be punished."

He slapped her face hard, knocking her backward, bringing tears to her eyes. When she would have been driven back by the blow, his hand holding her ponytail kept her from falling. He rained blows on her, using his fist as well as his open hand.

Lexi barely felt the attack after the initial slap, managing to kick out with her legs, as she'd practiced over and over in the gym with her brothers-in-law. She hit him hard in one knee and a thigh with the heels of her boots. He cursed at her as he fell into the gate. She rolled, astonished that the move actually worked.

Slamming her fists as deep as possible into the soil, she directed the seismic energy straight at the man who had turned her life into a living hell. She put every ounce of fear and anger, helplessness and despair he'd made her feel into the blow. All the pain. The grief at the loss of her family. All of it went into the terrible strike directed at him.

The earth shook beneath her fists, the ripples spreading out, rushing beneath the ground straight at its target. Caine struggled to his feet, dragging himself up using the fence post.

"You bitch. You're going to pay for that." He winced when he tried to take a step, and his knee crumpled out from under him.

A vein appeared in the ground, zigzagging like a snake, widening as it approached Caine. Her eyes widened in horror and she pulled her fists out of the earth fast, but it was too late. The crack became an abyss, opening directly under Caine and the gate, dropping them both into the fissure. The crevice wasn't extraordinarily deep and it slammed closed on Caine's legs, crushing them, trapping them in the ground. He screamed and screamed.

Horrified, she stumbled backward. Two men raced toward her from the other side of the fence, leaping over it, one breaking off to try to aid their leader while the other rushed her. He held a very large knife in his fist. She recognized both men. They had been training under Caine, doing enforcing and punishing of members who committed any infraction against the cult when she'd been there.

Peter Rogers was the man desperately trying to dig Caine free while Darrin Jorgenson came at her with a knife.

"Kill her. Kill the bitch," Caine screamed over and over, tears running down his face. His upper torso flopped over the ground, his face suddenly buried in the dirt.

She tried to make her brain work, tried to remember what Levi had told her to do, but she couldn't think, couldn't move. She stood waiting for the death blow, thankful that at least she'd managed to stop Caine from taking her away with him.

There was no sound. None. Later, when she thought about it, she felt as if the very earth had taken a breath. Time slowed down. She saw each step Darrin took as if he was in slow motion. She literally could see every breath he drew and the lines of fanatical hatred on his face.

She didn't take her eyes from him, watching him come closer and closer, waiting for him, relieved now that it was over.

A hole blossomed in the middle of Darrin's forehead, a bright red crater that knocked him backward, the blow hard enough to jerk his head back and send his body flying through the air to land in a heap on the ground.

Lexi stared at the body, uncomprehending. A hard arm circled her waist and dragged her backward, thrusting her behind a man she'd never seen before. He was tall, with axe handle shoulders, a thick chest and shaggy hair. At first she thought it was Levi, Rikki's husband, but he moved differently and he was . . . bigger. More muscular.

He strode toward Caine and Rogers, covering the ground as if he moved above it rather than on it. He was smooth and fluid and something out of a movie with his long coat swirling around him. He raised his hand as he approached the two men and squeezed the trigger of his pistol just once. Peter Rogers dropped to the ground like a stone. Lexi jammed her fist into her mouth to keep from making a sound.

Gavriil crouched down beside Caine, lifting his head by his hair, staring into his eyes. Evil stared back at him malevolently. Caine's legs were crushed, but Lexi had managed to keep the crevice from killing him. Caine looked past Gavriil to Lexi and spat on the ground.

"You whore. You're dead. I'll kill you slow. Your devil won't save you. No one can save you. Your name is written in the book of the reaper in blood."

"Save it for your parishioners in hell." Gavriil kept his voice soft, so there was no way Lexi could hear. Deliberately he dropped Caine's head harder than necessary so that his face landed in the dirt. He leaned down, putting his mouth close to Caine's ear. "I'll be coming back without her, and I know more ways to make you welcome death than you can possibly imagine. Stay alive for me, will you?"

Gavriil rose, turning back to Lexi. Her face was stark white, her eyes enormous. "Are you all right? Any broken bones?"

She still couldn't move, not even when he reached her, holstering his gun in the shoulder harness and reaching out to run both hands over her, searching for damage. Terrible tremors wracked her body and she couldn't catch her breath. She didn't dare look at him or she'd cry. If she looked at Caine or the two dead men, she'd throw up.

"Lexi, talk to me. Look at me. Look at my eyes." His fingers smoothed over a bruise already marring her cheek. The pad of his thumb removed a small trickle of blood at the corner of her mouth.

There was something commanding, compelling in his voice—not at all like Caine, but more in a velvet soft, mesmerizing, *worried* tone. As if her health was the most important thing in this man's world. Lexi forced her gaze upward, over his broad chest where the thin black shirt he wore beneath his open coat was stretched tight over well-defined muscles. Her gaze continued upward, past his strong, shadowed jaw and straight nose until she found herself staring into eyes as dark as midnight. Beautiful eyes. Eyes she was certain she'd seen before. Her breath caught in her throat.

She let herself fall into his dark blue gaze, her only refuge. The world around her receded until there was only this man and his amazing eyes holding her safe.

"Do you know who I am?" His voice was infinitely gentle. A wisp of sound with no impatience, no threat, only concern.

She shook her head mutely. She couldn't find her voice. Her hands trembled, and she twisted her fingers together to try to get the shaking under control. She was definitely in shock. Violence was abhorrent to her, although she *had* defended herself. She just couldn't look at the dead bodies, or Caine, still alive, still a threat.

Her gaze, in spite of it all, began to shift toward him.

"Have you heard the name Gavriil before? Or Prakenskii?"

Gavriil deliberately spoke softly in a Russian accent as he framed her face with his hands. "Look only at me, *angel moy*, nowhere else. Only at me."

He watched her eyes widen. She nodded, some of the shock receding. "I'm here, and I'm going to take care of this. Don't look at them. Don't look at him. I need to know if you're hurt."

She swallowed hard, her breath still shallow and labored, her eyes still bouncing a little, but she didn't pull away from him and her gaze was steadier on his.

"No. No broken bones. He's very good at beating up a woman but making certain she can work the next day."

"You know this man?"

"I'm the whore's husband," Caine shrieked. "She's a Jezebel. Look what she's done to me. She made a deal with the devil. She's a witch, worshiping Satan, holding him hostage between her legs."

Her face went completely white. She looked as if she might faint. Gavriil held her head firmly to prevent her from looking at the man claiming to be her husband. "Don't look at him. He's nothing. He can't hurt you, not ever again," Gavriil said, keeping his voice as gentle as ever. "I need you to go sit in your wagon there for a moment. I'll be right with you. Can you walk?"

She nodded, and Gavriil turned her around, away from Caine and the obscenities he continued to shout in between screaming and crying and desperately digging at the dirt holding his legs captive. Gavriil waited until she had crossed the road to slip into the trail wagon before once more crouching down beside Caine. He gripped Caine's hair in a vicious grip, dragging his head up.

"We'll have a conversation very soon, you and me, but not right now. Never call yourself her husband again. Not out loud and not in your mind." As he held up Caine's head by his hair with one hand, the other took a fistful of dirt, shoving it in, packing it tight and then holding his hand over his mouth and nose. "I don't have soap with me, so this will have to do."

Gavriil was strong and he made certain Caine could see the casual way he cut off all air one-handed before he dropped the man's head on the ground again and left him to try to pry and spit the dirt from his mouth. He kept his body between Lexi and Caine so she couldn't see the man or what he'd done to him. He leaned into the trail wagon.

"He's not my husband. They told me the marriage wasn't legal. I was eight years old and he kidnapped me. He's not my husband," she denied, tears shimmering in her eyes. A few trickled down her face.

"I'm well aware of that," Gavriil said, and used the pads of his fingers to brush the tears away. "I don't want you to think about him ever again. He's totally insignificant. A worm. Less than that."

"He'll never stop coming after me. He won't. I have to call the sheriff right away and tell him what I've done," Lexi said. "They'll send me away from here and I don't know what I'll do. I can't start all over again. I just don't . . ." She trailed off, tears swimming in her eyes.

"There's no need to call the sheriff," he said gently. "I want you to let me take care of this. You go back to your home and call Levi, Thomas and Max. Tell them what happened, but don't let anyone overhear. I know Max has children. We don't want to frighten them after all they've been through."

"They'll make me leave," she whispered again, her hand going protectively to her throat.

"Who? No one can make you leave," Gavriil assured her, struggling to understand.

"I'm in witness protection. I'm supposed to call a number and they'll come and get me. They'll take me away from everyone, and I'll never get to see my sisters or the farm again." Tears tracked down her face. "He's got followers, others who will come for me. They kill entire families. They killed mine."

Gavriil felt everything in him go still. It took control not to look back at the man who had kidnapped a child and then murdered her family, forcing her to become his "wife." "Look at me, Lexi. Right now. Don't think about anything else. Just look at me."

Lexi's tear-drenched eyes met his. He smiled at her, more a showing of his teeth than an actual smile, because he wanted to kill the son of a bitch right then. He watched her take a deep, shuddering breath.

"We'll handle this. You'll never see these men again. We'll figure out how they found you and we'll make certain it doesn't happen again. The farm is safe. They couldn't get on the farm without any of you knowing."

She frowned and looked around her, back toward the farm. "But you did, didn't you?" she asked suddenly, comprehending. "You were following me."

"I belong on the farm," Gavriil said, keeping his voice as gentle as he could. Caine was back to shouting obscenities at Lexi, clearly not learning his lesson. "The warning system already in place recognized me—recognized that I belonged here." He reiterated it, wanting her to begin to accept it as fact.

She nodded slowly. "Thank you for saving my life. They would have killed me."

"I'm sorry I was slow getting here. I don't move quite as fast as I used to." His body was screaming at him, protesting every step he took, every move he made now.

Lexi's frown deepened and she leaned toward him, her hand smoothing over his jaw. "You're hurt."

He stilled inside. No one ever saw his physical pain. He didn't allow it to show on his face or body, in his eyes. Only someone who saw into him, saw beyond the surface, could have seen pain in him. There was no doubt this woman was his. He took her hand and pressed his palm to hers. "Wait for me at your house. I'll come to you. Send my brothers to me and don't think about this anymore. Don't call or talk to anyone else until I've come to you."

"But my sisters . . . We made a pact to tell one another everything."

"We'll tell your sisters," Gavriil said. "But I'll be with you. Remember, I'm the one who did all the damage here, not you."

"Caine has to go to the hospital," Lexi pointed out. "The cops will know for certain then." She looked down at her hand, still enveloped in his.

"Let me worry about that. You go get my brothers and wait for me."

"Gavriil, they'll all come to my house. They'll know. We always know when one of us is in trouble."

He nodded. "That's okay. Just don't allow any of them to call the sheriff." His gaze was steady on her. "Will you do that for me?"

Lexi's eyes clung to his. "That's the least I can do after you saved my life." She started to look past him to Caine, but Gavriil blocked her view.

"Don't. Don't give him that satisfaction. He's nothing to you. Just look at me and then go." He tightened his fingers around hers. "Don't see him. Only me."

Lexi pressed her lips together and nodded. Reluctantly he let go of her and watched as she drove away. He turned back toward Caine, and there was nothing at all left of the warm, gentle man. The one striding toward Caine was utterly stone cold, inside and out.

2

"THEY'VE been gone a really long time," Lexi said, looking anxiously around the circle of women gathered on her porch. These five women had become family to her. They weren't bound by birth, but in every other way they had become sisters.

"Do you think something happened to them?" She pushed her thumbnail between her teeth and frowned, looking toward the back part of the property. "I shouldn't have run away like a coward. This was my mess."

"You're not a coward, Lexi," Rikki Hammond assured her. "Stop worrying so much about them. I'd know if something happened to Levi."

Married to Lev Prakenskii, whom they now called Levi Hammond, Rikki was both autistic and bound to water, an element of great power. She loved the ocean and captained her own vessel, diving for sea urchins with Levi to help provide cash for the farm.

Rikki leaned over and brushed a kiss against Lexi's cheek, a rare gesture of affection from her. "I'll go make tea. It seems longer than it really has been."

Airiana nodded. "Same with me," she agreed. "I'd know if something happened to Max."

"Where are the children?" Lexi asked, suddenly aware that if Max was gone and Airiana was with her, the four children Max and Airiana were adopting were alone.

"I thought it best to leave them at the house. Lucia and Benito know what to do, and they're watching over Siena and Nicia. They know something's wrong, so I'll have to keep an eye out for Benito. He has a tendency to spy."

That made them all laugh. Benito took protecting his sisters seriously and had become Max's shadow ever since Max had saved them all from a human trafficking ring. He walked like Max and had begun to take on his mannerisms, and he'd been on the farm less than two weeks.

"It's all right if you need to get back," Lexi assured Airiana. "I wouldn't want them to be afraid. Being alone after losing their parents and going through what they all did can't be good."

"Lexi," Airiana reminded softly, "they're in their new home. They're aware of all the security we have, and they know we're at your house. They'll be fine. The entire farm is their home. *I* need to be with *you* right now."

Airiana was bound to air, and Max appeared to be as well. The Prakenskiis had a number of gifts, but Max was an element, just as Airiana was, and that made them a very powerful couple.

Lexi blinked back tears. "I'm glad you are. I should have let the earth swallow Caine." The admission burst out of her unexpectedly and she clapped her hand over her mouth. "I'm sorry, I didn't mean that." But she did. She knew she did. She was terrified that with Caine alive, he would eventually come for her. He wouldn't stop. Nothing would ever stop him.

Her stomach rebelled at the idea of ever being alone with him again. She touched her ponytail, the one he'd yanked so viciously. "You once asked me why I never cut my hair, Airiana. I grew out my hair after I escaped because Caine cut it off repeatedly to humiliate me when he punished me. He shaved my head once. I promised myself I would wear my hair long if I ever escaped."

There was a collective gasp from the other women. She didn't want to see the sympathy on their faces—she'd break down. Falling apart wasn't going to help. She didn't understand why she couldn't stop thinking about Gavriil and feeling guilty for leaving him there alone to deal with her mess.

She turned away from her sisters, wrapping her arms tightly around herself. The memories were too close—on top of her now—and she wanted to vomit, to curl up in the fetal position and hide away. All of her hard-won armor had deserted her and all she could do was feel like a helpless child.

"Of course you would wish the earth had swallowed Caine," Lissa Piner said. "Who wouldn't? That man was . . . is . . ." She broke off, looking at the other women sitting on Lexi's sprawling porch, annoyed at such a mistake. She was bound to fire, and sometimes her passionate nature rose to the surface when she wanted to protect her youngest sister.

Lissa had no doubts that the man who had abducted Lexi from the safety of her home and forced her into a life of rape and terror by night and work by day wouldn't ever make it to the hospital.

Hastily she changed tactics. "What's Gavriil like? I'm amazed that he would actually use his own name so openly, almost as if he was daring Uri Sorbacov or Uri's father to come after him."

Lexi frowned again, a little distracted, trying to follow what they were all saying. She knew they were trying to divert her attention. She tried to remember who Uri Sorbacov was. He was the son of the man who had murdered the Prakenskiis' parents and abducted all seven brothers, separating them and forcing them into schools to become covert operatives and worse. He also had been the one to order a hit on most of the Prakenskii brothers and had tried to abduct Airiana. He had a litany of sins to answer for, but was safe in Russia, far from retaliation.

"Aren't they all on a hit list?" Lexi asked, suddenly worried about why Gavriil would use his real identity. Her thumbnail found its way back between her teeth—exasperated, she pulled it out.

"Not Ilya," Blythe Daniels said. "He's the youngest Prakenskii brother, and for some reason he seems to be able to live out in the open with no threat."

Lexi found Blythe's voice incredibly soothing. She was always the one who calmed every situation down. She wasn't bound to an element, but she had incredible gifts of her own and always was the voice of reason in the middle of a storm. She had brought them all together and had found the farm for them to purchase. Lexi would be forever grateful for that alone.

Judith Vincent swung her feet up onto the wide railing of the porch. "Tell us about Gavriil. When Thomas or Levi talk about him, it's always with this sort of reservation in their voices. A tone."

Married to Stefan Prakenskii, Judith was bound to spirit and could amplify all the other elements. Stefan had taken the name Thomas Vincent and the two of them were never far apart.

Airiana nodded. "Almost as if they're in awe of him—or afraid of him. I can't imagine Max, Levi or Thomas afraid of anyone, but they definitely talk differently about him."

Lexi scowled at them. "He was gentle and kind to me. He had no choice when he shot those two men. They were going to kill me. I'm sure he didn't want to kill them, but if he hadn't, I'd be dead. And he was hurt. I could see it."

"Hurt?" Judith asked. "You didn't tell us that. Was he shot? Stabbed? Should we have told Thomas to take him to a hospital?"

Lexi shook her head. "I think he came here with some injury."

"That's right," Airiana said, snapping her fingers. "Gavriil was stabbed like seven times guarding my dear old dad, Theodotus Solovyov. Gavriil nearly died."

Judith sat up straighter. "Thomas told me about him. He should have died. It was really bad. And Sorbacov put out a hit on him because he didn't die, and according to Sorbacov, Gavriil was useless to them. But that was a long time ago, his injuries should have healed."

"He worked for their government all those years and they just threw him away, threw all the Prakenskiis away. That's so wrong." Lexi's sympathy was entirely with Gavriil and had been from the moment she felt his pain.

"If he's using his own name, and he knows Sorbacov put a hit out on him," Blythe said, "he came here to say good-bye to his brothers. He's planning to lead them away from Thomas, Levi and Max. That's the only reason he would use his real name."

Rikki came through the front entrance bearing a tray with a teapot and cups on it. The women turned to her gratefully. They had met one another in group therapy. Each of them had gone as a last resort. It was a special group for women who had relatives murdered and in some way felt they were to blame for the death of their loved ones. They had grown close and realized that together they were far stronger and more powerful than apart.

"Thank you," Lexi murmured, taking one of the cups and pouring a little milk into it. She turned back to her sisters, her small frown still very much in evidence. "Maybe he just told me his name to reassure me."

"Whatever the reason, honey," Judith said, "we're grateful to him for saving your life." She put her teacup on the railing and looked out over the farm. "We have to be more careful about listening to the men. We're always rolling our eyes when they give us orders on where we can go and how we're supposed to get there, but we all have too many enemies to pretend we're always going to be safe."

Lexi sighed. "I may as well tell you the truth. I'm in witness protection. The things I told you about the cult and the kidnapping and the murder of my entire family is all true, but I testified against several key members of the cult and the rest scattered and were able to get away, including Caine, the man who forced me into being his wife. My real name is Alexia Wilson, not Lexi Thompson."

"I suspected as much," Blythe said. "It was all over the news when it happened."

"You weren't his wife," Lissa said fiercely. "You were a little girl he beat and raped. There was no marriage, no sacred vows. He was no man of God, and anyone who would perform a ceremony uniting an eight-year-old child and a grown man is certainly no ordained minister."

Lexi ducked her head. "I know. That's what they told me. The point is, if Caine found me, other members of the cult probably know where I am as well. It was just luck that Gavriil had come here. I saw my family for about three hours, and the feds moved me into a safe house before the trial. While I was there, these people went into my home, murdered my parents as they slept, went down the hall and killed my two brothers and my baby sister. We have children here." Her eyes met Airiana's. "Your children. They've been through far too much already."

"No." Blythe said it firmly. "You aren't leaving."

Airiana leaned forward and took Lexi's hand. "I had to ask myself the same question about coming back here. I'm working for the government now, and everyone wants my work. Sorbacov tried to take me to Russia. I've got Evan Shackler-Gratsos trying to kidnap me, and if it hadn't been for Max, I'd be with one of them right now."

Evan Shackler-Gratsos, Lexi remembered, was a billionaire who had inherited not only a major shipping company from his brother, but his brother's side of human, arms and drug trafficking as well. Lexi hugged Airiana tightly. "I'm so glad Max was there."

"I am terrified of allowing Evan to get anywhere near the children, after what they've been through—and he was responsible," Airiana admitted. "But, and you have to listen to me, baby, we're better and stronger together than apart. Even if you disappear, they would still come here to us. You know that. You were in protective custody and they went after your family. They'd still come after us."

Lexi shook her head. "I froze. After I trapped Caine in the ground, and realized there were others, I couldn't move."

Lissa hugged her tightly. "You saved yourself. Caine obviously beat you. Look at you, all covered in bruises, but you still saved yourself. You executed the moves Levi taught us in class, and you broke away from him just like you were supposed to."

Lexi chewed on her thumbnail, wishing she could be more like the rest of them. They all had confidence in themselves in spite of the things that had happened to them. "If it hadn't been for Gavriil, I'd be dead right now. I don't want to be the weak link. What happens if I'm here alone on the farm with Lucia and the younger children and they come?"

"I have no doubt that you would protect the children," Airiana said. "No doubt at all. Max said women often are much more willing to fight for their children than themselves."

"Do you really want to take that chance?" Lexi persisted, terrified that they couldn't see inside of her.

She was a mess—a terrible, unholy mess. No amount of practice in the gym or on the gun range made her feel any different. She was afraid all the time. Now, she feared, she would always remember that she'd nearly killed a man with her most precious, sacred gift. She felt inadequate and more terrified than ever.

She'd stopped being afraid for a moment when she'd looked into Gavriil Prakenskii's eyes. She secretly hugged that moment to her. She'd felt—alive. For the first time she really felt she could breathe. She could see the world in his eyes. She could see herself there, strong like she wanted to be.

It was peculiar and a little crazy—he was a complete stranger—but maybe she'd connected with him because she sensed he was as broken as she was. All she knew for certain was that she wasn't going to allow Gavriil Prakenskii to throw away his life, and she was fairly certain that's what he'd come here to do.

"Yes," Airiana answered the question firmly. "Absolutely yes."

"I think your Gavriil was right," Lissa said. "I don't think we need to call anyone over this little incident. The boys can handle it, and we'll just keep working on security and watch you a little closer."

"Maybe Gavriil will stick around and help you with the farm," Judith added. "He was your guardian angel. Maybe he won't mind being your bodyguard."

Lexi shook her head. "I don't want him in danger. He really has something physically wrong with him. If I can get him to let me take a look, I might be able to help, and if I can't, Libby Drake is back in town. I can ask her . . ." She trailed off when she realized the other women were staring at her in astonishment. "What?"

"You're going to take a look at him?" Blythe echoed. "Honey, you don't even talk to people let alone take a look at them."

Airiana gave a little snicker. "Presumably without clothes. You know, just for an inspection."

Lexi felt her color rise, her skin turning bright red. "Well, if I'm going to help him, I'll need to see the problem, won't I?" She glared at them, daring them to contradict her.

"Of course," Lissa soothed. "We're only teasing you."

"But honey," Judith reminded, "the stabbing was some time ago, and it may be impossible to help him after all this time. In any event, he's no wounded creature for you to look after."

"Of course he is," Lexi said. "You didn't see him."

"We're about to," Blythe said. "The men are coming back and your Gavriil is right in the middle of them."

Lexi stood up, slowly putting the teacup down. Gavriil moved over the ground with a dancer's fluid step rather than a fighter's, which was how she always saw Levi and

Thomas. Max was just out there for the world to see, a tough, rough man anyone would think twice before messing with. But Gavriil . . .

"Oh, my God," Judith whispered, her hand going defensively to her throat. "And I thought Levi was frightening. Airiana, are you seeing what I'm seeing?"

Airiana touched Judith's hand to quiet her. She saw the aura, dark and dangerous and extremely violent, surrounding Gavriil Prakenskii. The thought of him ever being alone with their little fragile Lexi was almost shocking. Truly horrifying. What made the situation so much worse was the fact that he was walking with his brothers, all very dangerous men, and yet his aura was fully colored in violence, outdoing every one of theirs.

Gavriil Prakenskii wore his cloak of darkness as casually as another man wore a coat. Airiana wouldn't have been surprised to see him sprout horns. He was the coldest, hardest man she'd ever seen in her life.

Judith nudged her and indicated Lexi with her chin. The other women had fallen silent as well, staring at the newcomer as if he might be the devil walking up to them in his blue jeans and long, swirling trench coat.

"He's got a million weapons inside that coat," Rikki murmured. "Maybe more than a million. He's just scary."

Lexi didn't seem to hear her. She didn't seem to see anyone other than Gavriil. His dark gaze fastened on hers, and she had the strange sensation of falling into him. She didn't like strangers, especially men, yet he didn't feel like a stranger. No one else could see the pain in him, which surprised her. Normally, Lissa and Airiana were very good at using healing energy when it was needed.

That didn't matter to her. She wanted to go to him, take his hand and lead him to a chair to get him off his feet. He needed to sit down. She was fairly certain he hadn't slept in days, and she hated the exhaustion she could feel pouring off of him.

"Is there any tea left?" Levi asked, and leaned down to

brush a kiss over Rikki's upturned mouth. His hand slipped into hers. "I'm sorry about having to miss a dive day."

"Oh no, Rikki," Lexi said instantly. "I didn't realize I kept you from diving. I'm so sorry. I shouldn't have called you, Levi," she added. "I could have just asked Thomas and Max."

Levi put his arm around her and gave her a brief, rare hug. "You did exactly what you were supposed to do. And Gavriil tells me you used the kick we worked on like a pro. I'm proud of you."

Gavriil moved up the stairs straight toward them, and scowled at his brother. Levi instantly dropped his arm and stepped away from Lexi.

Gavriil ignored the others and went to Lexi, taking both her hands in his. "Are you all right?"

Lexi nodded and patted the porch swing, feeling sick with his pain. She couldn't understand how the others didn't see or feel it. His pain was so severe it was nearly tangible. She couldn't help stroking a hand down his arm, silently urging him to sit.

Gavriil allowed Lexi to coax him into the swing, knowing her sisters were horrified that she was standing so close to him. They'd be even more horrified if they realized just what she was to him. He didn't care. Nothing mattered to him but this young woman, so fragile and broken, but with a heart of gold and a steel spine she didn't even know she had.

He read the compassion in her eyes easily, and knew that was his best "in" with her. She would run at the first hint of interest, of a takeover, but she would be drawn to him if she thought he needed her help.

He sank into the swing and tugged her hand so that she slowly, almost reluctantly sat beside him. Clearly she wasn't used to being with a man, a stranger, but still, she was more worried about him than about herself in that moment, and he had no compunction against capitalizing on her compassionate nature.

Her shoulder fit beneath his. His thigh was tight along hers. He wanted to close his eyes and rest, to just sit with her on the porch swing, something he'd never done in his life, but suddenly it was the most important thing in the world to do. He allowed her to feel his exhaustion, even his pain, although he sensed she did so on her own, that she saw far more than he would ever want another human being to see.

"Did you take Caine to the hospital?" Lexi asked.

Levi and Thomas exchanged a long glance with Max. Caine had been in no shape to go to the hospital or anywhere else for that matter. He'd been long gone by the time they'd arrived and probably begged for death long before he'd ever seen it coming for him. Gavriil hadn't even broken a sweat. He'd straightened up slowly, looking at them, not with the eyes of a long lost brother, but rather the eyes of a killer, a man long lost to the world of humanity.

"I'm sorry, honey," Thomas said. "Well, maybe I'm not. He was dead by the time we got there."

"But . . ." she protested. "He was yelling at me, calling me names. He was alive . . ."

"He bled to death, Lexi," Max said.

"I *murdered* him then." She started to cover her face with her hands, but Gavriil caught her one hand and brought it to his chest.

"Self-defense isn't the same as murder, *solnyshko moya*, and you acted in self-defense," he said. He opened her fist and pressed her palm over his heart.

Max exchanged a quick look with his brothers. Gavriil was using a very tender version of "my sun," in Russian, an unusual endearment to call a woman he'd just met. "It isn't any different than when we fought off the men coming to take Airiana away," Max added. "We used every means possible to defend ourselves and those we love."

"I wanted him dead," Lexi confessed in a little rush. "I hit the ground too hard because I wanted him dead."

"He was an evil man," Gavriil said. "Believe me, Lexi,

I know evil when I see it. I've come across it enough in my lifetime."

That brought her attention immediately back to him. She tilted her head to look up at him. "You need to rest. You were up all night, weren't you?"

He nodded his head. "I traveled a long way to find Ilya and to see all of you. Sorbacov put a hit out on Ilya."

"I didn't expect that," Levi said.

Thomas shook his head. "Sooner or later one of us is going to have to kill that man. There's no reason to go after Ilya other than pure spite."

"Why are you using your real name?" Max asked. "That's a beacon for Sorbacov. You know that. Unless you're just using it because you're with family."

Gavriil shrugged. "I want him to know where I am after I leave here. Once I'm well away from all of you, I'll establish a trail. He'll send someone after me, and I can lead them away from Ilya and this farm." That had been his plan all along. But now there was Lexi. What did a man like him do about a woman like her? He sure as hell had no intention of giving her up, or leaving her to Caine's cult.

His admission was rewarded with Lexi's swift intake of breath and a quick shake of her head. He felt a spark of energy from the center of her palm through his shirt, straight to his heart.

"No." A single word. Softly spoken. Just *no*. He wasn't even certain anyone else had heard her. Her green eyes drifted over his face, and she shook her head.

His heart reacted as if she'd used an electrical charge on him. He didn't have physical reactions to anything or anyone unless he allowed it. He hadn't given his body permission to feel—not in the middle of so many people—yet there was no denying the almost painful response of his heart to her.

He had never expected to find himself in such a position, and he needed a plan of action. For that he needed a clear mind, and right now he was exhausted. He was seventy-two hours without sleep and needed to lie down for a short while. He didn't release Lexi's hand, although he made certain there was no pressure, just his hand lightly over hers, pressing her palm gently against his heart.

"I don't want you to worry anymore about losing your farm," he said, allowing his lashes to drift down as if he might be falling asleep right there.

What the hell are you doing? Levi demanded. *Gavriil, there's no way you'd fall asleep in the middle of this group. Don't play her. She's off-limits. No woman on this farm is to be used for whatever reason.*

Go to hell, Lev. He didn't lift his lashes or look at his brother. His voice said it all.

"You're welcome to stay with Rikki and me," Levi said aloud, his tone a low whip. There was so sharp of an edge that his brothers and the women looked at him.

Rikki didn't speak, but she looked as if she might faint. She rocked back and forth, her fingers twisting together in agitation. She had difficulties with strangers, particularly anyone entering her home. It was significant that Levi didn't soothe her or retract his invitation.

"Levi," Lexi said, "what in the world is wrong with you? You know that wouldn't work."

Gavriil remained motionless. Absolutely still. Just waiting.

"Perhaps it would be better if you stayed with us," Airiana volunteered, putting her hand gently over Rikki's and frowning at Levi.

"You have four children," Lexi protested. "He'd never get any sleep there."

Gavriil let the talk swirl around him, leaving them to debate where he should stay. At least they were giving him an opening to remain on the farm. He studied his brothers through hooded eyes. All three looked fit and happy. All three were happy to see him and yet wanted him gone— away from Lexi. It was very clear to him that they all protected her.

"It's logical to come to our place," Thomas said. "We

have plenty of room, right, Judith?" He put his arm around her.

"Yes. That would be lovely. Of course you should stay with us, we'd love to have you," Judith said, almost painfully.

Gavriil shifted his weight slightly, bringing his thigh tighter against Lexi's. Her security and safety was his job now, and he wouldn't be staying at any of their houses. He was staying with Lexi, right where he was. He waited, tempted to suppress a slight groan to galvanize her into action, but Levi might take out a gun and shoot him. The idea was a little amusing.

"That's just silly," Lexi said. "I've got a huge house and it wouldn't be inconvenient for him to stay here. He needs rest, and I'll feel much safer with him close. Gavriil, if you want to stay here, you're welcome. You'll have plenty of peace and quiet."

He'd noticed the sleeping bag rolled up in the far corner, tucked against the railing. He was fairly certain she spent most nights on the porch and not in her house. In her mind, she figured she would just let him have the house. He let her think it. "If it would make you feel safer," he said, opening his eyes and looking directly at her, "of course I'll stay. I don't want to be any trouble though. A couch is good."

Levi snorted, and Max made a growling sound deep in his throat.

Gavriil, she's very fragile, Levi said again. *What the hell are you doing?*

What the hell was he doing? He didn't know. He didn't even care. He sent his brother one hard look telling him without words to back off. He couldn't reassure Levi that he'd leave Lexi alone because he didn't know exactly what he was going to do with her. He only knew he couldn't leave her. She belonged to him, and nothing, not a single person, had ever belonged to him.

More than that, he'd never had anyone look at him the way she did. Or see inside him the way she saw him. Her safety was paramount to everything else now. He'd never

had anything in his life he cared about. That was dangerous. He didn't get attached. He didn't have a home or an
expectation of one.

His life consisted of hotel rooms and apartments that
had nothing in them. He stashed money and passports all
over for emergencies and never stayed long in any one
place. No matter how grave an injury, he moved locations
every few days, not leaving so much as a fingerprint behind. Until now. Until Lexi. He was going to stop here—at
least for a while.

Lexi stood up abruptly, taking matters into her own
hands. "I know you've all got work to do. If we're not calling the sheriff and I don't have to leave, then we need to let
Gavriil rest. I have plenty to do."

The others had no choice. Airiana gathered up the teacups and took them inside while the women started down the
steps, clearly reluctant to leave. His brothers hadn't budged.

I'll need some kind of answer, Gavriil. She's family.

*I'm your family. And you know you're treading on very
thin ice.*

Levi shrugged but he didn't move, and Gavriil admired
him for that. Levi was well aware Gavriil could kill them
all from his position, just sitting there on the swing, but he
didn't so much as flinch. He stared at Gavriil with steady,
watchful eyes.

Gavriil reached out almost lazily and caught Lexi's
wrist, tugging until she turned. She smiled at him. Innocent. Sweet. Her green eyes soft and too trusting. She had
no idea that he was a monster rocking gently back and forth
on her porch swing. She saw him as her broken bird and
she was determined to make certain he was safe and secure. He lifted her palm into the air facing him. Her small,
delicate hand, roughened from so much work.

Gavriil lifted his own palm and pressed it toward hers.
His palm pushed energy against hers and he felt a rise of
power from his deepest core, the very essence of who he
was. It was strong, extremely so, his spirit, his will, the man
he was forged in hell. Electricity leapt between them,

sparks dancing like fireflies in the air around their palms.
It hit her hard, a jolt that sank through flesh to bone.

"No," Levi and Thomas both said simultaneously. Max
took a step toward him and halted abruptly when sparks
arced in the air between the two palms.

Lexi yelped, pulling her hand back, pressing it tightly
against her body as if she'd been injured. "You zapped me."
There was a mixture of laughter and tears in her voice, telling him it hurt more than she wanted to let on.

It was too late for all of them. Gavriil had no idea why
he gave into the compulsion to answer his brother in such a
way. He hadn't thought about it, he hadn't even considered
or planned for it. Energy rose from somewhere deep inside
him. That onetime gift that couldn't be taken back and was
never given lightly.

A commitment. A vow. Binding brands, embedded
deep, more than bone deep, sinking into flesh, sinking into
his soul, her soul. They would be forever bound together.
That rise of energy from a Prakenskii to the one woman he
claimed as his own, weaving that connection tight from his
soul to hers.

"Let me see." He tugged at Lexi's wrist until she reluctantly allowed him to examine her palm. Satisfaction rose
when he saw that faint brand, two circles intertwined, embedded into her palm, under her skin, already disappearing
from prying eyes. It was an intimate, private mark that was
for no one else to see but the two of them.

He lifted his gaze to his brothers. He knew what they
saw, and it wasn't going to give them much reassurance. He
wouldn't pretend he was anything but who and what he was.
But they'd better heed his warning. He wouldn't give them
another, not now that they knew.

Levi cursed under his breath and turned away abruptly.
He'd been on the farm the longest and he clearly loved Lexi
as a sister. Thomas scowled at him but didn't say a word.
He turned on his heel and took the steps two at a time.

Max stood there looking at him. "I hope you know what
you're doing, Gavriil. I really do."

Gavriil didn't bother with a reply. Of course he didn't know what the hell he was doing, he was in brand-new territory, but he'd figure it out. He had time. Ignoring Max, he pressed his mouth to the center of Lexi's palm, brushing his lips over the wound in a brief kiss.

"I'm sorry, *solnyshko moya*, I didn't mean to hurt you."

"Lexi," Levi commanded her attention, forcing her to look at him. "If you need anything at all. If you want help, just call."

She smiled at him. "I may be asking for you to cook after a day or two. You're awesome, and I'm sort of mediocre in that department."

Clearly she didn't comprehend the danger she was in. Gavriil realized she was still thrown by what had happened earlier. He'd already dismissed the incident, clearing his mind of Caine and his associates. They were dead and gone and no one would ever find the bodies, but Lexi hadn't dismissed them.

Levi shook his head and reluctantly followed his brothers and Airiana, leaving them alone.

Lexi stared after her brothers-in-law, realizing for the first time that her safety net was gone and somehow, without knowing how or why, she'd insisted Gavriil Prakenskii stay with her. She turned away from him to give herself a moment to think. Her sisters were frequently at her house, running in and out, and lately, Airiana's children often did the same thing. But no one stayed.

She spent long hours alone and wasn't certain she knew how to talk to anyone without being awkward.

"Lexi." Gavriil spoke softly. "If you don't want me to stay, I can find somewhere else to sleep. I'm not really picky about where. I'm a stranger to you. You don't owe me anything, and I'd never want you uncomfortable."

She spun around to face him. Exhaustion was in every line of his face. He looked . . . alone. Pain clung to him like a second skin. The pain was so severe, she couldn't understand how Airiana and Judith hadn't seen or felt it.

"I don't want you to leave, Gavriil. I know it's a little

awkward because we don't know each other, but I think we can get past that. I do have to say something to you though." She bit down on her thumbnail and then her eyes met his.

He felt the impact like a physical blow. It was almost terrifying the way his body and his mind reacted to this woman. He had no idea it was even possible for him to react to a woman, to another human being, the way he did to her. She moved him. She moved the earth beneath his feet. There was something very satisfying in knowing he still had a few human qualities left in him. There might not be much in the way of humanity, but if he had anything at all, if there was something left of his soul, it belonged to this young woman.

"Tell me, *solnyshko moya*." He kept his tone soft, coaxing, as gentle as he knew how to be. He'd never felt gentle or tender toward anyone, he hadn't known he was capable outside of faking it, yet he actually *felt* those softer emotions toward her.

"I'm sorry you had to shoot those men. I know you did it to save me. You had no idea who I was. I didn't mean a thing to you, but you still shot them both and you didn't have to. It must have been terrible for you. I'm sorry I put you in that position." Her apology came out in a little rush.

He didn't even know how to respond. She meant every word, he could hear the sincerity in her voice, and see it on her face. She left him speechless. Completely enamored. She was winding herself around his little finger, his heart and probably his soul. That brand had been stamped into his bones, not just hers.

"Levi warned me not to go outside the existing boundaries of the farm, but I just couldn't help myself," she continued. "I wanted to really take some time and look over that acreage to see what I could do with it. By being so selfish and careless, I put you in a terrible position, and I'm really very, very sorry."

He had the unexpected urge to kiss her. The compulsion welled up strong and was nearly impossible to ignore. He was grateful for all the years of discipline. Lexi Thompson would run like a rabbit if he made one wrong move. He held himself still, his gaze drifting over her, more possessive than he would have liked, but then she was shifting her weight anxiously from one foot to the other, waiting for him to say something and not paying attention to the fact that he was a tiger with teeth and not the lamb she thought him.

"I'm not going to lie to you, Lexi. It didn't bother me in the least to shoot the two bastards. It's what I do. I exterminate rodents. You've been around my brothers enough to know what we did. I've been at it a few years longer than they have. I started when I was fourteen years old. Don't think for one moment that you put me in a bad position. I had a choice, and truthfully, it didn't bother me. They were going to kill you."

Relief showed on her face. In that moment, he realized just what Levi had been trying to tell him. Lexi had been taken at the age of eight and beaten into submission. Her family had been murdered. Everyone she loved had been taken from her, and her life had been one of subjugation to a criminally insane man. She was more than fragile.

She'd gone from a government safe house to the farm. She knew no other way of life. Here she was beginning to know who she was and little by little was gaining self-esteem and confidence. Now he came along, and she was going to have to make new changes and adjustments—ones that might be more difficult than he first considered.

Gavriil sighed. He couldn't change who he was. He was as cold-blooded as a man could be and still actually call himself human.

"You're very nice to say that. Are you hungry? Do you want to lie down for a while? I can get back to work . . ." she offered, her voice fading shyly.

She didn't need to be going back to work, not after the trauma of the morning. He ran a hand through his hair. "Stay with me. I haven't talked to anyone for a long time, and I like the sound of your voice."

He found her soothing, her voice reminding him of perfectly pitched music softly riding on the wind. He held out his hand to her, afraid going into the house would be too intimate. She needed care. Great care. He approached everything logically and intellectually, thinking things through thoroughly so that he could come at a problem or a job from many different angles, and he was prepared for anything. This was going to be his most difficult and, hopefully, his most rewarding challenge.

She moistened her lips. "I'm not very good at conversation. I've never had company before. Not someone who isn't family."

He smiled at her. "But I am family in a way." The last thing he needed was for her to see him as a brother. He didn't make the mistake of snagging her wrist, although he could have. He waited, his hand extended, willing her to take that first step toward him and their future relationship.

Lexi glanced almost longingly out toward the beds of herbs and flowers surrounding her house and then, as if making up her mind, put her hand in his and sank down onto the swing beside him again.

Gavriil put his feet up on the railing and stared out at all the lush green. So many colors. There was no doubt she was an earth element. No one could grow so many varieties of plants and have them thrive like they were here. The way to her heart was right in front of him. She loved her plants, loved the farm. Everything she was she poured into her home.

"It's beautiful here."

"I think so," Lexi agreed, sounding pleased.

"Who helps you? It's a lot of work to maintain this many acres." He took care to sound casual, to keep his gaze away from her, studying the layout of the farm and wishing the house was positioned just a little bit better. Clearly when it had been built, his brothers hadn't been living there to give them advice on where to build. Still, he could make security work with what they had.

"In the beginning all of us did the planting. Everyone helps out as best they can. We needed money when we first started, before the farm began to produce, so everyone else worked in businesses off the farm."

He allowed his lashes to drift down, watching her closely out of the side of his vision. He'd managed to retain possession of her hand. She was very aware of it, but she didn't seem to know how to take it back from him. She moistened her lips nervously, but she didn't pull away. He idly began to draw circles with the pad of his fingers, keeping the patterns feather-light and nonthreatening.

"I worked on a farm a time or two." That was strictly the truth. Both times he'd assassinated the landowner, but that wasn't really relevant. One had been a fairly large opiate farm and the drug lord had crossed Sorbacov one too many times. The other had been owned by a very successful hit man who had made a try for Sorbacov himself. He'd thought himself safe on his vast and well-guarded farm. "None of the places were as beautiful as this place. It's almost a work of art."

Some of the tension drained out of Lexi. "Sometimes I think of it that way, a canvas waiting to be painted. I like to put splashes of color here and there to show off all the shades of green. Judith is really our artist, but this is my attempt. I try creating beauty with living plants."

She turned her head and looked directly at him. He felt her hand tremble and instantly that deadly part of him coiled, went still, ready for anything.

"Is he really dead? Caine? Is he dead? I'm not certain I can believe it. I've spent most of my life terrified of him. To hear that he's dead and not see it . . ." She shook her head. "He seemed invincible to me. Protected by the devil. I knew he'd find me one day. It's hard to believe he's really dead."

3

THIS was the moment Gavriil had dreaded, had feared would come. He had known Lexi would ask about Caine. How could she not? The man had destroyed everyone she loved. He'd turned her life into a nightmare. She couldn't believe he was dead without seeing the body, and that wasn't going to happen. He took his time, trying to think of a satisfactory answer, one he could give her without revealing the fact that another monster sat right beside her.

"Gavriil? Is Caine really dead?" Lexi asked again. "He was very much alive when I left him. I can still hear the horrible things he called me. I need to know the truth."

The truth would scare her to death. Gavriil shifted his weight just a little, enough to slide his thigh along hers. He still retained possession of her hand and he continued the lazy, soothing circles, tracing the pattern of the intertwining rings that had sunk beneath her skin right in the middle of her palm.

"He's dead, Lexi. I can guarantee you that." He made it a statement. His eyes met hers, allowed her for one moment to see a brief glimpse of who he was, what he could be, when he wasn't sitting on the porch swing with her.

Her eyes went wide with shock. She saw him all right. Again she surprised him. She didn't flinch or move away, she just continued to look at him with her steady gaze. "Did you kill him?"

Gavriil shrugged. "He's dead, isn't that enough?" It was impossible to look away from her vibrant green eyes. She was earth all right, cool and steady and stubborn. She was beautiful, there was no doubt about it, but he realized it was the brightness in her he was attracted to.

She continued to look at him without blinking, one eyebrow raised.

"I'm not going to lie to you," he said, his voice dropping low and harsh. "The rest of the world, maybe, but not you. Be very sure you want an answer before you ask me a question."

He was her exact opposite. Their childhoods were somewhat comparable, but she'd gone one way and he another. She had retained compassion and the softer emotions, while he had had every emotion beaten out of him.

"Did you kill him?" she repeated.

"Yes." He wasn't going to lie to her. He might skirt the truth, he might plot to win her over, but he wasn't going to lie to her. "I killed him. And no, it didn't bother me to kill him. He was evil and he would never have stopped coming after you. His legs were broken and we would have had to take him to a hospital, and you would have lost your home and family once again because of a monster. He needed killing."

Lexi sighed softly, chewing on her lower lip while she turned over and over in her mind what she was going to say. Gavriil was very lost, but he didn't know it. He was so much like her, so shrouded in his past, shaped by monsters and then forced to live in a civilized world.

Truthfully, Gavriil had never lived in a civilized world. He knew nothing about it. He'd never had the chance to stay in one place or forge a relationship with anyone else, in-

cluding his brothers. There was weariness and pain in
every line of his face. He was a big man, solid and muscular, yet he flowed like water over the ground. When he
stopped moving, he was utterly still, like a great jungle cat.
She thought of him that way. Feral.

She looked down at her hand in his. There was a connection between them, perhaps because they shared a similar
past and understood each other. Instinctively, she knew
Gavriil was acting out of character with her. He wasn't a
man to sit on a porch swing and take a woman's hand so
gently. Normally he would have slipped back into the shadows and been long gone.

He needed help. This was probably his only chance at
any kind of a life. She had found peace on the farm and
she'd learned how to trust a few people as well as bond with
them. She was happy here. Her past hadn't let go of her, and
she knew it wouldn't, but that hadn't stopped the magic of
the connections the six women had created together.

She bit her lower lip, and looked down at her hand in his.
"Gavriil, you do know that killing is wrong, don't you? You
know it is."

He frowned as if thinking over her statement. She wasn't
surprised when he shook his head. "No. I think there are
mistakes, people who are twisted and evil and go through
life hurting others. I don't think they should be allowed to
survive."

How was she supposed to respond to that? His world had
been one of violence. His job was to find and eliminate
targets. She doubted if he knew and liked a single family.
He wasn't in one place long enough to get to actually know
real people. Good people. In his world, everyone was violent and depraved and greedy.

"Still." How did she put so much denial into one word
without it sounding preachy? Or holier-than-thou? "Taking
a life should be difficult, Gavriil."

"I'm not going to tell you the things I've seen in my life,
but I've looked at pure evil and known there was no way to
redeem or save them. Caine was a man like that."

"Yes, he was. But we don't get to judge who lives and who dies," Lexi said.

He smiled at her and brought her palm to his mouth. Her heart jumped and began to beat a little wildly. She wasn't certain if her response was to his smile or to the feel of the gentle, featherlight brush of his mouth on her palm.

He was physically beautiful. His face was carved from stone, a masterpiece in masculinity. His eyes were absolutely gorgeous, a dark midnight blue, heavily fringed with black lashes. His hair was glorious, an unruly, thick glossy mop of black waves streaked with silver she was tempted to try to tame.

Looking into Lexi's eyes, Gavriil realized for the first time that there was a chink in his armor. He'd worn armor his entire life; it had been forged in hell. No one could get to him. No one could get inside of him. Or touch him. He knew more ways to hurt or kill than most men could conceive of, and he could disappear in the blink of an eye. But not here. Not with her.

Lexi saw him. She saw into him. Hell. She probably knew every secret he had. If he had a brain in his head, he'd kill her and be done with it, but she kept looking at him with those big green eyes filled with compassion and invitation. She was far too innocent and naïve to realize what that look could do to a man like him.

"I might be one of those monsters, Lexi, the kind that shouldn't live. I've asked myself that a few times," he confessed, telling the strict truth, making a half-hearted attempt to save her. "I judge who lives and who dies all the time. The people I go after aren't human. But then, I doubt I am either."

She did the most unexpected thing. She brushed back his hair, her fingers moving along his scalp with a whisper of a caress. Gentle. Soothing. She ripped his heart out with the small gesture. He felt the actual pain and couldn't help himself. He pressed the hand he was holding hard over his heart, to try to keep the dried-out organ inside his body. It was too late. She had it. It belonged to her.

One small act of kindness and he was gone. Shredded. Taken over. He wanted to curse. Weep. Fight. There was a part of him that coiled tight, ready to attack. He'd been shot, beaten, tortured and stabbed numerous times. This was far worse. With one touch she had disarmed him. She'd destroyed him. Utterly destroyed him.

"You're just tired, Gavriil. Like me, everything that mattered to you was ripped away from you and with it, your heart. Maybe even your soul."

He winced. She was striking far too close to the truth, and she'd already gotten under his skin, taken his heart and now she was looking into him. No one did that. No one. He protected himself at all times, yet her green eyes saw right through his armor and now she'd turned the spotlight on him.

His hand slid up her arm to her throat, his fingers sliding around her neck. She was so small. So vulnerable. He felt her pulse fluttering in his palm. One movement and she would be dead. It was that simple. To save himself he simply had to crush her throat. It would be so easy. So simple. He could be back in the shadows, in the wind and no one would ever find him. No one would ever see him.

She didn't move. Didn't pull away from him. Her eyes never looked away from his. If she saw danger—or death—in his gaze—and he was damned sure that she did—she didn't flinch. She just accepted him.

"What the hell is wrong with you, Lexi? Do you have any idea what I am?" He bit the question out harshly between his teeth, wanting to shake her. She was so close to death but she didn't realize it—or she didn't care. "I'm a fuckin' monster. I don't belong anywhere near you. Take a good look."

He was strong, enormously so. He was twice her size, his palm wrapping around her delicate throat easily. She stood still, one hand locked over his heart, the other resting lightly on his shoulder. Not once did her incredible green eyes waver from his. He realized in that moment she was fighting for him.

Once more her hand slipped into his hair, her fingers combing through the unruly strands. "Gavriil, you were forced to work for monsters. I know how that feels. I know what it's like to know you can't ever see the world or the people in it the way others do."

Her fingers continued to move through his hair, stroking him, taming him with her gentle hand. His hand, wrapped around her throat, was all about violence. Hers, moving through his hair, was calming, even caressing. He felt fear. Real fear.

He'd never been afraid of dying. He didn't have anything to lose. They'd taken everything he cared about from him. But she was asking him to live. To come out of the shadows where he'd existed and actually live.

"I stay here on this farm because I can live a fantasy life. I have my sisters who love and protect me. And they do. Without them, I wouldn't survive."

His entire being rebelled at her revelation. He actually had a physical reaction to her words. She *had* to survive. She had to be in his world. He might be so far gone that he was not redeemable, but if he had one chance, it was with the woman beside him. In any case, with or without him, she was worth far more in the world than he was. He allowed his hand to slip from her throat, back down her arm to her wrist.

"Never make the mistake of thinking we're the same, Lexi," he cautioned. "I'm capable of terrible things. You're not."

"I'm trying to learn," she admitted.

He shook his head. "You be who you are. It isn't necessary to learn anything but defense."

"Levi told me every defense is an offense."

She wasn't running, screaming for help. She hadn't even condemned him and she had known what had been in his mind when his hand circled her throat. He had seen the knowledge in her eyes. Knowledge, not condemnation. "Levi's right, *solnyshko moya*, a good defense should be an offense as well."

His body was beginning to signal he'd had enough. Pain could be pushed back for only so long. He had forgotten the pain wracking his body every second of every day, just for a while, just while he was with her. Now it was coming back full force and he could do nothing but allow it to wash over him.

"I need to lie down for a few minutes."

He needed to try to formulate a plan, to consider his best course of action and what to do about Lexi. He was terrified for her. He understood why Levi and the others were so protective of her. Like him, she didn't fear death. She'd had too much taken from her, and she was willing to put herself in harm's way to give him a chance.

She wasn't as naïve as he'd suspected. She knew he was the devil. She knew he was a wild animal capable of destroying her, yet she stood there in front of him with her wide-open, all-seeing eyes and invited him inside. Invited him to do his worst and promised silently that she'd stand by to catch him.

No one had ever done such a thing for him. No one. He was humbled by her. Shocked. Outraged. He feared her complete power over him—and she had all the power whether she knew it or not.

"Of course. Come into the house."

Lexi found herself nervous all over again—this time not because she was bringing a stranger into her home—but because she was attracted to him. She'd never been attracted to any man. She hadn't thought it possible. He was lost just as she was. Maybe worse. He'd gone down a path she so easily could have gone down without her sisters.

He'd thought about killing her. She saw him, the wounded animal that he hid from everyone else, and he'd been so fearful that he actually had considered striking out at her. Just the way a cornered, wounded animal would. She'd stayed very still, breathing for both of them, accepting his decision. Waiting for him to make up his mind. Was he going back to the shadows, or was he going to try to live.

Gavriil Prakenskii was a man worth fighting for. He

needed someone to throw him a lifeline. Everyone saw the violence in him, but no one seemed to see his pain—or his worth. She did. She identified with him.

She knew Gavriil had to be more uncomfortable than she was and that helped her to move with confidence through her house, pointing out the bathrooms and showing him each bedroom so he could choose the one he'd feel safest in while he slept—if he could actually sleep.

Lexi preferred wide-open spaces so she could see what was coming at her. Her house, unlike most of her sisters', was a single story. She didn't want to be trapped upstairs and not have an easy escape. The house was long and branched out in all four directions, east, west, south and north, with the living room being the central location. Great arches led the way to the various directions.

The kitchen was situated to the east. She liked to look out over the sink when she worked, either cooking or cleaning, out the large windows to the forest toward the back of the property. Two bedrooms were located on the southern side, opening from the great room via the arches. A large sunroom was located to the west. A jungle of plants grew everywhere and the sound of running water could be heard. The main bedroom was situated on the northern side.

Situated in the very back leading to a large verandah was an immense atrium, a lush indoor rain forest with a jungle of plants, water flowing into a small pond and tiny birds flitting from one plant to the next. The atrium ran the length of the house. He'd never seen anything like it. The sound of water was soothing, and the floor-to-ceiling plants definitely made one feel serenity and far from the craziness of crowds.

Her furniture was Asian. She surrounded herself with calm. Prevailing colors were black, white and red. She hoped Gavriil felt at peace in her home. Each piece of furniture was something she loved, but she didn't have much of it.

"Where do you sleep?" Gavriil asked. He'd looked into each of the three bedrooms and none of them looked lived in. Her house was beautiful and comfortable, but she didn't live there. She lived outside among the trees and vegetation.

"The bedroom to the north is my bedroom."

"Have you ever actually slept in it?"

She ducked her head and smiled at the hardwood floor. "No one's ever asked me that before. No. I never have."

"Where do you sleep?" he repeated.

"Outside. On the porch," she admitted.

"That's why you have the sleeping bag stashed out there." He shook his head, fighting not to touch her. "It gets cold here."

Lexi lifted her head, smiling at him. Her smile had a way of turning his insides to mush. Everything about her was a new experience for him. He was finding out more about himself the longer he was in her company, more than he'd ever known.

"It does," she admitted. "But I feel safe when I'm outside."

"We'll have to see what we can do to change that."

"Then you'll stay?"

Her green gaze collided with his. His palm itched. His body hardened. She was beautiful from the inside out.

"Do you actually have even an ounce of self-preservation left in you?" he demanded harshly.

She winced. Her gaze skittered away from his. She shrugged. Gavriil cursed himself. He hadn't meant to hurt her, but what she was doing, knowing what he was, was just plain stupid. Or she had a death wish.

Lexi turned to walk out of the room, but he shackled her wrist, careful to be gentle when he wasn't feeling that way at all.

"I didn't mean that the way it came out."

Her gaze jumped to his again and he found himself falling into her green eyes. He wasn't certain which one of them was the prisoner. He had her by the wrist, preventing movement, but he couldn't get out of her eyes.

"Yes, you did. Don't patronize me, Gavriil. I'm not a little puppy you just kicked. I'm a grown woman and I make my own decisions. I choose to let you stay here with me because when I look at you, I see myself. I was given a chance here. I'm just extending that same chance to you. Take it or leave it. That's up to you."

They stared at each other a long time. He found himself smiling. For the first time, his smile was actually genuine. "Believe that's the only reason if you like. I'll let you get away with it for a little while. And next time I hurt your feelings, kick me."

She raised her chin. "I'd probably break my toe." A small answering smile curved her soft mouth, drawing his attention to her lips. "In any case, I'm supposed to be teaching you, by example, that violence is not the answer."

"If I stay with you, are we going to have rules?" Now he was just plain amused. He lived a life without contact with others and he certainly wasn't civilized, nor did he follow rules.

"I've been giving that some thought," she admitted, watching him as he crossed the room to look into the closet.

The northern bedroom was the largest of the three, with a private, very spacious bath and an enormous walk-in closet. He glanced inside. She didn't have much in the way of clothing. Old faded jeans with holes in them and soft flannel shirts seemed to be her apparel of preference. Well . . . he might change that as well. At least put a dress or two in her closet.

"Gavriil."

Her voice was tentative, as if she wanted to say something but was shy about it. She looked shy, faint color stealing beneath her skin. She put her thumbnail in between her teeth and bit down.

Gavriil gently tugged on her wrist until she released the thumbnail. "There isn't anything you can't talk to me about. It's just us. You and me. Say it."

"I know you're in pain. I can see it. I was told that you'd been stabbed several times and that the wounds were extremely severe."

"It was a long time ago," he said, keeping his tone neutral, not understanding why she was having such a difficult time coming out with whatever she had to say.

"I know. And sometimes when a wound is too old, there's nothing I can do about it, but once in a while, I can do some good."

He tilted his head to one side and studied her face. She was really embarrassed now. Her face was red and she definitely avoided his gaze. He caught her chin, forcing her eyes up to his face.

"Are you telling me you think you can do something to reduce the pain? When every doctor I've gone to says I have to live with it and take drugs to get by?" There was no way he could take drugs or drink. That would get him killed eventually.

She nodded. "I hope I can. I can sometimes feel where the pain is coming from and unblock or redirect the path of the nerve. For you to have this much pain, it has to be more than chronic inflammation."

"Mostly nerve damage," he admitted.

"I really think I could help—at least I'd like to try."

"What's making you so nervous?" He didn't let go of her chin or allow her gaze to shift from his.

She touched the tip of her tongue to her lower lip. Her lashes swept down to veil her eyes for a moment, and then he felt her take a breath as if making up her mind.

"I have to see the damage to your body. Put my hands on you. I mean like your bare skin."

She was red from her head to her toes. He was certain if he could see her scalp even that would be red.

"I'm not making a pass at you. I can't do that sort of thing . . . I just want to help you. I mean . . ." Her thumbnail came back up toward her mouth.

He caught her hand to prevent the movement. "You're trying to say you're not going to jump me the minute you have me naked on the bed."

He'd never teased anyone, not since his parents had been

murdered, but he couldn't possibly help himself. He thought he'd forgotten how it was done, but she was priceless trying to convince him she wasn't attempting to seduce him.

Lexi cleared her throat twice. "Yes. That's exactly what I'm trying to say."

"Why do you think you can't do *that* sort of thing?" He kept the amusement out of his voice. He could ensure she would be quite pleased to do that sort of thing—with him. "I'm very good, just in case you were considering it." He couldn't help teasing.

She stared at him in horror and then burst out laughing. "Very funny. I wasn't wondering."

He was fairly certain that was the strict truth, but she would be now that he'd planted the thought. Sex clearly was a taboo subject, and he couldn't blame her. Her introduction had been a nightmare.

"I'll concede that you're just going to . . . um . . . *inspect* my body for completely altruistic reasons. What do you want me to do?"

"I'll go get the herbs I need and some needles and incense and you can take a shower and get under the sheets. They're clean. I don't sleep on the bed, but I do the laundry every week."

He shook his head. "Do you have any idea how bizarre that is? You wash the sheets once a week but you don't sleep on the bed?"

"My sisters usually come over on Saturday, so it's just simpler not to have to explain. They'd get all worried and want me to go back to the counselor, and I've made as much peace with the situation as I'll ever be able to. I don't want to keep talking about it." Lexi folded back the thick down comforter to reveal bamboo sheets.

Gavriil didn't know what to say. He was going to let her try to work her magic on him, but he knew it wouldn't work. Every doctor he'd gone to—and there had been many in various countries—had told him there was no hope. His body was too damaged. But still . . . She'd worked up the courage to tell him she might be able to help even though she was horribly embarrassed that she had to ask him to let her see his body.

"The towels are on the rack. There's soap and shampoo, and I keep extra toothbrushes in the drawer. I'm always losing them," Lexi said.

He raised his eyebrow for an explanation. She flashed a small, enigmatic smile, shrugged and left the room. He took a long, deep breath. This had been the most he'd talked with someone in a very long time. It was the first time he'd spoken with someone he considered "good."

He undressed slowly, stashing weapons around the room and under the pillow. He hung his coat in the closet, ensuring the weapons and ammunition in the loops inside the coat didn't show. He folded his clothes neatly and set them on the floor beside the bed with a gun under his shirt. Another knife and gun were stashed inside his boots, positioned on the other side of the bed.

He measured the distance across the bed, certain he could reach either side with his long arms from the center of the mattress. Before stepping into the shower, he took careful stock of the room, the exits and entrances, the visual from outside from every conceivable spot in the room. He observed everything in the room that could be used as a weapon, including the pen and paper she had on top of her bureau.

Only when he was certain he knew every inch of the room, including where floorboards creaked, did he enter the bathroom. There was an Asian feeling to the bathroom as well. The shower stall was spacious, as was the tub. He liked that he could see anything coming at him and wondered if Lexi had drawn up the layout of the room with that in mind.

As he allowed the hot water to pour down over him, he faced the door, left slightly open to ensure he would be aware the moment anyone entered the bedroom. His favorite hold-out gun, plastic and small, was always inches from his fingers. Three throwing knives were just in reach, laid out on top of the towel.

He realized the shower was one of the places he always felt vulnerable. He often attacked his target in a bathroom. Most people were busy relaxing there, thinking they had complete privacy. Certainly Lexi would feel vulnerable in a shower, probably whenever she was in the bathroom. He knew immediately why she lost her toothbrushes—she didn't brush her teeth there. She probably wandered around outside where she could see anything or anyone coming near her home.

Caine had attacked her in the bathroom, in the shower. He wanted her terrorized, afraid of him coming from any direction. He took her safety from her. He'd abducted her from her home and then went back and murdered her family years later. He sent the message that nowhere was safe and no one could keep her safe.

"Gavriil? I'm coming in to lay everything out," Lexi called, warning him.

He considered walking out naked, but after his revelations, and he was certain he was right, he shut off the water, managed a cursory drying and wrapped a towel around his hips. He slipped the gun into the small of his back, tucking it into the towel, and left the throwing knives.

"I'm going to warn you, *solnyshko moya*, the front of me isn't a pretty sight." He had never given a damn what he looked like. The web of scars was horrendous, and that meant working out to stretch the scar tissue so he could move fast and easy when he needed to. He told himself it still didn't matter, but he hesitated, just for one moment. No one else would have ever noticed, but he did.

He kept his features expressionless and breezed into the room, watching her closely as she turned toward him. Her gaze jumped to his chest and she let out a small gasp. His gut tightened. Immediately she came toward him, her face a mask of concern, her eyes soft. The pads of her fingers went to the raised scars just to the right of his heart.

"The blade nicked your heart. It had to have. How in the

world did you survive this? No one could survive such a wound."

He nearly grabbed her wrist and pulled her hand down. Her touch sent streaks of fire racing through his bloodstream. His cock stirred in spite of the rigid control he imposed on himself, and that *never* happened. Never. Yet now it had happened twice.

She indicated the bed, without seeming to notice he was a man. That didn't do anything for his ego. He'd been afraid of alarming her, and she hadn't even glanced down. Not once. He knew because he didn't take his eyes from her. He'd made up his mind to keep everything between them absolutely platonic, but perversely, when she didn't look at him, he wanted nothing else.

"Woman," he said, exasperated with himself. "You're enough to drive a man to drink."

She blinked and looked up at his face, into his eyes. "I'm sorry. It's just that I'm so shocked that you survived. Get on the bed and just relax. It will take a few minutes."

He shook his head. If someone had told him he'd be lying naked on a bed for a woman to "examine" his old injuries, he would have told them they were insane. He found himself obediently following her instructions, pulling up the sheet and tossing the towel aside, taking time to slide the gun under the other pillow.

He watched her moving around the room, lighting candles and incense, and found her soothing. There was a bowl of herbs on the nightstand. He had a sense of the surreal, a dreamworld that didn't exist, one where his woman enjoyed caring for him.

Lexi returned to the bed, a look of concentration on her face. Her hand brushed back the hair on his forehead, the lightest of gestures, barely there, but it could have been a burning brand pressing her straight through skin and muscle to bone. She was taking him over, and he was just lying there, allowing her to do it.

He forced himself not to react, staying very still while

she climbed up on the bed, her gaze on his chest. He was a mass of scars and he'd never really thought about it before. Front and back, there was hardly a place that had normal skin. She knelt close to his body, bending over him.

The first touch of her hands nearly had him coming off the bed in alarm. Her eyes were closed, but her hands lay against his skin lightly, palms down. Every muscle in his body tightened. Every cell responded to her touch. The feel of her skin against his skin took his breath away. He'd felt a woman's hand on his body many times, strokes and caresses meant to inflame him, to arouse him, yet not a single one had ever affected him the way her touch did.

She wasn't trying to be sensual. Her lashes were long and dark against her fair skin. Her face was a mask of concentration, not sensuality, yet his body reacted naturally to her touch, coming alive under the pads of her fingers and the stroke of her palms. His heart beat too fast. His breath came in ragged, labored gasps. If she looked at him, she'd see his features carved with harsh sensuality, when she felt none of that terrible arousal threatening to consume him.

He tried to breathe away the sensation. It was absurd how much pleasure her touch generated when she wasn't trying to arouse him. It was illogical and irrational how much he wanted her when such things were completely foreign to his nature. He was always logical, unemotional and detached. She turned his well-ordered world upside down.

The energy Lexi generated was so intense heat flashed through his entire body as her palms and fingers slipped over his chest. She stopped in places and the most adorable little frown would appear, then smooth out when she found whatever she was looking for and she would continue on.

Her hands moved over the heavy muscles of his chest, covering each of the three stab wounds there with the ridges of scars and then began to move lower. Gavriil gritted his teeth. This was worse than the training when he'd been a boy and they'd sent women to arouse him, doing all sorts of things to his body. He'd been beaten if he reacted—or didn't react—depending on what he was told to do. The lesson had been all about control and discipline, and he had that—or did, until Lexi.

There was no controlling his body's reaction when her hands slid lower over the defined muscles of his abdomen and the four stab wounds surrounded by scar tissue. If her eyes hadn't been closed and her concentration hadn't been so complete, she would have run screaming from the room.

His cock raged at him, hard and thick and long, coming alive and making urgent, savage demands. He swore between his teeth, his breath hissing out. That part of his anatomy had become a separate entity, and was totally out of control. His hips moved subtly, beneath the sheet, trying to ease the painful ache between his legs.

"Shush, I'm almost done," she whispered, without opening her eyes. "I think I've got this. I'll have to do a small bit of work at a time, but the worst damage is around your heart."

She moved her hands back up to the largest area of scar tissue. "He must have stabbed you and twisted the knife as he brought it out of you."

He remembered that moment. The blade going into his body, the pain and near paralysis that had almost cost him his life. He had such control of his body, of his heart and lungs, that he'd nearly shut them down to keep from bleeding out. He couldn't actually repair his heart himself, but he'd managed to shore it up until he got to a hospital.

Lexi opened her eyes. "I'm going to try to open up the pathways that have been broken. Just try to relax. I'll just work on this one, right near your heart. The first session probably won't make a huge difference, but you should feel it."

She worked the acupuncture needles like a pro. He'd been in China several times over the years and had done his own studies there. He recognized good work when he saw and felt it. "Where did you learn this?"

For a few minutes he didn't think she'd answer him. She placed the needles carefully. He felt the burn of each one sizzling along a nerve ending that had dead-ended long ago, leaving him with so much damage the pain never stopped. Right then, it seemed, the fire burned hot right through the blockage.

"There was a woman in the compound, a doctor from China. Her American husband had become part of the cult and she couldn't leave. She tried to help me. We spent a great deal of time together. She taught me what she knew about herbs and healing. I knew how to read of course, we had to read the bible every day, but math and other subjects weren't considered important for someone like me . . ."

"What does that mean, someone like you?"

Again there was silence. She flicked at another needle. He felt a splash of something wet on his chest and his gaze jumped from the needle to her face.

"Lexi, don't. Don't cry. He's not worth your tears. Whatever he told you, whatever he called you, none of that is true."

"I know. I do know. It's just a little close right now." She forced her head up and gave him a watery smile. "You'll need to rest. The needles will make you sleepy. I'll be back in about forty minutes to remove them. Don't shoot me."

"I wouldn't consider it. Strangling is so much more personal."

That got a real smile out of her.

"While you're drifting off to sleep, please think about staying here. Your brothers have found peace here. I did too. I think you would, Gavriil, if you gave it a chance. None of us here would have chosen what happened to us, but we can change our futures. We can choose how we want to live and with whom."

"Sweetheart, no one's going to give me the chance to stay here. I'll be lucky if I get half an hour's rest, and I can't say as I blame them."

She turned abruptly and came back to the bed. "What do you mean?"

"Do you really think your sisters and my brothers are going to leave you with the wolf? They think of you as a little lamb, and they know what I am. Right at this moment, they're deciding how best to handle throwing me out without hurting my feelings—or getting hurt." He gave a small, humorless laugh. "They really should have said their piece before they left me alone with you."

She smiled. That reaction was the last one he expected, because it was a genuine smile with love softening her eyes. "Aren't they wonderful? All of them? See, Gavriil, that's exactly what I'm talking about. It doesn't matter how the world around me might be falling apart or whether or not I'm having a bad day, they care. They always care. It's nice to have that, and you need it."

He wasn't sure what he needed. He only knew that when he was away from her, he had no feelings. He felt no emotion. He had no idea why the Prakenskii connection had worked on a woman like her, or why when he was in her company, he was a better person, a human rather than a machine. Yet with her, his emotions seemed to be out of control and nearly overwhelming.

"Stay here. Stay with me, in this house. If you need to be alone, I can make do somewhere else." She looked around her bedroom. "They built me a house because they love me and they felt I needed a home." She indicated the window, the farm beyond it. "That's home. That and everyone who lives here on this farm."

"Lexi, you have no idea what you're offering." Was she insane? Did she not see him? Could she really be so blind that even when he told her what he'd done, she didn't understand who and what he was?

"Of course I do. When you look at me, Gavriil, what do you see? A child?"

Hell no, he didn't see a child, he almost wished he did. They wouldn't be having this conversation and she'd be safe. "I see a beautiful woman with compassion in her heart, too much maybe."

She smiled, and this time it was all for him. When she smiled like that he was fairly certain she could shatter him if this thing between them went much further.

"I knew you saw more than the rest of the world." She

seemed very pleased that he could see into her when he was appalled that she could see him so clearly.

"It was in your eyes when you looked at me. I know I'm broken. I know that. But that's all they see. They don't see that I'm happy. I'm okay with being broken. I have severe panic attacks and I hate them, but every day I get up and I go to work and I deal with whatever comes my way."

"You're the youngest, naturally they'd be protective. You're all protective of Rikki because she's different."

"We're protective of one another for various reasons, even the men. But I'm not nearly as fragile as everyone thinks I am. I choose not to go into town, not because I can't, I just don't enjoy it. If necessary, I go. The point here is, no one can say who stays in my home and who goes. I choose to allow you to stay. I want you to at least give yourself a chance, even if it's just for a day, to experience something different. You don't have to worry about going to sleep. I'll sit on the porch and watch over things until you wake up."

Good God, she was actually offering to guard him. Gavriil felt as if she was bringing him to his knees. What in the hell was he supposed to do with a woman like Lexi? He didn't have softer emotions. She needed care. He was going to stay because he *had* to stay, not because it was the right thing. He could offer her protection. No one would ever harm her with him around. That much he could give her.

"I'll stay for a little while whether or not the others like it. Caine felt the need to confess his sins before he died. He admitted to me that there are several cult members who were aware that you were here, on the farm."

She went rigid, flinging her hand out to catch the door-frame for support. "We have children here. Airiana's four children. Their parents were murdered so they could be used as sex slaves. One sister, Nicia's twin, was killed. Nicia and Benito were both . . ." she broke off.

"They'll be safe. Look at me, Lexi. See who I am." He waited until her eyes met his. He let her see the cold-blooded killer in him. She didn't move, didn't run. She looked at him as if he was an angel, not a devil. "I give you my word I won't let anything happen to you or those children. I don't give my word lightly. No one will get through me to any of you."

She looked into his eyes for a long time and the tension slowly eased out of her. She nodded her head. "Go to sleep for a little while, Gavriil. I'll be just outside on the porch. No one will get past me to you."

He heard the honesty and determination in her voice and wanted to weep.

4

"TELL me why you're so upset, Levi," Rikki demanded. She pushed a hand through her thick, sun-kissed dark blond hair, clearly agitated.

"I don't know what you mean," Levi hedged. Since they'd been together he'd never once deceived his wife, and yet his older brother had been on the property a few hours and he was already dodging her question.

Rikki shot him a look, the one that said he'd better answer truthfully. She might be autistic, but she was highly intelligent and she knew her husband very well. He would never have invited someone to their home without first talking it over with her—and certainly not to spend the night.

"You didn't want Gavriil staying with Lexi. I need to know why," Rikki insisted. "I don't like that you're keeping something from me, especially when I can plainly see that you're worried about Lexi."

Levi glanced at Thomas. Judith sat beside him on the railing. Thomas folded his arms across his chest. He looked formidable. That wasn't going to help them now. It was too late. Gavriil had made that abundantly clear.

"I don't know how to explain it," Levi admitted. "Gavriil's my brother."

"So are Thomas and Max, but you didn't have this kind of reaction with them," Judith pointed out.

"That's not true," Thomas clarified. "He met me late at night and threatened to take my head off if I hurt you the first time I ever really saw him here."

"You did?" Judith looked pleased. "That's so sweet, Levi."

Levi groaned. Thomas smirked.

"Not sweet, Judith," Levi corrected. "You can't ever call me sweet. I was willing to kick his ass, which is manly and macho, *not* sweet. I've completely lost my reputation with you women."

"You're not getting off track that easily," Lissa said, her red hair throwing off sparks. "What's wrong with your brother? All of you are uneasy with him being here. Right at this moment he's alone with our little sister."

Max shook his head. "We're glad he's here. You have no idea what it's like to lay eyes on one another and actually have a conversation after the years apart."

"But you didn't," Airiana pointed out. "You didn't converse with him, at least not when we were with you."

The three men exchanged long looks, but none of them answered the question.

"When we started this farm," Blythe said, "all of us agreed to be truthful with one another, and to talk things out when there were problems. We've all had a voice in every decision. You came here and took on those same rules. We're loyal to one another. Of course your brother is welcome here, but if you know something we don't, or if Lexi is in any kind of danger, you owe it to us to tell us."

"His aura is very powerful," Judith added. "And violent. When Levi first came here, I was terrified for Rikki because Levi's aura seemed extremely dark, but Gavriil's is worse. Far worse." She looked to Airiana for confirmation.

Airiana nodded, slipping her hand into Max's. "I'm sorry to say it, but it's true. His aura was unrelentingly dark. I couldn't catch a glimpse of anything, any other trait than pure violence."

"He's not a psychopath," Levi snapped, and then shook his head. "I'm sorry. It's just that, it's difficult for someone else to know what we've been through, especially Gavriil and Viktor, our older brothers. They bore the worst of it."

Rikki rubbed her hand down Levi's back and leaned close to him, her body brushing up against his, a rare gesture for her in public, even around her sisters. Usually Levi was the one to touch her or show affection openly. In private, Rikki was extremely loving to him, but when she did something others would think of as insignificant such as her small gesture, to Levi, it was a huge declaration of love.

He brought her hand to his mouth and pressed a kiss along her knuckles. "I'm sorry, Rikki. I knew better than to offer our home to Gavriil. I didn't want him to leave, but I didn't want him alone with Lexi. I just didn't know the right thing to do."

She brushed her fingertips down his jaw, looking at him with eyes the color of obsidian. "It's all right, Levi. I would rather you protect Lexi than worry about how I might handle your brother in our home. We could have worked that out. Do you think she's in danger?"

"From Gavriil?" Levi hesitated, uncertain what he thought. Gavriil had marked Lexi in the way of their family, claiming her for his own, but the women were right, violence had been Gavriil's way of life. Levi didn't really know him at all. How could he assure the women that Lexi was safe with him when he didn't know himself?

"Yes, Levi," Lissa persisted. "From Gavriil."

"I don't know." He had to be honest. He looked a little helplessly at his brothers.

Lissa muttered something that sounded like a curse and jumped off of Rikki's porch. "I'm going back to her house. If that man has touched one hair on her head, I'm going to kill him myself."

"Lissa, hang on," Max cautioned. "Gavriil is different. You can't come at him like a runaway freight train. He isn't going to respond. He's a shadow. He took apart Caine and found out that other cult members know Lexi's here. Gavriil seemed determined to protect her from them. If that's the case, he isn't going to budge until he gets the job done. Nothing you say or do will change his mind."

"And quite frankly," Thomas added, "you can't kill him. You would never lay a hand on him. He's a scary bastard, even for one of us to take on. Hell, for all three of us to take on. If we knew Lexi was in trouble, we'd do it, but . . ."

"He marked her," Levi interrupted abruptly. "I saw him. Palm to palm. Right in front of me. Deliberately in front of me to warn me to back off."

There was a silence. Airiana, Judith and Rikki rubbed their palms down their thighs. Blythe looked alarmed, and Lissa frowned at them.

"What do you all know that I don't? What does that mean?" Lissa demanded.

"In our family, generations back," Thomas explained, "we've always had this strange gift." He reached for Judith's hand and turned her palm over, running his thumb across the center. Two intertwined circles rose beneath the skin for one moment and then receded.

Lissa gasped. Thomas brought Judith's palm to his mouth and pressed a kiss into the center right over the mark.

"I have one as well," he added. "We all do. It can only happen with one woman. Once she's chosen, and our gift accepts her, we can choose to use our onetime connection that binds us closer. As far as I know, no Prakenskii would ever choose a woman, bind her and then walk away. If he did, he would have to have a powerful reason."

"He did that to Lexi?" Lissa asked incredulously. "Does he have any idea what she's been through? She'll be so afraid. She isn't ready for any kind of a relationship."

"Honestly," Max said, "I don't think Gavriil is either. However traumatized Lexi's been, I can assure you, Gavriil's had equal or more. Viktor, my oldest brother, and Gavriil were taken to the worst training schools. The conditions were brutal; all of us in the other schools knew about those places and how harsh they were. We were brutalized enough, and the thought of being sent to one of the other schools was enough to keep most of the students in line."

"I'm sorry about that," Lissa said, "I really am, but he can't force Lexi into anything she doesn't want. She's been forced enough times in her life without having it happen again."

"What can we do?" Judith asked.

"I'm not willing to tell my brother he isn't welcome here," Thomas added. "Not unless he does something that upsets Lexi. We're all speculating here because we're uneasy, but we don't know what's going on at her house."

"Then we need to find out," Blythe said firmly. "One of us needs to go back there and check on her. If we all go, it will look as if we're attacking Gavriil in some way."

"I know Lexi. If she thinks we're all in some way going after him," Lissa added, "she'll defend him. She doesn't want to hurt a snail in her gardens let alone someone she considers wounded. If we make her look at him like that, she'll fight for him and not think about the consequences to herself."

They all looked at one another. Airiana glanced toward her land. Each of them had five acres of their own within the farm's acreage, and right now, she was concerned with what was going on with the children. She wouldn't put it past Benito to be spying on them all.

"I'll go if you want me to," she volunteered, reaching for Max's hand. "But probably Benito will follow us."

"Let me do it," Blythe said. "If I go alone, no one is going to see me as a threat. I can take some food over. Levi, can you whip something up for me, sandwiches maybe?"

"*Not* peanut butter," Lissa said, referring to Rikki's beloved ingredient she thought was a perfect meal for breakfast, lunch and dinner.

"Hey! I eat more than peanut butter," Rikki said. "I actually can eat a few other things now, can't I, Levi?"

He ruffled her hair. "You do, and I'm so proud of you. I'll see what I can find, Blythe. That's a good idea." He went into the kitchen. Their door was generally open, leaving just the screen closed. He would be able to hear their conversation while he put together a lunch.

"And then you'll call us," Lissa said anxiously to Blythe. "I won't be able to work on anything until I know she's safe."

"I think Lexi's the safest person on this farm," Max said. "Gavriil will protect her with his life. If you've got him, you don't need the rest of us. He's a one-man army."

"I just don't want him making any demands on her," Lissa said. "What exactly happened this morning? Lexi was so upset she cried a lot when she was telling us."

Thomas shrugged. "Gavriil came to the farm to see us, and he spotted Lexi. He followed her to the other piece of property, but he was on foot and she was in the trail wagon. When he spotted her, one of the men was rushing her with a knife and he shot him first and then the second man who was armed as well."

"But not Caine," Judith said.

"Caine was already trapped in the ground. Lexi used the kick-out move we've been working on and she connected with Caine's knee and thigh, driving him away from her. That gave her enough time to open a crack in the ground. He sank to his thighs and the ground closed, trapping his legs there," Max explained.

"But he wasn't dead?" Lissa persisted.

"Not right away," Thomas said. "He lived a little longer, just long enough to tell Gavriil others would be coming after Lexi."

"Why would he tell Gavriil that?" Rikki asked.

"Gavriil said he felt the need to confess," Thomas said, using a tone that said that avenue of conversation was closed.

The women exchanged a long look of comprehension.

"Don't look now," Max cautioned, "but we're under surveillance, and it's not Benito this time."

Airiana scooted over to casually lean her hip against the railing beside Max, fitting beneath his shoulder. She tried not to laugh. "Nicia and Siena? They're babies. What in the world are they doing over here?"

"They've got Benito's binoculars, and he's never far from them," Max said.

"I think the strap has grown right into his neck," Airiana agreed. "If the girls are here, Lucia must be as well. She doesn't let them out of her sight, and this is her first official big babysitting opportunity. I told her I'd pay her to watch the children for an hour or two, but that I'd be on the property if they needed us."

"Where is that little devil?" Max asked. "He's got to be close by."

Airiana tilted her head up to Max's face. "Surely you're not referring to our son as a 'devil.' He's so like you."

"My point exactly."

"If you can't see him," Blythe said, "he's really becoming like you. When have you never been able to spot someone sneaking up on you? I think it's so great that he's emulating you."

"They spend every night in our bedroom," Max groused. "All four of them. The two little girls are in our bed. Lucia sleeps on Airiana's side on the floor, and Benito sleeps on my side on the floor. We've taken to escaping through the upstairs window to the gazebo. Of course they position themselves perfectly to know if we get up and try to sneak out. That boy has actually tried to follow us."

Rikki snickered. Lissa burst out laughing. Judith covered her mouth and buried her face in Thomas's shirt. Thomas and Levi laughed uproariously.

"I can see I'm not getting any sympathy from the lot of you," Max said, but his eyes were laughing, and there was no doubt that he was proud of Benito's blossoming abilities.

"Fortunately for you," Levi said, returning to the porch with a picnic basket filled with food, "it isn't easy to get close to this house. All the ground cover is low, and fireproof. He can't have overheard us."

"I wouldn't put it past him to have some sort of a listening device," Max said. He frowned as he surveyed the food

Levi handed over to Blythe. "Is that a picnic basket? I mean like a real one? With a handle and plates and silverware?"

"Does it have a checkered cloth as well?" Thomas asked innocently.

"Go to hell, both of you," Levi suggested, with a rude gesture behind Rikki's back. "You're jealous because I'm civilized and know what a picnic basket is."

"Is there something wrong with a picnic basket?" Rikki asked, her eyes widening. She turned as though looking to Levi for an answer.

Levi scowled darkly at his brothers. "They're trolls, baby, of course there's nothing wrong with using a picnic basket."

"Oh. I thought maybe you bought it as a joke or something," she said, looking serious.

Thomas and Max nearly fell to the porch floor laughing. Thomas actually held his sides. Levi couldn't help laughing either. It was rare for Rikki to tease him. He definitely hadn't bought the picnic basket. Judith had given it to Rikki, thinking she might use it on her boat when she went diving. Rikki used a cooler, but she treasured the basket because it had been a gift.

"He's on the roof," Max said suddenly, his head snapping around. He glared up at the rooftop. "Benito, get down from there right this minute."

"That's awesome," Levi said. "He made it all the way across the open yard and didn't tip any of us off to his presence. He's getting good, Max."

"Benito, I'm warning you. Get your butt down from that roof right this minute," Max said. "Airiana's about to have a heart attack."

Airiana raised her eyebrow. Clearly Max was the one worried about Benito's safety, but she didn't contradict him. "Do come down, Benito," she encouraged.

"Did you come in from the other side of the house?" Levi asked, as the boy shimmied down from the top of the roof to the overhang of the porch.

Before he could answer, Max reached up and caught the

boy around the waist, pulling him down and setting him down beside him none too gently. "Stop scaring Airiana."

"Sorry, Airiana," Benito murmured, his eyes bright with his accomplishment. He couldn't stop smiling. "I did it, Max. All three of you and the women. I snuck up on you, and no one even noticed me."

"You used your sisters as bait, keeping our eyes on them, didn't you?" Thomas asked.

Benito nodded. "Max said to use any distraction that might seem natural. I knew it would tip you off that I was close, but if you weren't looking at them, you might have felt me getting close to the house."

Max dropped his hand on top of the boy's head and carelessly ruffled his hair. "That was good thinking. What did you use to get up on the roof? There's nothing to climb on to make that kind of height."

He knew Levi wouldn't keep a ladder that close to the house and there were no trees to use the branches.

Benito looked smug. "Rikki always sleeps with the window open. I've never seen it closed, not once when I've come around. I just used the windowsill."

Max narrowed his eyes at the boy. "You're not that tall."

Benito shrugged, but he looked a little apprehensive. "I jumped and caught the beam and swung my legs up."

Airiana gasped. "Benito, you could have missed and broken something."

"I know. I realized it wasn't the smartest idea," he hastily admitted. "I won't do it again. I was going to ask Max what would have been a better way to do it, but I was going to wait until you weren't around."

Max groaned and looked away from Airiana's darkening frown.

"Wait until I wasn't around? What exactly do you two discuss when I'm not around?"

"Man things," Benito said, puffing out his chest. "Not for women's ears."

Max clapped his hand over Benito's mouth and pulled the boy into him, pretending to strangle him. "You can't say things like that. How many times do I have to have this conversation with you?"

Airiana made a face at Max. "I see, Benito. How often do you and Max have these little manly talks?"

"Lucia!" Max raised his voice and signaled to the three children still hiding in the brush. "Now would be a really good time for you girls to join us."

"Coward," Airiana hissed, and winked at her sisters.

"I'd better go check on Lexi," Blythe said, tucking her arm through the handle of the picnic basket. "I'll call as soon as I've spoken with her and know what's going on."

"She's safe with him," Max said. "I'm certain of it."

"Who's safe with who?" Benito asked, looking from one to the other.

Blythe laughed. "You have your hands full, Max."

Siena, the youngest child, ran to Airiana and wrapped her arms tightly around her legs. Nicia raced to leap into Max's arms. Lucia sauntered after them. At fourteen, she was trying hard to be grown-up for her younger sisters and brother. Benito and Max had a bond, forged on the ship when Max rescued him, the same with Nicia. Siena naturally gravitated to Airiana, but Lucia hadn't quite made up her mind yet.

Airiana knew she wanted to stay, but she'd trusted the man who had betrayed them and sold them into the human trafficking ring. She was more reserved, watching everyone closely and keeping her sisters and brothers very near to her. This was the first time she'd ever participated in one of Benito's plots to spy.

Lucia seemed to feel most comfortable when she was close to Airiana. She enjoyed being around the others, but she was always very quiet and watchful. Airiana couldn't blame the girl. She'd barely had a chance to process her parents' murder when the man claiming to be their uncle had turned them over to be used and discarded by sex traffickers. Then Nicia's twin sister was murdered and Nicia and Benito assaulted.

How did a fourteen-year-old girl ever trust again? Or

smile or laugh? Lucia was trying for the sake of her younger siblings, but more than once, when she was alone with Airiana, she broke down completely.

Airiana held her hand out to Lucia, smiling in welcome. "Lucia is giving me a lesson in making pasta the way her mother made it. I'm very excited about it. When we finish, we're going to put on a big spaghetti feed for everyone."

Lucia nodded a little shyly.

Judith's eyes lit up. "I would love to learn. I bought a book on it, but failed miserably. Is there room for me? I'm not going into work today, so it would be a perfect day for it."

Lucia glanced up at Airiana, who shrugged. "It's up to you, honey. If it would be difficult with an audience, we'll just do it together."

Lucia was silent a moment, and then she looked up at Judith with her very large, dark eyes. "It would be nice if you could join us. When my mother made noodles, we always had a big group of women all working together. It was fun."

"Then I'll come for certain," Judith said.

"I want in on this," Lissa said. "I can bring fresh sourdough bread to the spaghetti feed if you'd like."

"She gave me a starter," Lucia said to Airiana. "For the sourdough bread. She made it for us when you and Max were gone."

"Of course Lissa can come," Airiana said.

Airiana liked having Lissa around Lucia. Lissa was an outgoing personality and she seemed to enjoy being with the children. She loved board games and often dropped by the house to play with the children in the evenings. She managed to get Benito, Nicia and Siena laughing, but Lucia rarely even smiled. Airiana hoped being in the kitchen, where Lucia excelled, would make Lucia much more comfortable.

Rikki pushed Levi toward the women. "Levi cooks. He's a great cook. I'm . . . um . . . working on gear this afternoon, but Levi could join you."

Everyone knew Rikki didn't cook. Levi had to do the cooking if he wanted to eat. She would have been quite happy living on her beloved peanut butter, something she considered the perfect food.

"He looks good in an apron," Rikki added.

Thomas and Max snorted and the women burst out laughing. Benito pointed at him and roared with laughter.

Levi scooped Rikki up in his arms. "Woman, you're just getting out of hand. Keep it up and you'll be the tender on the boat and I'll be the diver."

"As if." Rikki sniffed disdainfully. "I'm captain *always*."

"You're a pretty cute captain, so I guess I'll follow you around," Levi said, putting her back on her feet. He kept his arm around her. "I would love to learn how to make pasta noodles, Lucia, if you'll have me in your kitchen." He gave her a courtly bow, ignoring his brothers and Benito as they laughed wildly.

For the first time, Lucia gave a small, brief smile. She gave Levi a little curtsy. "You are most welcome in my kitchen, Levi. Benito, you and your two friends can eat out of a box tonight. No fresh pasta for you three," she scolded.

Instantly all three males sobered. "Whoa, now," Thomas said. "We need to rethink this. I look pretty darn good in an apron."

"Is that true, Judith?" Airiana asked. "I can't picture Thomas in the kitchen let alone with an apron on."

Judith raised her eyebrow at her husband. "You've never actually worn an apron that I've ever seen."

"But I'm in the kitchen *all* the time," Thomas pointed out. "It's one of my favorite places."

"Lucia!" Benito burst into a spate of Italian, talking rapidly, trying to get himself out of trouble. He was at his most charming when he spoke his native language. He had no problem using his eyes and good looks to get his way.

"Advocate for both of us," Max reminded.

Lucia threw her hands into the air. "Fine. But stop picking on Levi. He's a brave man to come to my cooking class."

"Yes. Yes, very brave," Benito agreed.

"What time are you giving everyone the lesson?" Blythe asked. "I'm just going to take some lunch to Lexi and talk to her for a few minutes. I'd like to come if I have time."

"We thought we'd start the lesson around one," Airiana answered, glancing at her watch. "I still have to feed the children lunch and then we'll be ready."

"I'll definitely be there," Blythe said.

As Blythe turned to walk away, Lucia stepped forward. Her fingers clutched at Airiana's hand. "You can invite Lexi to join us as well," Lucia managed to get out, her voice painfully shy.

"I'll be happy to, thank you, Lucia," Blythe said. "It's kind of you to include her. Lexi stays too much to herself."

It would be natural for Lucia to recognize Lexi had gone through a similar experience. She had to have noticed how they all checked on Lexi often.

Blythe waved to the others and set out briskly to walk to Lexi's home. She ran several miles every day and the distance wasn't far enough to bother her. She needed the time to think. Gavriil Prakenskii was family. There was no getting around that. His brothers would be upset if he was asked to leave the farm, yet clearly, in some way, they recognized that he was different from them. That worried her.

Without conscious thought she ran her palm down her thigh. Doing the kind of work the brothers had done for so many years would take its toll. Men could go either way. Levi had wanted a different life, and he'd grabbed it with both hands when he'd met Rikki. Thomas had done the same. She hadn't known Max long enough to tell which way he'd gone. He seemed rougher than both Thomas and Levi, but no one could observe him with the children and Airiana and think anything but that he was a family man.

So what was different about Gavriil that had his brothers tense and anxious for Lexi? Had they believed her life was in danger, Blythe was certain they never would have left her alone with the man. She'd been a little shocked that Lexi had insisted Gavriil stay with her. As far as Blythe could remember, Lexi was never alone with any of the men, not even the ones she'd come to consider her brothers.

When they all worked out together in the gym, or practiced self-defense moves, the doors were always open and there was always at least one other woman in the room. Blythe knew Lexi felt affection for Levi and Thomas. She'd only just met Max, but she accepted him on the farm. Still, she stayed away from the men as a rule. She probably was closest to Levi than the others, and even with him, Lexi held herself apart.

Blythe went through the fields of various crops, taking a shortcut to get to Lexi's house. She was surprised at the variety of vegetables that were growing. She hadn't really been paying attention to the farm and how much it had grown.

Lexi sat in her porch swing watching her approach. Blythe waved at her and then gestured around her. "How in the world do you do everything by yourself? You need help. I had no idea the farm had gotten so big."

Lexi smiled in welcome. "It's really doing well. But you're right, it's getting to be too much for me. I've been working longer hours, but sometimes my back hurts so bad I can barely straighten up."

Blythe paused, frowning. "You should have told us, Lexi. You work too hard, and we need to get you help."

Blythe set the picnic basket on the railing and sank into one of the large, comfortable chairs on Lexi's porch. The wraparound deck had been important to Lexi. She'd wanted it large and spacious, but covered from the weather. They spent more time on Lexi's deck when they all visited than in the house.

"Levi sent lunch. He thought you might not be up to cooking yet, after this morning."

"That was thoughtful of him," Lexi said.

"And before I forget, Lucia is giving a lesson on making pasta noodles around one today at Airiana's if you're up for that. She especially asked me to invite you. It seemed important to her."

Blythe studied Lexi's face. She'd been crying. Weeping silently. Lexi rarely made a sound when she cried. Blythe was certain that when she was a child, Caine had beaten her if she made a sound. It always broke her heart when Lexi cried so quietly.

"Are you all right? This morning must have been a nightmare for you."

Lexi nodded slowly. "It certainly brought everything back again. All those memories I try so hard to lock away. I think I close the door and lock it and I won't think about it ever again, but that never works. Somehow, every night that horrible man haunts me. Now, he's taken away my feeling of safety here on the farm. Worse, I'm worried about all of you."

Blythe nodded. "Of course you would be worried about us after what happened to your family, Lexi. It's natural. I've seen the same thing in Lucia. She's so traumatized that she can't let her siblings out of her sight."

"Poor babies. All of them. I hope we can give them some peace here. Although now . . . with Caine finding me . . . I don't know if it's fair to them to have me stay. I've been thinking about that a lot. I don't want to leave, but I can't be selfish either. Those children need stability, and Max and Airiana will give it to them. With Levi and Thomas here, I think they'll be safe."

Blythe leaned toward Lexi. "Is that why you wanted Gavriil to stay with you? Does he make you feel safer?"

Lexi looked surprised. "No. No, I wouldn't use him like that. He's been through enough and it was bad enough that he had to kill someone to save my life. I feel terrible about that, although he just dismisses it like it wasn't anything. But it is, Blythe. Taking a life is always difficult."

Blythe nodded. "That's true. I'm sorry he had to do that too, but I'm grateful to him that he did. I'd much rather have you alive."

Lexi smiled at her. "Thanks, Blythe. I'm grateful as well."

"Is that why you've got him here with you?" Blythe persisted. When Lexi frowned, she continued. "I'm just worried that you're uncomfortable. We all are. We know you don't like being alone with men, and I wouldn't want you to think you have to take him in if you'd rather one of us give him a place to stay. He could even stay in the community building. We could easily make up a room for him there."

Lexi shook her head. "I didn't ask him to stay because I felt beholden to him, Blythe. I wouldn't do that. You know me better than that. I want him here because I feel he needs to be here. I can't explain it any better than that. I'll let him know he has other options, and if he prefers to take anyone else up on their offer or he wants his own place—which he might—I'll call you."

Blythe nodded her head, her gaze steady on Lexi's. "You're certain this is what you want to do?"

"Yes," Lexi said firmly. "I hope that when he's rested, he'll choose to stay. He's worked on farms before." A note of eagerness crept into her voice. "I could use the help, especially if he knows how to run the equipment."

"I thought Thomas volunteered."

Lexi rolled her eyes. "Thomas doesn't know a vegetable from a flower. He wouldn't know a weed if it jumped out of the ground and bit him. And he certainly isn't touching my tractor." A brief smile came and went. "I've had to keep the keys with me at all times since Benito has come to live with us. That boy is curious about everything."

"I'll have Max talk to him."

"Max is the only person he listens to. If Gavriil stays awhile, I might be able to get by without hiring anyone else this year. I'll need more equipment and someone else to work with me for certain, especially if we get that other piece of property. And llamas."

"You and your llamas."

"I want a dog too. I know we're all supposed to vote on that, but I'm here by myself a lot. Dogs would help alert if strangers were around."

The conversation had gotten away from her and there was no way for Blythe to bring it back to Gavriil. She sighed and stood up, conceding the sparring victory to Lexi. She wasn't going to get her younger sister to reveal the real reason she wanted Gavriil to stay with her, but it was clear she was determined that he remain exactly where he was.

"Don't forget we'll be trying to learn how to make pasta at one," Blythe said. "Enjoy your lunch."

"I doubt if I can make it, but I'll try," Lexi said. "I have tons of work to do, and I want to make certain Gavriil gets plenty of sleep."

"He can sleep while you're with us," Blythe pointed out, but kept walking away with a cheery little wave. She'd done her best. As far as she could see, not only was Lexi all right, but she was going to be stubborn about anyone trying to force Gavriil Prakenskii out of her home or off the farm.

5

GAVRIIL lay listening to the voices out on the porch. The window was open and he could hear the conversation easily. Lexi's sister had come to get him out of her house, but somehow Lexi had diverted her from the main subject, and Blythe couldn't do much about it. He found himself smiling in spite of the electricity zinging through his body. His nerve endings felt on fire.

Lexi hadn't told Blythe that he was in chronic, unrelenting pain. She knew how badly his body was damaged, but she hadn't said a word. He wasn't fooling himself. Lexi hadn't taken one look at him and fallen head over heels. She barely noticed he was a man—she viewed him as a wounded animal—but she hadn't given away his secrets.

Lexi was determined to save him. Not fix him, exactly— she wasn't naïve enough to believe that was possible—but she wanted to give him a semblance of peace and that was amazing to him. No one had ever done for him what she was attempting. He was uncomfortable in the presence of others, yet not with her.

The strange thing was, he'd actually dozed off a couple

of times. Sheer madness when he was in such a dangerous position. He couldn't understand why he was so mesmerized by everything about Lexi—but he was and he had to deal with it.

He knew the moment Lexi left the porch and entered the house. She didn't really make much of a sound, just a whisper of footsteps on her hardwood floor, but he had a built-in radar that seemed to follow her every movement. He waited, his heart pounding a little too fast, a little too loud.

It was a bit ridiculous when he could defeat a polygraph by controlling his pulse and breath so easily. He could slow the beating of his heart or any other organ. He controlled every bodily function from his sex drive to his respiration, and yet when Lexi was near, she threw him into complete chaos.

"You're back," he greeted. He hadn't realized how much he wanted to see her, to feel her close to him. He was used to being alone and he'd always preferred that, but suddenly he seemed to be so enamored with her that he didn't want to be apart from her.

"Were you able to sleep at all?"

Just the sound of her voice, her beautiful green eyes drifting over his face as if she enjoyed looking at him, was enough to cause his body to stir.

She came straight to him, leaning over him to examine his chest. Her hair tumbled forward to brush over his skin, the slide like a waterfall of silk where her ponytail swept across his chest. She began to remove the needles one by one. Each time she pulled one from his body, she placed her palm over the spot and closed her eyes for a moment.

"You didn't answer me, Gavriil," she said. "Did you manage to get any sleep?"

He didn't answer, waiting for her to look at him. He wanted to feel the impact of her eyes. Each time he had dozed off he saw her eyes looking at him. Soft. Gentle. Looking into him. Seeing him. He needed to know if it was real, or if the incense and aromatic candles were causing a hallucination of some sort.

Lexi didn't lift her head but her gaze jumped to his. He saw sparkling emeralds. Not light green, but a deep, very dark green, like the cool of the forest.

"A man would kill to have you notice him." The words slipped out before he could stop them. He didn't want her to run from him—to realize he was plotting to find a way to make her fall in love with him.

She looked at him for a long time, searching his eyes as if looking into his soul and seeing how vulnerable she made him feel. A slow smile curved her soft mouth. "Well, you did that already and I definitely have noticed you, so there's no need to do that again."

The teasing note in her voice whispered over him like the stroke of fingers. "I did sleep, thank you. Right now, though, I think I could use a very strong cup of coffee."

"Chamomile tea. With lavender and honey in it," she contradicted, and went back to removing needles. "I know you're probably very uncomfortable right now. Opening up those pathways can be painful. I figured you were already in pain and you handle it, so if it takes a few sessions to get them open and functioning properly without them short-circuiting like they are now, it will be worth it."

"You do realize my nerves are damaged. The doctors say they won't ever heal." He caught her ponytail in his hand, closing the thick mass of hair in his fist. "I went to several different countries and got numerous opinions."

"I'm very aware they are damaged, Gavriil. I could feel the paths blocked and broken. I'm not saying it will work for certain, but usually if I can feel the damage I can fix it." She picked up the tray of needles and started to turn away from him. Her hair, captured in his fist, prevented movement.

Lexi lifted one eyebrow. "I'm betting you haven't eaten in a while."

"I'm used to doing things for myself."

"That's good, because I can barely take care of myself, but just for the next few days, until we get this nerve thing under control, I thought maybe we could compromise."

"How does that work?"

She smiled at him again. Her mouth was beautiful, her lips full and soft, a terrible temptation. "You do everything I say, of course. Right now, I need my hair back so I can make the tea and get the lunch Levi sent over for us."

"Can you cook? I might consider letting you boss me around for a couple of days if you can cook."

"Of course I can cook. And I always use fresh, organic vegetables and herbs." She managed a haughty look even with her sparkling eyes. "Believe me, doing everything I say will be totally worth it. I'm a very good cook, although I tell my sisters I'm not so they occasionally feed me after I've worked all day."

"I didn't notice a lot of use in that kitchen of yours," he hedged. "Letting you boss me around won't be easy. I have to know what you're saying is true." He tugged on her hair as if he was considering the proposal.

"What's to think about? I stick needles in you daily and make you drink all kinds of concoctions that I won't tell you what's in them, boss you around and feed you wonderful meals. I'll even let you have this bed. It's the most comfortable. That's a *huge* concession right there."

"You never sleep in it."

"Exactly. It's brand-new, never been used. Totally comfortable. Judith made certain it was the best. Bamboo, no nasty creatures or fungus would dare touch that mattress. You'll be so safe. And I'll guard you when you sleep."

"This sounds like a dream come true. Really. How could a man go wrong?"

"There's more," Lexi added. Her smile widened, taking his breath away.

"I can't wait," he said.

"When you're all better and forever beholden to me because I'm such a good healer, you can work the farm with me. I might even let you drive my tractor, although I'm not making any promises. That's my baby and I don't let just anyone drive it."

"This proposition of yours just gets better and better," he

replied. He sat up. He had to. Otherwise the thin sheet was going to give away the fact that his body had stirred to life all over again. His cock was really becoming a nuisance. The damn thing had decided to rebel, taking on a life of its own. He discovered that moving around too much with a whale of a hard-on wasn't particularly a great idea.

"Isn't it though? If you have clean clothes, I can wash the ones you were wearing." She indicated his neatly folded stack of clothes. "There's blood on your shirt. I'm always nicking myself, so I'm fairly adept at removing a bloodstain."

He frowned, allowing her ponytail to slide through his fingers, freeing her. "What do you mean, nicking yourself?"

"On tools. I cut myself all the time. I wear leather gloves, but sometimes they're just in the way."

She was so matter-of-fact about injuring herself that it set his teeth on edge. Someone needed to care for her, not the other way around. He found he was irritated at his brothers and the other women on the farm. Clearly they didn't help Lexi, yet they were definitely reaping the rewards of her work.

"Doesn't anyone help you out around here?" His voice was harsh, a low, demanding tone that had her turning away from him.

"Of course they do, when they can. Everyone works. I told you that. At harvest, they all help."

She was quick to defend her family members from any perceived slight. He realized he would have to guard his opinions of the others—and he *was* annoyed with them— no matter what she said. The farm, from what he could see, was huge. It was far too much work for one person.

"That's good," he said, using a neutral, almost casual tone, as if they were discussing things in the abstract. "Because a farm this size definitely needs more than one person working it." He wasn't going to make the mistake of firing her up, forcing her to defend the others. He needed her defending him, not them.

"I don't like strangers around me," Lexi confessed. "The farm is kind of my haven and the thought of someone I don't know hanging around bothers me. I keep thinking I'll hire someone to help out, but so far, I haven't been able to make myself do it. The others have mentioned hiring someone several times but I keep putting it off."

She sounded apprehensive and a little ashamed, as if, by not hiring an outsider, she was a coward. The idea of someone outside the circle of family didn't sit well with him, after all. He didn't want another man working alongside Lexi.

"I suppose there's nothing else for it then," he said, with an exaggerated sigh. "I'll have to take you up on your generous offer and let you boss me around for a few days in order to drive that tractor of yours."

He was rewarded with a quick flick of those deadly green eyes. She fastened her gaze on him, and he felt the bed shifting out from under him. He lifted the sheet enough to keep his body from scaring the hell out of her. She was damned beautiful. She moved like a summer breeze. He hadn't known women like Lexi really existed.

"Why are you suddenly looking so sad?" Lexi asked, concern on her face. She put the tray of needles down on the bureau and came back to him. "What is it, Gavriil? I'm really not bossy. I was teasing you."

"I know that."

Her fingers were back in his hair, stroking it back, massaging his scalp, a comforting, soothing gesture a woman might make to a child. She was petting the wild animal, taming him with her touch.

"What is it?"

He caught her hand before she could inflame his body any further. He'd been fourteen years old when he gained control over that part of his anatomy. He still bore the scars on his back and thighs from the punishments when he wasn't able to. All that training, all those years of discipline were gone in the blink of an eye and she wasn't even trying to seduce him.

"I haven't spent this much time with another human being since I was a child."

She pressed her lips together, her forest-cool eyes never wavering. "You don't have to spend time with me, Gavriil. I have tons of work to do, and I can stay on my porch. There's also a building we all share. Blythe mentioned it and said you could stay there if you preferred being alone."

He couldn't help himself. He brought her fingertips to his mouth and bit gently, his teeth scraping back and forth. It was that or kiss her, and he thought biting at her fingers was far safer for both of them than kissing her. Her eyes darkened. A small frown appeared, but she didn't pull away from him.

He realized she didn't recognize foreplay or seduction. She'd been a child with an evil man and he'd never taken his time with her, or made love to her. Caine had used her, but he had never made her aware of her own sexual appetite. At least Gavriil had been made aware early on that sex could be pleasurable. He doubted if Lexi had a clue.

There had been a few moments between them, like now, where something stirred in her eyes, a flare of sexual confusion, as if he was causing a reaction in her body. She looked a little frightened, as if she didn't know what was happening to her.

"I'm just fine where I am," Gavriil said. "I like being around you. You soothe me. There's something very peaceful about you. I've never been teased before. Do you realize how many 'firsts' you're giving me?"

She smiled and her eyes were like the sun's rays beaming through a canopy of leaves. Her entire face lit up, showing off all her creamy, flawless skin and her full, soft—very tempting—lips. She was killing him without trying. He needed to get his libido under control before he blew his every chance.

"I'm glad."

Awareness crept down his spine. His grip tightened on her hand. "Lexi. I want you to walk into the bathroom and close the door. Casually. Just go into it as if you're going to use it. Keep smiling at me. No questions."

She looked frightened but she nodded her head. She

touched his face, featherlight, but he felt it all the way to his bones.

"It's probably nothing, but I prefer to stay alert," he added quietly.

Lexi held it together, following his instructions exactly, going to the bathroom and closing the door. She moved with unhurried steps, looking natural should anyone be watching.

The moment the door was shut, Gavriil reached for his jeans, turned and slipped into them almost in one motion. He shoved his feet into his boots, and concealed the weapons in their usual places. He was dressed and armed in seconds. He moved with casual grace to the open window. He waited there, just to the left, out of sight. Still. Patient. Baiting his prey. His knife was in his palm, a familiar extension.

There was silence. His heart rate remained exactly the same. His pulse never changed. This, he understood. This was his world. Here he had control. Discipline. Power. He understood the rules.

A whisper of movement told him his prey was growing restless. A shadow moved. Stopped. Gavriil didn't so much as tense. Deep inside, he was coiled and ready to spring, but for the moment he remained utterly still. His mind didn't race. There was no chaos or fear. He was in complete command.

A head appeared in the window and he struck with lightning speed. Grabbing the thick dark hair, he dragged the head all the way inside, exposing the neck, pressing the razor-sharp blade of his knife against the throat. Dark eyes stared up at him. Shocked. Scared. A child's eyes.

"What the hell are you doing here?" Gavriil demanded. "Who sent you?"

"Lexi!" The boy screamed her name.

Lexi emerged from the bathroom at a run. Gavriil, still holding the knife to the boy's throat, blocked her rush, shoving her back behind him.

"Do you know this boy?" Gavriil asked. He didn't take his cold gaze—or the knife—from the boy, not once. In his experience a child could be just as deadly as an adult. He'd made his first kill at fourteen.

"Let him up. That's Benito, Max's boy." Lexi peered around his larger body, staring at the knife that bit just enough into the boy's throat to cause a thin line of blood. "Please don't kill him."

Gavriil removed the knife from the boy's throat, and not so gently dragged him into the room, mostly by his hair.

With one hand he patted the kid down; the other kept him immobile. He retrieved a Glock from the waistband of the boy's jeans and held it up in the air.

"What's this? Were you planning on killing me, boy?" Gavriil kept searching for more weapons. He never just carried one on a job. Evidently the kid felt the same way— he had a hell of a big knife shoved down into his boot.

"Benito! What were you thinking?" Lexi asked, trying to step around Gavriil.

He cut her off with a sweep of his arm. "Stay behind me until we straighten this out. I don't give a damn whose kid he is, not when he comes sneaking around with a gun and knife."

"He's twelve years old," Lexi said. "A child."

"He's not a child when he's armed." Gavriil transferred his hand from the boy's hair to his throat. "You'd better start talking, kid, I can break your neck just as fast as I can cut your throat. Were you hired to kill Lexi?"

"Oh, for God's sake," Lexi said, exasperation in her voice. "He wouldn't do that. He lives here on the farm with Max."

"Then *he* can convince me. You stay behind me, Lexi, or I'm going to have to hurt this kid. I'm not taking chances with your safety."

"Are you her bodyguard?" Benito asked, his eyes nearly rolling back in his head with fear.

The boy didn't move though. Not even a tiny inch to try

to get away from the deadly grip Gavriil had him in. Gavriil had to give him credit for that. Benito was terrified, but he was thinking it all out.

"If you didn't come here to kill Lexi, or me, what the hell were you doing outside the bedroom window? Are you some kind of Peeping Tom?"

Benito shook his head. His gaze clung to Lexi's. He didn't look at Gavriil. "No sir. I was practicing."

"Practicing what? Scaring Lexi?"

His voice was a low whip of menace. What the hell was the kid doing? Did he have any idea just how close to death he'd come?

Lexi started around Gavriil once again to comfort the boy, but he shifted just enough to keep his body between hers and the kid's. She put her hand on the small of his back. For a split second, he was more aware of that contact than anything else.

"He's working on his skills. Guarding all of us. Moving quietly without detection," Lexi explained.

"Is that true?" Gavriil asked, slowly allowing his hand to drop away from the boy's neck.

Benito touched his fingers to his throat and looked at the blood smeared on his fingertips. He nodded. "Yes sir."

Gavriil let his breath out slowly. The kid had guts, and even though he was clearly a pain in the ass, one had to admire him. He willed Lexi to let him handle the situation without her. The kid needed a scare thrown into him—which Gavriil had given him. Now he needed to feel as if he was going to learn something from the experience.

"Lexi was about to make me some tea and we were going to eat lunch. I'll clean up your throat there and then we'll sit down and I'll tell you where you went wrong."

Lexi's fingers slipped down his bare back to the pocket of his jeans. She curled her fingers there. He glanced at her over his shoulder.

"Are you all right?"

"I was afraid," she admitted. "I really thought some of Caine's people might have come after me. Now that I know there's nothing wrong, I think my knees are a little weak, but I'm really okay. I am."

He wanted to blast the kid all over again. He turned back to the boy. "That's another reason you don't slink around and scare people. Everyone has a history. You don't want to make it worse for them, do you?"

Benito shook his head. "I'm really sorry, Lexi."

For a moment, Lexi pressed her face against the small of his bare back, right where her hand had been. Right over a series of scars from a whip tearing his flesh open when he was a child. Gavriil wanted to pull her into his arms and comfort her, but he stopped the impulse.

"I really am sorry, sir," Benito said, the fright fading that fast. "And I want to know what I did wrong. I mean aside from coming here in the first place," he added hastily.

Gavriil reached behind him without turning, and put his hand over Lexi's, pressing her palm into his buttocks where she held on to his pocket. "Never try sneaking up on me again. Not ever. It isn't safe. You're very lucky I was in the mood to ask questions. Otherwise, you'd be dead and Max would be coming after me. Do you understand? You can't play around with this kind of thing. If you're going to learn, you need to understand the difference between playing and coming after someone like me."

Benito nodded his head several times, wincing a little. The cut was shallow, but it had to hurt.

Lexi lifted her head. He felt the warmth of her breath against his skin. Her fingers traced the long, numerous scars crisscrossing his back, a whisper of movement only, barely there, but his body stirred and his gut tightened into knots.

"Didn't Max tell you to stay away from here?" He caught Lexi's hand and pulled it down, away from his bare skin. She had to stop if he was going to be able to think clearly. All that did was bring her attention back to Benito's plight.

Gavriil held her still, preventing her from going to the boy. The kid had to learn, and being babied wasn't going to help. "Lexi, would you mind making me that cup of tea?"

She was silent a moment, clearly making up her mind whether or not to let him handle the situation without her. In the end she capitulated. "Benito, would you like some as well?"

He shook his head, looking a little apprehensive now that she was leaving.

"Lexi, I left my war bag just outside the greenhouse, concealed in the brush on the west corner. I wouldn't want a child to find that bag. It also has clean clothes in it. Would you mind getting it for me while I make certain this wound doesn't get infected?"

Lexi studied his face for a long time, clearly trying to read his stone-cold features. "Benito is very much treasured here, Gavriil. He's trying hard to be a man under difficult circumstances."

Gavriil had lived through difficult circumstances. He wasn't going to allow that to be an excuse. The kid was spying on them, looking through bedroom windows. That wasn't okay in his book. Benito also needed to know that that kind of behavior could get a person killed.

"The west corner," he repeated, his tone implacable.

"See. I knew you'd forget our deal at the first opportunity," she accused.

He caught her chin, forcing her green eyes to meet his dark blue ones. "Just this one time, *solnyshko moya*, while I'm seeing to your safety."

"Well don't shoot him. Or stab him. Or beat him up either. I want him in good condition when we return him to Max and Airiana."

Out of the corner of his eye, Gavriil noticed the boy squirming. He didn't much like the idea of Max or Airiana finding out what he'd done. "That leaves me a lot of room, Lexi."

She winked at him. "I'm well aware of that. Just make certain he's alive when I come back. Benito, you do everything he says. He isn't nearly as patient as Max."

She shot Benito a warning glance and then left the room, taking the tray of needles with her. Gavriil was pretty certain, if he were capable, he would have fallen in love with her right then and there. He had no clue how love felt, so he dismissed the idea and turned his attention back to Benito.

"Let's get you cleaned up, kid," Gavriil said. He blew out a couple of candles as he went by them on his way to the bathroom. The first aid kit was under the sink. "Sit in that chair over there. You never let a knife wound go. Not ever. Sometimes the germs on the blade are worse than the cut. Always clean it as soon as possible."

Benito sank into the chair, staring with wide eyes at the massive scars covering Gavriil's body. There was everything from burns to what looked like grated skin as well as bullet and knife scars. There were whip marks across his back and a large shiny indentation from a shotgun. The scars on his chest were the worst, the ridges circular from where the knife had been twisting as it was brought out of his flesh.

"Yeah. Take a good look, kid. This isn't the high life. You don't want to go into this business and end up with no life, no family and a body like mine. Raise your chin. This is going to sting."

Gavriil pressed an alcohol wipe to the seeping wound. The boy didn't make a sound. Tears welled in his eyes but he sat absolutely still. Grudging respect had Gavriil hastily applying the soothing ointment that contained a triple antibiotic. He sank into the chair across from the kid.

"I'm Gavriil. Gavriil Prakenskii. You're Max's boy?" He crossed his arms across his chest, allowing his legs to stretch out in front of him. He was well within striking distance. Both arms could swing up or down easily blocking any attack, and both feet, in that lazy sprawl, could easily kick a target. The position was very deceptive and one he'd cultivated to look as if he was completely relaxed.

Benito cleared his throat. "He's adopting us. My sisters and me."

Gavriil nodded slowly. "I hear you lost your parents."

"They were murdered." Benito nearly spat the words, rage welling up.

"Tough. That's tough. My parents were murdered too. You have to be careful, kid. That burn you feel in your gut can be dangerous and lead you down paths you don't want to go. Max is a good man. He's tough as nails and he's a scary son of a bitch, but he's a good man. You listen to him and learn from him."

"He told me to stay away from here."

"But you didn't listen. Why?"

"Something bad happened this morning but they don't want to tell us. I think it happened to Lexi. She's . . . like us. She knows."

"And that makes her one of you," Gavriil said, making the jump in the boy's thinking.

Benito nodded. "We wanted to make sure she was all right. If she was alone, I was going to ask her to tell me what happened so I could tell my sisters. Lucia is really upset and having a hard time. She likes Lexi. We all do."

Gavriil studied the boy's face. There was more to it than what the kid was admitting. He softened his voice, reminding himself he was talking to a child and a traumatized one at that. "You came here to protect her, didn't you?"

Benito ducked his head. "Yeah."

"That's why you brought the weapons, isn't it?"

Benito squirmed, looking extremely uncomfortable. "Yeah," he admitted, looking down at the floor.

The kid was priceless. He was capable of being a little assassin if Max didn't watch out. "Do you know how to use either of them properly?"

"Max has been teaching me," the boy mumbled.

"The fact that you won't look at me tells me you know you were wrong to touch those weapons, Benito. Playing with guns or knives is a really bad idea. Protecting the people you love is a serious business. You don't do silly things. If you take possession of a weapon, you need to know what you're doing. You don't get to be a kid playing a game. The moment you pick up that gun or knife, you're a man making a man's decisions and they'd better be right, they'd better be something you can live with."

Gavriil felt Lexi's approach. She moved across the ground lightly, a part of nature, but he had her imprint inside of him and he knew the flow of her, the feel of her. The moment she was near, the pull on him was strong, as if they were two magnets drawn to each other. He wondered if she felt the same way.

He wasn't entirely certain what the Prakenskii connection did in terms of sealing or binding Lexi to him, but he felt that bond in every cell of his body. He knew he would always know when she was close. She wasn't alone either.

"Lexi's coming back and someone's with her," he announced.

Benito looked so panic-stricken he thought the kid might try to dive out through the window. "It's not Max."

The relief told him Max's opinion mattered.

Benito pushed his hand through his hair. It was shaking. "I really am sorry. If they'd told us what happened and that she had a bodyguard, I wouldn't have come like that." He broke off abruptly and then suddenly looked up, his eyes meeting Gavriil's. "I might have come anyway, but I wouldn't have been so sneaky."

"Never stick your head in a window like that. If the top of your head goes into the room, you're not looking to see what's inside."

Benito nodded. He rubbed his scalp as if it was still a little tender from Gavriil using his hair to pull him inside. "Will you tell me what happened? Airiana and Max say we live here now, this is our home. But they don't tell us anything."

"You're children. They're adults and have to make hard decisions."

Benito shrugged. "I don't feel like a kid, and neither does Lucia. How do we go back to playing like other kids after what happened to us? If this is our home and our family, we need to know what's going on."

"I think grown-ups want to make you feel safe after what happened, Benito. Telling you about problems outside of your control won't accomplish that."

"I'd rather know what I'm facing."

Gavriil sighed. "I can't break a confidence. Each of the women here have had someone they loved murdered. Lexi's story is hers, and it's up to her to tell you. You wouldn't want Max or Airiana telling me what happened to you aboard that ship, would you?"

Benito turned red. His eyes burned with anger and his fists clenched.

"Only you can decide who you trust enough to tell things to. Lexi's past came back to haunt her this morning. She's on edge and extremely upset."

"Is she in danger?"

"I believe she is, but I intend to stick around and keep her safe. Along with me, Max and the others to watch over her, whoever might wish to harm her doesn't stand much of a chance," Gavriil said.

Lexi came into the house and moved straight for the kitchen, presumably to make the tea. Airiana knocked on the bedroom doorjamb and stood there regarding her errant son, with a mixture of relief and exasperation on her face.

Benito launched himself out of the chair where he'd been holding himself together after the fright. His arms slid around her waist and he buried his face against her shoulder, holding her tight. Airiana stroked his hair in little caresses, her gaze meeting Gavriil's as he stood up slowly.

"It's all right. I trust Gavriil has opened your eyes to the danger of spying on people." Airiana handed Gavriil his war bag with her free hand.

"Benito had the best of intentions," Gavriil said. "He may have gone about it the wrong way, but he came here thinking he might have to protect Lexi. Apparently his sister, Lucia, is very worried. They know something happened, asked you or Max, weren't satisfied with the answer and decided to try to find out on their own."

Gavriil shrugged into a fresh shirt.

Airiana pulled Benito's head back and inspected the raw slice around the boy's neck. Her eyes met Gavriil's. "You did this?"

Gavriil nodded. "He was very lucky I didn't kill him when he stuck his head through that window."

Airiana closed her eyes for a moment and then took a deep breath. "You know we're going to have to talk to Max about this, right, Benito? We don't keep things from one another."

Benito's face darkened. "Yes we do. You refused to tell us what happened to Lexi this morning."

"Because it wasn't Airiana's place to tell you," Gavriil reiterated, his voice a low whip. He didn't like repeating himself, and he didn't want the kid to shove off his own responsibility. "If you want to know something, don't expect others to gossip. Be a man. Ask the primary source. If she doesn't want to tell you, respect her wishes, but don't blame Airiana or Max for keeping a confidence."

"You know Max is going to want to have a discussion with you about this," Airiana warned.

Gavriil sighed. "You tell him I'm not so good at discussions. I've said my piece on the subject. If he has any questions, Benito can fill him in. I trust that the kid doesn't lie to you. He can tell Max what happened and Max can take it from there."

It wasn't difficult to understand that he was done with the entire matter. The warning note in his voice was very clear and unmistakable. Airiana glanced over her shoulder to look at Lexi, who stood in the hallway. Their eyes met for a very long time, Airiana trying to silently convey her fear for her youngest sister.

Lexi broke the silence, ignoring Airiana's warning look. "Tea's ready, if anyone wants it. And Gavriil, lunch is ready. We can eat out on the porch."

6

"I thought they'd be staying for lunch," Gavriil said, leaning back in the comfortable chair on the porch, his long legs sprawled out in front of him. With great satisfaction he watched Airiana and Benito disappearing down the path that cut through the property up to the road where her car was parked.

Lexi rolled her eyes. "Really? We're going to have to work on your people skills."

"I have great people skills." He took a cautious sip of the tea, making an issue out of it as if he thought she might be trying to poison him. "I excel at people skills. I am succinct when speaking and get my point across immediately."

"If I didn't know better, I would have thought you ran the two of them off on purpose," Lexi said.

He smiled at her. A deliberate wolf's smirk. "I can't imagine why you would think such a thing."

She tried—and failed—to look stern. "Perhaps because you look so pleased with yourself."

"I'm just pointing out I have mad people skills." He picked up a sandwich and took a bite, chewing thoughtfully, waiting for her to settle into the chair opposite him. The tray of food was on the small table between them, the pile of sandwiches facing him.

Lexi sipped at her tea, regarding Gavriil over the top of the teacup. He appeared invincible and tough to others—she read it in the way they looked and acted with him. *She* could see pain etched into every line of his face, in the smoky heat of his blue eyes.

"You're too trusting, Lexi," Gavriil said suddenly.

She didn't take her gaze from his face. She loved to look at him, but wasn't certain why. She should have been intimidated like everyone else, especially because he had had his hand around her throat at one point and definitely had been considering ending her life. She wasn't certain how she knew that had been in his mind, or why she was just as certain that he wouldn't do it.

"Because I'm sitting here with you?" She especially loved his voice. She'd never heard that particular combination before, of smoke and edginess. There was a sensual intimate quality to his tone that mesmerized and intrigued her.

"That and you would have rushed to save that boy without ever checking for weapons on him. Three times you had your back to him."

"He's twelve and traumatized."

"He had a gun and a knife on him." Gavriil took another bite of his sandwich. "You never ran across fanatical children? Not ever?"

She knew she went pale. She felt the blood draining from her face. Her stomach lurched. Memories crowded too close. Once, she'd confided in a girl she thought was her friend. They'd worked together for over a year, and Lexi told her she detested Caine. The girl had rushed right to him, eager to please him with the bit of news that his "wife" hated him and wished he'd die.

"Yes." Her mouth went dry and she tasted blood, a faint coppery taste that sometimes haunted her dreams. In the early days, after she'd managed to escape, that horrible reminder was often in her mouth.

Gavriil's eyes went dark. He leaned toward her, holding her gaze so that it was impossible to escape. She had the feeling he could see right into her—into all the ugliness that she tried desperately to hide away.

"Tell me."

She shook her head. She didn't tell anyone. Not details. She'd always gotten away with it because she could tell herself she was in witness protection and no one could know, but his eyes didn't blink. His silence was as compelling as his command.

"Most of the children in the compound were as fanatical as their parents." She moistened her lips. Her throat felt as if it was closing, swelling on her so that she had to clear it several times. "If you were stupid enough to confide in them, they told everything you said to the leaders. The punishments were terrible."

His expression didn't change, but somehow, with her last four words, she felt a difference in him. He'd been relaxed, sprawling out in front of her, eating his sandwich and asking questions. Now, darkness swirled in him. In his eyes, maybe, but certainly in his heart, and in his soul.

"What kinds of punishments?"

"I don't want to talk about this, Gavriil. I don't ask you personal questions. I don't for a reason. I can't talk about this."

"Who better than with me."

"I don't even know you."

"You know me." He sank back against the thick cushion, his dark blue eyes never leaving her face.

His gaze was unrelenting, merciless even, yet his eyes were so dark blue she felt as if she might be falling into the night sky. How could he look both lethal and attractive at the same time?

"I thought she was my friend. Carla Shore. She was my age and we'd worked and played together for over a year. Caine liked to be rough and sometimes it hurt just to move the next day. I told her I hated him. She immediately told him. Of course, it's a sin to hate one's husband."

She shrugged, and a small smile briefly touched her mouth. "I hated him even more after his beating. You know those whips marks you have on your back? I've got them too. He shaved my head, stripped me in front of the congregation and flogged me."

Lexi did her best to sound matter-of-fact, but Gavriil could see the pain in her eyes and hear it in her voice. She had shoved her past behind a door and locked it, but she wasn't healed. Neither was he, and he was a lot older than she was.

"I would have to say it would be a sin *not* to hate that man in those circumstances. The man was no husband cherishing his wife, he was a child molester drunk on his own power." He folded his arms just to be safe. He wanted to kill something—or someone.

She was so damned young. Inside of her was a brightness that even Caine with all his evil hadn't managed to obliterate. Why hadn't the man wanted to protect her? Caine had wanted to destroy her. That was why he couldn't give her up, why he obsessed over her. He had to have seen that light in her and it must have sickened him every time he looked in the mirror. He *needed* to destroy her and he hadn't been able to. No matter what he'd done to her, she hadn't become as ugly as Caine was.

"I wish my many beatings had been for as good a reason as that," he confided, because he had to give her something, offer something of himself back to her. "I fought them quite a bit. I tried to leave the school, to go find my brothers. Viktor and I promised my father that we'd watch over the others. The worst beating came when I failed to control an arousal. The girl was punished if she couldn't arouse me, and I was punished if she could. Control and discipline." He shrugged.

"That's terrible. Why would they do that?"

"So we were always in charge of the performance. Sex

is used for a lot of reasons." He kept his voice as matter-of-fact as hers had been. "It's a very effective weapon, Lexi."

She sent him another wan smile. "Maybe we are more alike than you thought."

He couldn't imagine two people more unalike. He had embraced the underbelly of life, the seedy, dark violence of a different realm. She had embraced a family and found a way to love them without reservation.

"The doctor, the one who taught you acupuncture, what happened to her?"

She went very still. Her face froze. The teacup slipped from her fingers. His hand snaked out to catch it in his palm before it could crash onto the tabletop between them. Hot tea splashed, but he barely felt the burn. He never once took his gaze from hers.

The pain in her was every bit as acute as his physical pain—maybe more. He lived with pain every single moment of his life now, yet he was just beginning to discover once again that emotional pain was far worse.

"Just before I turned sixteen, her husband decided he wanted to marry someone much younger. She said no. She was told she had to leave. No one left, Gavriil. No one could ever leave. We all knew that. There were too many secrets. She packed just as if she would go, her head up, shoulders straight. When she kissed me good-bye, she told me to be brave, and Caine drove her away. A few weeks later when he was angry with me, he told me she screamed and screamed when he raped her. He used that word. He told me she wasn't brave at all."

"He preferred children. Why would he touch her?"

"He preferred power. Sex was power to him. He controlled everyone around him using any means, brute force, sex, his punishments, promises of life in the hereafter. All that mattered was control."

She had good insight to the man. Caine had wanted control over all of them. He'd hurt Lexi over and over to cower her, to drain her spirit. When she broke away from him and he'd lost control, he'd sought it out again by murdering her family.

Gavriil had to give her something. He set the teacup carefully on the small table. "I know all about that kind of control. First they beat you and strip you of all dignity. They keep you alone and scared and in pain. Then there's the threat. The only way you can be controlled if you're like us, refusing to give them every part of us. They threatened my brothers—to torture and kill them one by one in front of me, starting with the baby."

She swallowed hard, her lashes fluttered again and again, but her color wasn't quite as pale. "Is that why, even though you don't want anyone else around, you are able to tolerate me?" Lexi asked.

Gavriil chose another sandwich. He was far hungrier than he thought. "Have you asked yourself why it's okay for me to stay with you when you don't want anyone else around?" he countered.

She leaned into him. "I'm the only person you've ever truly been afraid of, Gavriil. Why would you stay here with me?"

The woman knew how to throw a punch. He was proud of her though. She *had* recognized the danger she was in. He felt a little mesmerized by her, hypnotized by those eyes that either blazed like the brightest emerald, or, like now, went cool forest green.

"Sometimes, *solnyshko moya*, the answer is impossible to explain. The truth is, I don't know. I like your company. You soothe me. You intrigue me. I'm not going to lie to you and say I'm not attracted to you as a man is to a woman. I am. That's a first for me—real physical attraction. Everything about you turns my world upside down."

She blinked rapidly, and sank back in her chair. "You're a strange man, Gavriil. I would think you would want to stay far away from me."

"That's the real question, isn't it? Why don't I? I should have turned and walked away the moment I saw you coming out of that cornfield, but I knew then that I was already lost."

Lexi rubbed her palm as if it might be itching. His was. Discipline kept him from touching it.

"What did you do to me? To my palm when you zapped me?"

He remained silent. His sins were catching up with him fast, and he didn't want her to run from him. He was a hunter and giving chase was instinctive.

"It's some sort of Prakenskii thing, isn't it? I've seen Rikki, Judith and Airiana all rub their palms as if they itched. It can't be a coincidence. I know we're not supposed to know the name Prakenskii, but you all have the same eyes. What did you do to me?"

The idea that he had claimed her without her consent didn't sit well with him. Not after knowing about her life and what Caine had done to her. She had to make that choice, not him. Still, his claim couldn't be taken back, nor would he do so if he could. He was that selfish. He didn't know what he was going to do with her, he hadn't really gotten that far, but no one was going to harm her.

"Gavriil, you use silence the way others use words."

She pressed her thumb into the center of her palm. He felt the push on his own skin. He turned his palm over and, keeping the image of her face in his mind, stroked a caress down the center, watching her closely. She gasped and pressed her hand to her face, her eyes going wide.

"What did you just do?"

"It's a connection between us. If you needed me, you could easily call me to you through that connection." That was one way to look at it, and very true. He would know the moment she was in trouble if she touched the center of her palm.

Lexi pressed her lips together, closing her fingers around her palm as if holding it to her. He couldn't read the gesture or her reaction. That was rare as well. He finished the sandwich and washed it down with tea.

"There's more to it than that, and you don't want to tell me."

He was grateful for the years of discipline. He kept his face pure stone. "No, I don't want to tell you. I shouldn't have put that mark on you. I don't have any idea why I couldn't overcome the compulsion to do it. It was wrong of me, but there's no taking it back, and I can't say that I even want to."

Lexi continued to look him in the eye. He'd never had trouble looking anyone in the eye. Never. But her gaze saw far more than others' did, and sitting in the spotlight, knowing she was looking inside of him and seeing things he might not even know about himself, was difficult. He did it because she deserved that window into him. He had tied them together without her consent and she needed to know what kind of man he was.

Lexi shook her head. "You shouldn't have done it."

"I couldn't stop myself. Again, that's a first for me. I'm sitting here across from you, and realize how close I am to mimicking Caine."

Her swift gasp and quick shake of her head were gratifying, but he held up his hand to stop her from speaking. "It's true, *angel moy*. I'm all about control. Controlling those around me, my environment, everything in my world. I put my claim on you without your consent, and I knew what I was doing."

"You said you couldn't stop yourself, that it was a compulsion stronger than your discipline and control."

"So what kind of a man does that make me, Lexi?"

"A very confused one."

She tilted her head to one side and her ponytail fell over one shoulder, and all that thick silk tumbling down stirred his body. This time he managed to clamp down on the rush of hot blood coursing through his veins seeking a willing target in his cock. He managed to suppress the savage urge, a small triumph, but he'd take it.

"Why confused?"

"I'm not going to lie either, Gavriil. I've never so much as looked at a man in a sexual way, not ever, not until you. Do I find you attractive? How could I not? But I'm terrified of a relationship. Not just a sexual one, but an actual relationship. I could never be with someone as commanding as you are. You're intimidating . . ."

"I don't intimidate you."

"Because we're not in a relationship. I don't know how to be in one. I don't know anything about a good relationship between a man and a woman." Her confession came in a little rush, as if she needed to get it over with, as if he might not understand.

"I don't know how to be in a relationship either, Lexi," he said. "Not at all. Like you, I live alone, and I've always preferred it that way. I don't relate to others. You said yourself I need people skills. How the hell would I know how to be with a woman? You're my first attempt at civilized conversation and I've already made a few mistakes."

She laughed softly. "You're doing fine, Gavriil. Better than you know." The smile faded, leaving her eyes dark and haunted. "I don't want to be afraid of you. I don't want to worry that you'll try to force me into something I don't want."

"You want me to give you reassurance? Would you even believe me after I put my mark on your palm?"

"Yes."

"I would never force you, Lexi, but I can't say I won't try to court you." If he was being strictly honest, he'd already begun.

"It won't work."

He shrugged. "Maybe not. I don't know the first thing about courting a woman. I don't even think it's done anymore. Now it's all about seduction, getting a woman in bed as quickly as possible."

"And you don't want that?" Her gaze slid over his face.

Gavriil had to smile. There was a certain disappointment in her eyes. "Of course I want that. I'm a man, *solnyshko moya*, it's easy enough to take a look at me and figure that part out for yourself. Still, whether or not it's still in practice, I think you deserve someone to court you. I may be totally inept, but I'm going to give it my best shot."

Lexi shook her head, but her eyes were soft, the perfect forest green he had come to look forward to falling into. She had found peace on a far different path than he had, and he found he wanted to go there with her.

"That's such a sweet thing to say, Gavriil, that you want to court me. I don't know if it's old-fashioned or not, because I've never even been out on a date. Not once in my entire life, but I don't want to lead you on, I just know I couldn't be in a relationship, it would be too scary for me."

He hadn't known until she told him the story of her friend, the Chinese doctor, what he was going to do with Lexi Thompson. He knew now. He was going to keep her. He was going to defend her. He was going to do his best to walk the same path she walked.

"You're not afraid of me, Lexi, and that gives me more than I've ever had in my life. I'll take that for now and we'll see where we go from there."

"You deliberately push people away from you by making them afraid, just the way you did with Airiana and Benito," she pointed out. "Others might give you the same chance I have if you let them."

"I did the same thing with you, but you stood by me," Gavriil said. "In fact, I did worse, and yet there you sit, looking beautiful and quite unafraid."

"I'm not beautiful, but thank you all the same." Lexi reached for the small teapot beneath the cozy to pour herself more tea.

"Sure you are. Apparently you don't see very well. I'll overlook that because we have this deal and you get to be bossy for a couple of days."

She laughed. The sound of her laughter was like music playing, soft and melodic.

"How do you feel about dogs?" Gavriil asked, watching her face closely.

Lexi paused in the act of bringing the teacup up to her

mouth. "Dogs? Who doesn't love or want dogs? I'm here by myself a lot, so I wish I had one, but we all have to agree. Everyone seems to be in agreement. I don't think Lissa is very fond of dogs, but not because she doesn't like animals. I suspect she got bit at one time, because she isn't afraid of very much."

"I love dogs and I've been working with them for a while, since I recovered from my last dance with a knife. I couldn't work so I found a little place way out in the middle of nowhere and brought a couple of dogs with me. They're beautiful."

"Here? In the United States?"

"In Russia. But I brought them with me."

"How can you do that? Get them into the country without anyone knowing. I presume they aren't in quarantine somewhere."

He could see she was getting excited. Somehow the idea that she might like animals, especially dogs, only served to make him want her more. He was falling pretty hard and very fast and it shook him. Still, he was going to stay. She'd offered, and Lexi wasn't a woman to take back an offer. The others couldn't do anything about it.

"There are all kinds of ways to slip in and out of a country, Lexi, and over the years, I've made a few connections that have helped. Also, I'm very adept at paperwork."

"You look very smug right now. Where is the dog?"

"Dogs," he corrected. "I have a breeding pair and the female is pregnant."

Lexi leaned toward him. "Gavriil, I know you came here to say good-bye to your brothers. You used your real name. You've admitted that you were going to lead any hit man away from your brothers. What would you be doing with these dogs?"

The more time he spent with her, and saw the expressions chasing across her face, saw the way she became animated, especially when she thought about him leading assassins away from the farm, he found himself falling all the harder.

"I wanted them safe," he admitted.

Abruptly, Lexi put down her teacup. For a moment he thought he saw tears swimming in her eyes, but she looked away from him, out toward the farm.

"What is it, Lexi?" he asked softly. "How have I upset you?" He reached across the small table to lay his hand on her thigh, needing to touch her, to know what he'd done wrong.

The moment his hand curved along her thigh, she stiffened. He was extremely careful to keep the gesture non-threatening and platonic. He waited until she relaxed. "If you don't tell me what I do wrong, I'll never know."

"It's just that I don't want you to ever compare yourself with Caine again. Not ever."

She turned and looked at him, straight in the eye. He felt the impact of her gaze like a dagger to his heart. Her eyes swam with tears. A few sparkled on her lashes. Several others tracked down her face. He couldn't stop himself, he reached over the table and brushed them from her face.

"I don't understand."

"You're willing to sacrifice yourself for your family, but before you do, you need to know your dogs are in good hands." She shook her head. "Gavriil, do you have any idea how truly lost you are? I'm broken and I know it, but I also know better than to throw away my life. I'm not afraid of death, and it's not like I have tons to live for, but life is something precious. A gift. I've learned that much. You're so ready to throw it away."

"I don't have much to live for either, Lexi. My brothers have a life here. I knew that. I was happy for them. I want them to thrive here, but they can't do that with a death sentence always hanging over their heads. I would go after Sorbacov, but I'd never get close to him or his son. They both have to die for all this to stop."

"Your brothers wouldn't want you to sacrifice yourself, Gavriil. And I don't want you to. You're far more broken than I am. You don't see yourself at all."

He sank back into the chair. "You persist in thinking I'm a good man."

"I know you are. Good men make certain their animals are cared for. Good men rescue women who are strangers to them."

He didn't know what to say to her. Good men didn't go around killing for a living, but he didn't want to remind her of that. Something, a small ripple in the air near them, disturbed him. He let his gaze move from Lexi to the surrounding forest. Someone was close to them, had moved into hearing distance. They were good at stealth, barely moving the air around them. It smacked of a professional.

"Lexi." He said her name softly.

A woman emerged from the brush near the pathway, hopping a couple of steps as if she might have a pebble in her shoe. She dropped to her knee, nearly out of sight again as she tugged at her left shoe to remove it. The sun turned her hair into a blaze of glory, a wealth of fiery red.

Lexi stood up immediately, a smile of greeting on her face. "Lissa! Are you all right?"

Soft laughter floated toward them. "I took the shortcut and got a little rock in my shoe for my efforts. I came over to see if you might go to this thing Lucia's putting on. The cooking class. I know you've got to be shaken up by everything, but she's especially asked for you and so I thought maybe going might help you as well."

Lissa's head popped up above the bushes as she stood. Gavriil watched her come toward them through narrow, hooded eyes. He kept his expression blank, but suddenly, Lissa intrigued him. There was something about the way she moved, an awareness about her.

"Who is she?" he asked softly.

"Lissa Piner. One of my sisters. She was here earlier."

He had seen her of course, with her red hair, how did anyone miss her? But he hadn't noticed her. Not like this. Not with his warning system blaring at him.

"What does she do?"

"She's a glassblower. She's an amazing artist."

Lissa Piner might be an amazing artist, but he would bet his last dollar that she was far more than that.

"How long have you known her?" he asked. Even as the woman approached, the way she moved intrigued him. She didn't make a sound. She wasn't just light on her feet, it was more than that. She moved with absolute grace, a flowing rhythm that spoke of stealth and shadows. She'd triggered his alarms and yet, the expression on her face when she looked at Lexi was very real, very open. Lissa genuinely loved Lexi.

Gavriil realized all the women had secrets just as his brothers did. Whatever those secrets were didn't seem to matter on the farm. They accepted one another for who they were. They'd formed a tight-knit family and their loyalty to one another ran deep. For the very first time he longed to be a part of that.

Lexi stepped to the edge of the railing, so close to him he caught that faint scent she gave off of the forest and the earth itself. She smelled clean and fresh, the air after a rainstorm.

"I've known Lissa for five years," she answered. "She's wonderful."

Gavriil stood too. He needed space and felt crowded all of a sudden. There were too many people here with too many secrets, all trusting one another, yet he trusted none of them—with the exception of Lexi—and that was unexplainable.

He stepped back into the wider section of porch, giving himself plenty of room. The threat he felt was vague, nearly nonexistent. Something about Lissa put him on edge.

Lissa hurried up the stairs without so much as glancing at Gavriil, throwing her arms around Lexi and hugging her. "You look alive to me." She grinned at her sister and then tossed Gavriil a smile. "We did speculate on whether or not you were going to do her in."

"I resisted, although she forced me to make a deal with her that she could boss me around. I'm officially working with her on the farm." He deliberately engaged in the conversation, watching Lissa closely to see how she would react to his revelation.

Lissa's open, friendly expression didn't change. Her mouth continued to smile, but her eyes flickered for a just a moment, a fraction of a second, but he caught it. She watched him the way a hunter might watch a large jungle cat.

"Baby, are you going to this thing with me?" she asked Lexi, but she didn't take her eyes from Gavriil.

"Is it really that important to Lucia?"

"Yes. She asked several times if you were coming. I figured Gavriil might need to sleep, so unless you were working like the madwoman you are, I thought I could persuade you to join in on the fun. It will be good for Lucia. She's still in the first stages of grief and acceptance. Living here with all of us is new and difficult."

Lissa was good. Gavriil had to hand her that. Lexi had far too much compassion to turn down the invitation. If a fourteen-year-old girl who had just lost her parents and sister as well as going through a terrible traumatic event needed her, she would help. Lissa had worded her summons so carefully. She'd even managed to make it sound as if Lexi would be giving Gavriil much-needed room to allow him to sleep.

"Will you be all right?" Lexi asked him.

He could so easily make a fool of himself over her. He knew that. He was old enough to know he was walking in dangerous territory. There was no way for him to prevent himself from falling deeper when she looked at him like that. All eyes. All cool green. All worried.

No one worried about him. Not ever. Not that he knew of anyway. "I'll be fine. I've got a few things to do. If you need me, I'll come. I'll find you, no matter what. You know how to call me." He ignored that steady stare from Lissa and the raised eyebrow when he'd promised Lexi he'd get to her.

Lexi smiled at him and nodded. "I'll be at Airiana and Max's house. Do you know which one it is?"

He'd studied the layout of the farm before he'd ever arrived. Lev had sent the schematics to their private message drop after he had married Rikki.

"Apparently it's important to Lucia that you're there. Of course you should go," he said, all reasonable. He ignored the gathering knots in his gut.

"The house is all yours. Getting some sleep might be appropriate, but if Benito, for some reason, hasn't learned his lesson, please don't cut his throat," she teased.

"I'll do my best to behave." Now that she was really leaving, he found he was reluctant to part with her.

"Baby, would you mind lending me one of your sweaters," Lissa said, rubbing her arms, "I didn't realize it was going to stay so cool."

Oh yeah. He'd been right about Lissa Piner. She had something to say, and he could predict exactly what it was going to be.

"Sure, it will only take a minute." Lexi gathered up the tea and sandwich plates and restacked them neatly on the tray. "I'll leave these in the kitchen. The sandwiches should be good if you get hungry. Levi wrapped them nicely."

His gaze drifted over her deliberately. He allowed possession to show on his face. He felt possessive. He felt edgy and a little desperate that she was leaving him and going to her family. They'd do their best to get her to throw him out.

The moment Lexi disappeared inside, he turned his full attention to Lissa. "I presume you have something you wanted to say to me." He lobbed the first ball in an even tone, waiting to hear her out.

"Lexi's special. Beautiful, inside and out. Don't hurt her, Gavriil. I know you're a Prakenskii and you're tough as nails, but if you hurt her, I'll come after you."

Lissa spoke quietly. Calmly. She meant every word.

"You didn't tell me to stay away from her."

Lissa shook her head slowly. "I don't think you can stay away from her. I'm very aware that there is some kind of connection between your family and all of us. It can't be a coincidence that three of my sisters are madly in love with three of your brothers. I can see the way you look at her. I know you're here for the long haul. I'm just telling you, she's amazing and I don't want her hurt. She's been hurt enough."

"Why didn't you go after Caine?" he asked quietly.

"I would have, but I didn't know who he was. Lexi was in witness protection and she didn't give names. I tried to piece her past together from old newspaper articles, but I couldn't be certain," Lissa admitted.

"I think we understand each other perfectly," Gavriil said. "I can assure you, Lexi is safer with me than she would ever be without me, and I have no intention of ever hurting her. I appreciate that you've been here and will be here to look after her."

"Don't stay now if you're not going to stay permanently. She can't suffer any more losses."

Gavriil smiled at her. There was something about tough little Lissa he liked. She didn't play games. She wanted Lexi safe and she told him herself. She looked him straight in the eye and she clearly was willing to risk her life for her youngest sister. Standing up to a man like him wasn't easy. He knew how intimidating he was. The thing was—Lissa wasn't all that intimidated, and she saw him for what he was. Unlike Lexi who looked inside of him, Lissa saw the cold-eyed killer.

"I'm staying." He made it a statement, delivered in his implacable tone.

"Lexi needs careful handling. She's not a rush job."

"I'm well aware of that," Gavriil said. "I might not be charming or sophisticated, but I'll keep her safe, Lissa. And I have no intention of hurting her. That I can promise you."

"Then that's enough for me."

Lissa smiled at him, and he felt as if he might actually have an ally. It was unexpected, and it touched him more than he wanted to admit.

7

ILYA Prakenskii's massive estate was located across the highway from the ocean and well back into the forest. Large iron gates guarded the entrance. Security cameras were everywhere. Being married to Joley Drake, one of the biggest superstars in the music industry, meant tremendous security and the money needed to provide that security.

Ilya's acreage butted up next to that of Sheriff Jonas Harrington and his wife Hannah, who just happened to be Joley's sister. Both properties were beautiful and mostly forest, but the Harrington side was easier to access. They had the same security cameras—Gavriil was certain Ilya had been instrumental in positioning them—but they weren't nearly as well kept as they should have been.

Gavriil entered through the Harrington property. He moved with ease through the heavier forest toward the back of Ilya's estate. He knew how to avoid cameras, where the best locations would be for motion sensors and how to spot them.

Ilya's house was spectacular. Gavriil stood in the shadows admiring it; the large, sprawling structure had to be ten thousand square feet. It was a lot of house to guard. Gavriil shook his head. Ilya didn't have a security force, another mistake, not that they would be of much help against someone Sorbacov would send, but just the absence of one member would alert Ilya.

He timed the swing of the camera and moved between each rotation. Normally, his body screamed at him, and he definitely felt the pain—that terrible unrelenting burn along his nerve endings—but whatever Lexi had done to him had eased it for a short while. He'd almost forgotten pain until this moment and that meant it had slipped for a short while into the background.

His heart contracted at the thought that she might actually have helped him when he'd suffered for so many years and had given up hope. Was that even possible? But then he hadn't thought it possible that he could ever find a place of peace. That he might find a woman of his own and dare to sleep more than a night or two in one place.

He knew Sorbacov would come after them all, but together they were strong. Uri Sorbacov's father, Kostya, had discovered the key to keeping them all in line. Not beatings, not torture, it had been the threat of him harming a sibling—particularly Ilya. Both Viktor and Gavriil had tried to watch over him throughout his life. Twice Gavriil had taken out several men who were out for blood when Ilya, acting in his capacity as an Interpol agent, had interfered with their business. He knew Viktor had done the same.

Gavriil chose to enter the house through the music studio. It was large and filled with equipment. He could see they could shoot music videos as well as work on music itself in the room. Information told him Joley was very pregnant and no one would be in or near that room.

He was cautious now that he'd gained entrance into the house. Ilya was inside. He'd watched him drop his wife at Harrington's house and go back home. Gavriil knew there was no possible way he'd been detected, but Ilya's instincts had to be kicking in. As the seventh son, he was extremely powerful and had all the gifts. They would be hunting each other through the house, and Ilya knew the hunting ground better than he did—although he'd studied blueprints of the place.

Gavriil slipped inside the wide hallway, a work of art in itself. He couldn't help the stab of pride he felt for his brother as he moved through the house, placing each foot carefully to ensure the floorboards didn't creak. The rooms were spacious and open, the ceilings high.

He had been in the homes of millionaires many times, and once even a billionaire's, but Ilya's two-story sprawling home was classy, elegant even. From the wood floors throughout the home to the stainless steel in the kitchen, everything was well made and looked beautiful as well as functional.

Clearly the woman had chosen the house. It was a security nightmare, from its location to the many entrances and exits. He would never live in such a place; he couldn't. The walls were a soft color, but the lighting and the furniture were white in several of the rooms. All he could see was a perfect backdrop for targets.

A whisper of movement alerted him. He stilled, his breath moving slowly through his lungs, while he waited for his brother to come to him. He melted into the ornate staircase, the glowing golden wood, becoming, in his mind, part of the very grain.

Ilya moved around the bottom circular stair, staying in close to the wood, so close Gavriil could have reached out and touched him. There was a gun in Ilya's hand, but all Gavriil could do was stare at his brother—the baby that had been wrenched from their mother's arms and was moving in stealth and silence through his home.

Ilya was a fine man. He looked fit and handsome. The years hadn't touched him in the same way they had the others in the family, and Gavriil was happy for that. Had he not met Lexi, it would have been enough for him just to see Ilya in his home, grown and happy, doing well.

Gavriil waited for Ilya to step past him and he moved in

behind him, careful not to touch him, not to get too close. "Put the gun down very slowly and turn around. I'm your brother and don't particularly want to shoot you, but if you move against me, I will." Gavriil's voice was steady, so was his hand. He wasn't lying, he would shoot Ilya in a heart-beat—he'd just make certain it was somewhere not lethal.

Ilya stilled. He didn't stiffen, if anything his muscles were relaxed and ready. Gavriil found himself smiling.

"I have a lot of brothers," Ilya said, his voice just as even. "Which one?"

"Gavriil." He hadn't expected to be choked up. His voice came out husky with emotion. He had enjoyed seeing his other brothers, was equally as proud of them, but Ilya had been the one he had been the most afraid for. He'd been a baby, so young. He hadn't had the chance to know his parents or brothers. He didn't have the anchor that they all had.

For one moment, staring at the back of Ilya's head, he could see his mother's desperate face, the terror and sorrow in her eyes as Ilya was ripped from her arms and she was shot through the head. He and Viktor had both tried to take the baby from the soldier who had taken him. Both had been pistol-whipped viciously. Both still carried the scars.

"Walk forward, you know the drill, into the room and move over by the fireplace. You're a difficult man to get in touch with."

"My wife was finishing out her tour." Ilya placed his weapon carefully on the mantel, using two fingers. He turned slowly around, his hands in the air, empty palms facing Gavriil. He looked about as vulnerable as a tiger. "I don't get many messages when we're on the road."

Gavriil wasn't fooled for a moment into thinking Ilya was no longer armed. He most likely carried several weap-ons. "I'm going to put my gun away." He slipped the gun in his holster, all the time watching his brother carefully.

More like feasting his eyes on him. Ilya had grown up into a Prakenskii in spite of being separated from them almost from birth. His shoulders were wide. His eyes a crystal, piercing blue. He definitely had all the gifts of the

Prakenskii family; Gavriil could feel the power in him. He appeared ice-cold and completely confident.

"That's a good idea, I wouldn't want Joley walking in and getting upset."

"Joley is with her sister Hannah," Gavriil said. "That isn't about to happen."

"You did your homework." For the first time, Ilya smiled, as if he might actually believe Gavriil was his brother.

Gavriil knew he looked like an angel of death. There was no getting around the years of working in the shadows, but the kid should at least recognize his eyes. "Of course, didn't you expect I would?"

"I've never seen you before, not that I remember, but no brother of mine would come here without knowing where my wife was first. An assassin wouldn't care." Ilya waved Gavriil toward a chair. "I expect I'm on someone's hit list or you wouldn't be here."

Gavriil nodded. Clearly Ilya wasn't quite as excited to see him as he was to see his youngest brother. He forced air through his lungs and blamed his emotions on Lexi. Without her, he would still be stone cold. He'd deliver his message and not be a little hurt that Ilya didn't share in his excitement.

"Uri Sorbacov is making his bid for the presidency and he can't allow his father's sins to surface. Anyone connected with the schools is being targeted. It isn't as if you're difficult to find." Gavriil conveyed the message in a low monotone, careful to keep any expression from his face. He refused to appear vulnerable to this man, not now.

He'd risked his life time and again to give his youngest brother the opportunity to live life as close to normal as possible. He'd succeeded, and he knew Viktor would be pleased as well. Ilya didn't have the scars on his face or body, or the lines that marked so many kills a man eventually lost himself. Gavriil was grateful for that, and it would have to be enough.

"I half expected it," Ilya said, studying his brother's

face. "I might have actually picked you out in a crowd, now that I can really look at your eyes. I don't really remember too much about any of you."

"Were you aware that Lev, Stefan and Maxim all live here in Sea Haven?" Gavriil watched his face carefully. There was a problem between the Drake family, which Ilya considered himself a part of, and Lev Prakenskii. Gavriil didn't like the fact that his youngest brother had aligned himself against his own family.

"Jonas let me know they were in town. I expected one of them, not you."

"I'm in town as well," Gavriil said. "And I'm here to stay. I don't want there to be a problem with the Drakes and with us." He leaned toward Ilya, his eyes pure ice. "Is there going to be a problem, Ilya?"

"Because of Elle Drake?" Ilya shrugged. "Lev would have gotten her away from Gratsos if he could have, and I'm certain Elle will say the same thing. Whether or not her husband Jackson lets it go, we won't know until they return."

"And where do you stand in all this?"

"I tried to warn Lev to get off that yacht. He chose to stay on it," Ilya said. "Why do you ask?"

"Lexi Thompson," Gavriil replied. "She's mine. I will defend her with every breath in my body." Just saying her name made his palm itch. He suddenly needed to see her. To breathe her into his lungs. He'd put his psychic mark on her, but he was just as branded as she was. "Know that if it comes to some kind of decision on whether or not to push her family out of the area because of Levi. We're family. You're ours. You belong with us."

"I don't know any of you," Ilya reiterated.

Gavriil shrugged. "You know us. In your heart you know who we are. When the times comes, Ilya, do the right thing."

Ilya sighed. "Family loyalty runs strong in us. Joley's my family too. That makes her sisters and their husbands my family as well."

For the first time, Gavriil could read the conflict in his youngest brother. Deep down he even understood it. Ilya couldn't possibly know the sacrifices they'd made in order for him to have the life he had.

"We will defend the Drakes, just as we do one another, but I won't allow anyone to threaten Levi or try to take Lexi's home from her."

"The Drakes aren't like that."

"Perhaps they aren't, but Levi was warned that Elle's husband, Jackson, just may well be exactly like that. Handle him, Ilya. That's all the warning I'm going to give." Gavriil meant that, and he allowed Ilya to see that he did. Ilya knew dangerous men. Gavriil wasn't going to hide who or what he was from his brother. "I'm a ghost. You know what that means. You know my reputation."

"I appreciate the warning, Gavriil, although it isn't necessary to give me one. I know who you are. You have a certain reputation in our country, and being my brother, I always looked for word of you."

The tight knots in Gavriil's gut unraveled just a little. It was the first sign that Ilya acknowledged he was a Prakenskii and that his family meant something to him.

"We kept track of you as well. You were in Brussels, following the pedophile ring. You'd gotten too close and they sent a team after you. I heard a rumor there was a contract out on you and I went to Brussels and cleaned them out when they came at you in the hotel."

"That was you? We never could figure out who took out the team. There's been a couple of times while I was working I seemed to have an angel or two on my shoulder. Was that you in Montreal? That was a very close call. Without my guardian angel, I'd be dead."

"That was Viktor. He and the others kept as close as we could," Gavriil said. He didn't want his younger brother to think he was the only one who had cared enough to keep tabs on him. They all had.

"But none of you approached me."

"For the same reason you didn't come looking for us.

Sorbacov would have known and one of us would have
been killed."

Ilya sat back against the thick cushion of the tapestry-
covered chair. "I'd like to get to know all of my brothers
better. Do you know where Viktor and Casimir are?
They're the only ones unaccounted for."

"Viktor is somewhere in the wind. He went deep under-
cover and hasn't surfaced even to check our emergency
system."

Ilya caught the note of worry in Gavriil's voice and
looked up sharply. "Do you think he's in trouble? Dead?"

Gavriil shook his head. "Viktor would be damned hard
to kill. It would take a pro, and whoever managed it would
eventually crow about it. They'd want the reputation as the
man who killed Viktor Prakenskii."

"And Casimir?"

"The last I heard he was in Russia. I hope he's not considering anything foolish such as going after Sorbacov."

"Someone needs to kill that man and his father," Ilya
said. "I should have done it a long time ago."

Gavriil frowned. The last thing he wanted was for the
child they had all tried so hard to protect to put himself in
danger. Gavriil and Viktor had made a deal, even then,
when they were just children with Kostya Sorbacov. They
would cooperate if Ilya was given a different direction,
something not so soul-destroying.

"Don't try it, Ilya. You have a wife and a child on the
way. He knows us, knows our faces, and he's ready for that
move. He's surrounded himself with an army. I have no
doubt one of us might slip in, but I doubt we'd get to him
and it would be a suicide mission."

"What name are you using?"

"My own. I came here to lead them away from all of you
and then I met Lexi. She was . . . unexpected." Gavriil
spread his hands out in front of him. "I'm not used to this.
The house, the things. A woman. I don't know if I can do
it, but I want to try."

"She's the youngest one, isn't she? They moved in some

five years ago, Joley told me. Her cousin Blythe owns the farm with them."

Gavriil narrowed his eyes, trying to see into that statement. She's the youngest. She was significantly younger than he was in terms of years, but not in her soul. Ilya was the youngest of the brothers, and he couldn't help but view Gavriil, with his reputation and his loss of humanity, as far too old for someone like Lexi.

The brothers had been stepping-stones in terms of age. Viktor was the oldest, then Gavriil and Stefan. Casimir hit solidly in the middle with Maxim, Lev and Ilya following. In actual years, Gavriil wasn't that much older than the rest, but he felt every rip in his soul.

He pressed his thumb deeply into the psychic mark. He'd never needed anyone. He'd always lived alone and preferred relying only on himself. Everyone else was an enemy. Loved ones were liabilities. Friends were liabilities. He would never look at Lexi that way. She was a path to peace. Maybe even freedom. Still, to need someone was far different than wanting them, and right at that moment he felt as if he needed her and that didn't sit well with him at all.

"Yes." He suddenly realized Ilya was waiting for an answer. "Lexi is the youngest. She runs the farm and I'll be helping her out there."

Ilya smiled and shook his head. "You? On a farm?"

"I can run a tractor and other machinery needed. Security was beefed up, and I'll see what I can do to improve it. If necessary, if it gets bad, bring your wife and stay until we figure a way to get Sorbacov and stop all of this." He looked around the house. "This place is too big, and you're only one man."

"How much time do you think I have before a wet team shows up?"

"Sorbacov will send assassins from the school first. He won't want to draw attention to what he's doing. If he sent a team after you, he'd be an idiot. Your wife is famous. No, he'll try to pit the graduates of the school against one another and hope they kill one another off. If you're still alive after the first few attempts, then he'll begin sending teams that can't be traced back to him."

"You think I can expect him soon," Ilya said.

"I had to make arrangements to get here. It wasn't easy. I used an assumed name until I reached the States, but then I wanted Sorbacov to know I was here. I hoped it would divert attention from you. My paperwork is in order and I used credit cards and my passport, both traceable. He'll take the bait, he won't be able to stop himself. He'll get word to whoever he sent after you and they'll come at me."

"You're still protecting me."

Gavriil shrugged. "You and the others. It's a habit. I didn't have anything to live for, Ilya. You and the others did."

Ilya sighed. "I'm all grown up."

"I see that. You look good." Gavriil looked around him at the elegant room. "Are you happy?"

"With Joley? She's my world. She always will be. I'm excited about the baby. You should have seen her face when I told her birth control wasn't going to work."

"I'm happy for you. I really am. Beef up your security and get word to us the moment you think Sorbacov's man has arrived. We'll come." He would be watching as best he could over his youngest brother.

"Jonas Harrington is married to Hannah Drake and lives next door," Ilya said unnecessarily. "He's the local sheriff. I'll let him know I'm going to have company soon. He's good. He's had my back more than once."

Gavriil nodded. "Levi told me he's a good man."

"So you and Lexi?" Ilya said. "Lexi keeps to herself. She sells at the farmer's market sometimes, although often the other women do it for her, as she's quite shy."

Gavriil was already restless, needing to leave, needing to get back to Lexi. He had one more stop to make before he could go back to the farm. Ilya had to sense that Gavriil wanted to leave and he was trying to hold him there with small talk. Gavriil found himself happy about that when normally he would have been annoyed at any delay to his plans.

"She's comfortable on the farm."

"Jonas tells me that all the women have had traumatic events in their lives. Murders of loved ones."

"It's possible that the reason these women can be with us is because they've suffered similar events," Gavriil said. "That, or the universe is lining up to give us something wonderful after so many years of nothing."

He stood up. He couldn't stay any longer. The restless need was on him, an urgent demand he couldn't ignore. "It was good to see you, Ilya . . ." He trailed off, holding up his hand to silence his brother.

Ilya didn't ask questions but slid a gun from his boot. Gavriil indicated the southern end of the property. More than once he pondered the question of why he could feel the presence of an actual threat to his life, but he could. He had been careful when he'd pulled Benito through the window, because that life-or-death reflex hadn't kicked in, nor had it done so with Lissa. It was out in full force now.

"I guess they managed to get here sooner than you thought," Ilya said softly.

"They aren't in the house yet, but I can feel them." Gavriil was already on the move, making his way unerringly toward the southern side of the long building, back toward the kitchen.

Ilya paced to the right of him, moving in silence. Gavriil shook his head. "Make sure your wife is all right. I've got this."

"She's fine. Jonas is with her, and they aren't going to risk killing her, not when these assassins might be traced back to Sorbacov, you said so yourself. I've already texted him to put the women and his baby in a safe room. And don't worry," Ilya added when Gavriil shot him a disgusted look, "he won't come to try to help. He knows better. His job is to look after Joley and Hannah."

"You'd better be right, because these two will kill anyone on the property. You know how they work."

They had reached the kitchen. "Not that way," Ilya said. "Don't risk opening the door." He took the lead, sliding his hand into a hidden notch behind a wall of hanging pots and pans. A panel slid aside. He stepped inside a narrow corridor.

"I should have known you'd play around with the building itself."

"Actually, this was here. It was never put in the blueprints," Ilya said. "The original owner was a smuggler. He actually had a tunnel built that runs under the road to the sea. He used steel and concrete and the thing is insane. There are several escape exits."

"Nice. You're a Prakenskii. I have a lot of work to do on Lexi's house."

"I wasn't happy with this one until I was told about the hidden corridors, rooms and escapes. I added a few refinements. Cash. Passports. New identities for us."

"Weapons," Gavriil guessed.

"An arsenal," Ilya said. "That farm is probably outfitted to fight several wars."

"I haven't been there long enough to know what they have, but they've intertwined their gifts with those of the women and built some kind of power grid. I could feel it the moment I stepped onto the grounds."

Ilya opened a door cautiously. It led out into the pavilion surrounded by heavy plants and brush. A narrow path allowed them to move through the foliage rapidly and with ease. Ilya signaled that there was a branching path ahead. He went to the left, circling in an arc that brought him out along a creek bed and much closer to the fence between the two properties.

Gavriil took the right, his path taking him into the forest, a much more direct line to the two intruders making their way toward the house. Both men were adept at avoiding cameras, just as Gavriil and his brothers were. Gavriil recognized them immediately. The older of the two, Efrim Goraya, had been in one or two of the same hand-to-hand combat classes. The younger, Georgii Yenotov, had been in a language class. Both were older than Gavriil.

He'd been the youngest in all of his classes, easily excelling, partly because his parents had passed their genius on to their children and partly because he was naturally athletic as well as having physic gifts.

Efrim had been a quiet man, about five years older than Gavriil. He was very good at martial arts and hadn't been pleased when Gavriil had exceeded his training and became the top student in the classes—until he saw the way Gavriil took so many beatings from the instructors. He hadn't been the least bit bitter then. Twice, he'd snuck into Gavriil's dormitory room and handed off salve to him. That had been one of the few acts of kindness Gavriil could remember.

Georgii Yenotov had been a kid who should never have gone to such a school. Gavriil was shocked that he was still alive. He'd been the inept student, awkward and clumsy, but he'd been brilliant in languages. He could create a perfect accent the first time he heard it.

Gavriil put aside everything human he knew of the two men and concentrated only on their fighting abilities. Georgii would be dangerous in that he would use his automatic weapon the moment he felt threatened, spraying everything and everybody with a million bullets before he ran.

Efrim was calm and steady. He would move with complete confidence, and his specialty was hand-to-hand combat. He would be the one in the lead, holding Georgii together, wanting a quiet kill. Over the years, Gavriil had heard of some of his hits. All had been deemed accidents, and it didn't surprise him that Uri Sorbacov would send Efrim in first.

Efrim's specialty was taking out a target and making it look as if it was a natural death, suicide or an accident, even if that meant taking out a number of innocents around his target. Gavriil knew he would make for the house, looking for a quick kill and getting out as fast as possible if Sorbacov had given him the information that Gavriil and his brothers were close.

Gavriil went very still. Of course Sorbacov hadn't told the two assassins. Georgii wouldn't have come. Efrim, yes, but not Georgii.

Gavriil positioned himself in the deepest shadows along the route the two would take to enter through the kitchen. He used his gift of blurring every line, fooling the human eye into thinking he was part of his surroundings, in this case, heavy brush. He crouched low and stayed very still, not moving, but keeping his blood moving to keep his muscles warm. His breath was controlled so that air barely moved around him.

He heard them. They were a few feet apart and moving with stealth. He thought they sounded a bit like elephants. Three times twigs snapped, and the leaves crunched beneath their feet. He spotted Ilya several yards away, dropping in behind them. He didn't want his younger brother anywhere near the automatic weapons.

Gavriil had wanted to kill Efrim first, but he knew exactly how Georgii would react. He palmed his knife and waited, allowing them to close the distance between them. As they came toward him, he shot Georgii between the eyes as he threw the knife at Efrim.

Georgii went down hard. The knife lodged in Efrim's arm, slicing through muscle and tendons so that the weapon cradled in his hands fell to the ground. Efrim swore, and rushed him, drawing Gavriil's knife from his body. He threw just as Ilya and Gavriil shot simultaneously.

Gavriil twisted his body as he shot, but the knife sliced through his biceps, burning like hell and separating far too much skin and muscle. Ilya jogged toward him as he stepped out of the shadows and stared down at the two dead assassins.

"They didn't know you were anywhere around, did they?" Ilya asked, his eyes on his brother's wound and not the two dead men.

"No. They should have been more cautious. Sorbacov expected you to kill them both," Gavriil said. "He's using

us to do his dirty work for him. He knows we'll dispose of
the bodies."

Gritting his teeth, he moved away from the two dead
men, careful not to allow his blood to drip onto the ground.
"Nothing like getting cut with my own knife." He'd forgotten the fire. The feeling of a sharp blade penetrating his
skin, separating muscle and tissue, tearing through his
body like a hot brand.

He worked to keep his expression pure stone as the
memories rose along with the pain to swamp him. He'd
been stabbed seven times, and each time the knife went in,
his attacker had twisted it as it came out, leaving behind
maximum damage.

"Gavriil, that blade was covered with his blood." Ilya
frowned down at Efrim. "You have no idea what kind of
diseases you could contract. At the very least you could get
a terrible infection."

If anyone knew about infection from stab wounds, it was
Gavriil. He'd had to be on intravenous antibiotics for months.
He'd had to go to an old doctor he'd done a favor for to get
the medicine. He'd been barely able to move, let alone care
for himself. He'd been lucky no one had found him during
those days.

"I'll take care of it," Gavriil said grimly. The thought of
what was to come wasn't pleasant.

Ilya shook his head. "Libby Drake is home. She's an
amazing healer. She'll come if I ask her to."

Gavriil shook his head. "We've got to take care of this
mess. I've still got a couple of things to do." He had to get
back to Lexi. Suddenly that was the most important thing
he could imagine. He felt the compulsion growing stronger
with every passing minute.

"Let me call Jonas. I'll report two intruders with automatic weapons. I've got permits for my guns."

"I shot Georgii, and one of my slugs is in Efrim," Gavriil
said, exhausted. He'd had enough of killing for the day. He
wanted to go back to Lexi and feel her hands moving over

his skin, breathe her in and feel at peace again, just for a little while.

"Give me your gun." Ilya held out his hand. "Come up to the house with me. I'll take care of that wound and then you get out of here. I'll call Jonas."

Gavriil hesitated. The last thing he wanted was trouble with the police. He wiped his prints off the weapon and using his shirt, handed it over.

"Your sheriff friend has probably already called for backup. He had to have heard the shots." Gavriil backed away. "Handle this however you think best, Ilya. I'll be at Lexi's. You need to come by and see your brothers."

Gavriil waited until he was back in his truck and had his first aid kit out before he pulled the knife blade out of his arm. He'd waited to keep the blood loss to a minimum, but it took discipline to walk back with the blade in his arm.

He slapped a compress bandage on it fast and sat breathing slow, concentrating until the pain subsided enough for him to function.

His dogs were waiting for him, and he couldn't take much longer to go pick them up. They were well-trained, but he didn't want to take a chance that someone would accidently stumble across them. Still, it was slow going. The wound needed stitches. He could sew the damn thing up himself, but it was an awkward angle and he had the feeling that Lexi was very good with a needle when it came to wounds.

His dogs were exactly where he'd left them. He signaled them up and to do their business. Both obeyed instantly and then came running to him. He crouched down to scratch behind their ears and on their chins. They were massive, intimidating animals. Black Russian Terriers, bred in the Red Star Kennel of Moscow in the 1930s, the breed was confident, loyal, intelligent and very protective.

Gavriil had a natural ability with dogs, one of the many gifts passed on to him from his mother and father. He had run across the breed a number of times and had been intrigued with their intelligence. He had found them to be

calm, confident and very self-assured, and in need of an
equally confident handler.

All black, robust with big, solid bones and heavy muscles, the Black Russian Terrier was a great guard dog. He
felt if there was anywhere a dog was needed, it was on
Lexi's farm. This pair, Drago, shortened from Fierce Black
Dragon, and Kiss, short for Kiss of Death, had saved his
life.

The recovery after being stabbed so many times had
been horrendous. He wasn't a man who could recover in a
hospital or in physical therapy. He had hidden in the mountains and forests of Russia, but first, he had acquired a male
and a female from champion bloodlines. Both had been
puppies and required daily walks and training. He had been
forced to get up and move even when he thought it would
kill him.

The dogs had been his constant companions and he'd
spent nearly two years alone in their company, working
with them until they were inseparable and totally trusted
one another. The dogs were naturally wary around strangers and he would have to introduce them to the family
members on the farm slowly. Kiss was pregnant with her
first litter and getting close to her time. He needed to get
her home and find her a place she would approve of to have
her puppies.

Gavriil glanced at his watch for what seemed the two
hundredth time. He had to get home to Lexi. Who was he
kidding? The anxiety wasn't over his wound or the dog
having her pups, it was the need to see her again. What
had happened to him that he was so obsessed with Lexi
Thompson?

"Load up, we're going to our new home. And don't get
ugly with her. I'll expect you both to protect her, same as
me." He had little doubt that she would manage to win the
dogs over just as she had him.

8

GAVRIIL was grateful he had plenty of time in the house to allow the two Black Russian Terriers to get used to Lexi's scent. She was all over the house. He tried to inhale her, tried to take her in, letting the dogs explore their new home while he sank into one of the deep, cozy chairs in the large sitting room. Maybe it was all those days without sleep, or loss of blood, or possibly the memories of the stab wounds so close, but he felt very weak. If he didn't get Lexi home, and he passed out, the dogs would never allow her into the house.

He let his breath out slowly, stretched his legs out comfortably in front of him and slowly turned his hand over, looking down at it. He drew one finger down the center of his palm and the psychic mark blazed into life, two perfect circles joined together. He whispered her name softly and pressed his lips into the brand on his palm.

Come home to me, angel moy, *I need you,* he whispered in his mind, reaching for her with every cell, every fiber of his being.

He closed his eyes, allowing his body to absorb the pain.

There was no fighting the burn along his nerve endings, or the terrible agony consuming his shoulder and arm. He was no stranger to pain, but still, even allowing it to take him over didn't stop the initial feeling of hopelessness.

He pressed his thumb tightly over the two rings and let his eyes close. He didn't know how long he'd been drifting in a sea of pain when both dogs, lying at his feet, leapt up and gave low, rumbling growls. He lifted his gun from the arm of the chair and sent both back to the floor with a command.

Lexi pushed open the door and stood there, framed in the gathering dusk, her hair disheveled as if she'd been running, her gaze jumping to the dogs and then moving over him, assessing how badly he was hurt.

"Is it safe to come near you?"

He couldn't help the smile coming out of nowhere, the way she made him feel. She didn't panic, when she should have been having one of her panic attacks. The dogs were huge and both targeted her instantly, never taking their wary, threatening gaze from her. The only thing keeping them from attacking her was his command to stay.

"Stay very still. I'm in a vulnerable position and they don't like it."

"So am I." She hung on to the door, ready to slam it closed if either dog moved. "And put the gun down. You don't look in any shape to be using that right now and it might accidently go off."

He raised an eyebrow. The gun felt like an extension of his arm, so familiar in his hand he knew it was impossible for him to make that kind of mistake, but he put it down on the arm of his chair and stood up, surprised at his weakness. He led the dogs into the other room. Neither liked it, but they settled when he gave them a hand signal.

"It's safe to come in," he said, and collapsed back in the chair. "Just don't go into the back bedroom."

"Let me see your arm. You have blood all over you." Lexi rushed across the room to pull back his sleeve. The bandage was soaked in blood. She shook her head. "Is this

the way I'm going to find you every time I leave you by
yourself?"

He put his head back and closed his eyes. Her touch was
gentle on his body. He felt power run through her. He could
have slowed the bleeding had he tried, but he'd been too
tired. He didn't want to move. The sound of her bustling
around the house, getting things together to take care of the
wound soothed him.

"Unfortunately," he murmured without opening his
eyes, "the blade was in someone else before it was in me.
That makes it doubly dangerous." The thought of another
massive infection was daunting.

"Don't worry about anything right now. Just rest. Honestly, Gavriil, I don't know how you've survived this long
without me."

Her voice whispered over his skin, over his senses, dull-
ing the pain as nothing else could. Her hands were sure,
filled with healing warmth as they stripped away the
soaked bandage and cleansed the wound thoroughly with
some kind of strong antiseptic. The burn robbed him of his
breath, and he forced his body into a meditative trance,
putting himself far from the pain, a technique he'd used
numerous times to survive.

He was aware of Lexi working on the wound, patiently
sewing it up. She had to stitch inside as well as out and he
was a little surprised at her skill. When she was finished
and went to move away from him, he caught her wrist and
held her close.

"What was her name?"

"Who?"

"The doctor. The woman who taught you so much. What
was her name?"

He felt the tremor that ran through her, but he didn't let
go. He needed to know the name of the woman who had
treated her like a human being. The woman who knew she
would eventually be thrown away, but had reached out to a
young, traumatized child and given her the best of herself.
A worthwhile human being.

"Daiyu Zhang. Her name was Daiyu Zhang."

Lexi's voice was filled with tears. His heart bled for her. Gavriil turned her palm up and pulled it to his mouth. He pressed kisses into it, as if that could take away the years of hurt.

"I'm sorry, Lexi. She was an extraordinary woman. I wish I could have known her." Gavriil closed her fingers over the center of her palm and brought her fist to his mouth again. His teeth scraped gently back and forth over her knuckles. "If we ever have a relationship and we do decide to stay together, if we end up with a child, we'll have to honor her with the name Daiyu."

Lexi pressed her lips together tightly for a moment, her eyes swimming with tears, turning them into sparkling jewels. "It means black jade. She would have liked that, having a child named after her. She always wanted children, but she couldn't have them. That was part of the excuse her husband used to get rid of her."

"Is that why you have so many pieces of black jade in the house? I noticed a piece in every room. I thought at the time that the jade was part of your Chinese décor."

"She used to say her black jade was the stone of protection. And that was what she was, how she lived her life, as a human shield against anger and aggression. She said the stone was important to ward those things off because it had an elemental shield of energy against both physical and psychic attacks. It can also be used as a powerful healing stone."

"So you filled your house with it."

"With her," Lexi said, and pulled away from him. "I filled my house with the things she taught me. I never went to school after he took me. I didn't have the opportunities other children had. She was my only teacher. She was the only adult who took an interest in me with no other agenda. She was the one person there who never betrayed me."

"In essence, Daiyu was your mother."

Lexi slowly nodded her head. "She's all I had. Caine took her away, the same way he took my family."

Gavriil hooked his one good arm around her waist and pulled her down into his lap. "I'm just going to comfort you, nothing more. You're breaking my heart right now. Maybe I need the comfort more than you do, but all the same, just curl up here for one moment and let me hold you."

Gavriil thought she would resist, or hold herself away from him. He was well aware no one had ever held her like he was doing. He kept his arm around her and waited patiently, not forcing her, or putting more pressure on her. Slowly she relaxed into him, and in that moment, he felt as if he'd just been given the most precious gift in the world— her trust.

"Tell me how your lesson went. Was Lucia happy to see you?" He dropped his chin on the top of her head, nuzzling all that dark reddish silk.

Her fingers curled in his shirt. "Yes. Her face lit up when I went in with Lissa. Levi was there, and he wore an apron. It was all manly but I know he wore it for Lucia. I thought it was awesome that he'd do that for her."

"You like Levi."

"Very much. I had trouble at first, being around him. I don't usually go near men, but he's so wrapped up in Rikki, anyone can see that, so I didn't feel threatened. He hasn't been here that long, but he works wherever he's needed and he already feels part of us—like a big brother looking out for us."

"That's good," Gavriil said. "What about Thomas?" Levi to Lev was an easy switch, but Stefan to Thomas was a little more difficult for him. He was going to have to work at getting used to that name.

"Thomas is more reserved than Levi. He's definitely crazy about Judith, but I don't know him as well."

She didn't realize that she was just as reserved as Thomas was. Gavriil leaned his head back again and closed his eyes, inhaling her scent. She would always feel like peace to him, like cool forest and the earth after a summer rain. Clean and fresh. She represented a new life. He was grabbing hold with both hands now that he'd made up his mind.

Lexi's body heat melted into his. It was a first for him to hold a woman on his lap, to simply cherish her. Offer comfort with no strings attached.

"And Maxim?"

"Maxim." She smiled. He couldn't see it because her face was buried in his chest, but he heard it in her voice.

"He's Mr. Tough Guy. He's not as intimidating to everyone as you are, because he has four shadows. Seriously, he can't take a step without the four children somewhere close. All of them look at him like the sun rises and sets with him. He tries to act like he doesn't like it. He gets all gruff, but you should see him with them. It's beautiful to watch."

"So you like him."

"I don't know him. He's only been here a couple of weeks, and we've had a few crazy things going on."

Gavriil remained silent, just waiting.

"Yes, I guess I do like him. How can you not like a man who takes on the responsibility of four children? I like Thomas as well. They definitely would protect all of us." She turned her head and looked up at him. "Tell me about your dogs."

"They saved my life. They gave me a reason to get up in the morning and to force my body to work when it didn't want to. They're the first real companionship I've ever had since I was taken." He hadn't known until that moment just how much he loved both animals. "The male is Drago and the female is Kiss."

"Kiss? As in the band KISS?"

"Kiss, as in Kiss of Death."

"Oh." She sat up and slipped off his lap. "You'd better introduce us. You need to go to bed. The sun's gone down, and you still haven't told me what happened to you this afternoon."

"You didn't ask," he pointed out.

"I figured you would tell me, but you're not getting to it."

She was very careful of his injured biceps. He noticed even when she melted into him, she didn't jostle him in the least.

"Because it wasn't important," he replied.

"I think you need to revise your opinion of what you consider important, Gavriil. When you come home with blood all over you and a wound that takes some fifty-six stitches to close, that's important."

She'd said, *"Come home."* He wanted to smile, but she had her little schoolmarm expression on her face and he figured she considered the conversation serious.

"I'm sorry. Yes. Of course. You're right. I should have told you what happened right away. It was more like a gun-fight than a knife fight." At her gasp, he hastily amended his explanation. "It wasn't much of a fight at all."

"Gavriil Prakenskii, cough it up." She put her hands on her hips. "What exactly did you do now?"

He did laugh. "I'm not Benito."

"You could be," she said. "Spill."

"A couple of would-be assassins went after my youngest brother, Ilya."

"Oh no." Her hand flew to her throat. "Is he all right? Is Joley okay?"

"She was at her sister's house. He was with me."

She stood there a moment looking down at his face. She suddenly leaned down, framing his face with her hands, her gaze capturing his. "He was with you, meaning of course he's fine. Of course you took care of it, Gavriil. One of these days you aren't going to be fast enough and you're going to die. I don't want that. Do you understand me? I don't want that."

"If you keep looking at me like that, Lexi, I might have to kiss you, and then we'd have all sorts of problems."

She didn't stop looking at him, but she blinked a few times. "I don't know what this connection is between us, but I don't want to lose you, Gavriil. Please, for me, be a little more careful with yourself." She dropped her hands before he could move into her, stepping back and frowning at him. "And don't ever kiss me because you feel sorry for me. I'm not your sister."

He felt the slow burn start in his blood. "I wouldn't be kissing you if you were my sister. You told me you didn't want to be afraid I'd make a move on you, so I was politely warning you. You're not even making any sense."

She looked smug. "I'm a woman. I don't have to make sense. You need to be in bed, so eat and go to bed. I'm going to sit outside and contemplate what I'm going to do with you."

"You need to be introduced to the dogs. Kiss is pregnant and about to give birth to her first litter of puppies. I don't want her to get overprotective and not let you in the house."

"I'm quite happy on the porch. She can have the house. You do cook, don't you? When you're feeling up to it, you can cook me meals and bring them outside."

When she teased him, there was no way to resist her, no way to stop the spread of happiness slowly moving through him like some tsunami. "You really have a great sense of humor, don't you?" He grinned at her.

"Apparently. Fine. I'll meet your dogs, but if they kill me, it's on you."

The little tremor in her voice told him she was just a little afraid, now that she had taken care of his injury. Before, she'd been worried about him, but the dogs were large and intimidating.

He didn't feel like getting up and introducing her to the dogs. He considered just sleeping right there so he wouldn't have to move. His body hurt and his nerve endings burned until he felt raw and used up. But there she was, standing in front of him, looking nervous and determined, so beautiful she made his heart ache.

Lexi moved away from him to reach for the light switch. Dusk had turned to night, deepening the shadows he was more familiar with, more comfortable in.

"Don't," he said softly. "Leave them off."

He saw her take a deep breath before she nodded. "Just tell me why."

"We can see outside unless the lights are on. With them on, anyone outside has a bit of an advantage."

"I can put the blinds down."

"*Solnyshko moya*, you said you wanted me to stay. I know it feels as if I'm taking over, but I have to know we're safe. I prepare. I stash weapons around a house, and I know that won't bother you because I found your weapons. I leave money and passports in various places just in case. I've never spent more than a couple of nights in one place until I went to the mountains and forests to recover from this." He swept his arm over his body, indicating the stab wounds. "I want to be here. On this farm. With you. I have a chance to find something else here. It may be a slim one, but I'm willing to try. I just need . . ." He broke off, a little helplessly.

He didn't know the first thing about explaining himself to anyone. The conversations with her were the longest he'd had with another human being in more time than he could count.

"It's okay, Gavriil, I understand, I do. And I'm grateful to you for all the lessons in safety. I want to feel safe in my own home and I haven't. Not ever." She shivered and rubbed at the goose bumps on her arms. "Your dogs are just a little intimidating and they're black. In the dark I would think they would give someone a heart attack."

"Are you afraid? I wouldn't allow them to hurt you."

"A little."

"I'd shoot them before I'd allow them to harm you. And that's saying a lot, Lexi," he said quietly. "I owe my life to them."

"Tell me what to do." Her voice trembled but her chin was up.

Pain radiated from his biceps up to his shoulder, down his back and through his entire arm. He was going to have to lie down soon, there was no question about it, and he couldn't have the dogs killing her if she moved around the house.

Lexi thought she was going to sleep outside in her usual spot on the porch, but he had other ideas. She felt safer on the porch where she could see anything coming at her, but the house was safer with him in it and now, with the dogs and their incredible sense of smell and natural protective instincts, he could better protect her.

"Sit in the chair over there. I'll be on my feet. You won't pose a threat to me seated, especially when I'm standing."

"You aren't going to fall down are you? You're swaying a little. I've probably got some pain pills around here. If not, I can call Blythe and she'll call Libby. Libby's a doctor and she can—"

"I don't take painkillers. They dull the senses and I prefer to be sharp."

"Gavriil, you aren't going to heal fast if you hurt like that."

"You're going to heal me. I can feel the power in your hands. You'll do it, Lexi, so no worries. Sit down and let me call in the dogs. Then I'm going to bed."

"Have they already eaten?" she asked, her teeth chewing on her lower lip. He couldn't help but notice how full and perfectly curved her lip was even when he was making his way to the door.

Lexi sank into a chair and he called the dogs through, murmuring softly to them in his native language. He told them she was a friend, although, since he didn't have any friends, he'd never used that particular word before, so he changed it to his *mate* and introduced her as a pack member.

The dogs immediately went to her, smelling her. Her scent was on him and all around them. She belonged. Gavriil continued in his soft, commanding voice, every now and then running his hands over the two animals to reassure them all was well. He sank down onto the arm of her chair, his legs unable to support him.

Lexi slipped her arm around his waist. "You need to get in bed."

"Call them by name. Let them smell your hand. If they push against you, pet them. If not, just talk to them, let them get used to your voice."

Lexi followed his instructions, as well as his example. She spoke to the dogs in a low, calm voice. Drago smelled her hand and looked at Gavriil, and then, as if he understood, pushed his body against Lexi's. She dropped her hand into his silky, wavy coat. She smiled as she stroked the animal.

"He's beautiful, Gavriil."

Gavriil thought so as well. The male was sturdy, with strong bones and good conformation. Kiss was beautiful as well. Her body was heavy with puppies. Lexi was careful to make a fuss over the male and wait for the much more reluctant female to accept her.

Lexi was patient, taking her time talking to the male and allowing the female to check her out thoroughly. Gavriil let his breath out when Kiss finally signaled her acceptance of Lexi into her life. He had her pet Kiss, touch her, run her hands over the pregnant female while his hands mirrored hers to make certain Kiss accepted her fully.

"When will she have her puppies?"

"Very soon, any day. I tried to get her here, thinking I'd leave them with my brothers, so I'd know they were well taken care of."

"Before you sacrificed your life." Lexi shot him a look from under her long lashes. "Let's get you to bed."

He wanted to smile, but she had her little schoolmarm look on her face again. Every time they referred back to his original plan of leading Sorbacov's assassins away from his family, she got that particular expression. He was becoming rather fond of it.

He waved the dogs back and rose slowly from the arm of the chair, feeling as if a saw was cutting through his arm right down to the bone, and not a particularly sharp saw. Lexi stood up with him and slipped her arm back around his waist to steady him. He didn't need her help, but he liked the feel of her body close to his.

He couldn't believe the way she made him feel. His entire life he'd been closed off from human associations. He'd never wanted to be close to anyone, never could find a way to trust a woman far enough to be vulnerable around her. The first time he'd seen Lexi, he'd known. The earth itself had trembled beneath his feet and his heart had done a curious melting so that he was lost before he'd ever had a chance to retreat.

She left him at the bathroom door, and he heard her moving around the bedroom, pulling back covers and making up a bed for the dogs. The sounds were vaguely comforting. When he emerged, he wore nothing but a towel. He stood leaning against the door, watching her as she built a nest from blankets, presumably for Kiss.

She glanced up and went still. He knew he was devouring her with his gaze. She was beautiful to him. Everything about her, especially the care she was giving his animals. He hadn't prepared her ahead of time for them, but because they were his, she'd welcomed them.

"Thank you, Lexi," he said.

Lexi found she couldn't move. Gavriil leaned against the wall, a towel riding low on his hips, his eyes alive with pain, drifting over her possessively. No one had looked at her quite like that. He didn't look as if he owned her, but as if she was his, cherished and treasured and beautiful to him.

His face was ravaged with pain. Lines were etched deep. His shoulders were broad, his chest heavily muscled, his waist and hips narrow. He looked, in spite of his injury, invincible. He was battle-scarred, and right now, she could see exhaustion in every line of his body, but it didn't matter. She was completely and utterly captivated by him.

"Gavriil, please get in bed. If you don't, I'm going to sit on the floor and cry, right here." He was so wracked with pain he could barely move, yet he didn't seem to acknowledge it, or know how to just lay it all down for a while. "You've got the dogs, and I'm pretty good at keeping an eye out. I won't fall asleep, I promise."

There was something about him she just couldn't help but be drawn to. He was tragic, yet he didn't know it. He needed saving, but he didn't know that either. He was so alone standing there. He didn't know how to love, so broken, just like she was. She didn't know how either. Or maybe it was survival mode they both lived in, and they didn't dare allow anyone else in because if they were ripped apart a second time there would be no fixing either of them.

"I want you to lie down on the bed with me. Just stay there. I'll sleep under the sheet and you can have the blanket, but stay with me."

She was already shaking her head, an automatic reaction. She didn't sleep in a bed where someone could climb through the window and put a knife to her baby sister's throat. The air left her lungs and she couldn't catch her breath.

He moved so fast he seemed a blur, pushing her head down, his hand at the nape of her neck, strong, making her aware he could break her neck easily.

"Are you so afraid of me that you panic at the idea of lying on the same bed with me? Even when I have assured you that you're perfectly safe with me?"

There was no accusation in his tone, only a soft inquiry. His presence helped her to push air through her lungs. She shook her head and slowly straightened, her heart still pounding, blood still coursing through her veins, but she could breathe.

"It isn't you. It isn't, Gavriil. I'm sorry I made you think that." She glanced toward the window. He was so omnipotent and she felt fragile and a little hysterical with her panic attacks. She made up her mind to just tell him. Let him see what he was dealing with.

"He came through my bedroom window. Into my home. My sister was asleep in the bed next to mine and my parents were just down the hall. I had two older brothers and their bedroom was across from mine. They had cult members stationed at each of the rooms and if I didn't go with him, they would have gone in and killed all of them right there." She pressed her fingers against her mouth tightly.

Gavriil very gently laid his hand over hers, closed his fingers around hers and pulled her hand to his mouth. He kissed her fingertips, as if she had burned them. "Don't be ashamed because you don't like sleeping in a bedroom. That worthless excuse of a human being took your feeling of safety away. A home is supposed to be a sanctuary, a place that should never be violated. He took that away. You sleep on your porch to compensate. Why should that make you embarrassed?"

"Look at you. Intruders broke into your home. They ripped your family apart just as Caine did mine. They murdered your parents just as Caine did mine. You're strong and you don't have panic attacks . . ."

"Silly woman."

His voice twisted at her heart. There was a note in it she couldn't quite identify. Silky and soft. Tender.

"Look around this room. It's an armory. There are weapons stashed in every conceivable place, not only here in this bedroom, but throughout the house. I've brought two very protective dogs with me. I intend to build a safe room as well as an underground room to store more weapons. I'll turn our home into a fortress, and still that won't be enough for me. To protect you, Lexi, I'll go to lengths that will make you crazy. What's the difference between us? Not much if you ask me."

She couldn't help the smile. They were both so broken it was terrible, yet wonderful at the same time. She wasn't alone, and he didn't care about her panic attacks or her inability to stay in the bedroom all night.

He tugged at her hand. "You don't have to sleep here. Just lie down with me. I need to feel you next to me. You give me courage."

Lexi followed him to the bed, more because the fingers shackling her wrist hadn't let up for one moment. He wasn't holding her tight, but his hold was firm.

"I think you're the most courageous person I know."

Gavriil slipped beneath the sheet, pulled off the towel, folded it carefully and slipped a gun between the folds before he laid it on the floor nearly under the bed. He knew Lexi watched his every move intently. She sat on the other side of the bed rather gingerly, as if at any moment she would bolt.

He winced when he lay back, but lying down never felt so good. He found her wrist again, and settled his fingers around it, his thumb stroking over her pulse.

"I'm not courageous, Lexi. I live away from society, in the shadows where no one can see me. I slip in and out of countries, move constantly, form no attachments. How is that courageous?"

She frowned and turned toward him, hesitated and then stretched out beside him, propping her head up with one hand. Her gaze drifted slowly over his face as if she was puzzling something out.

"Gavriil, you're here with me now. How much courage did it take to stay? You actually weighed the idea of killing me for a moment . . ."

"Don't," he said. "I would never have been able to do it."

"I know that. I knew it at the time. I wasn't afraid of you. I'm still not."

He was still loosely holding her one wrist, but she lifted her other hand and reached out to brush strands of hair from his face. His breath caught in his lungs. He knew it was a mini miracle that she touched him at all, let alone with such an intimate gesture. She didn't even seem to notice she did it.

"You're safe with me." She was. No matter what, he would protect her, even from himself. Still, that didn't mean he wouldn't get her used to his close proximity, to his hands on her. He wanted to be the one exception in her life. She was uncomfortable with everyone else, and that was perfectly fine with him. He wanted her relaxed in his company, laughing, feeling that as long as she was with him, she could be in her house and feel safe.

"Lexi, put your hands on me, one on my shoulder, right above the wound and one below it." Deliberately he allowed his eyes to close, striving to portray the picture of a man who had nothing on his mind but the pain in his shoulder. "I'd like to try a little experiment."

Lexi didn't argue or hesitate. She came up on her knees and leaned over him, rubbing her hands together. She had a natural healing talent. He felt the power running through her body. He had many gifts, and one was the ability to boost the strength of elementals or psychic gifts.

She placed her hands on the positions he'd requested and closed her eyes, feeling his body, feeling the raw nerve endings and inflammation building around the wound. He reached up with his free hand and caught at the scrunchie securing her hair from around her face and tugged until all her glorious hair fell free.

He threaded his fingers through it, reveling in the feel of such thick silk. She had a lot of hair. "I like your hair down."

"It isn't practical when I'm working."

"You're not working when you're in the house," he pointed out. "You could carry your tie in your pocket and pull it back up when you're outside." He had to open his eyes and look at her face.

Her hair tumbled down around her face and shoulders, even longer than he'd imagined. The ends pooled on his skin, a dark, rich auburn, more red than brown, almost like a glass of dark wine. His body stirred in spite of every effort to stay relaxed.

"I like your hair long like this." His tone went low, caressing. He deliberately allowed his voice to brush over her skin the way her hair did over his.

"That's good, because I'm not ever going to cut it. I trim the ends, but that's all, just to keep it healthy."

There was a touch of defiance in her voice, a touch of fire and that fire blazed through her hands to the muscles of his body. The heat spread through his body, a slow burn that seemed to move from muscle to muscle, seeping into his blood where it grew scorching hot, but maintained a slow flow until it saturated every cell in his body. His cock grew full and hard, a savage ache that only added to the beauty of the moment.

He felt—loved. She couldn't possibly love him, she hadn't had time to fall in love with him, but still, no one had ever cared for him like this. No one had ever aroused his body as she did. The pads of her fingers moved on his skin, finding hidden trigger points, and he let her work on him, lying still and accepting the fact that he was drowning and it was far too late to save himself.

He wanted to close his eyes again and just absorb every touch, but the expression on her face was far too beautiful to miss. Her lashes were long, her lips slightly parted as she concentrated, wholly focused on his body, on taking the pain from his arm. She shifted her position, her hand sliding around his muscle, careful to keep away from the stitches, but her palm was a hot brand against his skin.

Her breasts skimmed his side, sending another flash of heat arcing over him. He forced his own hands into the mattress. He had absolute confidence in his ability to seduce her. He'd been trained and he knew every way there was to please a woman, but he didn't want that for her—or for him. He wanted her to come to him. To be ready in her mind, not just her body.

She suddenly opened her eyes and looked directly into his. Her wild green gaze hit him like a wicked punch. "Is that better? Do you think you can sleep?"

He nodded slowly, holding her gaze captive with his. "Get ready for bed and just lie with me until I drift off. Something happens when you're touching me and the nerve pain seems to recede. I don't know if it really does or I just think that it does, but either way, you've given me more relief than I've had since I was attacked."

She took a breath. He held his. Both waited. Finally she nodded and slipped off the bed. Gavriil didn't say another word. He felt as if he was holding his breath the entire time she got ready. She braided her hair and changed to thin sweatpants and a racerback tee. When she slipped on top of the comforter and pulled up a blanket, turning away from him, he turned toward her and wrapped his injured arm around her waist.

She went rigid. He didn't let go. He curled his body around hers and nuzzled against the nape of her neck with his face. "I promise you, Lexi, I won't make a move on you. I just need to hold you. I can give you a knife if that would make you feel safer."

"There's already a gun and a knife under my pillow." There was a hint of laughter in her voice and some of the tension eased out of her.

"Oh. That's right. I forgot that. See? You can shoot me if I'm not a man of my word."

"Don't think I won't," she cautioned.

He felt laughter rising and the fact that she could make him feel that emotion awed him. He had spent time trying to get her to relax and accept his presence, and all the while she was taming him like some wild animal.

"I know you would."

"It's starting to rain." She sounded excited. "Listen to the rain. Rikki's playing music over the farm."

He listened to the pattern of the rain. It fell softly in some places and much harder in others. Power pulsed through the air.

"That's Judith, boosting Rikki," Lexi said, awe in her voice. "Aren't they wonderful? Rikki can coax water out of practically nothing. When we're desperate, Airiana can move the clouds to us. If the rain is too heavy, Rikki can redirect to the redwoods and forest and keep it from killing our crops."

"And you read the earth, the soil. You can tell what it needs and when."

She snuggled deeper into the pillow. "Yes. We make a great team."

"I'll fit right in."

Lexi fell asleep somewhere around midnight. Gavriil had known she was exhausted and would eventually succumb to the warmth of his body, the sound of the rain and the comfort of the bed. He allowed himself to sleep in intervals, monitoring the area around their house—and already he thought of it as theirs. Occasionally wildlife came close but no humans, and he was grateful for the reprieve.

He woke at three to the sound of weeping. Drago and Kiss both pressed close, pushing against Lexi's side of the bed, anxious to comfort her. His heart jerked hard in his chest. His arm was still wrapped firmly around her, but his hand was under her shirt. How it got there, he had no idea, but she hadn't pulled away from him.

"*Angel moy*, what is it?"

She continued to weep. It took him a minute to realize she was sound asleep. Why the fact that she was crying in her sleep made it so much worse, he didn't know. He pressed his hand into her abdomen, his fingers splayed wide to take in as much of her skin as possible, as if he could somehow be part of her and take away the demons.

"Lexi, *solnyshko moya*, it's all right now. He's gone for good. He can't hurt you or anyone you love ever again. Your sisters are safe. Do you hear me? Wake up enough to know you're safe." He whispered the words, a sorcerer, determined to push her nightmares away.

When that didn't work, he sighed and turned her into his arms, raising her palm to his mouth. He pressed kisses into the exact center, breathed warm air there, and pushed their intimate connection even further.

I'm here with you, Lexi, and you're safe. I killed that man for you. I made sure he suffered before he died and told me who knew where you are. I'll find them and I'll kill them. Every one of them, until I know you're safe. He used telepathic communication, enabled by the connection between their palms as well as their gifts.

He told me details about what he'd done to you and I lost control. I've never lost control in my life. I'm not ashamed of it, but it did throw me for a long while, which is part of the reason I had my hand around your throat.

You can hate me if you want to, or despise what I am, but he's gone. Wiped out. He can't come back.

Her weeping lessened. He felt her stillness and knew he had her attention. *Now you know the worst of me. The very worst. You know what they made me, a monster capable of terrible things. I've done things beyond any hope of redemption and I couldn't feel a thing while I did them. I looked at him and could only see you—what he'd done to you.*

There was the faintest of stirrings in his mind. A brush of her mind against his. Her weeping stopped completely. She didn't move away from him as she should have. She didn't push at the hand spread out over her skin. She stayed very still, but he knew she was listening now.

I don't know what chance I have to be a civilized man, but if there's any way at all to be worth something to you, I want to be it.

You already are.

Three words. That was all it took, and she had his heart in the palm of her hand.

9

GAVRIIL had breakfast ready when Lexi stumbled into the kitchen just after five thirty. He felt tense and edgy, a wreck, another first for him and one he didn't care for at all. He'd given her every reason to throw him out. The reasons just piled up, one after another until he couldn't understand why she had allowed him there in the first place.

He heard her coming in her bare feet, and when he looked up, she was framed in the doorway. She'd taken a shower already and her hair was damp, tumbling around her face, falling in waves, a dark, rich color that reminded him of the earth itself. Dressed in her vintage blue jeans with several holes in them and her inevitable plaid flannel shirt, no makeup and glowing skin, she looked younger than ever—until you looked at her eyes.

"Good morning, Gavriil." She sent him a small smile and turned her attention to the dogs lying close to each other in the corner. "Good morning, Drago. Kiss, I hope you're feeling good this morning."

That was worse than if she'd walked in and slapped him hard across the face and told him to leave. He couldn't read her. He read everyone. That gift kept him alive, but there she stood, looking so beautiful it hurt, and he had no idea what she was going to do or say.

"They've had their run this morning," he said. "You don't own a coffeepot nor could I find coffee, so I made tea."

Her face brightened. "Tea is perfect. I always have a cup of tea before I go out to work. With milk," she added as he poured her a cup.

He held his breath as she walked into the room, straight toward him. He braced himself. Lexi took the mug, wrapping both hands around it. She stood right in front of him, looking up at his face, her eyes searching his for a long time. He knew what she must have felt like when he put his hand on her throat. She weighed his fate. Force him to leave because he was a monster beyond all hope, or . . . what? What was he thinking?

She couldn't possibly understand his life or what had been drilled into him and then required of him. The worlds he'd traveled in were far beyond her imagination. Her eyes, a deep forest green, moved over his face, looked into his, and he knew she saw him, not the person she'd believed him to be, a broken man so much like her, but the killer they'd shaped and trained and sent out into the world to do their bidding.

He had completed every job and he'd grown numb, a survival tactic he knew, his mind trying to save him from the insanity of his life. How far did one go to protect family? As far as he knew, he'd never killed an innocent man. He'd done his research on every job, and he'd spent his life in the underbelly with the men who didn't dare show their faces in the light of day.

Lexi reached up and cupped the side of his jaw, her thumb sliding along his face in the lightest of caresses. "All this time, Gavriil, I thought I was so broken you would eventually look at me and decide there was no hope. But you . . ." She shook her head and dropped her hand. "I think you need me."

She turned away from him and dropped into one of

the kitchen chairs, curling up in it, sipping at her tea. "I've got tons of work to do this morning. I'll come back around noon and try another session with acupuncture. Please don't do anything to aggravate that wound either. How does it feel?"

"Like someone shoved a knife through my arm." He put eggs and hash browns onto two plates and added fresh strawberries before carrying the plates to the table. "It doesn't hurt unless I breathe or move." He tried a tentative smile just to see if his face could actually change expression without shattering.

"That's good." Her answering smile was faint. "You really can cook. That's nice. I can, and I'm good, but I don't always feel like it. Maybe we can share the job."

"You might want to taste the food instead of pushing it around your plate first," Gavriil suggested.

Relief was overwhelming. He refused to allow it to register on his face, but emotion consumed him, made him feel shaky both inside and out. He sat across from her, expressionless, looking the picture of a confident, tough man, and yet he barely recognized himself. He had never felt so exposed and vulnerable in his life.

"We need to get some coffee. And a coffeepot."

"I never thought about it. I never drink coffee and no one ever comes here except for my sisters and they're happy with tea, even Rikki, who loves black coffee. She'll even drink tea with me. I did ask Judith to pick up chocolate the other day because Lucia came by one day and I didn't have anything to offer her."

"You don't have much in your cupboards."

She shrugged. "Mostly I eat what I grow and I pick it fresh. Everyone does that. We do have a communal storage room. There might be coffee and a pot in there. If not, I can go to the store late afternoon." She glanced at her watch. "I might finish up by then. I've tons to do because I didn't work yesterday. It rained though, so I don't have to worry about watering."

"Aren't your crops on an automatic watering system?"

"Most are now. And I have a system for the younger fruit trees as well. Some things just don't grow well here on the coast." She frowned and chewed her eggs thoughtfully. "When we bought the farm there were no watering systems. We've had to slowly install them as we've gotten the money for it, but it's a lot of money and we've never had that much extra. The farm is beginning to thrive and pay for itself, but prior to that, we siphoned money from the other businesses."

"They all benefit from the farm and produce," Gavriil pointed out. "You work the farm. They have separate money. Do you get paid?"

"Actually, we don't really separate the money. We all contribute. Lissa does the accounting for us all and we're all on budgets. We meet every other month to discuss how we're doing financially and how we can improve. All of us are allotted so much money per month."

"And when my brothers showed up, they didn't help out financially?" He couldn't keep the low, ominous note from his voice.

Her gaze flicked to his. "Of course they did. They've put a lot of money toward security and they're purchasing the land that borders ours—another five hundred acres. It's mostly forest, but I've coveted that land for some time, so I'm superexcited about it."

She pushed her plate away and stood up. For the first time he realized she was nervous and that realization settled him immediately. As she started to turn, he reached out and caught her wrist. She halted the moment his fingers settled around her wrist, but she stared straight ahead.

"Lexi. Turn around." His voice had gone low. Tender. He *felt* tenderness toward her. How could he not?

She turned very slowly to face him. Tears sparkled in her eyes, turning them from a forest green to a deep emerald. He tugged gently until she reluctantly took the two steps to bring her to his side.

"I'm sorry for what I am. I wish, for your sake, I was a better man."

She blinked to remove the tears, but one slid down her face in spite of her efforts. "Do you really think I didn't ever wish him dead? I plotted to kill him a million different ways. I wanted him dead. I prayed he would die."

"But you didn't kill him, Lexi," he pointed out gently. "Wishing him dead was natural under the circumstances. That doesn't make you like me."

"I didn't kill him because I was too much of a coward, not because I had a great moral conviction that it was wrong," she confessed. "I killed him a thousand times in my dreams. I made him suffer the way he made all of us suffer. I wasn't the only girl they brought there. Three girls ended up committing suicide. One died in childbirth. Do you have any idea what it's like to be chained up and put in a box the size of a small casket you can't move an inch in with the lid closed and locked? I hated him. I wanted him dead and I hated myself for not being strong enough to kill him."

"You aren't responsible for the deaths of those girls," he said, with sudden insight.

"If not me, then who? I was in his house. I fixed his food. I had access to knives. When he was asleep, I could have plunged one through his heart. I was too scared and because of that those girls died."

"Lexi, you can't believe that. You were a child and he stripped you of everything. You were lucky to survive."

"And they weren't so lucky. Do I think you were wrong for what you did to him, Gavriil? I wish I did. I wish I could sit in judgment and tell you once again, like I did the other day, that killing is wrong. I don't honestly know if it is."

She sighed. "When you came in and I thought I'd killed him using my gift, I was horrified and I don't even know why. I should have been shouting for joy, but instead all I could think about was how selfish I was, that I killed him to protect myself and not those other girls."

"You were a child, Lexi, a little girl who should have been playing with her friends, not living with a monster."

She didn't realize tears were spilling down her cheeks. He wiped them away with the pad of his thumb, wanting to kill Caine all over again for the trauma the man had done to her and so many others.

"It doesn't matter now, *solnyshko moya*, we're here and we're starting over. He's gone and he's never going to harm another girl."

"If I had killed him, Gavriil, if I had just found the courage, my parents, brothers and little sister would all be alive today. I was so afraid he'd catch me and put me in the terrible box. I tried so many times, but I couldn't make myself."

He pulled her into his arms, standing her between his thighs, and framing her face with his hands. His eyes searched hers for fear, for anything that told him to back off. When there was nothing but sorrow and pain, he bent his head to hers.

Gavriil kissed her eyes, soft little brushing caresses. He followed the tracks of her tears down first one cheek and then the other, tasting her tears. His lips found the corners of her mouth, brushing gently. He settled his mouth over hers. The briefest of kisses—to comfort not claim—to reassure not arouse.

He took great care to be gentler than he'd ever been in his life. When he lifted his head, she melted into him, circling his neck with her arms and resting her head on his shoulder, the uninjured side. Even in her time of distress, she was careful of him.

"I know I shouldn't say this to you, Gavriil. I know it's wrong of me, but thank you. I'm sorry you were the one who had to do it because I know you have to bear that burden for the rest of your life."

Gavriil started to protest but then realized she needed to tell him everything just as he had needed to confess to her.

"He would have killed me, and I still, after all of the

training both Lissa and Levi gave me, couldn't find the courage to kill him. He paralyzed me. I just froze. I felt like a terrified child. I'm so sorry." She lifted her head and looked him in the eyes. "I would be a total hypocrite if I told you how wrong you were in what you did. You were able to do what I should have so many years ago."

To his shock, Kiss rushed over to push her face against Lexi in an attempt to comfort her. The females of the breed were often less accepting of new relationships than the males, who just generally remained aloof. Lexi dropped her hand in the silky coat for a brief moment.

"I'm all right, Kiss," she murmured. "I just can't stop crying."

Gavriil signaled the dog back to the corner as Lexi laid her head on his shoulder again. He tightened his arms around her, holding her body close to his, aching for her. He'd done a lot of terrible things in his life and he suffered pain beyond what most could have taken, but being helpless when the one person in the world who meant the most suffered, that was true pain.

"I'm going to stay, Lexi. We're going to build a life for ourselves. We're going to find a way to be a family and be happy together. You know the worst of me and you seem to be able to accept me the way I am. I'll do my best to make you happy. I can give you my word on that. I know I can keep you safe."

She pulled back again to look into his eyes. "Will you really be happy cooped up on a farm after all your travels? With a woman so broken she doesn't know if she can have a normal relationship with a man?"

"I lived alone for two years in the hills and forests of Russia. I've spent my entire existence alone. The farm is the perfect place for a man like me who needs solitude as well as peace. I like the work, and you're the kind of woman who wouldn't mind if I needed space." He couldn't imagine needing space from her, but if so, she wouldn't be upset with him. She was too accepting.

Lexi moistened her lips with the tip of her tongue.

"What are we doing here? Are we really discussing trying to have an actual relationship? Like a man and woman? Not just roommates?"

"Like a *real* man and a *real* woman?" A slow smile came out of nowhere. This was what happiness felt like. This was sharing a moment with another human being that counted. She'd given him so many firsts now he could hardly believe it. "Yes. I think that's what we're talking about, Lexi, but I don't want you to panic."

"I am. I'm totally panicking. I'll let you down, Gavriil, and you deserve so much more than I'll ever be able to give you. I'm a hard worker and I could be a good companion, but the womanly thing totally eludes me."

He took her hand and gently opened her fingers, exposing her palm. "I can see the panic in your eyes, *solnyshko moya*. Truly there is no need for it. If the man-woman thing is meant to be, then it will happen. We can live as companions, although, honestly, I will never see you as a sister." He brushed his thumb over the center of her palm, watching her face, watching the hint of desire creep into those forest green eyes.

She made a face at him. "I think you're the proverbial devil in blue jeans come here to seduce me."

"You got that right." He brought her hand to his mouth and pressed a kiss into the center. "I might point out before you get afraid, that you slept in your bed last night and I was very, very gentlemanly."

She smiled and this time it reached her eyes, lighting her face. "I did, didn't I? That was my very first night in my own bed. And you were a perfect gentleman."

"Where will you be working? I've got a couple of things to do here and then I'll catch up with you."

"You aren't going to rig the house with bombs or something equally as crazy, are you?" she asked, suspicion in her voice.

He laughed. He couldn't help it. "I'm going to have Levi and Rikki come over and I'll introduce the dogs to them. Then I'll ask Maxim and Airiana to bring the children. I need to make certain they accept everyone on the farm as part of their pack before Kiss has her puppies. She's looking more and more as if she might have them sooner rather than later."

"When is she supposed to have them?"

"She's about a week out, but she's already showing signs. I don't want her to be so protective over the puppies that she has a difficult time accepting the others who live here. Lucia and your sisters have to feel comfortable coming to visit."

"I'll need to tell Lissa about them," Lexi said. "She's skittish about the subject."

"You said she was bitten?"

Lexi frowned. "I actually can't remember if she said that or not, but she acts like she may have been. Lissa isn't afraid of much."

"I imagine she isn't," Gavriil said.

"What does that mean?"

"Only that she's fierce," he said. "Has she ever kicked one of my brothers' butts in training?"

"She says they're always just a little faster, but she comes close."

He nodded. "Why don't you let me talk to Lissa this morning? I like her. I don't want to alienate her in any way. She's seems closest to you."

Lexi stepped away from him, shrugging. "I love them all, but Lissa seems to know I'm not the sweet, fragile child the others see me as."

"You are sweet, Lexi, and whether you want to admit it to yourself or not, you're fragile. That doesn't mean you can't be strong or courageous, both of which you are. It means this hard-won peace that you found can be ripped away. You need to stay here, on the farm. You've made a home and life here. Your sisters obviously worry about Rikki having to move, but they should be worried about you as well."

"I could do it."

"Of course you could, but that doesn't mean you should.

In any case, it isn't going to happen, so put that worry to rest. I've spoken to Ilya and we've come to an understanding. I think he'll make certain the Drakes will be accepting of us. After all, in a way, we're all family or will be soon."

She shot him a quick look but refrained from asking what he meant. "I'm heading out to check the lettuce field. I had to replant this last week and I want to finish up there."

"Kiss me."

"What?"

"Before you go, kiss me. Isn't that the accepted practice when the woman of a man's heart and soul exits the home to go to work? I'm fairly certain I'm right. If you don't know the answer, we can always call one of your sisters and ask."

Her eyes had gone wide with shock, dark with excitement and maybe a little fear. "You wouldn't dare."

"Of course I would." He forced innocence into his voice. "How else are we going to learn anything?"

Lexi stalked back across the room. He could almost hear her heart pounding. Her breath came a little too fast, her breasts rising and falling in agitation. She stood in front of him for a long time, staring down at his face, her hands behind her back.

"What is it, *dusha moya*?" he asked gently. She looked so lost his heart nearly broke for her.

"I don't know how."

He frowned. "What do you mean, you don't know how?"

"He made me do things to him, but kissing wasn't one of them."

He had never hated a man in his life. When he killed, he killed dispassionately. It was a job, and he did his job and left. But Caine . . . The man had taken a child and abused her in every way possible, stripping her of dignity and humanity in order to control her completely. He hadn't shown her a single kindness and he'd never tried to prepare her body for the brutality of what he would do to her.

"That's good. It's a good thing that man didn't subject you to a disgusting pretense of love. I was taught how to kiss. Like a damned robot, Lexi. No feeling. No purpose other than to arouse a woman I needed information from. I've never kissed a woman I felt affection for." Hell, he'd never felt affection—until now. "I guess this will be another first for both of us."

"What if I do it all wrong? Or worse? I totally freeze up and both of us will know for certain I'm not capable of any kind of kissing?"

"What kind of kiss are we talking about here? I'm all for diving straight to it if we want to figure this thing out fast, but I was taking the slower, much more careful approach. Letting you get to know what an all-around great prize you're getting. I come with an arsenal, two killer dogs and skills on my resume few others can ever claim."

The anxiety slowly left her face to be replaced by a small smile. "You're impossible, do you know that? I'll bet no one else knows you have a sense of humor."

"It's been a well-kept secret, so much so, even I didn't know."

She burst out laughing and the sound was prettier to him than any music he'd ever heard.

"Come here, woman." He stood up and pointed to the spot in front of him. When she complied, he caught her chin in his hand and leaned down to brush his mouth across hers. His heart nearly stopped and then began beating hard in his chest. He had intended to let it go at that. A chaste kiss, nothing to frighten her, but he couldn't stop, not after seeing her fears.

He brought her in closer to him. His mouth moved again, back and forth. Coaxing. Gentle. Her lips trembled beneath his. He felt the rise and fall of her breasts against him. He counted each breath she took. His tongue slid along the seam of her lips, asking for entry.

This is something I can give you. Something he had no part of. Give yourself to me, Lexi, put yourself into my keeping.

Lexi went very still, an untamed bird readying herself

for flight. He felt every inch of her body pressed against his. Her scent surrounded him, drifted into his lungs, filling him with . . . her. He didn't rush her decision, but teased her lower lip with his teeth, with his tongue, coaxing her response rather than demanding it.

His fingers curled around her neck, his thumb sweeping gently over her cheek. Her lashes fluttered and closed. Her lips parted and his tongue swept inside the hot sweetness of her mouth. His heart actually stuttered. The earth seemed to move beneath him. The world dropped away—everything—until there was only Lexi.

He was aware of everything about her. How small she was. How fragile and delicate in comparison to him. Yet her muscles were firm, her curves soft, her body fitting perfectly into his. Her mouth was pure honey, a hot, sweet confection he'd never tasted but would never get enough of. Warm molasses moved through his veins, thick with desire, spreading heat throughout his body.

He was good at seduction, even better at sex, a practiced art he was highly skilled in. Gavriil had been taught to always be in control. He allowed his body release when it was time, and of course it was always pleasant, but just kissing her was different than anything else had ever been. His heart, when it finished stuttering like mad, began to pound as if it might actually leap from his chest into hers.

He controlled his reactions to all women, every move he made totally rehearsed and deliberate. There was no way to be deliberate kissing Lexi. There had never been . . . this feeling. He couldn't describe it. He only knew that pure emotion overwhelmed him, consumed him and that it was the real thing. His stomach knotted and his body went hot with need.

Her mouth was a miracle, plain and simple. Heaven. He had never believed in heaven or God until that moment. Until he found it in her. The taste of her was intriguing, addicting, and he knew he would never get enough of her, never be able to kiss her long enough or often enough to sate his craving for her. She tasted like love. Pure love. He didn't even believe in love, but there it was, all in this one small woman he held in his arms.

Passion for her was real. There was no denying that his body demanded hers, and he wanted to rejoice because he had the ability to feel a real physical response to a woman— to his woman. She'd been so afraid she wouldn't be able to respond—he'd been equally afraid his training would take over.

He was gentle, kissing her over and over, his breath, hers. He didn't want to ever come up for air. Not ever. He wanted to weep for being granted such a gift.

Lexi stood very still in Gavriil's arms. She'd never imagined kissing someone could ever be like this. She'd never believed she ever would be kissed and if she were— she had been certain she wouldn't like it.

Gavriil's mouth on hers was hot and felt as if he was claiming her, not as a possession, but as someone to cherish and protect. More, there was actual desire. Real desire. Not a brutish, ugly use of her body, but something so different she felt tears burning in her eyes at the pure joy of the moment with him. With Gavriil.

She had never considered how a real man felt about a woman he chose—the true caring telling her that her pleasure, her response, was more important to him than his own. The evidence was in the way he held her. In the touch of his hand on her neck and his thumb caressing her face. The stroke of his tongue exploring her mouth so gently, not demanding, never asking anything of her.

She hadn't expected he would be gentle or tender, and that disarmed her as nothing else could have. She felt his response to her, the genuine desire, but more than that, the feeling. It came out of nowhere, rising like a tidal wave in her to match that generous feeling in him. She couldn't name it, didn't even want to feel the emotion because it made her too vulnerable, but she knew he felt it too.

Her body went hot. Her breasts ached. She felt dampness

between her legs. The sensations startled her to the point she nearly pulled away from him, but the pad of his thumb sliding over her skin and the taste of passion was too much of a temptation to miss. He opened the door to a world she never imagined she could be a part of. It was both exhilarating and terrifying.

He had to be every bit as scared as she was. He'd lost everything just as she had. He knew once they were together, they would both be vulnerable again. She hadn't expected to want to give back to him, but he was risking everything, and she refused to do less for him.

She slipped her tongue tentatively alongside his, trying to follow his lead. The taste of him, wild, masculine, and exciting, exploded in her mouth, seeped into her bloodstream, and ran hot through her veins. Every nerve ending in her body sizzled with an electrical charge. She knew she tasted passion. But there was love. She hadn't known love with a man, and how could it be? How could Gavriil Prakenskii love such a broken woman? He was . . . extraordinary. She hadn't known how extraordinary until this moment.

Lexi found something there in the absolute beauty of his mouth that she'd never really had—hope for a future. She wasn't certain a physical relationship was possible, but Gavriil had given her this moment, this first, gentle, amazing kiss that went on and on and robbed her of breath and sanity.

Her mind seemed to melt, her body on fire. Gavriil poured himself into her, giving her everything—giving her . . . him. He kissed her with complete and utter focus and passion and emotion. He swept her away from the real world of violence and uncertainty. He wiped out every bad memory that never left her consciousness until there was only Gavriil and the paradise of sheer feeling, his hard, strong body and the promise that there might be a future for her.

Tears clogged her throat, making it impossible to breathe. She gasped. At once he lifted his head and pressed his forehead against hers, drawing a ragged breath into his burning lungs. His hands held her upper arms as if he held on to a life raft.

Gavriil cleared his throat, trying to think when his brain had gone to mush. "Well, that changes things."

She offered a tentative smile, pressing her fingers to her lips. "I don't know about changing things, but it does give one hope, doesn't it?"

"Definitely. In the meantime, the ground needs to stop shaking and the room needs to stop spinning. I'd move, but it's impossible with all the activity going on around us." He drew his brows together. "You do feel it, don't you? I'm not alone in this?"

"I feel it, but I'm not certain what it means."

"It means we're definitely in a relationship." He gave a little sigh. "You know I'm going to be hell to live with now."

For one moment fear flickered in her eyes. She drew in her breath, but waited for him to finish.

He ran his finger down her face to her chin. "You're pretty much everything to me, Lexi, the only thing."

She frowned at him, shaking her head, but before she could speak, he pressed his finger against her mouth. "Let me say this. I barely know my brothers. I would protect them with my life, but are they capable of taking away the life I've lived? Holding me here? They aren't, Lexi. How could they be?"

"You love them."

"I don't know what love is unless it's standing in front of me. I'm loyal to them. Everyone has to have a reason to live. To stay alive and protect my brothers seemed a good reason. But then you came along and the ground's shifted right out from under my feet."

"Gavriil."

Her voice was soft. Sensual. He hadn't noticed that note before. Her voice slid over his skin like the touch of fingers, reached inside of him and grasped his heart.

"You love your dogs."

"I do care for my dogs and I want them safe, I care a great deal for them, but again, I would have left them with my brothers. I wouldn't have stayed for them. I'm staying for you. I have never needed or wanted anyone in my life until you. There's a connection between us, and I can't walk away from that. I don't want to."

"Do you have any idea how scary it is to think about this?"

"Yes. You make me vulnerable. I've never cared one way or the other if I lived or died. You gave yourself to me when I kissed you. You didn't have to. You had no reason to, but you did. I felt it."

She blinked rapidly and he could see that her lashes were wet. "You gave yourself to me first. If you were going to risk everything, I was going to as well."

"I'm going to turn into your shadow. And when I can't be with you, Drago and Kiss are going to be with you." He wasn't going to lie to her. He was no prize. He was going to be difficult to live with.

"I think Kiss is going to be staying right here at home." She looked around her, as if noticing the sun had come up for the first time. "I'm late. You made me late. I've got to go, Gavriil."

Reluctantly he stepped away from her, inwardly cursing that he hadn't already introduced the rest of the family members to his dogs. He would have sent Drago with her, but it was too dangerous. The breed had been bred to be independent thinkers, which meant, if Drago thought Lexi was in danger, he would act to protect her without her consent.

Lexi stood a moment looking at his face. He felt the impact of her gaze and wanted to sweep her back into his arms.

"Thank you, Gavriil. For that perfect moment. I felt whole. I wasn't guilty or filled with sorrow or thinking of what happened to my family. I saw only you and felt only sensation. It was a gift you gave me this morning and I'm going to hold it to me while I work. I'll be thinking of you this morning, not him. Not what he did to me or took from me. You can't know what you've done for me."

He stepped close to her again, cupping her chin in his palm and looking into the cool forest of her eyes. "I know more than you think, *solnyshko moya*, because you did the same for me. I had no idea a woman was capable of wiping out my past so eloquently."

Her eyebrow shot up. "A woman?"

He found himself smiling. "*The* woman. You. There is no other. I've been all over the world, and the first time I laid eyes on you, stepping out of the cornfield, I knew then I was lost. It never occurred to me that would ever happen."

"It still might not, Gavriil," she cautioned. "I have no idea if I can actually be comfortable or trust a man the way I would need to in order to be in a real relationship. A normal one."

He stroked his finger down her cheek. "I have news for you, *solnyshko moya*, our relationship will never be normal. We'll make it work for us, not other people. And we'll go slow. You kissed me. That's trust, and it's enough for now."

She nodded slowly. "You don't know it, Gavriil, but you truly are an extraordinary man."

"Only you think so. Go out to your lettuce field and I'll be there as soon as possible. I want to talk to Lissa first and then Airiana and Maxim. The others can wait."

"I'll be safe. Once I'm in the fields, the ground lets me know when someone's approaching. I won't be on the tractor."

He understood what she meant. She was bound to earth—an earth element—and she could feel danger through the soil itself. Up on the tractor, she had no way to feel trouble coming at her. "You must have felt very vulnerable working at the farm alone at times."

She shrugged. "It's our home. I'm good at growing things, but I'll admit, I did wish for a dog or two at times to guard my back."

"Now you've got the dogs and me."

"I don't know which is better," she teased.

His answering smile faded from his face as he watched her slip from the house. Immediately she took the sunshine with her. He felt the cold slipping back into his veins. Shadows drew him, settled around him. The dark blue eyes went glacier cold and he was once more the man he was far more familiar with.

10

LISSA Piner's home was situated on a small hill, surrounded by trees, but the trees were a good forty or fifty feet from her house. She had planted low-lying shrubs, flowers and ground cover all around her home. The grounds appeared well manicured, landscaped and beautiful. Metal structures adorned the landscaping surrounding the house. Each was a large, beautiful sculpture that flowed with the wind, creating movement. The house was two stories with the familiar wraparound porch the women all favored. At first glance it appeared to be the home of an artist. Gavriil wasn't deceived.

He studied the house from the shadows of the giant redwoods. She had the perfect spot for defense. There were no plants or trees that would offer cover to anyone sneaking up on her. He spotted several cameras as well as motion detectors. He would bet his last dollar that this woman not only had an arsenal in her home, but several escape routes involving one or more of the beautiful art pieces decorating the grounds around her house.

Out of habit he checked his favorite weapon, an FNP 45

Tactical with ambidextrous controls. It was accurate and had never let him down. He considered the weapon an extension of his body, and it felt that way in his hand. Fully loaded and ready, he slipped it out of sight and signaled to the dogs to stay.

Gavriil stepped out alone to cross the open space to Lissa's home. He knew within six steps that she was aware of his presence. He'd taken ten more before she appeared on her porch. She had one hand behind a column; the other she used to wave to him. There was no doubt she had a gun in her fist, hidden behind the large carved post. He didn't slow down or hesitate, but continued toward her.

"Is something wrong with Lexi?"

He read the anxiety in her eyes, although her face remained open and friendly. He shook his head. "I dropped by for another reason altogether. Lexi's working in her lettuce field. She said she had to finish planting or she would have come with me."

Lissa nodded. "The helicopter used to kidnap Airiana set down in her lettuce field and tore it up. Of course she would have replanted. I should have offered to help."

He had gained the stairs, and it forced her to take a step back. Her hidden hand went behind her for just a moment, and he guessed she had slipped the gun into the waistband of her jeans.

"Did I interrupt something?" He glanced through the screen to the front room where maps and brochures covered the floor. "I guess I should have called ahead, but I didn't think to ask for your phone number."

She shrugged. "I'm planning a trip. It's not a big deal. I like to get away to other countries. It inspires me to see different architecture. I love the museums and art galleries and I like to blend work with vacation. I've got three clients who want chandeliers, big money for the farm."

"Do you happen to have coffee?" He tried to look as innocent as possible but figured, when she shot him a look, that he'd failed. "Lexi doesn't have any."

She nodded slowly. "Come in. My house is a bit of a

mess right now, but if you can keep from stepping on anything, and find a place to sit, we can talk over coffee."

"Who designed your home?" he asked casually as he stepped inside. He felt an itch between his shoulder blades turning his back on her. He stepped aside politely, holding the screen to allow her to go in front of him.

"I did. I spent a long time trying to come up with the perfect home to suit me. I do a lot of glassblowing and metalwork. In the beginning I didn't have a studio so I had to improvise. I needed a basement until I could find a studio in town I could afford."

Gavriil took a slow, careful look around. She had beautiful chandeliers, hand blown, as well as paintings and sculptures worth a fortune. He had no doubt some of the paintings were done by Judith, but she had a few masterpieces.

The maps on the floor were mainly of St. Petersburg in Russia. She had books strewn around of buildings and architecture, all Russian.

"You're thinking of visiting St. Petersburg?"

She made no move to close the books or remove the maps, a mark of a true professional. She seemed perfectly at ease. "I've wanted to tour a few of the cities there for a long while. Some of the buildings are so ornate and beautiful. One of the clients interested in my chandeliers is in St. Petersburg, so this is an opportunity I can't pass up. Traveling is a hobby of mine. I've traveled extensively and have managed to see some extraordinary sights."

"Sicily?" He nodded toward the collection of photographs she had on the wall in her hallway.

"I think Sicily has the best examples of Baroque art and architecture you can find. Give me a minute. I just made a fresh pot of coffee. Do you take anything in it?"

He shook his head. "Just black is fine."

She was smooth. Lev, Stefan and Maxim had all been around her, and they were very good at scenting danger, but not one of them seemed aware of what Lissa Piner was. He studied the maps and the books.

Lissa returned with a mug of coffee for both of them. She waved him to a chair and sank into the one opposite him. He was fairly certain there were weapons in the chair she had chosen to sit in.

"What can I do for you, Gavriil?" Her eyes remained steady on his face.

"I brought a pair of dogs with me. Black Russian Terriers. Are you familiar with the breed?" It wasn't a common breed in the United States, but he was certain Lissa wasn't originally from the United States.

She didn't even blink. "Not really."

"They were bred in Russia's Red Star Kennel, a dog for military work. They have a high protective instinct, and my female is pregnant with her first litter. I was going to leave them with my brothers while I led Sorbacov's assassins away from here, but Lexi has convinced me to stay."

Lissa nodded. "That doesn't surprise me. The farm is overrun with Prakenskiis. There must be some connection between elements that draws other elements. I'm actually glad you're here. I know, without a doubt, you'll protect her. I can see it in your eyes. I just wasn't certain she would let you stay for long."

"It appears she has decided in my favor."

"That's good." She sat back in her chair, seemingly relaxed looking at him over the rim of her coffee mug. "Tell me about Sorbacov. Who is he and why does he want all of you dead?"

Her question didn't surprise him; in fact, he was waiting for it. "It's an old story."

"But one still going on. He's threatening the lives of my sisters and their husbands. He's capable of sending his assassins here, you've said so yourself. All of you have mad skills when it comes to assassinations, yet none of you have gone after him. Why is that?"

Gavriil sipped at his coffee, studying her face, determining whether or not to give her the information she required. She was patient, waiting for him to make up his mind.

She loved Lexi. She didn't question that he would stay

with her youngest sister. She not only expected it, but wanted him there. "Perhaps, if I am going to give you details about our greatest enemy, I should bring my dogs in for you to meet. Once the introductions are made, they will lie quietly while we discuss this."

"And they won't eat me when I come to visit."

"That is the plan. Lexi told me you were uncertain about having dogs on the property. You, of all your sisters, seem most concerned with security and I would think you would want them."

Lissa smiled at him, but there was no humor in the smile. "I've had a bad experience that colored my opinion. It's silly really. It shouldn't have. We had dogs when I was a child, and our handler betrayed my family. It was a long time ago."

He felt the difference in the room temperature almost immediately. The warmth was subtle, but it was there. Lissa looked perfectly calm, her hands as steady as a rock around her coffee mug, her eyes as cool and serene as ever, but he knew the memory he'd just brought back was a trigger.

"Tell me what happened."

"It doesn't matter."

"You're asking me to treat you like a sister, to give you information I wouldn't ordinarily share with anyone. Give me that same courtesy. I know your real name isn't Lissa Piner and you aren't from this country. English is your second language, not your first, although your accent is impeccable. I know you've done work very similar to mine. You favor your left leg, just a little when you're tired, although it doesn't hamper your speed in the least, so it's an old injury that has healed but still causes pain once in a while."

They stared at each other, two warriors who had recognized each other almost immediately. Lissa took another sip of coffee.

"Your home is a fortress, and you have an arsenal here. You're far better at hand-to-hand combat and self-defense than you let on, and to be with these women, you've lost a family member to murder, which probably started you on your path."

He was guessing on most of the latter, but it was a fairly safe bet.

Lissa shrugged. "I guess you did recognize me, and here I was trying so hard to cover my tracks."

"Not that hard. You needed help for your next project so you let me see what you wanted me to see."

She smiled for the first time. "So true."

"So tell me about the dogs that attacked you. It's important to Lexi that you're comfortable here on the farm. My dogs saved my life. I wouldn't want them to frighten you to the point that you felt the need to protect yourself. They make good protection dogs, and Kiss should have six to ten pups. If each family takes at least one, they'll bond with that owner and protect the house and farm for everyone."

"It's a good plan but . . ." Lissa pulled up the denim covering her left leg.

The scars were horrific. From her knee to her ankle she carried the evidence of a vicious attack. He waited until she pulled the material back into place.

"What happened?"

"My father was born into a certain family. I won't say he was a good man, but he was a good father. I was too young to know that he was mixed up in things he shouldn't have been, but his father before him had been, so he did what most sons did and became part of the family business."

Lissa put her mug down. Her hands were still and steady as ever, but her eyes went hot. There was no doubt the room temperature rose another degree or two. He felt sweat begin to bead on his skin and he breathed evenly to accommodate the difference.

"There was a man from a rival family who saw my mother. Their family was much more dangerous than ours, more men, more territory, more money. He went after my mother and she turned him down. I heard her telling my father about it."

In spite of how casual she tried to appear, her tone grew tighter. He expected the chair beneath her to burst into flames at any moment. The room actually took on a glow, as if the early morning sun had come inside.

"He told my mother to pack a suitcase fast, that we were leaving the country that night. He told my mother the man was psychotic and all of us would be in danger. His father protected him, and he would come after her for turning him down."

She pressed her lips together, and for the first time he saw her hand shake as she lifted it to her bright red hair.

"Northern Italy," he guessed to give her some time. "You don't find red hair often in southern Italy, but it's there in the north and your hair is natural." There was no denying it now. The moment he said it, he could see the fair skin and very red hair, thick and luxurious as Italian hair often was, along with her striking deep blue eyes. The combination was unforgettable, not necessarily an asset in the work he suspected she must have done.

"Ferrara. A beautiful city. We had a wonderful home. I loved it. All the classic architecture. Of course there were men, guards, all the time, but I didn't really understand why at the time. They came as we were leaving, four carloads cutting us off from our ride and the men who would have protected us. I'll never forget the sound of gunfire or the smell of blood as the intruders killed everyone. Our servants. Our protectors. Even our gardener and his family. He had four young children."

Gavriil inhaled deeply. He could almost smell the scent of gunpowder. He could hear the screams of his mother and the cries of the baby. His father calling out his love to his sons, telling them to be strong, making them promise they would always protect and look after the younger ones.

He lived in Russia, Lexi in the United States, and Lissa in Italy, and all three had been visited by men with guns, men who had destroyed their families. It was no wonder Lissa identified with Lexi and looked after her.

"Our dog handler, a man who had eaten frequently at

our table and even played with me in the gardens, a man my father trusted, betrayed us that night. He was working for the other family and he set the dogs after us. One of the dogs caught up with me and dragged me down. I couldn't keep up with my parents and they both turned back to help me. My father shot the dog but more kept coming."

"You couldn't run with your leg so chewed up."

She shook her head. "My father told my mother to keep going, but more dogs came and they took her down. There was a cemetery on the property and he told me to hide in a certain crypt until my uncle came for me. He said to wrap my leg and get there. He pushed a large bag into my hands, kissed me hard and shoved me away from him. I did what he said."

"You saw them kill your parents."

She nodded slowly. "I could see the men laughing, watching the dogs tear them apart. I never forgot any of their faces. Not a single one."

He studied her expression. "Your uncle came for you and he was a hit man for the mob, wasn't he? He taught you how to survive as well as how to hunt."

"Every last one of them."

There was a finality in her tone he couldn't help but admire. He found himself not only respecting Lissa, but liking her.

"I understand why you would hesitate to bring dogs onto the property. But if you were the one training the dog . . ."

"I wouldn't know how."

"I'd help you. Let me introduce you to my dogs. They'll be the ones protecting Lexi. I'd like to add them to the security here on the farm. I know we can make this farm impossible to infiltrate in spite of how large it is. We have only to protect, first the homes and then the places anyone works, such as the fields."

Lissa took a deep breath, her deep blue eyes moving over his face as if looking for something. He knew he wasn't much to look at.

"First tell me what happened to your arm."

"Sorbacov sent a couple of men after Ilya, my youngest brother."

"I know who he is. He can handle himself."

"Does Lexi know what happened to you? The others?"

"They know some of it. Enough to know my family was killed, but not what I am, or my real name. I'm not that person anymore."

His eyebrow shot up. "Then why the interest in Sorbacov? Why St. Petersburg?"

She shrugged again. "Bring in your dogs, but you'd better be able to control them or I'll shoot them."

Gavriil felt it was very important that Lissa see how well-trained an animal could be and what an asset the Black Russian Terriers would be on the farm. He went to the door and called them in, using only a hand signal. His past didn't allow him to turn his back completely on Lissa, but he tried to be polite about it, presenting a side target.

Drago and Kiss rushed to him and both sat squarely in front of him, but Drago's eyes were on Lissa, not on him. He was already targeting potential trouble.

"See how quickly they alert, but he's waiting to see whether you're a friend or enemy because I'm with you," he said, keeping his tone low and matter-of-fact. He gave the dogs the hand signal he used to let them know the person close wasn't to be attacked before bringing them in by his side to meet her.

"They'll accept you much better if you allow them to smell you."

"I said I'd do it." Her tone was tight, but she had nerves of steel. She held out her hand to the dogs, allowing them to catch her scent.

"Call them by their names and when you feel safe enough, pet them. They'll be a little aloof, but that's the way they should be."

Lissa followed his instructions to the letter. He could see she was surprised at how silky and soft their coats were. Both dogs allowed her to touch them, accepting her into their circle because Gavriil had decreed it.

Gavriil sank into the chair again and waved the dogs to the floor at his feet. Only then did Lissa settle enough to pick up her coffee mug. He knew she'd had one hand on the dogs and the other on her hidden weapon.

"I told you about my family. I would like you to tell me about Sorbacov."

"This vacation you're taking to St. Petersburg doesn't have anything to do with him, does it? Because he's surrounded by security at all times. The place where he stays is impregnable. If he could have been gotten to, one of us would have done so."

"I'm taking a vacation to St. Petersburg to make certain I'm nowhere near the farm or in Sea Haven just in case another of your brothers decides to show up. That, and it's worth several thousand dollars to the farm if I can land this client." She rested her chin on her palm, her elbow on the arm of the chair. "Is Sorbacov in St. Petersburg? I would have thought Moscow."

Gavriil shook his head. "Not Moscow. Sorbacov is staying in St. Petersburg at the moment while he cleans up his father's mess. He's trying to keep a low profile even while he's moving behind the scenes to become president."

"Why does he hate your family so much?"

"I honestly don't think it's personal. At least not until Maxim kept him from acquiring Airiana and her brains to become his own little captive think tank. He can't afford for his father's experiments to ever see the light of day, so he's sweeping the entire special unit of assassins his father created under the rug, so to speak. In order to do that, he has to execute the students who attended the schools his father set up."

"How did your family get involved?"

"When my father was alive, he was a very influential man. He had many gifts, and his political opponents feared him. At that time the country was in the beginning stages of unrest. It was all beneath the surface, and several men were trying to orchestrate a change in power. One of those, a man by the name of Kostya Sorbacov, was on the rise. He was very careful to always be in the background. He wanted anonymity to carry out his plans."

"The power behind the throne so to speak."

Gavriil nodded. "Yes. Unfortunately for him, there were several very powerful men who were outspoken against his chosen candidate. So he went to work systematically destroying them. One night soldiers broke into our home. We were taken, our parents murdered. Sorbacov didn't want us together. He feared we would be too strong and loyal to one another, so we were taken to separate cities and placed in schools."

"The spy/assassin schools for children. I heard whispers of them, but no one knew if they really existed."

"He called us operatives. I was Operative Prakenskii. We had brutal instructors and learned everything from languages to art, but mostly how to kill people. It was . . . difficult and the punishments for failure ranged from beatings to death. It was a big range."

Lissa sighed. "Let me get you another cup of coffee. Keep talking." She glanced at the dogs, straightened her shoulders and stood up gracefully. Both dogs alerted, watching her closely, but neither moved a muscle.

"There isn't much to tell. We did our jobs. And then Sorbacov's son grew up, and politics in Russia changed. Uri, his son, doesn't want to be the man behind the scenes. He wants to run the country, but he can't do that if there is any evidence of these schools Russia had been denying all along. So he set out to make certain all evidence of the schools was wiped out. Before he did, Lissa . . ."

Gavriil took the mug of hot coffee she handed him. "Before he did, Uri and his father went to St. Petersburg to their 'safe' house. To try to get to them would be suicide. It may be possible later, but now they're expecting it and have prepared. They know the faces and identities of everyone who attended the schools, and their security forces are on the lookout for those specific individuals as well as strangers."

Lissa curled her feet under her. "You're suddenly warning me off, Gavriil, why?"

"I didn't expect to care one way or the other," Gavriil admitted. "I'm not a caring man. I think Lexi did something to me the other day and ruined my ability to stay distant." He was half joking and half serious.

Lissa burst out laughing. "That's Lexi all right. She definitely can put a spell on you, and she isn't even aware of it." The smile faded from her face. "You know it won't be easy with her, right?"

"Do you think she'll have it easy with me?" he countered. He indicated the maps. "Are you really going?"

"Sometime in the next couple of weeks, when I know Lexi is safe from these cult members. I really love to get away now and then. It inspires me." A slow smile teased her mouth. "I wasn't kidding when I said I'd feel safer there than here. I'm not the kind of woman who could put up with an overbearing man. I can't imagine anything else in a Prakenskii, and it's down to two of us now. Blythe and me. I'd rather not take any chances."

"I see your point. I'd love to stay and chat more, but I need to make certain Airiana and the children have been introduced to the dogs. It seems Benito likes to sneak around spying."

"He does," Lissa agreed. "I've caught him a time or two lurking in the trees. He hasn't figured out a way to cross the open area to the house."

Gavriil laughed as he stood up. "He's industrious if nothing else."

"Their parents were killed, just like ours. They lost a little sister as well. Maxim is worried Benito is going to go down a wrong path. None of us want that for him, so we're all trying to redirect his rage and feelings of helplessness into a more protective mode." She shrugged. "Who knows if it will work?"

"One thing I do know for certain, Lissa," Gavriil said, "this farm is a place of healing. If there's any way that boy

can put his life back together and become something other
than a killer, it's here."

"That's a nice thing to hear," Lissa replied. "We tried
hard to make new lives for ourselves and to build not only
a haven of peace, but something productive."

"I think you've accomplished that. Before you make up
your mind to go on this trip, give it a little more thought,
given the things I've told you. If you really feel you want to
try, I can give you the schematics I have on the Sorbacov
estate as well as all information I've accrued. Which isn't
as much as I'd like. But you have to promise me that you'll
think about this."

Lissa nodded. "Thank you, Gavriil. And I wouldn't
mind knowing how to train a dog the way yours have been
trained. Do they scare me? You bet."

"I don't think much scares you, Lissa." He signaled the
two dogs to his side.

"Don't kid yourself. Dogs terrify me, but I'm willing to
try to get over it for everyone else's sake."

SHE'D kissed Gavriil Prakenskii. Lexi looked up at the
sky, expecting it to fall. A miracle had happened and no
one was around to witness it. Not that she wanted anyone
to see her kissing Gavriil, but really? She'd *kissed* him. She
touched her lips. She was smiling like an idiot and couldn't
seem to stop.

She wasn't going to ruin the morning by thinking of
anything that came next. She'd achieved a milestone, more
than that. She'd actually kissed a man, and she hadn't panicked or thrown up. She threw her arms out and did a slow
circle, happiness blossoming. Her feet did a little happy
dance right there in the lettuce field.

"Lexi?"

She whirled around, her heart in her throat, jerked back
to the present, to reality, to her life. The breath rushed from
her lungs and her throat closed. Adrenaline poured through
her body, paralyzing her. She could only stare at the young

girl who had come up behind her. It took many long moments before panic receded and her mind allowed her to recognize Lucia.

The girl was crying, tears pouring down her face. She looked so young and lost, Lexi stepped up to her and gathered her into her arms, holding her close while she wept. She didn't ask what was wrong, or what had triggered the storm. She knew. How could she not?

When Lucia finally began hiccupping and clearing her throat in an effort to stop, Lexi pulled back, her hands on the girl's shoulders. "Do you want to go up to the house and I can make tea for us? We'll talk."

"I can't stop crying this morning," Lucia admitted. "I didn't want the kids to see me. Siena and Nicia both fall completely apart if they see me crying. I just can't stop thinking about my little sister Sofia and what she suffered before she died. I couldn't stop them from taking her. I tried, Lexi, but they knocked me down and dragged her out." She pressed both hands over her ears. "I can't get her screams out of my mind. I've never heard anything like that, so frightened. So . . ." She broke off, staring at Lexi helplessly with her enormous dark eyes.

Lexi had screamed. She'd heard other girls scream, and she knew exactly the sound Lucia was trying to describe. She nodded slowly. "It seems as if those screams will never fade and leave you alone, leave you in peace, even for a moment. And then you worry they will fade and that means you're forgetting and the guilt and shame come."

Lucia nodded. "I can hardly stand it sometimes, Lexi, and I have to smile and laugh for the girls. Benito tries not to cry, and he won't tell me what happened to him, so I know that it had to be very bad. Nicia cries in her sleep and calls for Sofia. Airiana is so good to us, and I hate adding more of a burden to her by falling apart too, but I am. I'm completely falling apart."

She began to sob, pushing her fist into her mouth to try to choke back the heartbroken weeping. Lexi gathered her into her arms again.

"Airiana doesn't think you or your sisters and brother are a burden, Lucia. She knows what it's like to lose someone she loves in a terrible way. I do too. I lost my parents, two brothers and a little sister."

"Why? I don't understand why. My mother and father were good people. They didn't do anything wrong. It doesn't make any sense to me."

"Honey, it doesn't make any sense to anyone. There are bad people all over the world. I have no idea what shapes them into the monsters they are, but they ruin lives. They do. We have to fight back by not allowing them to ruin our lives. We're here together, building another family, learning to live all over again without the people we love and with the scars we carry. We're defiant and determined."

"I'm just sad all the time. More than sad. I feel as if something heavy is weighing me down and I can't get out from under it."

"That's grief, Lucia, and you're supposed to feel it. You lost your family. Please let Airiana take you to our counselor. She specializes in working with people who have lost loved ones through violence. I know she'll help you through this time."

"I feel guilty for clinging to Airiana and Max," Lucia admitted in a small voice. "It's okay for Siena and Nicia. They're young. Babies. Little Nicia was assaulted by that horrible man. She talks to Airiana and Max and that's a good thing. She needs to. They both need parents, and so does Benito, but when I find myself clinging to Airiana and Max, I'm so afraid I'm betraying my mother and father."

Lexi put her arm around the girl and started her back toward the house. "Your parents would want you to be happy and loved. They would want Airiana and Max to be in your lives, loving and caring for you and most of all, protecting you. If you find yourself loving them in return, that doesn't ever mean that you love your parents less. Do you understand?"

Lucia sniffed and shook her head.

Lexi kept her walking. Lucia shivered several times.

Airiana had told Lexi during the cooking lesson that she was worried about the teenager. Lucia was so busy looking after the younger children that she hadn't really dealt with her own traumas. Lucia was overwhelmed now, the reality of her situation hitting her at once.

"You love people differently. You love your parents, Lucia, and you love your siblings. You probably even feel maternal toward Nicia and Siena, right?"

Lucia nodded. "I always wanted little sisters, and when they came along, I pretended I was their mother, especially the twins." She choked up again.

Lexi settled her arm more protectively around the girl's waist as they made their way up the path toward the house. She felt a little desperate. She didn't know the right thing to say to Lucia, and right now, the child needed to hear something that would help her. Lexi wasn't certain she was the right person to come to.

"Of course," she said. "That would be so natural to pretend at your age that the babies were your own. The girls love you so much, Lucia, but it didn't lessen their love for their parents. Accepting and loving Airiana and Max won't take away the love you have for your parents. It won't. Love doesn't work that way."

Lexi had no idea if she was even making sense. Lucia continued to weep, only much more quietly, reminding Lexi of her own terrible grief—a grief so deep she could barely express it.

"Max makes me feel safe," Lucia said.

There was guilt in her voice. Shame. Lexi frowned. Now they were in precarious waters. She had to figure out for herself what was bothering Lucia so much. She had made the confession in a little rush, as if confessing her sins.

Lexi was silent, her mind turning over and over the way Lucia had made her declaration. "Honey, are you feeling angry with Max? You? Or your father?"

The moment she voiced the question, Lexi knew she was right. Lucia felt guilty because she was angry that her father hadn't protected them. She was angry at herself for feeling that way and angry at Max because she felt he was capable of protecting them—something her beloved father hadn't done.

A fresh flood of tears was her answer. Lexi stopped again to hold the girl tightly. "It's okay," she murmured softly. "That's natural too. There are stages of grief, and anger is one of them. Max would understand and so would your father."

Lucia shook her head. "How? How could they possibly?"

"Max grew up in a world of brutality. Every single day of his life, he saw men like those who murdered your parents. He trained to go after them. That was his job. Your father lived in a completely different world, Lucia. You had money and privilege. You went to great schools. That was the world your father grew up in and knew. How could he possibly see the danger? How could he know someone would plot such a heinous crime against him and his family?"

"I know. I know that. In my heart I know that, but in my head . . ." Lucia trailed off, once more flinging herself into Lexi's arms.

"It's all right to feel what you're feeling, Lucia," Lexi said, rubbing her back and smoothing her hair. She had to talk around a lump in her throat. "I felt exactly the same way. I wanted my father to protect me and I questioned how he could let such a thing happen to me. It's normal. Intellectually we know they couldn't do anything, but it hurts so bad that our hearts ache and we ask ourselves why."

There was a kind of cleansing in admitting to another human being that she felt those raw emotions so intensely, just as Lucia did. She knew, more than most could, just how guilty and ashamed she felt for having such thoughts. More and more she identified with little Lucia. How could she not?

"You did, Lexi?" Lucia asked, lifting her head from Lexi's shoulder. Her eyes searched Lexi's. "You're not just saying that? You were angry at your father?"

"Sometimes I still am," Lexi admitted. "Most of the

time I'm realistic and I know he couldn't have done anything, but then I have nightmares or a panic attack and I'm angry. I freeze and can't move, can't breathe, and it makes me feel cowardly and weak. Then I really get angry. Mostly at myself, but sometimes at him."

Lucia took a deep breath. "I'm glad you're here, Lexi."

"Me too, honey. Let's go in and put the teakettle on. Did you tell Airiana that you were coming to see me this morning?"

Lucia nodded. "She looked . . . sad. I knew she wanted me to talk to her, but I couldn't look at her every day if she knew how angry I was with my father. I didn't want to hurt Max and she would have told him how angry I get with him. Seeing her face I just felt guiltier. I feel ashamed and guilty all the time."

"I did too, for a very long time, and then I met Airiana and my other sisters. They changed my life and gave me peace. We'll find that for you as well. It may take time, honey, but we'll do it."

Lucia hugged her hard and then pulled away, giving her a watery smile. "I'm learning how to make tea the way all of you like it. Let me try."

Lexi watched her run up the stairs into the house, knowing she needed to be alone for a few minutes.

11

GAVRIIL dropped his hand on Drago's head, watching Lexi take Lucia into the house—his home. The word tasted strange to him, but was exhilarating at the same time. He had never thought he'd have a permanent home and the thought was daunting. He'd never stayed in one place long and he knew, sooner rather than later, he would become restless. He would have to find a way to deal with that.

Lucia was as tall as Lexi, all arms and legs, much like a gangly filly. His heart went out to her—another first for him. This place—the farm—was changing him faster than he had thought possible.

Gavriil spent an hour with Airiana and Max, letting the children fuss over his dogs. Both Drago and Kiss remained somewhat aloof, but tolerant of all the attention. Lucia was very withdrawn, and when she got up abruptly, muttering she was going to find Lexi, he couldn't help but see the hurt flash in Airiana's eyes. Max reached over and took her hand to comfort her.

Max's gaze met his and he nodded, knowing his brother

wanted him to follow the child and make certain she was all right. He waited a few minutes to give her a head start. He didn't have a clue how to deal with the girl's grief and trauma. He counted himself lucky that he hadn't made too many mistakes with Lexi. A fourteen-year-old girl? No way.

He took several deep breaths and then pressed his thumb into the center of his palm, reaching for Lexi. *Is it safe to come inside? Is she still crying?*

There was silence. He felt her warmth first as she came to him, pouring into his mind to fill every lonely place. The intimacy of her entrance stole his breath and sent heat rushing through his veins. He could almost smell her clean, forest scent and see the moss and cool streams. He definitely felt peace stealing into him.

I wouldn't mind the help with her. I don't have a clue how to comfort her.

He remained very still, not moving a muscle. *That's your department. You're good at that kind of thing.*

She made a little annoyed sound that didn't bode well for his future. *Because I'm a woman? I have no experience with teenagers. You're older and wiser.*

That's going to come back to bite you in your pretty little butt. Rather than bother you right now, maybe I should finish up in the lettuce field. Didn't you have some planting to do?

It's done. Don't be a coward. Come have tea with us. I already told Lucia you were on your way home. She's expecting you now.

Treacherous woman.

There was clearly nothing else for it but to go. It didn't really bother him, not when Lexi was waiting for him as well. He had a need to see her. To touch her. The obsession only seemed to grow stronger the more he was with her.

She likes the dogs. How did Lissa react?

She was very brave, Lexi. You would have been proud of her. She had been attacked when she was a child and she's never gotten over it. She does think it's a good idea to have protection dogs on the farm with each family. She will take one of the puppies. I promised her I'd help her train it.

Lexi came out of the house onto the porch and stood at the top of the stairs, her arm curled around the column, waiting for him. Just looking at her gave him a strange sensation of the earth moving beneath his feet. He wasn't a fanciful man, in fact he was quite cynical, but there was no denying the overwhelming emotions pouring into him when he was close to her.

Her smile greeting him as he came up the stairs to her made his heart stutter just a little bit. He leaned down and brushed a kiss across her mouth. "Hi. I missed you."

"I missed you too." She sounded a little shy.

Lexi touched his face with the pads of her fingers briefly, but she might as well have branded him. He found himself falling into the coolness of her green eyes. The dogs pushed against her in greeting, breaking the spell. Lexi rubbed their coats and murmured a greeting, telling them Lucia was in the house.

"I've got a tray," Lucia called. "Can you open the screen?"

Gavriil stepped around Lexi to open the door for her, partially blocking the dogs from the teenager as she came outside with the wooden tray. On it was the teapot and three cups. He smiled at her.

"I see you found Lexi."

Lucia nodded. "She was in the lettuce field. Yesterday she mentioned she had to plant." She sent Gavriil a shy smile. "She was dancing around. I think it was some kind of ancient rain dance."

Lexi burst out laughing, the sound contagious, but there was a hint of color creeping up her neck into her face and her gaze slid away from his.

What were you really doing? He couldn't help but be curious the way she reacted.

Dancing because you kissed me and I kissed you back. She was strictly honest.

He sank onto the porch swing abruptly before he could make the mistake of kissing her all over again. She could have torn out his heart with her admission. Her eyes were soft, almost luminous, and he couldn't quite stop looking at her mouth.

"I wouldn't put it past her, Lucia," he said aloud. "She's fond of her plants. She talks and sings to them."

"I talk to them because they like it," Lexi said. "Singing on the other hand might make them wither."

Lucia poured the tea into the cups, trying to look very adult. Gavriil dutifully didn't notice that her eyes were swollen and red and her skin was splotchy from crying.

"Plants like people talking to them?" Lucia asked, her voice filled with curiosity. "Really?"

Lexi nodded. "Yes. They respond to music as well. Not my singing voice, although, okay, I do sing to them, but only when no one's around. But I often play classical music in the atrium and the plants thrive."

"I *love* your atrium," Lucia said. "It's the coolest thing I've ever seen."

"Do the plants thrive because of the music, or because of you?" Gavriil asked, taking the tea from Lucia. She'd added milk to his cup because Lexi drank hers that way. He thanked her and took a sip, nodding to let her know it was good.

"Maybe both, but the point is, they like positive attention."

"Did you really mean it when you told Airiana and Max that we could have one of the puppies, Gavriil?" Lucia asked.

Gavriil noticed that Drago pushed against Lexi's legs again. The dog had definitely taken to her. She evidently liked him as well, because she didn't seem to realize she was petting him. Kiss lay at his feet, which didn't surprise him. She had done her duty, meeting several people, and she wanted to rest.

"Yes, I meant it. Do you like dogs?"

Lucia nodded. "These dogs are big and their fur is very soft. I wouldn't mind one sleeping in my room with me."

She sleeps in Airiana and Max's room with all the other children, Lexi informed him.

The phone rang in the house. Lexi didn't move. "That's the farm line. People leave orders on it," she said. "I take the orders down at the end of the day. It's just easier. If someone needs to talk to me directly, they know to leave their number."

It was clear to him she didn't like talking on the phone. "That seems like a good system, otherwise you'd be answering all day long and you wouldn't get any work done."

"That was the idea when I started it," she admitted. "Lucia, the tea is excellent. You really did a good job."

"So was the pasta," Gavriil said. "I really enjoyed it. Lexi brought some home to me and it was pretty amazing."

Lucia ducked her head, looking pleased. "It was my mother's recipe. I used to cook with her. I love cooking."

"Do you do the cooking at your house now?"

"Sometimes I ask Airiana if she minds, and she always lets me. When she's cooking, I help her."

Kiss got up abruptly, whining a little, and moved restlessly around the room, drawing Gavriil's attention. Just as suddenly she dropped back onto the floor, this time in the corner, near Lexi's sleeping bag. He glanced at Lexi. She had her eyes on the dog. Suddenly, she looked up and smiled at him directly. It was another first. One of those moments shared between a couple he'd seen from a distance—intimate—closing off the world until it was only the two of them in perfect understanding.

His body reacted, not with the savage ache he had come to recognize, but with something so much more, a complete and utter giving of himself to this woman. He felt an exchange between them. There were no words to describe the emotion settling over and into him—and in some ways it was more frightening than any job he'd ever pulled.

I can't lose you, now that I've found you. The thought was terrifying. He would be ferocious in his protection of her, cold and deadly, always her shadow. Just the thought that she could be harmed in any way left his gut in knots and a slow burn spreading through his body.

Lexi sent him a small smile. *Just remember who the boss is.*

Her eyes sparkled at him with a hint of mischief and the knots in his stomach unraveled just a little.

"Gavriil, I like your dogs," Lucia said, dragging his attention back to the child.

"I like them too, Lucia," Gavriil said. "For a long time, I was very ill and they helped me get out of bed and exercise. Dogs are more than just companions or pets. These two have been my only family for over two years. They have protective instincts in their DNA."

"I always wanted a dog," Lucia confessed. "My father entertained a lot, and he said a dog would be in the way."

This is dangerous territory, Gavriil. Be careful how you answer her, Lexi cautioned. *Her father may not have been an animal person, but he was her father.*

She had a point. He didn't want to say anything that might have Lucia thinking he didn't respect her father's opinions. He nodded his head slowly, aware the teenager was watching him closely.

"Your father is right in that dogs are not right for all families. And a dog that isn't well-trained can be all kinds of trouble. We live on a farm and these dogs are working dogs, so for us, living here, they make sense."

The phone rang again, a sharp insistent jangle he found annoying, always a bad sign. When anything mundane disturbed him, he knew he was at the point where he couldn't successfully block the pain. It was only a matter of time before the burning overcame his ability to keep it at bay.

Lexi must have noticed his discomfort. "I'm sorry about the phone. It's a workday and ordinarily I'm away from the house, so I don't even hear it. I can turn the ringer down." *You should lie down for a while. I'll come in as soon as Lucia leaves and work on you again if you don't mind.*

His body shivered in memory of her hands on his skin.

Craving took over. He could taste her in his mouth. Smell her scent. She seemed to surround him, so that he breathed her into his lungs and she moved through his bloodstream, heating him. She was fast becoming necessary to him, and both the speed and depth of his need shocked him.

"Lucia, let's gather the teacups and take them inside." Deliberately Lexi glanced at her watch. "I've got a few things to do that can't wait."

Lucia nodded and immediately began gathering the cups. She glanced several times at Kiss, who appeared to be asleep. "Do you think she's going to have the puppies soon?"

Gavriil nodded his head. "She's close. Larger breeds take a little longer than very small ones, but you can't predict the exact day. She's restless and she rarely makes a sound, so I think she'll begin to have contractions tonight or early tomorrow morning."

He pushed a hand through his hair and the action immediately centered Lexi's attention on him. He could see the concern in her soft eyes. Her lips pressed together tightly and a small frown appeared. His heart reacted to her expression with a small stutter of sensation he didn't want to identify. He pressed his palm over his chest, aching with the unfamiliar emotion.

The first wash of pain always shook him. It came in a wave and set his teeth on edge. He'd learned over the last two years to be able to control pain, an exercise in regulating his breathing and heart, stopping the burn along the damaged nerve endings, but he found it impossible to keep up after a few hours. That was part of the reason he was no longer considered able to do his job.

Gavriil.

Lexi's voice whispered along his nerve endings, quieting the pain, soothing the burn. He glanced up and locked gazes with her. He could get lost forever in her eyes. They beckoned him into the cool of the forest, like the path to another world.

You can do your job. You choose not to do it. There's a difference.

How had she caught his thought? *I'm tired,* solnyshko moya. *I think I will lie down for a few minutes. When you can, come in with me.*

As soon as Lucia is safely home.

He closed his eyes and allowed his head to fall back against the swing. Lexi made him feel as if he had a home—and a woman—of his own. She was magical, a woman of the earth who moved with grace and filled her surroundings with lush plants.

Lexi sent one more anxious glance toward Gavriil and picked up the tray. She could see the telltale lines etched deeper into his face. The skin around his mouth was a little whiter, as if he'd drawn himself too tight. Drago, the large male, moved closer to Gavriil as if offering protection.

"What's wrong with him?" Lucia asked, as she rinsed out the teacups. "I can tell something is."

"Really?" Lexi eyed her carefully. Gavriil was very good at hiding his injuries. "How?"

Lucia frowned and rubbed her finger over her eyebrow, leaving a smear of soapy bubbles. "His eyes. He's a little scary."

"Like Max?" Lexi wiped the soap bubbles from Lucia's face with the hand towel.

Lucia shook her head. "Max isn't really scary when you get to know him. He's kind of tough at first, and he growls a lot like an old bear, but he doesn't even raise his voice to us." She smiled at Lexi. "Max is really good to us. I didn't think I'd like him and I didn't want to like Airiana because . . ."

"You felt it would betray your parents if you let yourself love them," Lexi finished for her.

Lucia nodded. "But I also felt if I loved them, they'd be taken away from us too." She took a deep breath. "I argued with my father that day. The day my parents died. Over having a dog. I had asked a million times and he always said no. My mother did everything my father said, so I knew she wouldn't help. I tried to do all my chores without complaining for several months before my birthday because he said when I was responsible enough, I could have a pet."

"You asked for a dog for your birthday and he told you no," Lexi said.

Lucia slowly put the last of the teacups on the sink. "I was so angry with him. I called him a liar. He sent me to my room. My mother came in to talk to me, but I was angry with her as well because I knew she wouldn't let me have a pet either. I turned away from her. They were dressed up to go out. They both looked so beautiful, but I didn't tell her that. I didn't even tell her I loved her."

Lexi put her arm around Lucia. "She knew. Parents know. Your anger didn't cause their deaths. A terrible man rigged the car. *He* caused them to die, not you. And right now, wherever they are, I'll bet they're happy that when Kiss has her puppies you'll be around to help her with them."

"I wanted to ask Gavriil if he'd let me come over and help with them, but I can't tell if he thinks I'm a nuisance or not. He looks very scary. His eyes are cold. They never warm up unless he looks at you."

"Lucia, Gavriil is a good man. He's gone through extremely difficult times and is injured at the moment. You should try to get to know him. I'm certain when Kiss has her puppies, he'll be more than happy for the help. I know it's really important to socialize this breed of dog. We'll be counting on everyone to help us."

The phone rang again, a jarring note that made Lexi laugh.

"Why don't you ever answer?" Lucia asked. "That might be important."

Lexi shook her head. "It's the farm line. My family would call on my personal cell. I have a little mini tower in the house to boost the signal, although truthfully, I don't even know where my phone is."

Lucia laughed. "The farm phone rings all the time. Doesn't it make you crazy not answering it?"

"Seriously, I'm never home when it happens. We sell our produce to specific stores and homes and we give quite a bit to the food bank. I never realized just how many calls come in throughout the day. At night I just listen to the messages, write down the orders and call it good. I rarely have to actually talk to someone."

The smile faded from Lucia's face. "I don't want to talk to anyone right now either. I wish I was an adult and could do what I want. Airiana says all of us have to talk to this counselor she knows. Benito is being really awful about it."

Lexi caught the note of worry in the child's voice. "Come on, I'll take you home in the trail wagon. I think all of us are getting used to Benito's ideas on what men and women do and their roles. No one gets upset with him."

"Gavriil did. Benito showed me his neck."

"That was an accident. Benito stuck his head inside the house, and Gavriil had no way of knowing who he was. He could have been someone trying to hurt me."

"I don't think Gavriil has accidents," Lucia said shrewdly. She climbed into the trail wagon and looked back at the dogs sitting on the porch beside Gavriil.

"You're probably right about that," Lexi admitted, with a little sideways grin. "He didn't really hurt Benito, but he scared him. Maybe he was trying to make a point. I know he's worried about him. Counseling would be good for that boy." She started the trail wagon.

"You're saying if I go to counseling without protesting, maybe Benito would as well." Lucia hung on to the sides of the vehicle as Lexi drove through the narrow trails leading back to Airiana's home.

"Exactly. All of you need it, of course. Did you know that's how we all met? My sisters and me? We went to a group therapy meeting for women who had a family member or loved one murdered. The counselor really helped all of us to realize we could still find a way to be happy. I can't say we all came away from it guilt- or issue-free, because unfortunately trauma doesn't work that way, but the point is, we found a way to live again."

Lucia's small teeth bit into her lower lip. "I don't want to disappoint Airiana or Max. Telling someone I feel guilty for having new parents would really hurt them."

Lexi drove the wagon up Airiana's drive almost right to the steps. "No, it wouldn't. Airiana and Max both know what it's like to feel guilt, even though the guilt is misplaced. They want you to be happy. You need someone safe to discuss how you feel, Lucia. Your counselor isn't going to tell them anything unless you want them to."

Lucia smiled at her unexpectedly. "Thanks, Lexi. You make me feel grounded. I'm glad you're here."

Lexi flashed her an answering grin. "I always wanted to be the favorite aunt."

"Definitely," Lucia said, and jumped out of the wagon to run up the stairs.

Lexi glanced up to see Airiana framed in the window. Max stood behind her, his arms around her. Airiana looked as if she'd been crying, but she lifted a hand and waved to Lexi. Lexi blew her a kiss. It had to be difficult to bring four children into one's home and try to integrate them into a family when they were all traumatized. She was proud of her sister for making the decision to bring the children home with her.

Lexi drove back to her house thinking of Airiana and Max. Airiana was brilliant and worked for the defense department in some capacity Lexi didn't want to think too much about. Still, Airiana had insisted on working out of her own home so she could be present in the lives of the children.

The wind picked up in a little rush off the ocean, bringing the scent of the sea with it. The trees around her swayed gently. A storm was coming in fast. Immediately she turned the wagon and drove out to her fields. She stopped her vehicle and got out at each field and, crouching low, rested her hands on the ground.

From his vantage point on the small rise above the

fields, Gavriil watched as Lexi drove around the farm. Each time she came to a different crop, she did the same thing. She touched the ground for a few minutes, so gently, almost as if she were touching a child. He imagined her talking softly to the crops, giving reassurance to them to remain calm in the wake of the gathering storm.

He had gone up to the ridge above the farm to watch over her. He hadn't been able to help himself. The pain didn't matter, or the fact that his arm was on fire. The compulsion to protect her was far too strong. Now, he was grateful he'd followed her outside. Seeing her communing with her crops was worth the hard run up to the ridge and his vantage point.

She was beautiful, like a young goddess, her hair flying in the wind, but her movements gentle, tender even. The earth seemed to welcome her, every living plant bending toward her rather than with the wind. She touched the ground, and on impulse, he crouched low and put his own palms on top of the soil. Almost immediately he felt the sweep of her influence, a calm, soothing warmth that invaded through his palms.

Gavriil felt the water beneath the ground, running in small veins. He felt the richness of the minerals, the smaller insects, worms that tunneled and aerated the soil. He knew the connection between Lexi's palm and his enabled him to feel what she felt. The earth itself spoke to her. The plants murmured softly, a different language, but he felt their energy directed toward Lexi. Everything on the farm was connected to Lexi—especially him.

Gavriil stood up a little reluctantly and once again looked down at the woman who had cast her spell so successfully. She wasn't getting a prize by any means, but she didn't seem to mind. She saw him for what he was, both the outside shell and the inner man he protected so carefully, and she accepted him.

In his wildest dreams he'd never thought he would find acceptance. She had somehow found the key to unlock his frozen emotions. It wasn't just being with Lexi. He had been genuinely happy to see his brothers, especially his youngest one. And he found he actually liked Lissa. Little Lucia tugged at his heartstrings. He wasn't quite the cold-blooded machine he thought himself. All because of one woman.

He saw she had entered the greenhouse and knew her next stop would be the orchard and then home. He began to jog back, and this time his body felt every jarring step. Still, he wouldn't have missed seeing her taking care of her plants for anything.

Drago greeted him instantly when he entered the house, but Kiss wasn't at the door waiting for him. She'd paced through the house and was just returning, unable to settle. He scratched under her chin and looked into her eyes, murmuring reassurance. This was her first litter and she was anxious.

The phone rang again. He felt the jarring jangle right through his body, tearing at his already burning nerve endings. He had the impulse to rip the thing from the wall and toss it away. He really needed to lie down. He started toward the bedroom when awareness hit him. The need to rip the phone from the wall had nothing to do with the pain coursing through his body.

He had accepted pain a long time ago. He didn't allow pain to influence his mood. Once it got to that level, he removed himself from anything distracting so he could focus on bringing his pain under control. He wasn't there quite yet. He turned and looked at the phone.

Without hesitation he lifted it from the cradle. "Harmony Farms," he answered.

There was a small, startled silence as if the person on the other end hadn't expected him to pick up—or had expected a woman.

"You harbor Jezebel, a woman of great evil. The innocent blood will be shed along with the guilty," the disembodied voice intoned.

"It isn't Jezebel you have to worry about," Gavriil said

in a low tone. "It's the devil she's with, and he'll be waiting for you." He hung up the phone and turned as Lexi entered the room.

She had heard—her face was as pale as a ghost's. He had known she'd come in, but he wasn't going to hide anything from her, he wasn't that kind of man. He had made a commitment to this woman and he wouldn't disrespect her by trying to hide information from her, even if he knew it would be upsetting to her. He didn't know the right thing to do in a relationship, and no doubt he would be making her life difficult many times, but he would give her honesty.

"Caine has a few friends out there."

"I knew it was them when you referred to me as Jezebel. He called me that whenever he was going to punish me in front of his congregation. Which one called?" Her voice quivered, but she tried hard to sound matter-of-fact.

"He wasn't brave enough to leave his name. A man. Deep voice. Trying to sound tough. It threw him off his game a little to have a man answer."

"He probably left a recording or two on the machine," Lexi said, stepping all the way into the room. Her hands were shaking and she put them behind her back when his gaze dropped to them.

"Would you recognize his voice if you heard it?"

"Only if he was one of the men from our farm. They had more than one. There was a man they referred to as the Reverend who started it all. He would come to the various work farms and preach. Mostly he would 'save' the younger girls by forcing them to have sex with him. After he died, I'm certain Caine and his brother took over what was left of the cult. Caine's brother was arrested, but all of them had lieutenants and enforcers. This man could be anybody."

He beckoned her to him, pointing to the spot right in front of him. She looked a little lost and very vulnerable. She tugged at his heartstrings with her pale face and large eyes and hands that wouldn't stop trembling.

Lexi walked slowly across the room to stand directly in

front of him, her gaze held captive by his. Gavriil took her chin in his hand and bent his head to hers. "I won't let anything happen to you or anyone else on this farm."

Her lashes fluttered, veiling her forest green eyes.

"Lexi, I'm a straight-up cold-blooded killer, we both know that. I'm not your average nice guy. These people who are coming for you can't possibly have any idea of the life my brothers or I have lived. They're pedophiles and sex offenders. They beat up women and children. They murder in the middle of the night, helpless people who are asleep in their beds. They have no concept of dealing with men who have been trained practically from birth to kill."

He brushed her mouth with his. Gently. Tenderly. With no passion when passion welled up like a volcano inside of him.

"Do you think I want to keep showing you what I am? Every time I reiterate what I am, I'm afraid of losing you, but it's important to me that you feel safe. I can make you safe. I'm not ever going to be the sweet man who remembers flowers and candy, or flowery words. I'm going to be rougher than either of us wants sometimes and I'll make mistakes, but I can promise you, absolutely promise you, I'll keep everyone on this farm safe. I can do that."

Her eyes searched his for what seemed an eternity. He found his breath refused to leave his lungs. She went up on her toes and brushed his lips with hers. Her gesture was just as gentle, just as tender, but he felt the hint of passion and tasted it when she drew away from him.

"Don't ever worry about showing me who or what you are, Gavriil. I don't want you to have to be anything you're not. Not for me and not for anyone else. I do feel safe with you, and that's a gift beyond measure. I haven't felt safe since I was ten years old." She touched his face, traced one line down to his jaw. "You need to lie down for a while. I'll work on you to help with the pain."

"You get the room ready while I contact my brothers to give them a heads-up. I want everyone to be alert until these idiots make their move."

"I'll give Blythe a call as well," Lexi said. "She can contact Jonas Harrington." She leveled her gaze at him. "I'm certain he'll be able to help."

It went against everything he was to contact a member of law enforcement, but he nodded his head. "Kiss is very close to giving birth. I'm guessing by the way she's acting that it could be tonight or tomorrow morning." The dog had pressed close to him for a moment and then continued wandering through the house. Drago paced alongside her, not understanding why she wouldn't settle.

Lexi left him before he could kiss her—and God knew he wanted to. He ached with the need to hold her close to him and taste the cool, deep forest he knew was waiting for him. Still, he had to be careful, to take his time with her, not push her too far from her comfort zone.

He made the calls to his brothers and Lissa, and then went into the bedroom. Already the room smelled of incense and aromatherapy candles. She had turned down the bed so that he could strip and easily slide beneath the sheet. He smiled when he noted the gun was still beneath the pillow where he'd placed it. Out of habit, he checked to make certain it hadn't been compromised and was still fully loaded.

Lexi had her tray of needles as well as a first aid kit ready and a pitcher of water beside the bed. "Come lie down, Gavriil. I want to look at your arm."

Keeping his gaze on hers, he pulled his boots off and then stood, dragging his shirt over his head. His arm protested the movement, but he refused to allow it to show on his face. She didn't look away from him, not even when he dropped his hands to the waistband of his jeans. He hadn't realized just how awkward the position was or how much his biceps would burn when he tried to unbuckle his belt.

Without a word, Lexi stepped close to him and pushed his hands out of the way. His heart jumped and then began a slow pounding. Her gaze was on his. Steady. Shy. Determined. He lifted his hands out and away from her, then spoiled his clear sign to her that he wouldn't take advantage of her when his biceps exploded with pain and he had to drop his arm to his side. His hand brushed her shoulder and slipped down her arm to bare skin. The feeling of her was exquisite.

Her fingers didn't fumble, but she was slow and deliberate as she unbuckled the belt and dropped her hands lower to his zipper. He didn't care how much control he had had in the past, there was no controlling his body in this situation. Her fingers brushed his growing cock through the material and he felt the answering jerk. Blood rushed through his veins to pool low and hot.

She didn't hesitate. She pushed the jeans from his hips, taking his shorts with them. He dropped his hand onto her shoulder for balance as he stepped out of them. She didn't step back, but slowly straightened, his jeans in her hands, her eyes on his groin and the large evidence of his desire for her.

He heard her take in a breath, a swift, ragged inhale, her eyes large as she stared at his thick, hard shaft and the drops of pearl leaking from the smooth, silky head. She touched his chest. Tentatively, her fingers moved down over his abdomen, brushing over his scars. She stepped closer, and he could feel the warmth of her breath against his shaft. His cock reacted with a hard jerk, growing stiffer than he ever thought possible.

"You're killing me here, woman," he said softly, honestly.

"I'm not certain I can ever be a proper lover to you, Gavriil," she replied, still not looking up. "You're very . . . intimidating."

He cupped the back of her head, sliding his fingers into the silk of her hair. "I'm not asking for anything."

"I know you're not, but I'm hoping the way I feel about you will allow me to overcome my fears." For the first time she met his gaze with her own. "I haven't had a panic attack, and that's a good start."

12

GAVRIIL looked down into her dark green eyes, so vibrant and cool, a place of peace as a rule, but at the moment, he saw desire smoldering there. He bent his head to hers and gently brushed his lips over her mouth. One small kiss, nothing more. He didn't dare hold her in his arms. Not yet. Not when she was still working it out. She needed time, and he had all the patience in the world when it came to Lexi.

"You know, someday, when you're ready, I want to marry you. Really marry you. In front of our family and the kids and the dogs. Right here on the farm or maybe a little chapel if you're more comfortable. I know a priest that would marry us."

She hadn't stepped away from him, so he did the honorable thing and slipped beneath the sheets, although his body felt as if it might shatter at any moment.

"Would that be the same priest who married Judith and Thomas and Rikki and Levi? We went to San Francisco in the dead of night."

"Probably. He's an old friend, someone we can trust— well as far as I ever trust anyone."

"Is he really a priest?" Lexi stood over him, looking down at his face.

He should have felt vulnerable, but instead he felt cherished and wanted. Her fingers brushed back his hair, lingering for a moment on his face. "He's a priest. He said he has a lot to make up for."

"I think you're incredibly beautiful, Gavriil. I like looking at you."

"I'm grateful you find me attractive, although I'm a little beat up in places."

"I know it isn't easy for you to let me take care of you, and I appreciate that you're willing for me to try to ease the pain I know you're in. It bothers me when I see it on your face, or feel it when I'm next to you."

"Like the earth. The farm. You feel the plants, don't you?"

She nodded slowly and bent to remove the bandage from his arm. "Yes. I'm connected to them, I always have been. Even when I was a little girl, I used to talk to the plants in our house and they grew wild and crazy. My mother always said it was like a jungle in our home."

"Like the atrium you have, filled with plants. You have birds in there, flying around sometimes."

"Canaries. They love the plants."

She placed her hands over the wound and instantly he felt the warmth.

"This is healing nicely and much faster than I expected. That's you, not so much me. You can control your body better than anyone I've ever heard of."

"I trained with some monks in China. They could do incredible things. That's how I kept from bleeding out when I was stabbed so many times," he admitted.

"I knew you had to have done something. That wound in your heart should have killed you. I'm going to try to open the pathway on the damaged nerves again. I know it doesn't feel great while I'm doing it, but if we're persistent, I think eventually it will take away most of your pain."

He almost didn't care if it worked or not. He liked the

way she fussed over him, touching him so gently and looking at him with such concern on her face. "You didn't say anything about my marriage proposal."

She inserted the first needle. "I wasn't aware I needed to say anything. It wasn't exactly a question. More like a statement." She closed her eyes and passed her hands over his body, lingering over the large raised ridges near his heart.

Gavriil didn't take his eyes from her face, the deep concentration, the reaching with her mind and heart as well as her gift. Part of her ability, he realized, was in her giving herself. She was willing to share the pain if need be. If he stayed very still and let go of his need to be on full alert, if he reached for her as she was reaching for him, he connected with her gift. He felt the healing warmth she poured into him, tracing the pathways of his damaged nerves and finding the places where they were blocked.

Her friend, the doctor, Daiyu Zhang, had to have been astonished when she taught Lexi acupuncture. Lexi had to have been accurate from the first time Daiyu Zhang had shown her what to do. Lexi could easily visualize the pathways and "see" the blockages. It was no wonder she could heal others. She placed needles in several places on his chest where she had the first session, but she added more this time.

Twice she passed her hands over a second stab wound and heat poured through his body. She smoothed back his hair again. "Go to sleep, Gavriil. I'll watch over you. You need complete rest for half an hour. Your brothers will take care of anyone coming near the farm, and the farm itself will warn us. When Airiana came back, we fixed a kind of power grid surrounding us." She made a face. "Of course it let you in."

"It recognized me the way it does all of you. I'm a Prakenskii, just like my brothers. Of course it would know me. And your farm probably recognized that I'm your significant other. Your partner. The man who is going to marry you." His eyes met hers. "If you'll have me."

She moistened her lips, wariness back. "If I know I can

make you happy, Gavriil, I'll say yes, but not until then. I'm not going to ruin your life because I can't have a physical relationship. I'm already more than halfway into falling in love with you. I know that. I'm not ashamed to admit it, but it isn't good enough just feeling the emotion. I have to be able to show you."

"Halfway?" He captured her hand and brought it to the edge of the bed. "Only halfway?"

"I said *more* than halfway."

"I'm all the way. I fell like a ton of bricks, and this halfway nonsense has to go. You have to be right there with me."

She gave a little mock sigh. "I'll see what I can do. Now go to sleep. I'm going to see if the dogs want to go outside for a few minutes to do their business, and I'm hoping Kiss will find the right spot to have her babies. *Not* on one of the beds."

"Did she get up on the beds? She knows better."

"No, she didn't, but she's checked out every single other possible place in the house, and I figure that was next on her list. Go to sleep. I'm not kidding, Gavriil. If you don't, I'm knocking you out with a frying pan."

He tried not to laugh. It hurt to laugh. He was stuck lying on his back with just a sheet over his naked body and needles sticking out of his chest when she threatened him—with a frying pan.

"Think about me while I'm sleeping, *solnyshko moya*, because I intend to dream about you."

Lexi smiled at him and left the room. She would have closed the door but she knew him well enough to know he would object. She went straight to the phone in the kitchen to play back the recording, wanting to see if she could identify the voice. If she could, maybe Jonas would find the man before Gavriil did. She wanted Gavriil to have a chance to lead a normal life—a peaceful one.

There were thirty messages, and of the thirty messages, only nine were legitimate business messages. The other twenty-one were threats and after listening to them repeatedly, she realized that six different voices had left the messages. Of the six, she was certain of one belonging to a man named Benjamin Frost. He had been an enforcer for the Reverend and when every compound had been raided, he hadn't been picked up. He'd been one of the most brutal of all enforcers, and many of the leaders of the other compounds feared he had too much influence over the Reverend.

She wrote the name down and put five more question marks on the notepaper. Kiss whined, and she whirled around. The dog nosed the door. If she let her out and she found a place outside to have her puppies, Lexi feared she wouldn't be able to get the dog back inside.

"All right," she said aloud, "but you have to mind me."

She stepped out the kitchen door and waved the dogs outside after her. The wind had increased in velocity, rushing toward the house, carrying droplets of water with it. She tasted salt and sea when she lifted her face toward the sky. Overhead the clouds spun in giant swirls of black and gray and white, rolling around to shoot upward in great spinning towers.

"Hurry," she cautioned. "The storm's about to break any moment and you don't want to be caught out here. You'll get soaked." The dogs had longer, curly coats and beards with hair growing in long sweeps over their eyes. Their coats soaked up water easily. She knew because both loved sticking their heads in the water dish and then shaking them to spread water from one end of the kitchen to the other. Gavriil had placed several small hand towels in each room and now she knew why.

"The storm's coming in, you two, hurry. Do your business right now." She did her best to sound authoritative. She was still just a little intimidated by the large dogs, although Drago seemed to like her, and she was beginning to feel sorry for Kiss.

The sky had already darkened, although it was only late afternoon. She loved storms. She loved sitting on her porch and watching them come in from the sea. Rikki always was careful to keep too much water from hurting their crops, so she didn't worry about damage, and she loved the way the trees and plants responded to the rain.

She walked around the house, surprised that both dogs followed her. When she stepped onto her front porch, both animals did the same.

"He told you to guard me, didn't he?" she asked, realizing Gavriil had given the two Black Russian Terriers the job of looking after her. "So much for you liking me, Drago. You had me fooled for a moment."

Kiss whined and started panting hard. "Uh oh. I think you need to find your spot, little momma," Lexi said, and opened the door to signal them inside the way she'd seen Gavriil do. Both dogs responded by nudging her leg, nearly pushing her into the house.

Lexi laughed and gave them a scratch under their chins. "Fine. I'll go in first, but you do realize being bossed around by the two of you is embarrassing. You can try when we're alone but not in front of anyone. It's going to be bad enough when Gavriil's feeling fine again. I'll bet he's the bossy type."

She closed the door just as the heavens burst open and rain poured down in solid sheets of glittering silver. Kiss hurried down the hall toward the bedroom where Gavriil was. There was no stopping her. Clearly, she wanted the companionship of the man who had raised her.

Lexi followed her through the open door. Gavriil appeared to be asleep, but she knew he wasn't. He would have alerted the moment they came into the house, but his eyes remained closed, and he looked younger, the lines in his face not etched quite as deep.

Lexi watched Kiss go to the corner, inside the open closet where Gavriil had made a nesting box for the dog. It was big enough for her and the puppies and fit nicely inside the walk-in closet in the deepest part, back in the corner. Lexi had put blankets, sheets and towels on the bottom of it, hoping Kiss would use it.

Kiss scratched around, piling the old sheets and towels into a more comfortable bed before she lay down. Once inside the closet, she was nearly impossible to see. It was dark and she had slipped far back into the shadows, but Lexi could hear her panting as if she was uncomfortable.

She made her way to Gavriil, placing her hands over his body to feel if the pathways were beginning to respond to the ancient therapy. She couldn't help herself, nor did she try to stop the sudden impulse to lean down and brush a kiss across his mouth. There was something in him that drew her.

He hadn't seemed to have much of a life. Together they could make something good, she was certain of it, and yet she feared she would be the one to hold them back. Her fears. Her trauma. They both were broken, there was no doubt about that. All along she thought she was saving him. She was certain of it until that moment. Looking down at his face, she knew it was the other way around. Gavriil was saving her.

He lifted his lashes and she found herself staring into his amazing dark blue eyes. It was a bit like falling into the night. He made her aware of herself as a woman, as feminine. She had never felt feminine before. Her body had always been something she covered up and didn't think about. Now she was aware of her aching breasts and jittery stomach, the heat between her legs. Her body temperature even went up as though she had a fever whenever she was close to him.

Worse, she was aware of him as a man. She couldn't take a breath without breathing him into her lungs. Her body was on fire because of this man. She'd been dead inside and out. Even the shell of her body had been broken, and suddenly she was alive again. It was both terrifying and exhilarating. Still, she didn't know what to do. Being the one doing the saving gave her a goal and purpose she could live with. If he was the one doing the saving . . .

She couldn't breathe. Couldn't find air. The room actually spun, and her legs turned to rubber. Her stomach lurched and the need to escape overtook her. She looked around for a place to run, to hide, but she was frozen.

Her heart pounded so hard, so rapidly, she feared a heart attack.

"What is it, *solnyshko moya*?" He caught her hand. "You have tears in your eyes."

She had to answer him. There had to be honesty between them, and he had been more than honest, taking a risk when others would have lied. Her voice trembled and it seemed impossible to get the words out when she couldn't find air. "It's you, Gavriil. I realized I'm the one who needs you."

"I don't understand, Lexi."

"You tempted me. That low whisper of yours. That soft voice and tortured feeling to you." She closed her eyes, feeling lost. "Almost as if you dared me to come to you. I kept getting closer and closer to the flame, I just couldn't stop myself." Her legs were going to give out and she would find herself on the floor in another minute.

"Lexi, take out the needles." Gavriil made it a command. He wasn't certain what had happened or why she was suddenly questioning their strange relationship, but he wasn't going to lose her.

"You weren't living much of a life. All this time I thought I could help you. I could make a difference in your life. Give you peace, take away your pain and maybe give you a better life. Something better than moving every two days and never trusting anyone. I pursued you. I asked you to stay with me." She looked around helplessly, the room spinning so fast she feared she would faint and be forever embarrassed by her inadequacies.

"Are you rescinding your offer?" His thumb slid over her inner wrist.

"I don't know how to feel now." She sounded lost. "What am I giving you after all? What is it you need from me?"

"Take these needles out, Lexi. I can't talk to you about something this important with such a handicap."

"I don't know what to do, now. I don't know what to feel or how to act."

She was completely panicked. He could see it in her eyes, and hear it in her breathing. He swore in Russian and began to pull out the needles himself. She made a single sound and tried to help him, but her hands trembled so badly she could barely grasp the small needles.

The moment he was free, he sat up and caught at her when she would have fled the room. He was fast, his reflexes honed and he had her wrist, tugging her back to his side and then down onto the bed beside him.

"No," he decreed. "You're going to stay right here and talk to me. What has you in a panic? You faced the dogs without batting an eye and now you're ready to crawl into a hole and hide."

Lexi shook her head, trying desperately to drag air into her lungs. He pushed her head down, his palm curled around the nape of her neck. "Take a breath, *solnyshko moya*, a nice slow breath, and then you can talk to me."

She tried for him. Her body trembled, but she worked at controlling her breathing. "It's you, Gavriil. You're this strong, courageous man. Look at you. Really take a look at yourself. I convinced myself that I could help you—that you were every bit as broken in your way as I am. I thought you needed me, but you don't. You don't need anyone, least of all someone like me."

"Where the hell is this coming from?" he demanded, allowing her to raise her head. He needed an enemy to blame. Nothing she said made a damn bit of sense.

She remained silent, refusing to look at him. Gavriil shook his head. "You really don't know, do you? You don't have a clue what you are to me. Not the least little clue."

She stole a quick glance from under long, spiky lashes. She gave a quick shake of her head.

"You're everything. That's what you are. *Everything.*" He enunciated the word. "You're the only person that has ever mattered to me enough to make me want to stay. To settle. You saved my life. I was going to die after saying good-bye to my family. I knew Sorbacov would send his assassins after me and sooner or later they'd get me. It didn't matter. Dying truly didn't because I didn't have anything to live for. You gave me a reason."

She shook her head again.

Gavriil caught her chin and forced her to look at him. "Do you know why you're having a panic attack? Have you even figured it out yet?"

"It isn't a panic attack," she said in a small voice.

"Of course it is. I mentioned marriage. Marriage is unholy to you. Chains. A dictatorship. And whom exactly would you be tying yourself to? A nice guy? A man who is sweet and easily led around? No, you went out and got yourself a wolf. He doesn't even look like a sheep. Of course you're having a panic attack. Marriage represents everything ugly that happened to you."

She looked horrified. "That's not true."

She didn't sound convinced. She sounded shocked and scared, but her tone told him he was on the right path.

"Of course it is, and your reaction is perfectly natural. Caine took you from your home and forced you to enter into what he called marriage. You endured years of abuse from a perverted, sadistic pedophile in the name of marriage. How could you not associate the word with something horrific?"

She leaned into the warmth of his body, not away from him, as if he gave her comfort and she wasn't quite aware of it. He wanted to pull her onto his lap, but she was stiff, her pulse pounding and her breath still ragged. She was at least thinking, listening to him.

"I thought it was beautiful when Rikki and Judith were married," she said in a small voice. "I'm looking forward to Airiana's wedding."

"They aren't you. We're already connected. We both know I did that without your permission. In a sense, just as Caine took away your choice, so did I."

"No." She whirled around to face him, right there on the bed, her green eyes dark with anger, the panic receding.

"You are *nothing* like Caine. *Nothing.* Don't ever compare yourself to him again. You're careful of my feelings and kind and I can't imagine you hurting me."

"Really, Lexi? I had my hand around your throat."

"I knew you wouldn't hurt me, Gavriil. When I'm with you, I feel safe. Even then, when we were together, I wanted to keep you here on the farm where I thought I could make your life better. I felt as if we belonged."

"Unless I mention marriage." Deliberately he pushed humor into his voice.

There was a small silence. A slow, reluctant smile touched her mouth briefly and faded. "I think you could be right. I didn't think about it. I know it wasn't a real marriage, that a union between a man and a woman should be a partnership. I know Caine was sadistic. I wasn't the only person he hurt."

"That's all intellectual, Lexi, not emotional. You can recite the truth all day long, but your emotions can't necessarily be dictated to."

"Yours are," she pointed out.

He shook his head. "Not when it comes to you. When you panicked and I wasn't certain what was wrong, I thought I might lose you and I began to panic as well."

"No you didn't. I was watching you. Your expression never changed."

"Just because I don't portray emotion, Lexi, doesn't mean I don't feel it. When it comes to you, you can bet I'm feeling something. I don't want you to ever think you aren't valued by me. Offering marriage was my way of showing you how much I value you, but I know we're connected. We don't have to go into a church and say vows to tie us together. If you need the freedom you have right now, then that's how we'll do this thing. More than anything else, Lexi, you have to know I've got your back. Just talk to me when something doesn't feel right."

"I didn't realize that was what upset me. I just felt all along that we were on equal footing. That I had something to offer you no one else could."

"Which is entirely the truth. Absolutely the truth. I wouldn't be sitting here with another woman."

"You don't know that. This is the right time for you, Gavriil. Maybe you were just open because your brothers . . ."

He put his finger over her mouth to cut her off. "Look at me. I'm no young man. I've traveled the world. I never had another woman, or wanted one. You're it. The only. We fit. And I'm okay with being broken. You are as well. There's no right or wrong here, *solnyshko moya*, it's only the two of us. We can make our own rules."

Lexi nodded. "I'm sorry, Gavriil. I had no idea that was going to happen. That's one of my biggest leftovers from my days at that compound. I can't seem to stop the panic attacks, and I have no idea what's going to trigger them. I hate leaving the farm because I'm afraid it will happen out in public."

"Do you think your having panic attacks is going to make me think less of you?"

"*I* think less of me. I should be able to control them, but I can't, no matter how hard I try. I learned all the tools they give someone like me and still, I can't overcome them. Of course I didn't want you to see that in me. I want you to feel like you're getting someone special."

He laughed. He couldn't help it. "Lexi, you're talking to a man who killed people for a living. I'm a machine my employer points at someone and orders them gone. I follow those orders. I don't think about it. I don't question it. I don't care. I just do it. What kind of a man do you think you're getting? Compared to my flaws, your one tiny failing seems a little trivial."

Lexi shook her head. "You aren't like that. You just think you are. I know it isn't true because you told me everyone you'd gone after was someone who was bad, which means you did your research, you didn't let them just point at a target. In any case, I can see past that man to the other one, the one you hide even from yourself."

"That man doesn't come out often, Lexi. In fact, he

doesn't come out for anyone but you." Gavriil stroked his hand down her hair. Her ponytail had to go. They were in the house and he wanted all that luxurious hair to cascade like a rippling waterfall down her back.

"He comes out with a little fourteen-year-old girl who needs help. And with a pair of Black Russian Terriers. I'll bet he comes out around his brothers as well."

"Don't paint me as a saint. It won't work. I think it's important you have an accurate picture of me at all times, otherwise you'll be bitterly disappointed someday and that's the last thing I want."

"Have no fear, Gavriil Prakenskii. I will never see you as a saint. Just being a Prakenskii prevents that from ever happening," she assured him, with a small laugh. "I have to go fix us something to eat."

"I'll give you a hand. Let me get my shirt."

"Don't forget your pants," she advised. "You never know who might drop by." She crossed to the door. "Like the sheriff," she added, and sauntered out.

Gavriil stared after her and then found himself laughing. She scared the hell out of him, and then somehow made everything all right again, so right he could laugh. That didn't make sense to him. He wasn't certain how he was going to live on a roller coaster after his well-ordered life, but he was determined to ride it all the way. The woman was worth every emotional upheaval.

He dragged on his clothes and went to check on Kiss. Her panting indicated she was in the beginning stages of labor. He caught her head between his hands and looked into her eyes, murmuring his reassurance, knowing he would be sitting there in the closet with her when she gave birth.

"You're beautiful, Kiss," he said softly. "You're going to make a wonderful mother, just like that woman who at the moment is driving me a little crazy. We're going to take care of her, the two of us, you and me. We'll make certain her life is happy. Right? She's going to love your babies."

Kiss licked his hand. She didn't show her affection very

often, and he was pleased that she did so when she was confused about what was happening to her.

Gavriil stood up and moved around the room, checking his weapons out of habit, and then followed after Lexi at a more leisurely pace. He found her in the kitchen, pulling all kinds of produce out of the refrigerator. He leaned one hip lazily against the doorjamb and crossed his arms over his chest.

"Who might be dropping by?"

"I'm certain you heard me," Lexi said, rinsing several bunches of different kinds of lettuce. "Jonas Harrington is going to come by to listen to the messages various members of the cult left me. I listened while you were sleeping."

"Without me." He kept his gaze fixed on her face.

"You knew they were threatening me. It was just more of the same. Seriously, there was no need for you to stand there with me listening to their vile threats."

"Of course there was need. It's called support. Don't shut me out because you think I might go hunting."

She paused in the act of tearing the lettuce leaves and throwing them into a bowl. Her gaze met his squarely. "Not might, Gavriil. You will and you know it. I don't want that life for you anymore. And I don't want to be the cause of you feeling as if you have to continue in it."

"Lexi, you're not going to shut me out of this. These people mean business. You already know what they're capable of. Do you really believe for one moment I'm going to hand them over to the sheriff and think it's done?"

"I believe you should have a chance at living in peace, Gavriil. Hunting criminals and killing them is not peaceful."

"To me it is, especially if I know those people will never have the chance of touching you or anyone you love."

She moved around the center island and came straight to him, standing in front of him, her eyes soft and more loving than he felt he deserved.

"Gavriil. No. You have to stop."

She placed her palm directly over one of the scars on his

abdomen. At once he felt the heat. Her energy was strong. He pressed his own hand over hers, holding her to him, wishing the material of his shirt was out of the way so they could be skin to skin.

"If they come on our property and we have to defend ourselves, then yes, we'll fight them any way that we can, but you can't go hunting them." Her hand seemed to melt right through the thin cotton of his shirt so that he felt hot where she was touching him. "Let Harrington handle it."

She moved him in ways he had never expected. He took her hand and raised it to his mouth to press a kiss into the center of her palm. "*Solnyshko moya*, you are asking an impossible task of me. I am incapable of giving you this thing you desire. I am a hunter of men. That's who I am."

She shook her head. "You're my man. That's who you are."

He framed her face with his hands and bent his head to hers. Her lips were soft and warm and melted under his. He kissed her gently at first. Tenderly. Love welled up and encompassed him. There was no better place to be than with her. Her mouth was paradise. Hot. Filled with passion.

She gave herself to him tentatively at first. Shyly. Then she let herself go and simply accepted the desire pouring into both of them. Electricity arced between them. Lightning flashed in their veins. A fever of need raged as if they had caught fire and burned hot and pure together.

Gavriil pulled her into his arms, holding her as close as possible. He wanted her in his bed, all skin and heat, her mouth moving over him, sating the urgent demands that were becoming difficult to ignore.

"I love that you want me to have this life with you. I want it too, but I can't be someone I'm not, Lexi. I can't have anyone threatening you and just stay on the sidelines. You know that, don't you?"

She rested her head over his heart. "I want you just as safe as you want me. Can you understand that? You feel invincible, even to me, but you're not. You told me I was your everything. That I'm your world. The reason you stayed alive. Did it ever occur to you that I feel that exact same way about you?"

He hadn't. He couldn't imagine that the overwhelming emotion he felt for her was duplicated in any way. It didn't seem possible. "I'm so connected to you, Lexi, I can't think straight sometimes," he admitted.

"You give me panic attacks," she pointed out, pulling out of his arms with a small smile on her face. "That should count for something."

He followed her to the center island, where she was clearly putting together a salad. She already had eggs boiling and there were various cuts of meat in bowls. She deftly cut up cucumbers and tomatoes while he chopped scallions.

"I'm serious, Lexi. I want you to tell me who these men are who have threatened you. I know you know them."

"Sadly, I know you're serious." She sighed and added fresh croutons to the mix. "I can't stop you, but you might consider you aren't protected here in the United States and if you're caught, you'll be put in jail."

"Did you think my government protected any of us?" Gavriil raised an eyebrow.

She added avocado to the growing mix of vegetables already in the bowl. "Didn't they?"

"Of course not. They would never admit they sent assassins after anyone. No government is going to admit they have them or would use them to eliminate someone of importance."

"Why didn't you just walk away from it all?"

He shrugged. "My youngest brother, Ilya, was out in the open. He worked as an Interpol agent, but earlier, they used him in a few compromising covert operations and then threatened to expose him. He would have been killed. When we were boys, both Viktor and I agreed to do whatever was needed as long as they gave Ilya a decent life. For the most part, Sorbacov kept his word and we kept ours."

"So you're an honorable man."

She set the bowl of salad on the table and added the various other smaller bowls with other ingredients. He carried the plates and silverware over while she went back for the dressing.

"I tried to be a man my father would be proud of," he said.

She smiled at him as she sank into a chair. "I can't imagine that he isn't proud of you. I am. I think you're extraordinary. I still can't believe, when I look at you, that you're sitting opposite me, telling me you want to stay with me."

"Panic attacks and all." He raised an eyebrow at her. "Not to mention the kissing is superb. I'm all about the kissing."

She laughed briefly, the worry fading from her eyes, but then she looked directly at him, serious again. "I guess you're going to do whatever it is you feel is right, but promise me, when you do, that you'll always come back to me."

"Nothing will ever stop me from coming home to you."

"I'm still going to have Jonas Harrington listen to the messages. I only recognized one voice. The Reverend set up several compounds, not just the one where I was held. The police raided them and quite a few of the key people were taken into custody, but not all of them were found guilty. And not all of them were arrested. I don't necessarily know the others threatening me."

Gavriil shrugged. "Ilya mentioned Harrington was a good man and that he's married to a Drake. I suppose it won't hurt to have him on our side."

"I have to work tomorrow. I didn't do much other than replant my lettuce field."

"This storm is going to last awhile."

"Through the night, but we'll be able to get a lot done tomorrow." She pinned him with what she considered was her sternest gaze. "Even if it rains."

He thought her "stern" eyes were beautiful—all cool mossy green. "Let's have our tea on the porch and watch the storm after dinner," he suggested.

Her eyes lit up, turned into sparkling emeralds. "I'd love that. I love storms."

"Wouldn't you know Kiss would deliver in a storm? I

know you don't like sleeping in the bed, but maybe it would be a good idea tonight if you stayed in the room with me so if something goes wrong, we can both help her deliver safely."

It was a gamble, but he needed a good reason to bring her back to the bedroom. She was obviously interested in the dogs, and she was very compassionate. She gave him a look, but she didn't protest. Gavriil knew when to stay silent now that he knew he was going to get his way.

13

GAVRIIL lay listening to the storm. As the night wore on, the rain increased in volume again. The wind howled through the trees and hurled water at the windows in a capricious manner, bending the boughs of the trees so that they sawed against one another loudly.

Lexi lay curled beside him with only a thin sheet separating their bodies. She stayed on her side, turned away from him, but she didn't protest when he curved his body protectively around hers and slid one arm around her waist to hold her to him.

He was aware of her every breath, every movement of her body. He'd taken the tie from her hair and it spilled around him, rich and luxurious, a wealth of dark ruby silk he couldn't stop burying his face in. Just inhaling her scent gave him a hard-on, a thick, painful reminder that his body came alive anytime she was near.

Neither spoke, both listening to the wild music of the night. He dragged her closer to him, pushing his hips tightly against her, so that the thick length of his aching cock pressed into her buttocks, finding a snug home. He heard her inhale, a raw gasp, but she remained still.

He waited until the tension dissipated before he slipped his hand beneath the thin material of her racerback tee, spreading his fingers to take in as much skin as possible over her narrow rib cage. The tips of his fingers nestled beneath her soft breasts. Again, she stiffened a little, but she didn't protest or move away from him. He held her, keeping his breathing slow and even, willing her to accept his touch on her bare skin.

Gavriil didn't try to hide his need of her or his body's reaction to her. For them to have any kind of a physical relationship, she would have to get used to him touching her, wanting her body, even needing it.

"Do you always sleep in pajamas?" he asked.

"Do you always sleep in the nude?" she countered.

He rubbed his knuckles back and forth gently along the underside of her breasts. "Yes. Clothes bunch up and I have a hard enough time sleeping without that."

She was silent a moment. He felt her relax even more against him, even pushing her bottom back tighter against his groin. Her buttocks rubbed against him just for a moment, an involuntary reaction he was certain, and he had to close his eyes and allow his body to absorb the rush of heat. For a moment he couldn't breathe with wanting her.

"He said it was wrong to sleep in the nude," she admitted. "That my body tempted men and dragged them down from their spiritual level. He made me sleep in thick sweats. The only time I didn't have clothes is when he punished me."

Gavriil felt a cold rage swelling into a tidal wave of pure hatred toward the dead Caine and his disgusting friends.

"I prefer you to tempt my body, *angel moy*. Everything he told you was a lie. Don't let him get into your head like that."

"Gavriil." She turned her head and looked at him.

The action pushed her breasts across his hand. He

opened his palm to cup the soft weight to him. She blinked several times, but she didn't protest.

"Tell me, *laskovaya moya*."

"They branded me. On my thigh. Up high. There's no way to get it off of me."

He closed his eyes briefly, his face buried in her hair. He'd done something similar and it had to have hurt her—a terrible reminder of Caine taking her freedom.

"Lexi." He breathed her name. "I'm so sorry. I did the same thing to you. I didn't know. I know it hurt when I put my mark on your palm. I should have waited. I should have asked your consent."

He slipped one hand free to capture her palm and bring it to his mouth. He pressed kisses into the center. "Believe me, *solnyshko moya*, I'm sorrier than I can tell you." The more he learned of Caine, the more he feared she would think there were too many similarities.

"Don't," she replied softly. "Don't even go there. I need to say this to you. I need you to hear what I'm saying."

He tucked his hand back under her top, needing to stay close and connected.

"I have scars. On my back and the back of my thighs. They're ugly."

If he could have killed Caine much slower than he had, he would have done so. He would never feel remorse for what he'd done to the man.

"I have scars all over me, front and back, and it doesn't bother you."

She turned back and snuggled deeper into the pillow. He kept his hand curled around her right breast. Her nipple pressed against the center of his palm.

"It isn't the same and you know it. A man looks . . . *manly* with scars. A woman can look horrible."

He listened to the rain pounding against their roof, slinging water onto the panes of glass, and he breathed her into his lungs. "You couldn't be ugly to me no matter how many scars you have, Lexi. If that's all that's keeping you from sleeping in the nude, take off your clothes. Let me see. Let's get it over with and you'll never have to worry about it again."

He felt her inhale deeply. There was more, and he had to let her get it out. He could tell it was difficult and very important to her.

"My breasts are too big. He made me bind them because . . ."

"Because he liked children not women. You're a woman, Lexi, not a child, and your body is beautiful. Especially to me. Caine can't reach you here, not unless you allow his garbage to color how you feel about your body. Believe me, not him. Take off your clothes and be free. You don't cut your hair and you have to know it's beautiful. Take them off and get rid of his poison."

He opened his hand and allowed his fingers to massage her breast gently, small caresses. He wanted his mouth there. He could spend hours playing with her full breasts and never tire. He could feel the reaction of her body. Her breasts were quite sensitive. Her hips moved subtly, a restless need building.

"I'm not certain I want to move." Her admission was shy. Embarrassed. Honest.

Caine really hadn't touched her body. She had served him, not the other way around. Lexi had never experienced a man arousing her in the way Gavriil was. He transferred his finger and thumb to her nipple, tugging and rolling it until he heard her audible gasp. She sat up abruptly, hugging herself, looking down at him with dazed eyes. Her lips were slightly parted and she looked shocked.

"That's how a man who loves a woman touches her, Lexi," he said, without moving. He watched her face carefully. "He loves her body. He worships her. The reason the sex act is often referred to as making love is because that's what he's doing—he's showing her with his body how much he loves her."

She nodded her head, her long hair spilling around her face as she sat on the side of the bed staring through the glass into the night. She took a deep breath. He saw the rise and fall of her breasts against the shine of the window. Very slowly she grasped the hem of her shirt and raised it above her head.

His breath left his lungs in a heated rush. Her rib cage was narrow, emphasizing the full swell of her breasts. She gave another tug and the shirt was off. She didn't hide her breasts from him, but rather turned slightly so he couldn't see her back.

"Do you know how else a man can show his woman how much he loves her?" His voice had gone low. He hooked his arm around her waist and pulled her back down so that her hair spilled across the pillow and her breasts thrust upward toward the ceiling. Toward his mouth as he rose above her.

He bent his head to her, his tongue tasting her skin, the soft, rose petal skin that drove him crazy. He lapped at her lush mound, stroking her nipple with his tongue, and then using his teeth gently before closing his mouth around her breast, drawing her into heat and fire. With his hand he caressed her other breast, tugging and rolling her nipple while he suckled strongly.

He felt her body's response, the electrical charge running from breast to groin. He slid his hand down her belly, needing the feeling of possession, as she writhed under him, her skin growing hot. She made a small, strangled sound in the back of her throat. At once he was alert, careful not to get lost in the wonder of her body. He lifted his head to look at her. Her eyes went wide with sheer panic.

Lexi's body burned with fever. Her breasts ached and begged for more. Electrical currents ran from her breasts to her most feminine core, a heated magic she hadn't known existed. This was what making love was. This was the feeling of utter and absolute need. Want. Her entire body felt as if it might burst into flames, and deep inside, tension wound tighter and tighter until she nearly screamed for release.

Her body no longer belonged to her. She was Gavriil's. His. His mouth and hands had claimed her, and before she had known what to expect, it was already too late. She

wanted more. Everything. She wanted his mouth and hands
on her forever . . .

A sob welled up. If he made her feel like this, what
would he expect from her? She knew. She'd had to do such
things a million times and the thought had bile rising. She
couldn't. She just couldn't. She would never be able to give
Gavriil such a beautiful and wondrous gift. She stiffened,
her hands going to his shoulder.

Gavriil pulled back immediately, smiling down at her,
tucking the hair tumbling around her face behind her ear.
"That's how a man should love his woman, Lexi. And that's
just the beginning."

She stared up at him, her breath coming in ragged gasps.
She was close to another panic attack; she could feel her
heart racing and there was no way to control her breathing.

His hands were gentle—loving even—as he stroked her
hair, small caresses meant to soothe, not arouse.

"Did I frighten you?" His voice low and matter-of-fact.

Lexi bit at her lower lip for a moment and then shook her
head, veiling her expression with her lashes. She had to say
something so she settled for the truth. "*I* frightened me. I've
never felt like that."

"Like what? Tell me how you felt."

She felt more confused than ever. He was so amazing.
How could he want her so much when she was so broken?
"Hot. Wanting. Needing. Really hot. My body didn't feel as
if it belonged to me at all."

"Was it a good feeling?"

She nodded slowly, her gaze fixed steadily on his face,
her anchor in a very violent storm. She loved his face, loved
everything about him, and she was going to have to save
him from himself. Her heart ached.

Gavriil smiled at her serious expression. "I'm going to
kiss you, so don't panic. Just a kiss because I find you so
adorable and I can't resist you."

He didn't wait for her consent, he bent his head to hers
and took possession of her mouth. Again, he was careful to
coax her response rather than demand it, but he was a little

more aggressive, sweeping his tongue into her mouth and dueling with her, holding her closer, his mouth insistent. She was definitely getting the hang of kissing, and just like always, he found himself slipping into another world—one of pure feeling.

Sex had always been rather rote to him, every movement planned and carried out. He dictated to his body when to feel and what to feel. But not with her. Everything was new and real. The world dropped away and there was only the feel of her body melting into his, skin to skin. Her mouth was paradise, a hotbed of pleasure taking him outside himself and pushing away every other experience he'd ever had.

She brushed her fingers through his hair, and his heart reacted. His blood surged hotly. He kissed her again and again because once wasn't enough and never would be.

Gavriil lifted his head, breathing deeply to bring his body under some semblance of control. He loved that she could destroy years and years of discipline and training so easily and not even realize she was doing it.

"You have tears in your eyes again," he accused.

"I know. You're just so amazing, Gavriil. I don't think there's another man like you in the world. I don't think men stop like you do when they obviously need to keep going." She took a deep, shuddering breath.

"They do if they love their partner. They should be in tune with her. Now please show me your scars so you never have to worry about that again."

She stiffened. Her gaze slid away from him. "This is even more difficult now. I want to be perfect for you."

Lexi wanted to weep until the entire bedroom was flooded with tears. She couldn't do this. She couldn't. He had swept her away from the ugly memories and taken her to a place she'd never been. She hadn't known a woman—or a man—could feel like that. Gavriil had so generously aroused her body and in doing so, she knew he was just as aroused. She would never be able to do the same thing to him. Not ever. The thought made her want to vomit.

No matter how many times she told herself it would be

different because it was Gavriil, she knew she couldn't do it. Now, realizing just how much need he felt, she had to admit defeat. She just couldn't do that to him—tie him to a woman who could never satisfy him in bed—and she couldn't.

She already knew her scars wouldn't matter to him. She looked into his eyes, and she knew he accepted her with all of her flaws. He wanted her. He deserved so much better. So much more. She would have to leave her beloved farm because he wouldn't leave her. She wanted him to have a home. A place of peace. She had found it here and the least she could do was pass it on to him, even if she couldn't stay with him.

Her throat clogged with tears. She ached with wanting him, not just her body, but her mind. She hadn't known a man like Gavriil existed. She barely remembered her father. Caine had managed to take away every good memory, telling her stories until she couldn't remember what was real and what he'd made up.

Lexi sat up slowly and scooted to the edge of the bed, slowly turning around to present her back to him. Her long hair tumbled down her back to pool on the sheet. He moved it slowly out of his way. A web of scars started near her bra line and continued down her back to disappear into her pajama bottoms.

He used both hands to lift her to her feet, pulling the bottoms down to inspect the scars there. She had them on her buttocks as well as on the backs of her thighs. The ones low were the worst, the ridges raised and ugly. She felt the touch of his fingers, so gentle, almost a caress as he traced the scars with his fingertip.

The scars didn't matter now. She felt defeated. Caine had won after all. He had ruined her chance at a real relationship with a decent, caring man. She couldn't overcome her fears and the ugly memories of what sex was like with a monster. She was not going to subject Gavriil to a half-life with her.

Abruptly she swept her hair back down and stood up.

She couldn't look at him, couldn't let him see her face. She went to the drawers and yanked out jeans and a tee. She had a bag stashed under the stairs for a quick getaway.

"I'm going to sit out on the porch for a few minutes and catch the end of the storm," she announced in a tight voice, and left the room.

She was going to run. Gavriil knew it just looking at her. He saw it in the slump of her shoulders and the way her head was down, but her walk was determined. He slid out from under the sheet, reached down and gathered his clothes, careful to stay silent.

He took a deep breath and tried to puzzle out what had gone wrong. She had felt exactly what she was supposed to feel. He hadn't gone too far, he'd been careful to just show her, not only how it could be wonderful between a man and a woman, but how he felt it should be. He'd never actually had that experience so maybe he'd blown it, gone too fast, tried to take her too far too quickly.

Out of habit he tucked a gun into the waistband of his jeans, pushed a knife into his boot and followed her. She hadn't turned on lights—neither did he. He only had a short time to figure out her thinking. Where had he gone wrong?

For the first time she had experienced true sexual desire. She had never known what it was to feel real desire for her partner. Her body had come alive under his mouth and hands. She'd been frightened of course, but not panicked, not sad—and he'd read sorrow in her eyes. What was it?

He went through the kitchen, avoiding the front of the house where he knew she stashed her sleeping bag as well as a "run" bag. And she was running from him, that much he was certain of. Why? He slipped out the back door, his mind turning over the problem while he circled around the house.

Lexi was a generous woman. A compassionate one. All along she had seen the man inside the body of a killer and she'd reached for him. She had offered him a sanctuary even knowing how dangerous he was. She wasn't afraid of him. She was afraid *for* him. Now everything clicked into place. She didn't believe she could ever satisfy him, or give back to him what he could give her.

He understood. How could he not? The things Caine must have made her do were reprehensible and criminal. She was terrified of a sexual relationship, but she'd made up her mind to try—until she really knew what it felt like.

Rain fell on his face but he barely noticed. His hunting instincts had been honed over many years, and he knew she would go to the greenhouse and write letters to her sisters. She would never leave them without an explanation. All she had to do was walk off the farm and call witness protection and someone would come and get her. Lexi Thompson would disappear, and somewhere, far away, another woman would be born.

Every cell in his body rebelled at the idea. She wasn't going anywhere. He knew they could make it work. The fever for her burned too hot, was too addicting. It wasn't all about sex, although he had to admit to himself he wanted a physical relationship with her, that the urge was strong and would be enduring.

Lexi had given him knowledge he hadn't possessed in all the years he'd been alive. She had taught him love was given freely without thought of self. She thought herself broken beyond repair, yet he was the one that needed saving. He couldn't live without her. He'd been existing, and she'd been living a half-life. Together they made a whole. He just had to find a way to get her to see that.

He heard her weeping the moment he stepped inside the greenhouse. It was a cocoon of warmth. Plants grew huge and lush, a jungle nearly impenetrable, but he followed the heartbreaking sound to the western corner. She was sitting on the floor, her back to the wall, knees drawn up, her head resting on them, crying as if her heart was broken.

He stood there watching her for a moment, feeling as if he might shatter seeing her utter despair and misery. He took a deep breath and looked down at his hands. They were actually trembling. He'd never had that happen before. Too much emotion was paralyzing. He couldn't make a mistake and he knew it. This was a defining moment and he had too much at stake.

He couldn't force her, even though a part of him wanted to lock her up until she understood they belonged together. It couldn't be that way. She had to want to be with him. It had to be her choice, not his. This was the most difficult moment of his life. He didn't want to lose, because if he lost her now, he would lose everything.

He skirted around the last row of tomatoes and came to a stop in front of her. She knew he was there, he actually felt her sudden awareness, but she didn't look up. Gavriil sank down beside her. Close but not touching. He wanted her to feel his warmth radiating toward her, but he didn't want her to feel he was forcing her to connect with him. She had to take that step herself.

"I don't want you to go, Lexi. I want you to choose me. Stay with me. I know I'm not much of a prize. I know my faults. I need a commitment from you. I need that, Lexi. Not marriage if you don't want it. If you give your word, that will be enough."

She didn't respond or lift her head. Her soft crying continued. It was all he could do not to lift his hand to her hair.

"We're always going to have these moments of doubts, but if we both make that commitment, we'll always know the other will stand with us through them. I need to know you'll stand with me. I've got this hole a mile deep inside of me, and only you manage to fill it. No one else. There's never going to be anyone else. Neither of us is perfect, but together I know we can be whole. I want you to choose me, Lexi. Give yourself to me. I'll always cherish you, I promise."

She lifted her head and leaned back against the wall, looking at him with tear-filled eyes. She looked so sad his heart hurt.

"You're the only reason I'm still alive, Lexi. Don't give up on us."

She closed her eyes briefly. "I can't leave you. I tried, but I can't. I don't know why. I know it isn't even fair to you. It's a selfish need I can't overcome. You're like the flame and I'm a moth fluttering around you. This is going to be bad for you and I can't stop. I can't make it stop. I feel like you woke me up and now I can't live without you. I can't go back to being alone all the time, but I have nothing to give you."

"Isn't that for me to decide?"

"I don't know if it is, Gavriil. I feel a need to protect you. You won't protect yourself. Someone has to look out for you."

"Then don't go. I've never been in love either, and it scares the hell out of me too, but I know it's real. When I touch you, kiss you, or just look at you, I know what I'm feeling is the real thing and I don't want to let that go."

"How long can this last if I can't give you what you gave me tonight?"

There it was. He was on very shaky ground. A minefield. She had a thing about equality when it came to their relationship. She wasn't going to let him be the one always giving and she was absolutely certain she couldn't give back.

"Do you think in all my years of being an operative, I haven't had a woman sucking my cock?" His voice was harsh, and she winced, but he couldn't help it. Emotions were raw and painful, far worse than physical pain.

"That's not what I want from you and it will never be what I want from you. Not ever. I don't want you in my life so I can use your body. I'm good at seduction, Lexi. I can go to a bar and pick up a woman and use her if that's what I wanted. I want love. When you touch me, I feel love in your hands. When you kiss me, I taste love. I'm not in a rush. I'm enjoying all the firsts you've given me."

"You're so certain, Gavriil." Her eyes had gone very dark again. "I wish I could be like you, but I feel so confused. I feel like I'm running in circles with you. I don't know how to feel right now. I don't ever want you to look at me with disappointment."

"I'm holding on by a thread, *solnyshko moya*." He hesitated. "Do you know what that means? *Solnyshko moya?* It means 'my sun.' That's what you are to me. The sun. The world. All the bright, good things in the world right here in this tiny little package. My world was dark. I lived in the shadows, and damn it all, I belonged there. I wasn't a good man until I found you. You make me a better man. I'm fighting for my life here, Lexi. I need you to fight for me, not against me."

"That's what I'm doing, Gavriil. I am. I want you to be happy. You're a good man whether you think so or not. I don't want to think about you with another woman. I want to be the one to be with you, but . . ." She trailed off, clearly miserable.

He reached over and threaded his fingers through hers, drawing her hand to his heart. "Just say yes and stop worrying about whether or not you can perform sexually. I can assure you, we're going to be fine in that area. *Both* of us. It isn't going to take much to arouse me, Lexi, not when you're the first and only woman who can do it naturally, without even touching me. You have no idea what an aphrodisiac that is. It's only been a couple of days. Give yourself time."

"It's not like I did a very good job of saving you, Gavriil," she said, her smile a little watery. "From yourself or from me."

"You have no idea what you've given me, Lexi. Say it to me. I need the words, the commitment. If you say it to me, I know you'll stay and work out anything with me."

She bit down hard on her lower lip. He brought her knuckles to his mouth, looking her in the eyes.

"You're so worried about the sex. It's so trivial compared to the other things we're going to have to work out, things you haven't thought about."

Her eyebrow went up. "Like what?"

"Like my personality. Who and what I am. Do you really believe the wolf is going to turn into the lamb? I'm not an easy man, and I'm very dominant. You've lived with submission and it was ugly. I'm going to make mistakes and trigger memories. I have to live with that fear and it's far more real and worrisome than whether every time we try to make love we succeed."

His teeth scraped back and forth very gently over her knuckles. She blinked several times at him before she shook her head, a small smile touching her mouth briefly.

"You're always very gentle with me, Gavriil. Always."

"Because you haven't crossed me over anything important. You know I'm going to hunt these men down and kill them, one by one if I have to, until they leave us alone. You're not exactly happy about it, but I *have* to do it. It's not something I want to do, it's a must. Any threat to you will be eliminated and you're going to object every time."

She leaned her head against his shoulder with a little sigh. "Can you imagine two more screwed up people? Seriously, Gavriil. What are we going to do?"

"Stay here and commit to me. We'll work the farm together and learn to laugh and love together. As much as it's all a first for me, it is for you as well. There's no urgent timetable. Sex isn't going to glue us together, love is. We have to build a solid foundation and work from there. I intend to treat you so wonderfully you won't ever want to walk out on me again."

"I was *saving* you, not walking out on you."

"It feels the same. I'm not going to play the I-need-you-in-my-life-to-survive card—even though it's the truth. Don't do it again to me. Stay. Say it. Look me in the eye and say it to me. Your word that you'll stick with me through everything."

"Do you really want me? Knowing everything about me?"

"You're the only one who can make me whole. I want you with every breath in my body. I need you that much, Lexi."

She lifted her head and looked into his eyes, her green gaze searching his carefully. The rain wept on the glass rooftop. The wind wailed at the glass walls. He held his breath. The dark, ugly place inside of him that was a hollow hole waited to swallow him.

She smiled. "Then I guess we're going to work it all out together. I'm in it for the long haul because I want to be with you more than anything else."

Air moved through his lungs. The dark hollow place receded, shrinking away from her light, not daring to compete with her. There was no competition, not when she loved him enough to try to overcome her fears. Not when she couldn't leave him. Not when she cried for him.

Love was damn painful. She was stamped into his bones, into every organ of his body. There was no way out for him. He wanted her to love him with that same intensity. Their love didn't have to be the way it was portrayed in storybooks. They burned hot and bright, not just for the chemistry, but because two broken souls who had no hope found a way to be whole. He would protect her with every means he'd been taught or he'd learned over a lifetime of brutal lessons.

"Come on, *solnyshko moya*, it's too cold out here for you. And Kiss was really uncomfortable. I could tell by her breathing. Let's go boil water or do whatever it is one does when their dog is about to give birth."

She let him pull her up and then stopped abruptly, tugging on his hand until he stopped. "Wait. You don't know how to help her? Do you know what to do?"

He grinned at her. "I know how to kill a man a thousand different ways. You need that, *angel moy*, and I'm your man. Dogs or anything else giving birth, I'm not an encyclopedia of knowledge."

He felt weak with relief now that the crisis had passed. He wasn't certain how to feel about the by-product of loving her so much. He was a man confident in every part of his life, yet she'd reduced him to something close to desperation. He felt vulnerable and exposed. There was no way he could ever allow any other living person to see him in such bad shape.

He tugged her to him, needing to hold her against him. She went into his arms and they clung to each other, just holding on, as if they had survived a terrible battle. He felt as if they had, as if he'd fought a war and come out victorious but exhausted. He nuzzled the top of her head with his chin.

"Don't ever do that to me again, Lexi. I don't know what I'd do. I don't know how to feel emotion. It's all or nothing with me. You're my all."

"I gave you my word," she replied, her voice muffled against his shirt.

He could tell she felt as exhausted as he did. "Come on, *solnyshko moya*, we may have a long night ahead of us. Let's go check on Kiss."

The storm had let up so that only a fine rain came down, turning the sky a dazzling silver. He tucked her beneath the shoulder of his injured arm, leaving his unhurt arm free. He was equally adept at using either hand to shoot or throw a knife and probably wouldn't have a problem because the injury was nearly healed, but he wasn't taking any chances.

"The farm is so beautiful at night," Lexi said. "I love sitting outside and just looking at all the trees and plants. I can breathe out here." She could also see enemies coming at her.

"I've been thinking about Lucia," Gavriil said. "She was very interested in the dogs. It would make Kiss uncomfortable to have her watch as she gave birth, but I think we could get Kiss to accept her near the puppies and she can help to socialize them. She needs something to immerse herself in."

Lexi glanced up at his face and then touched his jaw. "Do you hear yourself? You're looking out for a traumatized child when you barely know her. You're a good man whether you think you are or not." She flashed him a little smile.

His heart reacted as well as his somersaulting stomach. That was how far gone he was. A little ridiculous for a man like him, but no one was around to witness it and the night didn't care. The rain veiled his expression from her. It was difficult to admit how completely mesmerized he was by her. Just the way she moved, a turn of her head, a quick smile and a flash of her green eyes and he was lost.

"Gavriil?" Her hand slid down his arm and she linked her fingers with his. "I don't want you to think I was running away from you or running out on you. I wasn't. I think you deserve so much more than you may get. At least that was my thought process, as flawed as it may have been. I was leaving for the right reasons."

"There aren't any right reasons, Lexi," he said gruffly. "There never will be. Just talk to me. We'll find a way to work anything out. We'll never be like other people, but it doesn't matter. We'll have our own world and the people who love us will accept whatever that is."

"You give me confidence," she said, glancing up at his face. "I don't have a lot of confidence other than with my plants. Especially when it comes to being a woman."

He led her up the porch steps to the front door. "That's exactly where you should have the most confidence, *solnyshko moya.*"

She went up onto her toes and brushed a kiss on his chin. "Because I matter to you and you look at me the way you do, you give me confidence."

He reached past her to open the door for her. Drago and Kiss both rushed them. "They prefer to be with people. These aren't backyard dogs and no one can ever make the mistake of thinking one will be, just because they're large."

"I'll have to make certain Judith knows that," Lexi said. "Her house is beautiful and she's a meticulous housekeeper. Thomas is going to want one, but Judith will balk at the size. You didn't introduce them yet, did you?"

He shook his head, patting both dogs. He slid his hand gently down Kiss's side to her belly. "She's definitely in labor. She shouldn't be up and around. Let's get her back into the closet."

"I was surprised to find you'd made the whelping box," Lexi said. "I did my best by putting old sheets and towels in it and making certain the box was in the darkest part of the closet. It's a big closet and I think she'll be comfortable in it."

"She'll have her own room," he said, making his way back to the bedroom. "You don't keep any clothes in it."

She shrugged. "I don't need many clothes. I work most of the time and sit on my porch enjoying the sunset or visit with one of my sisters. When I go to the market, I wear my work clothes."

"I'm fond of your work clothes." He sank down onto the floor beside the closet when Kiss moved inside and lay down, panting.

"You're going to sit up all night with her, aren't you? I'll get us something to drink and warm some towels just in case."

"This could take hours," he warned. "You'll want to be comfortable." He tugged at his boots, set them aside and placed his weapons close.

Her laughter bubbled up, a soft melody that sent fingers of desire brushing down his chest to his belly, lower still so that his groin stirred. It was a gentle overtaking, unexpected and tender. It was . . . good.

"I can't believe you always have a gun about an inch from your fingertips."

He pulled the knife from his boot and showed it to her, baring his teeth at her. "I believe in being prepared."

"You're such a Boy Scout."

"I was going for wolf."

Her laughter drifted back to him as she left the room to get the things necessary to spend the night on the floor with the dog.

Kiss delivered six puppies—two females and the rest males. It took her most of the night, and Gavriil and Lexi sat with her the entire time. Lexi helped breathe life into one struggling little one when it seemed as if they might lose him. They rubbed him with a warm towel and showed him to Kiss, telling her how wonderful she was.

Twice, Kiss laid her head in Gavriil's lap as he petted and encouraged her, telling her how amazing she was. Lexi looked at him with stars in her eyes. "I don't understand why you can't see yourself the way I do."

"Silly woman. I don't understand why you can't see yourself the way I do." He repeated her words back to her and then leaned over and kissed her. "It doesn't matter, as long as you can see me."

14

GAVRIIL opened his eyes, instantly awake. Beside him, Lexi lay curled up, exhausted from staying up all night. He smoothed his hand over her hair as he slipped the other under the pillow to grasp his gun. He had never thought to wake up like this, his woman soft and warm against him. Every protective instinct he had welled up along with the feeling of love.

Lexi had laughed and cried when each puppy had entered the world, looking up at him with sparkling eyes. Sharing the birth, something he'd never experienced before, made him feel even closer to her. Each moment spent in her company only made him certain they belonged together.

Drago's large head pushed against him. The dog stood close to the bed, alerting silently as Gavriil had taught him.

"I feel them," Gavriil assured, and put his hand on the dog's head once to acknowledge the animal had done his job. He signaled Drago to the door and slipped from the bed.

Lexi turned over immediately, her lashes lifting, her gaze colliding with his. There was fear in her eyes when she realized he was dressing fast and he had his gun out and close to him.

"Everything's all right," he assured her hastily. "We've got company is all. I think your sheriff and one other. I believe my youngest brother has come with him. The others are on the way."

She sat up and pushed at her tumbling hair impatiently. "What others?"

She looked beautiful. Sexy. Her eyes were large, still drowsy. Her hair was gorgeous, a thick mass of auburn silk, falling in waves around her to pool on the sheets. He had a wild urge to crawl back into bed and make love to her for hours. She was all soft skin and bedroom eyes. He found her impossible to resist.

He moved around the bed and bent to brush a kiss across her upturned mouth. Her eyes widened and her lashes fluttered.

"My other brothers. No one is going to come onto the property without the land alerting all of us. Can't you feel it? The shifting?"

"You came," she pointed out, making a little face at him. "There was no shifting to warn me."

"The earth moved for me the moment I laid eyes on you," he said truthfully. He kissed her again, this time a little more possessively, his tongue teasing the seam of her mouth. He wanted to taste her, the cool forest that could bring passion or peace.

His fingers curled around the nape of her neck, his thumb tilting her chin up while his mouth coaxed hers to open for him. Her lips trembled once and then her hands came up to his shoulders and her lips parted.

There it was. Paradise. The heat and fire swept into him, burning over and into him. She was there inside him, the taste of her addicting, his need deepening. There was no living without this woman ever again. Now that he knew what life was with her in it, now that he had a home, something he hadn't known he craved until—Lexi.

He whispered her name as he pressed his forehead against hers. "So this is what love feels like." His fingers tightened possessively around the back of her neck, the pad of his thumb caressing her soft skin.

Her lashes fluttered, eyes going a vibrant green. Her mouth curved into a soft smile. "You say the most beautiful things, Gavriil. You should have been a poet."

He brushed a kiss over each eye and slipped his gun into the waistband at the small of his back before straightening. "I'm a poet with a knife or gun."

She drew her knees up and dropped her chin on the top of them, smiling at him. Watching him. Caressing him with soft eyes. "You're going to go out there and act all tough, aren't you?"

"That's my intention, yes." He slipped a knife into his boot. It took discipline to keep his face pure stone when she made him want to laugh.

She made his life fun—another first. He looked forward to every moment in her company. He could see the world with new eyes, not with his jaded, cynical vision. She had given him a life. Existing in a dark world of violence was no life. He had known that all along, but she'd awakened him from his complacency.

He hadn't known he needed saving or that there was a giant hole in him that needed to be filled to bring him to life. He wasn't certain how he'd gotten so lucky, but he intended to keep making her happy for the rest of her life.

"I'll get dressed and make some coffee. I brought back a coffeepot and coffee from Airiana's."

"Thanks. And if this sheriff upsets you, I'll throw him out, just give me a sign."

Her laughter teased his nerve endings, sending little darts of fire racing over his skin and into his belly. "Everything about you makes me happy," he admitted. "Just listening to the sound of your voice. Looking at you."

She blushed, clearly not used to compliments. He resolved to give her as many as possible without sounding like a lovesick idiot. He didn't mind that she thought he should have been a poet, as long as no one else thought it.

"Go before I turn so red I can never recover," she said, waving him away.

He laughed and went to the closet to peek in at Kiss and the puppies. "She's going to have to do her business soon. I'll take her out back when my brothers get here."

She pressed her lips together and shook her head. "Seriously, Gavriil, I can be alone with Jonas Harrington. He's a good man and he's been a friend to us."

"I'm sure he has. Ilya likes him as well, but I don't know him and he doesn't know me. My brothers do know me and what I'm capable of. They won't let anything happen to you."

"Like tripping and falling on the living room rug?"

"There isn't a rug. If you trip and fall, someone's going to pay."

She rolled her eyes at him and waved him out again. "Give me a couple of minutes to take a shower. I'll be right out."

"Great." He couldn't help teasing her. "You'll come out smelling like the early morning after a fresh rain. In a closed room surrounded by men. I'm going to need more than one gun."

She laughed softly. "You're impossible. Get moving, I think they're at the door."

"They're still standing at the edge of the walkway. Ilya's afraid I'll come out shooting so he's being polite and keeping the sheriff busy until the others show up and I come out and greet them."

"You have such a foul reputation, Gavriil."

"And totally deserved." He infused his voice with pride.

She wasn't impressed. She threw a pillow at him. He'd never played before. At least he couldn't remember doing so. Happiness was foreign to him. He moved through the shadows like a robot. There was no laughter, and certainly no fun. He didn't wake up in the morning looking forward to the day.

Her soft, teasing laughter followed him as he went to the door. She was truly his sun. His world. She was home. She'd gotten inside of him—into his bones—into his soul. When she smiled at him, the shadows of his other life receded so far he couldn't see them anymore.

He had to get away from the potency of her company before he ran the risk of making a fool of himself in front of the others. He didn't want to appear vulnerable, and loving Lexi was all encompassing. The men coming to the house were experts at reading others. Loving her left him completely exposed.

"Don't forget to keep the dogs locked in the bedroom." His voice had gone gruff, emotions too close. "They'll be nervous and protective with the puppies. Drago is very intelligent and highly trained, but this is a new situation for both of us."

"I have heard that dogs take on the traits of their owners." Deliberately she looked at the male Black Russian Terrier. "I can see the resemblance in that focused stare targeting victims and smiling with his teeth."

He bared his teeth at her and then left her to go meet the local sheriff. He moved through the house in silence, allowing the familiar man he'd been for so many years to take him over. He slipped into that persona easily, the fit exact. It was easy to blur his image a little as he stepped through the doorway, pushing energy into several directions around him to give him the time to move to the protection of the column before the sheriff and Ilya even knew he was on the porch.

"You're here early," he greeted.

Ilya turned slowly. His brother smiled at him and put a hand on Harrington's shoulder, a gesture meant to show Gavriil neither had a weapon drawn and that he was friends with the sheriff.

"Not that early," Ilya denied. "It's already light."

"Just barely," Harrington said.

"You just wanted to stay home with the baby," Ilya accused, as they came up the walkway to the steps leading to the porch. "It's just the fog."

The sheriff extended his hand toward Gavriil, his eyes steady, trying to read Gavriil. His handshake was firm, but he didn't try impressing with his strength.

"Jonas Harrington," he said briefly.

"Gavriil Prakenskii," Gavriil identified himself, watching the sheriff closely.

His blue eyes flickered just a moment. A muscle jerked in his jaw, but he didn't even glance at Ilya.

"Of course. I should have known." Jonas glanced at Ilya. "No wonder you were so insistent on joining me this morning."

Ilya shrugged, clearly unrepentant.

Gavriil kept his eyes on the sheriff as first Levi and then Thomas emerged from the surrounding foliage and joined them on the porch. Max sauntered nonchalantly around the house.

"Looks like I'm outnumbered," Jonas quipped. He didn't seem upset, in fact he seemed happy for Ilya, smiling as the other men approached them.

Gavriil had to respect the man. Five Prakenskiis in the same space was more than intimidating, yet Harrington didn't bat an eye and it was very obvious he knew who they were even though his brothers used different identities.

Max, Thomas and Levi stared at their youngest brother.

Levi looked a little choked up. "You grew up," he said. "I'm Lev. I go by Levi Hammond, and I married Rikki Sitmore."

Ilya took his hand. "The sea urchin diver."

Levi nodded. "Do you know her?"

Ilya shook his head. "Rikki has always kept to herself."

Gavriil kept his attention mainly on the sheriff, who had turned around to watch the brothers introduce themselves. He'd turned his back completely to Gavriil and that told him Harrington, who looked tough as nails, wasn't an operative. He would never have trusted an unknown, not even with Ilya watching his back.

"Stefan." Thomas was next. "I go by the name of Thomas. Thomas Vincent, and I married Judith Henderson. She owns an art store in the village. I bought the gallery."

"It's good to see you," Ilya said. "I'm married to Joley Drake."

"I actually do read the tabloids at the grocery store," Thomas said, nudging Levi. They grinned at one another. "You sure do look pretty."

Ilya growled low in his throat. Both brothers laughed at him.

Max stuck out his hand. "Maxim—Max. Airiana is my fiancée."

"You have the four children Jonas told me about. Your . . . nephew and nieces."

"That's right."

"How are the children doing?" Jonas asked.

"It's an adjustment after losing their parents and sister," Max said. "We've gotten them into counseling, although it's a process." He glanced around. "Benito likes to shadow me, so no one shoot him if he sneaks up on us." He looked up at Gavriil as he cautioned them all.

Gavriil bared his teeth at his brother, his eyes flat and cold, uncaring that Harrington suddenly swung around and caught him in the act.

"I think Benito learned his manners," Levi said, with a quick grin in Gavriil's direction.

"Scary kid, isn't he, Gavriil?" Thomas said.

Gavriil leveled a look at his brother and turned and went into the house, leaving the door open so they all could follow him, all the while keeping the lot of them in his field of vision without appearing to do so. He was acutely aware of the sheriff staring after him curiously.

When they entered the house, Gavriil waved them all toward chairs, a casual gesture that clearly showed he was comfortable in his role as host in Lexi's home. He wanted to immediately establish that not only did he belong there but he was at home there.

He took the chair that allowed him the best view of the room. He noticed Levi glancing around, clearly looking for Lexi. Twice he exchanged an uneasy look with Thomas. He deliberately allowed them to consider that the big bad wolf might have eaten the little lamb. He wasn't the least surprised when Levi gave him a cool stare.

"Where's Lexi?"

"She'll be right out," he said, noncommittally. "Ilya mentioned you and your wife just had a baby, Jonas. Congratulations."

Jonas smiled, but it didn't quite reach his eyes. He looked friendly enough, but clearly, with all the brothers showing up, he was suspicious. "Yes. She's beautiful, thank you." He looked around the room at the men who he knew to be highly trained operatives. Five of them, all in the same room. All brothers. "Would someone like to tell me what the hell is going on? Ilya?"

Ilya shrugged. "If I knew, I would have told you. When I heard you were headed this way, I wanted to come along for obvious reasons."

"Levi?" Jonas prompted.

Levi shook his head. "We have a warning system on the property and when someone shows up, we all check it out. I had no idea you were coming."

Max nodded. "Airiana's work could be considered dangerous, and we wanted to make certain everyone living on the farm would be safe. When the system goes off, we all come running. You probably know more than we do."

"I see." Jonas didn't sound convinced. "Lexi called me late last night and asked me to come out this morning. She said a threat had been made and recorded on the farm line?" He made it a question.

Gavriil nodded slowly. "Yes. I answered one of the calls, thinking to take an order, and the man on the other end threatened some dire consequences if we all continued to harbor Jezebel." Gavriil stretched his legs in front of him in a casual pose as if the entire matter was inconsequential.

Jonas raised his eyebrow. "Did Lexi know this person or why they would be threatening one of the women on the farm?"

Gavriil heard Lexi come out of the bedroom and stop abruptly. She definitely had overheard Jonas's question. She didn't move. He rose immediately. "Excuse me. I'll go find her. Levi, you know your way around a kitchen, would you mind making coffee? And tea for Lexi? The dog had her puppies last night so we were up very late. I didn't have time to make any this morning."

Levi pushed himself up, using the wide arms of the chair. "Sure. I can make a decent cup of coffee."

Gavriil nodded his head briefly and walked from the room, keeping each stride measured and deliberate, although everything in him urged him to run to her. He found her exactly where he thought she'd be—on the floor. Her fist was jammed in her mouth, although she was struggling to breathe.

He reached down and lifted her into his arms, ignoring the sudden flash of pain from his injured biceps. Cradling her against his chest, he went on down the hall to the back of the house, far from the others. He couldn't use the kitchen door because he'd sent his brother there. The only other exit was through the atrium. He yanked the door open and took her into the wild jungle of plants.

Lexi drew in deep shuddering breaths, clinging to him.

He looked down into her face. She was embarrassed, but still having trouble getting her pounding heart and labored breathing under control.

"If you aren't careful, woman," he said sternly, "you're going to completely blow the image I've worked so hard on." He was very aware of the tiny birds flitting from branch to branch as he moved through the leaves and flowers to the door leading outside to the wraparound porch.

A small laugh escaped Lexi and she buried her face against his shoulder. Her body relaxed a little bit more, curling into him. He stepped out into the open air. The fog touched their faces and wrapped them in a silvery cloak.

"Just take a deep breath and look around you. I'm always amazed when I see the plants and the flowers, the crops growing the way they do here. Even the trees are healthy and seem happy." He sank down into a large chair facing the forest, settling her into his lap.

Lexi lifted her head obediently and looked around her. Almost at once he noticed a difference in her breathing. His thumb moved over her inner wrist, stroking her pounding pulse with little soothing caresses.

"I can handle the sheriff for you, if you need me to, Lexi, but I don't think you do. I think you can walk into your own living room and tell him about these men—and women—who are a threat to you. Levi, Thomas and Max are here along with Ilya. You're family to them. They will protect you with their lives. And then there's me. We aren't going to talk about what I am or what I'd do to keep you safe."

She pressed her hand to the side of his jaw, looking at him with her forest green eyes, always so loving when she looked at him. "I'm not afraid of them. It's just memories. They're so terrible and I get caught up in them, like I'm still there, still that child trapped and beaten. I've got this amazing place, my wonderful sisters and you. I'm not beaten down, but it feels the same when I go there in my mind."

"I can understand that. I rarely allow myself to think of those earlier years of brutal training when there was no hope and no way out." He smoothed his hand down her long sweep of hair. "We're here now and we're dealing with everything together," he reminded her. "Even the memories."

She lay back in his arms, nuzzling his chest with her face. "You're always so good at making me feel like I'm not alone. I appreciate you sharing your own experiences with me. Very few men would do that."

"We're in this together. Our way, remember?"

She nodded. "I'm okay now. I can face this. I knew it might come back on me some day, and I'm glad it did with you and your brothers here rather than just me trying to keep my sisters safe. And now we've got the children."

He noticed the way all of the women and even his brothers considered the children as if they were a part of every household. He was beginning to understand the infrastructure of the farm and the way they were all connected to make their family work.

"We've got to go back inside. I don't trust that Drago won't come through the door and eat the sheriff while we're gone, especially if he gets it in his head to wander around looking for you. I think they all have the impression I've locked you up somewhere or worse, murdered you, buried your body in the forest and taken over your house."

"Gee. I wonder how they could possibly have gotten that idea." She laughed softly and shook her head. "You really were having fun in there playing the part of the big bad wolf, weren't you?"

"What do you mean, 'playing the part'? I *am* the big bad wolf and they all know it. You're the only one who doesn't."

She laughed and wrapped her arms around his neck, looking into his eyes. "You're a wolf, all right, but you're mine and I think you're amazing." She leaned in and kissed him.

Her lips brushed over his. Once. Twice. His heart stuttered. Her tongue teased the seam of his mouth so that he opened to her. His belly somersaulted. It was the first time she'd voluntarily initiated any contact between them that might be considered sensual—and it was sensual. Her mouth was a hot paradise impossible not to get lost in. Fire raced over him, spread through his veins in a rush toward his groin.

His fist bunched in the silk of her hair, anchoring her to him, his mouth insistent, possessive, taking command of hers. She didn't pull away in spite of the sudden surge of aggression on his part. If anything, she melted into him, kissing him back, pouring herself into him, giving herself to him.

Her reaction was so unexpected, so shocking to him, the gift of trust she suddenly gave to him. Love for her flooded his heart and mind, burst through his soul until he felt nearly overwhelmed with emotion. He was in unfamiliar territory with Lexi, but he wanted her trust more than anything else.

The world around him receded until there was only the woman in his arms, pouring her love into him like some secret crystal stream only she knew how to create. She wiped out every ugly memory of every depravity he'd witnessed over so many brutal years. She was innocence and everything good he had never thought to know and she was his, right there, giving herself to him.

He kissed her over and over, reveling in the fact that she responded with eagerness. His mouth was hard and demanding, and she kissed him just as thoroughly as he kissed her. She didn't hold back any part of herself, but melted into his skin and bones, hot and wild, every bit on the edge of control as he was.

He had to be the one to stop, to make certain neither of them pushed too far. The wildfire was already pushing to the very edges of control, spreading through both of them like a storm. He heard the roar of thunder in his ears, felt the burn along every nerve ending, a sizzling hot need that rushed from every part of his body to center in his groin.

"Lexi." He breathed her name. "You have no idea what you mean to me." Or what she did to him—and he didn't want her to know—not yet.

Her gaze drifted over his face, and for the first time he saw a hint of possession there, and that look only fed the fire in his body. She was beginning to stake her own claim on him whether she realized it or not. He hadn't known until that moment how important it was to him. He'd never seen that look in a woman's eyes before. From a predatory temptress—yes—but not out of love.

"Are you even going to acknowledge that you know me when we go back inside?" Lexi asked, a mischievous light gleaming in her eyes.

"That's a good question," he replied, deliberately thoughtful.

She leaned forward and unexpectedly bit him on the earlobe. The small sting traveled like an arrow straight to his cock. She was dangerous now, a sensuous woman who had no idea how tempting she was. She was being playful, and all he could do was try to tamp down his sexual response.

"Ow." He massaged his ear. "Fine, I suppose I can give you a nod or something, but don't expect kisses. That's out."

She raised her eyebrow. "Really? None? Not even a stolen one?"

She made a little moue with her lips, and instantly he had the urge to kiss her all over again. "You really are dangerous, woman." He caught her upper arms in a hard grip and shoved her backward. "Get off my lap."

She gave a little shocked cry and grabbed him with both hands, clutching his shoulders to keep from falling. He laughed and dragged her closer.

"Stop playing with fire, *solnyshko moya*, we've got company and we're neglecting them. Right now I can guarantee you, the lot of them are trying to find excuses to go through the house and make certain you're still alive."

"Your brothers won't think that." She slipped off his lap to stand close to him, between his thighs, her hands on his shoulders. "Don't worry so much about your big bad reputation. If someone ever sees the truth about you, I promise to protect you." She brushed a kiss along his forehead. "You're a good man, Gavriil Prakenskii, and I'm crazy about you."

She wasn't near enough crazy about him, but he intended to see to it that she had every reason to become more so with each passing day. She moved him like no other person had ever done in his life. He had never spent five minutes alone with another human being unless it was absolutely necessary. He couldn't get enough of spending time in her company—just one more sign that he was that far gone.

"Come on," he said abruptly, too overloaded from emotion and needing to shut down for a few minutes. "We've got work to do."

She flashed him a smile but took his outstretched hand and tugged as if she was really helping him up. He found her fingers threaded with his and wasn't certain how to gracefully take his hand back before he was anywhere near his brothers.

They slipped back through the atrium into the main part of the house. As they started down the hall, he felt the slightest tremor go through her body. Glancing down, he could only see the top of her head. Her hair spilled around her face and her lashes veiled her eyes.

"Lexi, seriously, you don't have to do this," he murmured softly.

She let go of his hand. "Of course I do. And so do you. You don't like it any more than I do, you're just better at knowing how to keep your feelings a secret."

"It's an art form." She was absolutely correct in her assessment. He was either slipping up or she was so connected and in tune with him that she was becoming adept at reading him. "Go ahead of me. I'll be right behind you."

Lexi would take the attention away from him if she went first. His brothers and the sheriff would be assessing her health and state of mind instead of watching him look at her. It would give him the moments needed to slip back into his much more familiar role.

Jonas Harrington stood up the moment Lexi entered the room. Gavriil's brothers followed suit. Lexi looked a little startled at the sign of respect and she glanced nervously back at Gavriil. He suppressed a groan, but kept his features expressionless, even when he reached out and skimmed a finger down her back to steady her.

Levi, Thomas and Max were all watching him, not Lexi. He should have known. He gave them his stone face, but kept his hand in the small of Lexi's back to remind her they were in this together.

"Lexi, it's good to see you," Jonas said. "Hannah sends her regards and said to stop by to meet our baby if you get the chance. She wanted to come but Libby wanted her resting. It was a bit of a tough birth."

Gavriil respected the man more and more, although he was leery of him. He gave something personal to Lexi to put her at ease. His smile was genuine and he kept his voice pitched low and sincere. He would be hell on wheels in an interrogation room.

Lexi didn't take a step back, but she leaned into Gavriil's palm even as she extended her hand to the sheriff. "Thank you for coming."

"I brought you a cup of tea, Lexi," Levi said, closing in on one side of her.

Thomas stepped close as well, so that when Lexi shook Jonas's hand she was surrounded on three sides by the Prakenskii brothers.

"We might as well be comfortable," Gavriil said. "Lexi, why don't you sit down over there." He swept his hand toward the chair he preferred she sit in. *Take the yellow striped one, Lexi. I have a complete view of the entire room as well as the window from the one beside it.*

Lexi nodded, took the steaming tea mug with a nod of thanks toward Levi, and immediately sank into the chair Gavriil had indicated. "Congratulations on the birth of your daughter, Jonas. You and Hannah must be so happy."

"She's beautiful," Jonas said. "Although she sleeps most of the time. I hold her anyway." He flashed an engaging grin.

Ilya leaned toward Lexi. "Someone threatened you? Recently?" His gaze shifted to Gavriil. Clearly it had occurred to him that Gavriil's presence might be the reason for the phone call.

Lexi shifted her body just a little toward Gavriil. She didn't look at him, but every man in the room caught that small sign of distress and knew she looked toward him for comfort. It was all he could do to remain aloof, to not reach out and put his hand over hers. He kept his face pure stone, his eyes cool and hooded.

"Yes. On the farm line." She glanced at Jonas. "When I was eight, I was kidnapped, taken out of my home to a compound where a man everyone called the Reverend performed a ceremony marrying me to one of his lieutenants. Basically, he was one of their enforcers. He was in his forties and he was very cruel. I worked on their farm and was held prisoner until I was seventeen. I managed to escape. The compound was raided and many of those in power were arrested. In retaliation, the cult sent their enforcers to murder my family. I wasn't home. They're all dead."

Lexi didn't look at any of them when she relayed the story she must have told many times to police and prosecutors. She looked into her teacup as if it might save her. Her voice didn't waver, but it was extremely soft.

Levi curled his fingers into a fist and sat staring in silence at her face. Thomas swore under his breath. Max hit the arm of the couch with exploding rage. Jonas sat very still, his gaze never leaving Lexi.

Gavriil couldn't stop himself. He had to touch her. She held herself utterly still, as if she feared moving would shatter her. She looked fragile, vulnerable, and he detested that anyone else could see her that way. Both of her hands curled around the teacup. He pressed his thumb into the center of his palm and then stroked caresses over the spot.

Her gaze shifted toward him just for a moment and then went back to her tea.

"To make a long story short," she continued, "I think they found me. I don't know how, but they know I'm here on the farm. To make matters worse, I'm in the witness protection program and I don't want to call them and have to leave my life here."

"That's not going to happen," Levi said.

"Tell me everything," Jonas prompted, ignoring Levi's declaration.

"Caine, that's the man who I was forced to marry, called me Jezebel. He said I was a whore and a liar, a bad woman who couldn't be trusted enough to be left alone. In every message I played, the speaker said the farm was harboring Jezebel. I only recognized one voice. They had several compounds scattered around the United States and they moved us at various times. Each compound had enforcers who punished members for breaking rules or perceived faults. They killed when told to. The man whose voice I recognized worked with the Reverend as one of his personal enforcers."

"The Reverend as in RJ?" Ilya glanced at Jonas. "Is this the same man who came after Joley? He harassed and stalked her." He switched his gaze to Lexi. "He was here, in Sea Haven. Did you know that? Did you see him?"

Lexi carefully put down the teacup. Her hands were shaking. Gavriil glanced at his youngest brother. *Watch your tone. You sound almost accusatory.*

Ilya shook his head. "Lexi, I'm sorry, that came out wrong. I didn't mean to imply that you could have done anything to stop the Reverend."

"I knew he was here," she admitted in a low tone. "The entire world knew. It was all over television. I never left the farm. I didn't dare. If he or any of the men he traveled with saw me, they would have killed me. I thought about leaving but I couldn't do it. I just stayed out of sight, and when he died, I thought the danger was over."

"If you had gone to the police then," Jonas said gently, "perhaps we could have arrested him and tried him for his crimes."

"And the other cult members would have murdered my sisters here on the farm. I lost one family, I wasn't about to lose another," Lexi said. "Even this time, I thought long and hard about whether or not to call you."

"Why did you?" Jonas asked.

"Because of the men sitting here in this room. They matter to me. If the cult members try to kill my sisters or me, they'll be the ones trying to protect us and I don't want them in trouble."

Max shifted toward Lexi. "You should have come to us, honey. We have a fortress here. With Airiana working out of her home, we've got the ability and the sanction to stop anybody who threatens any of you."

Jonas shook his head. "You aren't sanctioned to kill. Not here in Sea Haven. That's not going to happen."

Max didn't reply; he sat back and folded his arms across his chest.

Jonas swore. "Don't tell me the four of you clowns are working for the United States government. You're Russian citizens."

"Only Gavriil is," Levi pointed out. "At the moment. That could change. You never know."

"Leave it to the police," Jonas warned.

Levi shrugged. "If they come here after Lexi or any of us, we have the right to defend ourselves."

Jonas leaned back in his chair and looked at Lexi. "Do you have a name for me?"

"Frost. Benjamin Frost. He's about fifty-five and he's been in the service. I think he was a mercenary for a while. They say the Reverend recruited him personally. Whatever these men liked, he gave them and fed their egos until they would do anything for him. He created a world where they behaved in any way they wanted without interference."

"So if you were a sadist or a pedophile, he provided the women and children and the environment," Jonas said.

Lexi swallowed and nodded. "This is very difficult for me to talk about. I don't know how many of them are left, but the enforcers and the Reverend's lieutenants were the worst. I don't think too many of the others were violent. They were mostly sheep following the ones they perceived as strong."

"When you and the others bought the farm with Blythe," Jonas said, "I had you investigated. I couldn't find anything at all on you. Nothing. I even asked some friends who have clearances far beyond what I ever had, and they couldn't find out anything about you. I should have suspected witness protection."

Gavriil shifted, his cool gaze finding the sheriff. "Clearly she had to change her identity to survive. I think we're done here. She's told you everything she knows. I'll play the messages for you and you can take them with you.

Maybe you can find a way to identify the others on the tape." He stood up, towering over Lexi, letting the others know he meant business.

"The phone's in the other room. *Solnyshko moya*, I know you prefer to take your morning tea on the front porch. You don't need to listen to those vile messages again. I'll take the sheriff in myself." He held out his hand to her.

Lexi took his hand and let him walk her to the front door. Gavriil's four brothers followed Jonas and him into the kitchen to listen to the threats.

15

LEXI immersed herself in the familiar work of nurturing her plants, finding comfort in the familiar rhythm. The soil felt rich with minerals, and each time she pushed her hands deep into the dirt she felt connected to the farm itself.

Around her, the fog drifted through the trees, a gray smoky mist, looking like fingers threading through the forest. She'd always loved the effects of fog and the feeling that when she was wrapped in it, it was a veiled cloak that sheltered her. She liked to feel the drops on her face, reminding her she was alive. She still enjoyed the sensation, but she didn't need them as much—she had Gavriil, and he made her feel very much alive.

The soil around her hands rippled in a way she recognized as welcome. She turned to look over her shoulder to see Lissa emerging from the veil of gray. She sent her a welcoming smile.

"Good morning, Lissa," Lexi greeted. "You look amazing as always."

Lissa didn't respond but came right up to her and put her arms around her, something out of character for her.

Alarmed, Lexi hugged her tightly, trying not to get dirt on her clothes.

"What is it?"

"Nothing, babe. I just needed to talk to you before the others got here. There isn't any getting around the fact that Ilya and Jonas showed up and the boys all rushed to your house for some big meeting, presumably connected to the incident that happened a few days ago."

Lexi sank back onto her knees and pushed dirt around her plant lovingly, although she didn't really need to, she just needed the time. The other women showed their emotions easily, hugging one another and Lexi naturally. Lissa always seemed to have a little space between her and everyone else. It was difficult for her to show her affection, although Lexi knew it ran deep. She was touched, and a little alarmed.

"You aren't worried about me, are you?"

"Of course I'm worried about you. You let Gavriil Prakenskii into your life after we had a conversation about those men and how we weren't going to fall. You fell. Like a ton of bricks." There was a teasing note in Lissa's voice, but her eyes didn't smile. She looked worried.

"It was difficult not to fall," Lexi admitted. "He's so gentle and kind. I know he looks scary, but he's not. He reminds me a little of a wild animal, untamed and feral. He just needs someone to care about him."

Lissa groaned. "A wild animal bites when it's cornered. Where do you come up with this nonsense? You should be the world's most hardened, cynical, bitter woman, but instead you're our Lexi, sweet and kind and gentle. I can see why he would want to be with you, but Lexi . . ." She trailed off as Lexi shook her head.

"I'm not like that. Inside where no one ever sees, I'm not like that." It was a confession, and she hoped Lissa didn't dismiss it.

Lissa studied her face. Very gently she touched Lexi's long ponytail, the one Lexi had swept her hair into as she walked to the field. "I understand, honey. I really do. How could you not want the people who took everything you loved away from you punished? When they seem so powerful and invincible and by comparison you're insignificant, you feel powerless, but hatred can grow, the need for justice when you know there never will be."

Lexi nodded. "I know it isn't right or civilized to think that way, but even if Jonas arrests these men, others will take their place, and how is putting them in jail really punishing them for the things they did to my family? How can they ever pay the price for killing innocent children as well as my parents?"

"They can't, of course," Lissa said.

Lexi sighed. "Still."

"What is it?"

"I received some threats on the farm line and decided to call in Jonas. It's important to me that Gavriil have the chance to stop what he does."

Lissa choked and pressed a hand to her mouth.

"He can live peacefully, Lissa, given the chance."

"Don't kid yourself, babe, he's the kind of man you never want to cross."

"Maybe. I hope you're wrong for his sake. Jonas Harrington told Gavriil and the others to leave everything to law enforcement. I was watching Gavriil very carefully. He was wearing his 'stone' face—impossible to read—but he flicked his gaze at his youngest brother, Ilya, the one married to Joley Drake. I barely managed to catch the nod Ilya gave to Gavriil, but I know there was some kind of signal."

"I can't imagine that Levi, Thomas and Max wouldn't want to go after these people threatening you, but Ilya? That surprises me, but in a good way."

"Lissa, I don't want them to go backward. All of them are here to change their lives. They can't stop because of me."

"Baby, I hate to be the one to break it to you, but we're all going hunting."

"What do you mean?" Lexi stood up slowly and looked behind Lissa.

Emerging out of the fog were her other sisters. Blythe, tall and willowy, a beautiful woman who always appeared soft and feminine even in her favorite running clothes. Judith, a tall woman of Japanese descent, with board-straight hair, shiny as a raven's wing. Airiana, a small little pixie with nearly silver and platinum hair, looking smaller than ever beside her tallest sisters. Rikki, her cap of sun-kissed dark hair framing her face, autistic, yet determined to live life on her own terms. With Lissa, these were her sisters, the women who had come together to help one another—the women who had saved her life.

"Uh oh. This isn't one of your interventions, is it? Because I'm not giving up Gavriil Prakenskii. I've made up my mind and I'm keeping him," she greeted, in her firmest voice.

Blythe laughed. "You sound like he's a dog or something of that nature. Not a man."

"A man?" Judith echoed, exchanging a quick glance with Airiana. "More like a Bengal tiger."

"Don't worry, honey, no one is going to try to talk you out of staying with Gavriil. You're a grown woman," Lissa said. "If you want to live on the edge, far be it from us to stop you. But we did think we could find these idiots and put a stop to their attacks."

Lexi shook her head. "You don't understand how dangerous they are. You can't go anywhere near them."

"That wasn't exactly the plan," Blythe said. "We were thinking more of creating a biblical answer to their threats."

Airiana rubbed her hands up and down her arms. "I forgot my sweater again, darn it. I had to sneak out of the house and avoid Benito. He's gotten as bad as Max and thinks the women in his family need an escort everywhere we go."

"Maybe we should take this into the greenhouse," Lissa suggested. "I don't trust any of the men not to be listening."

"Good idea," Judith said. "Thomas can get a little out of hand when it comes to personal security."

"Tell me about it," Rikki said, rolling her eyes. "Levi is

so bossy sometimes I've had to push him overboard more than once."

Lexi couldn't help but laugh with the rest of them at the thought of Rikki shoving her beloved Levi into the sea. There was no doubt in any of their minds that she'd done it. "Come on. I couldn't come up with a solution. I hope you did."

"We think we can take care of the problem," Lissa said, as they all began to make their way to the greenhouse, "but don't think this will stop the men from going after them as well."

"Your Gavriil scares all of them just a little bit," Airiana said. "But they want to do this because they love you, Lexi. You're family to them. They aren't going to let anyone take their family from them ever again. You can't blame them."

"Doesn't he scare you?" Blythe asked. "Just a little bit?"

Lexi shook her head. "He's so kind and gentle with me there's no way I could be afraid of him. I'm afraid *for* him at times, but not *of* him. You should have seen him with Lucia, Airiana. He was so caring, and later he thought about ways to involve her with the puppies in order to try to help her."

"He was pretty blunt with Benito," Airiana pointed out.

Lexi bit her lip. "Benito had a gun on him."

"That's the only reason I didn't get upset with Gavriil and I kept Max from losing his temper over the incident," Airiana said. "You'd just been threatened, and Gavriil had no way of knowing Benito belonged to us all."

They entered the greenhouse and instantly were in a cocoon of warmth. They rarely came together in the greenhouse, but when they did, they instinctively headed to the very center of it, and sat on the floor in a tight circle, hidden among the giant leaves and jungle of vegetation.

"Can you find any of their compounds, Lexi?" Blythe asked. "Do you know where they are? I would guess it would be the one closest to us. I know the Reverend established more than one in this area."

"Maybe," Lexi hedged. "Why?"

"I would guess, if they suddenly found you, it was by chance. You nearly always stay on the farm and you're out of the spotlight, but somehow they figured out that you were here. The only place you really go is the farmer's market. If someone who could recognize your face was shopping there, they probably would live close," Blythe replied.

Judith nodded. "We looked at everything you've done in the last few months, and the only other place you went was to Elle Drake's wedding. Someone might have spotted you there, but they couldn't connect you with the farm. Had we been followed, we would have known. At least I think we would have."

"I've been to a place tucked back into the mountains between Booneville and Manchester. It's way out there and heavily guarded. It was on the list to be raided but the police told me it had been abandoned when they got there. Word went out after the first couple of raids, and I think the people left to escape arrest," Lexi said. "They may be using it again, but there can't be many of them left."

Her sisters exchanged pleasant smiles.

Lissa reached over and patted Lexi's knee. "That's perfect. Mountains. Oceans. Wow. We couldn't ask for a better scenario."

"You didn't tell Levi, did you? Or Gavriil?" Rikki asked.

"Or Jonas?" Blythe asked.

Lexi shook her head. "I did give them the name of one of the Reverend's enforcers though."

"No, that's good," Airiana said. "It will give them something to do while we put our plan into action."

"What's the plan?" Lexi asked.

"Well, they're all about the plagues and pestilence, aren't they?" Judith asked. "We can give them what they deserve."

"Winds," Airiana said.

"Fire," Lissa added.

"Water, lots of it." Rikki blew on the tips of her fingers, and this time it was deliberate. She grinned at Lexi.

"And earth," Blythe said. "We just need to make certain

they get the message that their god is punishing them for their mistaken belief that they can send their enforcers after you."

Lexi bit down hard on her lower lip. "It's a proactive plan," she agreed, "and more than anything I'd like to be proactive against them for once in my life. The biggest problem I see is getting the right message to them. Whoever is in charge is most likely going to put a different spin on it when things start to happen. He'll say they have to kill me or their god will continue to punish them."

Judith burst out laughing. "I love you, Lexi. I really do. Is that what you see as our biggest obstacle? That's going to be a piece of cake compared to slipping away from our husbands and getting this done. Do you think Gavriil is going to agree to you leaving the farm without him?"

Lexi frowned at her. "Well, he really doesn't have that kind of say in my life one way or the other, does he? I do what I want."

Blythe leaned toward Lexi. "Until you cross him. Honey, you have to be realistic if you're going to be with a man like Gavriil. Like any of the Prakenskiis, and that includes their younger brother, Ilya. If you are the one woman in the world they give up their former life for, do you really think they'll just let you walk into a dangerous situation? It won't ever happen."

"Well I'm not going to lie to him. If we do this, I'm going to be honest," Lexi said stubbornly. "He's honest with me, and I'm not giving him less than the strict truth."

"That's fine," Airiana agreed, "I feel the same way, but we're just warning you, be prepared for a battle."

"How do you think he's going to react when he finds out you know where some of these people are and you didn't tell him?" Lissa asked.

"He already knows." Lexi smiled at her. "I saw it in his eyes when I told the sheriff the name of one of the men on the tape. I'm certain he thinks he can worm the information out of me."

"Well if we're really going to do this," Lissa said, "we

need to do it in the next few days. I've got a trip planned. You know how I take off a couple of times a year. I'm heading to Europe. I've got a few appointments with customers interested in my chandeliers, and you know how much money they bring in. I've got to firm up the deals. I'm sorry, I didn't know all this was going to happen or I would have put off my trip. I've already made all the arrangements."

"That's awesome," Judith said. "Where?"

"Germany, an actual castle, and one in Italy and the last in Russia. I'm excited to see what they want. I sent them my brochure. The estate in Germany is particularly exciting because they've actually invited me to stay in the castle."

"Who would have thought that in just a few short years our businesses would take off and become international?" Judith said.

"Blythe." Rikki touched her arm lightly. "You were so right about us being stronger together. Not only emotionally, but definitely financially as well."

Blythe smiled at them. "We were so lucky to meet."

"This farm is healing," Airiana said. "I hope it does for the children what it did for us. They all still have nightmares, and I can't say that I blame them."

"Are they still sleeping in your bedroom?" Rikki asked.

Airiana nodded. "They try to stay in their own rooms, but they come in one by one. We don't mind. We've made the gazebo our getaway." She turned to Lexi. "Thank you for talking to Lucia. Whatever you said has helped. She's easier around both Max and me."

"I think the puppies will help too," Lexi said. "She's very interested in them, and I think if you encourage that, she'll be pulled closer into our circle."

"Did Gavriil have to have the biggest, scariest dog in the world have puppies?" Judith demanded. "Sheesh. Of course Thomas is all over that. The dog might as well be a horse. Can you imagine one racing through the house and knocking over everything?"

"Like Benito?" Airiana asked slyly. "He spends a lot of

time with you and I can't imagine that half your artwork isn't damaged."

Judith laughed. "He is rather coltish. He's talented, Airiana, and he loves to paint. I've gotten him interested in restoration as well."

A draft shifted the leaves and they fell silent, exchanging looks. There was no sound, but they knew they weren't alone. Gavriil came through the wealth of plants first, leaning one hip against the bed of tomatoes and crossing his arms over his chest. Max emerged next, with Thomas and Levi following suit until the women were surrounded.

Thomas leveled his gaze at Judith. "It looks to me as if you six are having a little war meeting without us. What do you think, Levi?"

Levi studied his wife's face. "Rikki, honey, never play poker. You look as guilty as sin."

"I don't *feel* guilty," Rikki said, giving him her haughty little glare.

"That's too bad, because I'm going to have to work on that one with you long and hard until you do feel guilt. Anytime you plan behind your husband's back, guilt should factor in."

Airiana snorted in derision. "Like it does with the four of you?"

Max stirred but he didn't say anything at all, just kept his eyes on her face until she blushed.

"Seriously, Max, you are plotting every minute."

"So that is what you're doing," Thomas said. "The minute I realized the six of you were together, I knew you were up to no good."

"What's the plan?" Levi asked.

"It isn't quite perfected yet," Blythe said. "But we thought we'd bring the bible down on them."

Lexi felt Gavriil's eyes on her. He didn't say a word, but she felt the weight, a dark promise that made her shiver. She wasn't afraid of him, but he was intimidating. He suddenly held out his hand to her. His blue eyes didn't waver, not for a moment. He didn't blink, entirely focused on her as if they were the only two people in the room.

The compulsion to take his hand was stronger than she could resist. But it was more than that. She knew the others were watching. She could either take his hand and seal the relationship in the eyes of her family or blow him off. She wasn't about to do that to him. She put her hand in his and allowed him to pull her to his feet.

Gavriil wrapped his arm around Lexi, uncaring that his brothers and her sisters would see him. He needed to hold her. She knew more than the others the kind of men they were dealing with. Whatever plan they had devised—good or bad—was not going to be implemented without the protection his brothers and he could provide.

"We need to get home," he said, keeping his voice low and persuasive. "I didn't like the look of the littlest puppy and wasn't certain just what he needed. Come home and take a look, please. You can talk on the way."

"Oh no." Lexi immediately turned to her sisters with a small wave. "I think we can do this and maybe avoid harming anyone. You tell them, and I'll fill Gavriil in."

"That's an excellent idea," Gavriil said, as they stepped out of the greenhouse. He kept her close to him, his arm securely around her waist. "Fill me in."

"The Reverend used the bible to intimidate and frighten the members of his congregation. He breathed fire and brimstone. We're all elements. We can use those elements against them. We just have to figure out how to make certain they interpret the floods, earthquakes, winds and fires sent to punish them for threatening me."

"I see." He kept her walking, sheltering her body from the wind coming off the ocean. It was cold, and the fog swirled around them with each step. The mist muffled sound and gave the illusion of walking in another world. He tightened his arm around her possessively. Protectively.

She glanced up at his face. He felt her eyes drifting over him. It didn't matter that fear had developed the moment he knew she was gone and perhaps making plans to try to deal with the cult members on her own. She warmed something dead and cold inside of him. No one else could breathe life into him the way she did.

"Are you upset with me, Gavriil?"

She sounded genuinely puzzled. She hadn't been defiant or trying to be independent in the face of extreme danger. He didn't understand why she wouldn't come to him first, and she didn't understand the terrible fear of losing her he just couldn't get a handle on.

Vulnerability wasn't his strong suit. Lexi made him more than vulnerable. She stripped him naked and left his weakness exposed.

"Gavriil? What is it?"

"I need a little time to adjust to all this," he said slowly. "I never expected to ever feel this way about a woman. I've fallen pretty damn hard. It doesn't make sense, and I'm a man who questions everything and never trusts what I don't understand. I'm cynical, Lexi. I deal in logic and probabilities. Emotion isn't part of that. I rarely feel emotion. It has no place in my life. And then you came along."

She leaned her face into his rib cage, a small brush of her cheek against his body. He felt the small touch like an electrical charge. He half expected the fog to light up with tiny little sparks. How did one explain that to her?

"When a man has had nothing at all, no future, no hope of one and no one to call his own falls like a ton of bricks, it takes a little getting used to."

"You aren't in this alone," she whispered.

"I know. I'm aware you're struggling too, but we've got to talk these things out. You know those panic attacks of yours? I think they're contagious. When you're out of my sight, and I don't know that you're safe, I can't breathe."

She was silent a moment. He waited. Lexi was a fair woman and more, she was compassionate. She recognized the struggle in him. He believed in her, in her sense of fairness. In her caring. She would put him first always—it was in her nature. His nature was dominant and one of absolute confidence. He knew he would always have to take precautions never to take advantage of her.

Lexi looked up at his face. It couldn't have been easy for a man like Gavriil to make such an admission. She could see raw pain etched into the lines of his face. More, she could feel his confusion and irritation with himself. He didn't understand what was happening to him—to both of them—but he was doing his best to figure it out.

He wasn't a man who ever allowed himself excuses. Not pain. Not injuries. He certainly didn't have panic attacks no matter what he claimed. He functioned no matter what condition he was in. His emotions for her, as intense as they were, and as quickly as the feelings had developed, had taken him to an unfamiliar place, one in which he didn't know how to maneuver.

There was honesty there. Stark truth. He physically reacted when he didn't know where she was. "I didn't mean to worry you, Gavriil. I have to work. Running the farm isn't easy, even though I'm bound to earth. When I'm upset, I find it comforting to get my hands in the soil. It's habit."

"I've had a little time to think things over. I know it won't be easy for you to tell me where you're going. You've been independent so long and to feel as if you're answering to someone will be . . . difficult." He raked his fingers through his hair. "If you tell me where you are, maybe over time I'll get rid of this panicky feeling when you disappear."

Gavriil detested feeling the way he was. Naked. Exposed. Completely vulnerable. He hadn't expected such a visceral reaction to her just leaving without telling him where she was going. He had known. On some level he had known she would seek something familiar after the sheriff had questioned her, but there had been that moment, walking the others back out onto the porch and finding her gone.

He didn't want to ever relive that moment. He hadn't cared if he'd covered his panic in front of his brothers or not. He only cared that he find her and fast.

"I don't mind telling you where I'm going," Lexi said.

"But I'll be honest with you. It will take some time for me to always get in the habit of it. My sisters have their own places. We aren't together twenty-four/seven. I'm used to being alone and never answering to anyone. I suspect you'll find it just as hard to have to tell me where you're going and what you're doing."

Air moved a little easier through his lungs. The constricted feeling eased in his chest. A few of the knots in his belly loosened. There was just something about her that moved him—that set up a need and a hunger, a drive he was unfamiliar with. He'd never believed in heaven or hell until he met her. She turned his world upside down, and he'd known from the moment he set eyes on her that she would. She was the one.

"Lexi, I want to be the perfect man for you. I do. I want to give you everything you've ever wanted or dreamt about. I want you happy every minute of the day. But I'm not perfect, and I don't know the first thing about making a woman happy. I do know the kind of man I am—the one I've been shaped into."

She sighed. "Gavriil, I know you'd never hurt me. I just know it, deep inside. There's no doubt, and you shouldn't have doubts either."

He stopped abruptly, right before the first stair of the porch to their home. "I have no doubts that I'd never hurt you." His hand brushed her hair, all that soft silk, once more pulled back into the inevitable ponytail. "But you can't ignore the fact that I'm a violent man. My mind goes there first when I'm threatened. Everyone around you is going to be in danger when I'm in that state of mind."

He waited, hearing his heart beating, the thunder of his pulse in his ears. She looked up at him, her cool green eyes searching his face for a long time. He hadn't wanted to make the admission. It went against his logic. Against his code. Against who he was, but there was no denying one of his biggest fears was that he would harm an innocent in trying to get to her or protect her.

She had every right to condemn him. She'd lived in a

violent world. His greatest fear was that she would associate him with Caine. He didn't want her to feel as if she was a prisoner tied to him. Or that he dictated her every move. He didn't know how to smooth out his rough edges.

Lexi cupped the side of his face with her palm, a curiously tender gesture, and it made his heart turn over. "I didn't think of that, Gavriil, and I'm sorry. I don't understand any of this, what's happened between us, but clearly we're both going to have to deal with each other's issues. I'm actually a little glad it isn't just me." She gave him a tentative smile and went up on her toes to brush a kiss along his chin. "We'll be okay. It's not that hard to learn to tell you where I'm going. I'll make every effort."

He should have known she would react that way. Lexi didn't have an ego. She looked past words to the man. Whatever she saw in him—and thank the universe she saw something worthwhile—she made her judgments based on what she saw. He felt more love for her than he thought possible.

He turned abruptly and went up the steps, unable to express to her what she meant to him. He took her with him because he wasn't quite ready to let go of her.

"I wasn't making it up about the puppy," Gavriil told her, as he nearly thrust her into the house. He was grateful he could change the subject and give her something else to think about. "Would you take a look at him?"

"Of course." She hurried down the hall to the bedroom.

He allowed himself to lean weakly against the wall, just for a moment. He was more of a monster than he'd ever considered himself. He'd known it the moment he'd emerged from their kitchen to find her gone. Every belief he'd held about himself shattered right there.

He had always known he was far gone from humanity. He'd crossed a line years earlier and there was no going back, but he had a code he didn't break. It was the only thing keeping him from becoming worse than those he hunted. He would have broken his code in a heartbeat to get to her.

Love wasn't only painful for a man like him, it was damned dangerous. He glided down the hall to the bedroom to lean one hip against the doorjamb, just watching her—drinking her in like some lovesick idiot. She sat on the floor, tailor fashion, concentration on her face, while her hands cradled the weak puppy. Drago nearly dwarfed her, crowding close, his nose anxiously pressed against her.

He could almost feel the warmth emanating from her hands as she held the puppy close. She was beautiful there, her head tilted down, every line in her body one of intense concentration. He waited, watching her, his world right again because she was close.

She turned her head slowly to look at him. There was worry in her eyes. "I don't think he's strong enough to eat properly. He won't latch on. Would you call Blythe and see if we can get some goat's milk? I might be able to feed him with an eyedropper just to make him strong enough to eat properly."

"Blythe?" His eyebrow shot up.

"Her number is there on the kitchen counter in my address book. Kiss is being very patient with me. I've been trying to stimulate the puppy to eat and she's lying there and occasionally licking him to give him encouragement." She held the tiny creature close. "We'll have to give him a name."

His heart lurched. "*Solnyshko moya*, it is better not to get too attached in case you lose him. He's very weak."

"I know. But he needs a name. Something brave, because he's really trying, Gavriil."

He shook his head. He didn't want heartbreak for her. "I'll be right back. I'll make the call and also ask her to see if anyone can order us puppy formula. When I come back we have to discuss this plan of yours to scare this cult away from you. I also would like an explanation of why you didn't tell me you knew how to find them."

She turned her head and looked at him over her shoulder. She looked so beautiful he would have wept if he were that kind of man. There was sheer tenderness on her face.

Pure love. An expression so terrifyingly beautiful his eyes burned and his throat threatened to close on him. "I was protecting you from yourself, of course."

He turned away from her. He had no other choice. She disarmed him so easily with her caring. He had no idea what to do or say when she was like that. He had command of every situation no matter how dicey, until it came to his woman. There, he was completely at a loss. How did one fall so hard and make it work? He didn't have a clue but it didn't matter. He'd never been happier.

Blythe was eager to help and said she'd get the goat's milk or formula and bring it right over as soon as she found some. He went back to Lexi.

She was sitting in the chair nearest the closet, holding the puppy close to her. She looked so sad his heart ached.

"You're right, Lexi. He needs a name. Lyutyj. We'll call him Lyutyj. It means *fierce*. He'll be a fierce warrior and he'll fight to survive."

She had the puppy close to her heart, wrapped carefully in a soft blanket. "That's a perfect name, Gavriil, thank you." She kissed the little dog's head. "I'm certain he'll pull through. His mother and father are both brave and strong. He will be too."

Gavriil sank into the chair beside hers—the one he'd repositioned just to the left of the window so he could see out without anyone being able to see him. His hand automatically felt along the cushion for the knife he'd placed there. It was right where he'd left it.

"Tell me about this idea and what it entails," he prompted.

"First, before anything, we have to make certain they're even there. The police raided the compound a few years ago, but no one was there. That's the closest property to us that I know of that they use. It was never confiscated because the church didn't own it. The property hadn't been signed over yet."

"I can scope it out. Preparation is everything," Gavriil said, at her sharp glance. "Levi and Thomas can go with me. Max can watch things here while we take a look and see if anyone's there and if so, what kind of defenses they have in place."

"If we can scare them away from us, really put the fear of God into them and make most of the members abandon the cult, it would be better than killing them," Lexi said.

He didn't agree with her, but he needed to know what they were up against, how many and who was the most dangerous. If anyone was there who had been taken from their homes, like Lexi, he wanted the sheriff involved after they had cleaned up any evidence of the women—or the Prakenskiis—being there.

Gavriil nodded. "Clearly the first step is to scout around and see if they're even there. What's the second step?"

"We have to come up with a way that the congregation will believe every bad thing that occurs naturally is because their leaders are going against their god's directives. They have to come together every evening for prayers, which mostly consists of listing people's sins and them begging forgiveness. We send fog into the meeting house and write in the fog." She shrugged. "Something along those lines. Something a little spooky and scary. Then all the problems will start."

It actually wasn't a bad plan if you took the church enforcers out of the mix. They would be troublesome, but he wasn't going to point that out to her. He already, with his brothers, had plans to track down the six men who had made death threats against Lexi. The Prakenskiis planned to do a little reading from their own book of justice to them. That was a certainty.

16

GAVRIIL had never been so tired—or so satisfied or frustrated in his life. Working on the farm meant long hours in the middle of lush green plants and rich soil. He actually found he enjoyed the work. He could understand how Lexi, even without her connection to the earth, would be drawn to the tasks.

Both of them were used to being alone. Working side by side with her outdoors without having to say anything other than asking an occasional question was actually restful. His mind found the land a place of peace and his body discovered peculiar aches and pains that had nothing to do with bullet or stab wounds.

He and his brothers hadn't wasted any time before scouting out the compound. There appeared to be around thirty men, women and children living on the property. They set up cameras and motion detectors to get a feel for the rhythm of the place. Gavriil had slipped inside after dark and managed to install cameras in a few of the buildings, including the one used for their gatherings. He wanted to see and hear who the ringleaders were.

Gavriil was satisfied that they could protect the women if the women chose to drive the congregation away from the leaders. On the other hand, he didn't believe for one moment that the six men would stop coming after Lexi, and if he found on camera or heard on tape that anyone had been taken there and held against their will, he wasn't going to promise Lexi he wouldn't take care of it his way.

He paced around the room restlessly on bare feet, wearing only a towel hitched low around his hips. If he were a drinking man, now would be the time he'd be drinking. He felt as if he had gotten on a merry-go-round with Lexi and both were unable to get off. They just continued to go around in circles. She was always just out of his reach.

He refused to use his training to seduce her. He wanted to make love to her, to show her how it should be between a man and a woman, but so far, he couldn't get beyond kissing her or touching her. The next step would come naturally or not at all.

He knew she wanted him. He could see it in her eyes, and read it in her body language, but she just couldn't seem to take that final step toward him. He pressed his fingers to his eyes and shook his head. He ached for her, not just for her body, but for her past. She was such an innocent, taken by a depraved sadist. That vile monster had tried to twist her into something of his own ugly making. It hadn't worked, but she was still trapped by her past and Gavriil didn't know how to free her.

She seemed to think Gavriil wouldn't be able to do without the things Caine had taught her. He'd been a monster, that man, taking a child and teaching her to hate her own body. He'd used her and then punished her for "tempting" him. Caine hadn't once made her feel anything but disgust and fear.

The thought of touching Gavriil or tasting him as he did her, was abhorrent to her. She didn't say it aloud, but he knew that was her biggest fear, that if they progressed in their relationship, he would want the things from her that Caine had wanted and she couldn't give that to him, and she feared he would eventually look elsewhere for satisfaction.

Gavriil raked both hands through his hair. What she didn't realize was that he couldn't imagine ever going back to a life without her. Before her, he hadn't been living. The last couple of weeks had taught him that. She gave his life purpose and form. Everything about her appealed to him, drew him, called to him on every level. Why couldn't he find a way to draw her closer to him? To help her understand that making love was so much more than mere sex. That it was passionate, beautiful, intimate and affirming, not something ugly and depraved.

He had had sex, many times, just about any way one could. He seduced women whenever he needed or wanted to. He'd been taught how to control his body, what techniques to use and how to get a woman to want more. And he'd enjoyed it. But what he felt for Lexi, with Lexi, was worlds apart. Touching Lexi, kissing Lexi, had taught him the difference between having sex and making love.

Her scent drifted to him through the open bathroom door—a fresh, clean forest smell that appealed to him as nothing else could. She was soaking in the deep bathtub, her one luxury. Outside the window, the rain fell softly, but in a steady pattern. He turned on the gas fireplace to take the chill from the room so that when she came out of her hot bath she'd be comfortable.

He'd taken his shower, deliberately leaving the door open after washing the farm dirt from his body and easing the aches and pains from various old wounds. His arm was healed, and somehow, the acupuncture seemed to be helping with the nerve damage from the old knife wounds. He sank down into his chair and tried to find a way to relax when his body was as hard as a rock.

The sound of her occasionally moving in the bathtub both soothed and aroused him. He liked hearing her in the house. He was always aware of exactly where she was, whether in the kitchen or on the front porch. The last few nights she'd gone to sleep in the bed beside him after staying up with tiny Lyutyj. The puppy did appear to be getting stronger and had finally latched on to his mother.

Small steps, just like Lexi.

Two nights in a row he'd lain beside Lexi, painfully hard, afraid if he moved, his body might shatter, but she actually had relaxed enough to sleep beside him—naked. He contemplated what to do next. She trusted him more and more, but it was definitely becoming difficult not touching her. He needed her body the same way she needed his—she just didn't know why she was growing restless and edgy.

He raked his fingers through his hair again. "What in the hell am I going to do about you?" he whispered aloud.

LEXI sat in the hot water, letting it soak away the aches of her body, but it didn't stop the endless hunger crawling through her bloodstream. Each moment she spent in Gavriil's company only served to make her fall harder for him. She was tired of being afraid of the physical side of a relationship between a man and a woman, yet she couldn't overcome her aversion to touching a man.

She closed her eyes against the burn of tears, and drew her knees up to hug them tightly, feeling more vulnerable than ever. The longer she was with Gavriil, the more she knew she didn't want to lose him. He never asked anything of her, but she knew it was becoming difficult for him to live and work beside her.

Her own body was betraying her. She found herself watching the way he moved, the strength in his hands, the gentle way he picked up the puppies and caressed Kiss and Drago. She knew his every expression. She found herself staring at him. Drinking him in, just absorbing him. She didn't know how to feel anymore, she was so confused.

Lexi pressed her fingers to her eyes, shaking her head. The hot water shimmered around her, lapping at her body, making her skin feel more sensitive than ever. She was aware of him in the next room moving around. He made her feel safe. He made her feel as if she were beautiful and special. Sexy. Sensual. Everything she was not.

She wanted him, pure and simple. Well . . . her body wanted his. Her heart wanted him. Her brain rebelled and screamed at her she would lose him if she tried—or didn't try. They seemed to be doing some strange dance, moving in circles around each other.

He gave and she took. She had been living a half-life, existing on her safe little farm. He had been existing in the shadows. Now they'd come together. He'd been the broken one, she'd been so certain of it when she met him, but somehow the truly broken one had been her all along.

Caine had made her ashamed of herself, of her body. He had told her how vile she was, nothing but a temptation for a man, a vessel to use when the temptation became too much to resist. He had forced her to do things to him and then beaten her for doing them. When she began to develop, he'd told her she was ugly and disgusting and forced her to bind her body and cover up at all times.

Tears spilled down her cheeks. Caine had ruined her chances for a real life. She would never be normal. She didn't even know what normal was. She wasn't living much of a life, that was certain, and she was dragging Gavriil down with her.

Gavriil offered her . . . everything. Without strings. Without asking for anything in return. What kind of relationship was that? She kissed him. She loved kissing him. But every time they kissed she could feel the need and hunger running so deep in him. He never tried to hide it from her. More, she felt that same need and hunger running just as deep in her.

Truthfully, she'd been in a constant state of arousal for the last few days and had no idea what to do about it. Twice she'd gone into the greenhouse and cried. She thought about talking to her sisters to get ideas, but this issue was between them. Gavriil and her. No one else.

She hadn't known a person could feel so desperate for another's body. For his touch. Or his kiss. For his hands. She rubbed her chin back and forth on the top of her knees. She had to find the courage to either let him go or take the next step. And God help her, she didn't want to let him go.

She couldn't continue to take without giving something in return, but she didn't know how to make herself give him what she knew he needed. The idea of losing him terrified her—absolutely terrified her.

She lifted her head and looked at the full-length mirror Judith had installed in her bathroom. She hadn't protested at the time, but she never looked at herself in it. A few times she'd even covered the mirror up, but was afraid one of her sisters would discover the sheet over it.

When she'd taken a shower at the farm, Caine had forced her to wear a shirt to cover her body. He'd drilled it into her not to expose herself, yet Gavriil was just the opposite. He wanted her to sleep without clothes. He enjoyed looking at her body; Caine had been repulsed by her figure as she grew older. He even made her bind her breasts when he deemed them too big.

She had complied with Gavriil's request to sleep without clothes, partly because it was one of the few things she could give him and partly in defiance of Caine.

She wasn't certain what to think about her body. She knew the scars on her back, buttocks and thighs were ugly. The raised ridges sometimes ached in the cold. She had been more embarrassed for Gavriil to see the scars than for him to see her big breasts.

Of course, unlike Caine, Gavriil didn't seem to think her breasts were too big at all. Her hands came up to cup the soft weight. Maybe they weren't too big. They fit easily enough into Gavriil's palms.

Blushing, she stood up slowly. The water poured off her body into the tub. Steam rose around her and lightly obscured her reflection in the mirror. Still, she could see herself.

What did Gavriil see when he looked at her? She wanted

to see through his eyes, not Caine's. Perhaps that was the real trouble, she was trying to see herself through someone else's vision, not her own. She took a deep breath and forced herself to really study her body in the mirror.

She wasn't very tall in comparison to Gavriil. Her hair, even wet, was beautiful and her one vanity, again because Caine despised it so much. The moment she was free of him she vowed to never cut it, and with the exception of an occasional trim on the ends to keep it healthy, she hadn't. Gavriil loved her hair. He even liked her wearing it down.

Her breasts were full, high, and didn't sag in the least. She refused to give in to the urge to look away from the soft, firm mounds. Caine had referred to them as a cow's udders and insisted she bind them and keep them from sight at all times. Gavriil was just the opposite. He lavished attention on her breasts. He loved to touch her there, to kiss and suck and tug and roll the nipples.

Her entire body turned bright red at the thought of Gavriil's mouth pulling so strongly on her breasts. Damp heat pooled between her legs as she touched herself, mimicking his fingers on her nipples. Streaks of sizzling electricity rushed from her breasts to her most feminine core. Sparks of arousal danced up and down her thighs.

Shocked, she dropped her hands and almost sank back into the water, but then stopped herself. No, she was done with giving into fear and shame. She wanted to be free of Caine and his ugly influence. She was realistic enough to know she would never get over her panic attacks and that he would creep into her nightmares, but she didn't want him ruling her life.

Gavriil had been courageous enough to change his life. He had given her more pleasure than she thought existed. Caine hurt her in every way a man could possibly hurt a woman. Gavriil's mouth and hands on her breasts excited her beyond anything she'd known. He'd awakened her body to the pleasures a man could bring to a woman, and he'd asked nothing for himself.

Gavriil's kisses were amazing, even earth-shattering. Caine would never have kissed her. He had told her that her mouth was made for only one purpose.

Deliberately Lexi ran her fingers down her flat belly, watching her hand in the mirror. Sometimes Judith wore a gold chain around her waist, and Lexi had dreamt a few times that she had been bold enough to do such a thing. She wanted one that hooked to a piercing and rode a little lower than her waist. She wanted little bells that jingled with each step she took, reminding her of her freedom to dance in the fields. She'd never worked up the courage to go to a place where they'd do such a thing, because she'd been too ashamed to show her body to anyone.

Dreams and fantasies were far different than reality. This time, she had everything to lose. Gavriil was worth fighting for. He fought for her with every breath he took. Could she do less for him? He wanted her. He'd asked her time and again to trust him, to give herself to him.

She whispered his name as she brought both hands down over her thighs and back up to the junction at her legs. Love for him was there. She felt it rising inside her like a towering wave. Her body ached for him. She started to touch herself and then pulled her hand away as if she'd been burned.

Memories surfaced, ugly horrible fragments that wouldn't leave her alone. The pain. The humiliation. The disgust and shame. She sank slowly back into the water and drew up her knees, making herself as small as possible. Tears tracked down her face and dropped into the steaming water. She covered her face with her hands, not knowing what to do.

She felt Gavriil close. Moving in her mind. A caress. Gentle. Intimate. Her stomach muscles tightened. Fear lived and breathed in her. Fear, not so much for her but for him. He wouldn't leave her or give up on her. She had to be just as brave. She just needed to find the courage.

"*Solnyshko moya*, enough. Stop hiding in there and come to bed." Gavriil's voice was low and brushed over her

skin the same way he had the walls of her mind. Intimate
and gentle—hard to resist.

She bit her lip. She was hiding. From him. From herself.
From what she was and what she wasn't. He would know
the moment he saw her body that she was in a fierce state
of arousal. She couldn't possibly spend another night beside
him, skin to skin, his heat spreading through her until she
was afraid she would burn right there in the bed.

"I'm too tired to get out. I think I'll sleep right here." It
was a lie. Her voice betrayed her. She didn't talk in that
soft, silky voice meant for satin sheets and candlelight. An
invitation. Not only did her face turn red, but so did her
entire body.

"You're going to turn into a prune."

She heard him move and closed her eyes like a child
afraid to face her greatest fear. Silence. Long, heartbreaking silence. Lexi lifted her lashes, and there he was, his
wide shoulders filling the doorway, his dark blue eyes like
the midnight sky, drifting over her possessively.

She shivered, her nipples tightening. He was beautiful
draped so casually there. All man. His muscles defined.
Strong and confident. Everything she wasn't. He didn't
have to touch her to make her want him. He just looked at
her with his blue eyes and she was lost, caught in his spell.

She looked at him helplessly. Wanting had gone to craving. To needing.

"Baby, just come to me. Don't do this to yourself." His
soft whisper ran like fingers over her body to tease her
thighs.

She took a deep breath. Gavriil wore his skin comfortably. The towel dipped low around his hips and she knew
he wore it only as a condition to her modesty, not his. He
was a man who preferred not to show emotion, but was
completely casual naked.

She moistened her lips, determined to claim him. Determined to rise like the phoenix from the ashes of her past.
Gripping the edges of the tub until her knuckles turned

white, she slowly stood, forcing herself to stand naked in front of him. The light was low, but still, it illuminated her wet skin, playing over her body with the drifting steam.

She froze, her breath refusing to leave her lungs. She couldn't let go of the death grip she had on the tub. "Gavriil." She whispered his name, willing him to understand what she was trying to do—come to him in her own skin.

Gavriil nearly groaned aloud. She was killing him with her need to please him. She didn't understand he would wait a lifetime for her. She sounded sexy. Scared. Innocent. There was a note of raw courage in her voice that whispered over his skin and reached deep inside of him to turn him inside out.

He caught up a towel, and plunged his hand into the warm water to pull out the plug. She trembled, her gaze clinging to his. He wrapped his arm around her waist and lifted her right out of the bathtub.

She leaned away from him. "Are you crazy? You'll be soaked. We'll have water all over the floor." Her hands went to her long, thick hair, wringing it out hastily over the tub so that water streamed from the silky mass.

He set her feet on the bathmat and wrapped her in a towel. "I don't have a stitch on other than a towel. A little water never hurt anyone." He began drying her, using a slow, deliberately sensual massage, paying attention to every part of her body.

Lexi stood frozen, one hand on his shoulder. He could feel the tremors running through her body as she stood very still for him. His heart swelled. He felt almost overwhelmed with love for her. She was so frightened, yet she refused to give in.

In spite of the towel moving over her, little shivers shook her body. He took his time, warming her gently. The towel rasped gently over her nipples and teased at the undersides of her breasts. As he dipped the towel a little lower to wipe the water from her rib cage, he bent his head to her breasts, a slow, seductive descent, waiting for her to protest. When she didn't, he licked at her nipples, breathed warm air over them and drew one breast into the heat of his mouth.

She made a little sound, a breathy, soft moan, and her arm came up to cradle his head. He forgot for a moment he was drying her off, losing himself in the sheer pleasure of her soft body. His tongue flicked her nipple, his teeth tugged gently. He suckled first one, then the other.

You're so brave, Lexi. I'm proud of you. He teased at her nipple, drawing her deep in the heat of his mouth.

I don't know what I'm doing.

You're showing me you love me. He couldn't help kissing his way over the curve of her breasts back up to her mouth. Her lips trembled just like the rest of her, but were soft and warm and welcoming under his.

She had no idea just what it meant to him that she had gathered her courage and stood up stark naked in the bathtub, offering herself to him. As seductions went, most wouldn't consider it sexy. He found her the sexiest woman alive.

She was fragile and innocent in spite of the years she'd spent as a prisoner to a depraved madman. He felt privileged and humbled that she chose him and had worked hard to conquer her fears in order to come to him.

He could spend a lifetime kissing her. She gave herself without reservation to him when he kissed her. He left her mouth reluctantly to kiss his way back down to the tips of her breasts.

You're so beautiful. I love your body. You're warm and so damned soft, Lexi. When I touch you, I feel as if I've found my way home.

Her arms crept around his head again, holding him to her. Her long lashes fluttered and veiled the expression in her eyes, but it didn't matter. He felt her moving in his mind.

You are home here with me.

Her voice was tentative. Shy. Loving. His heart contracted. She could bring him to his knees so easily, and she didn't even know the power she wielded.

You are my home. You. Not a place. Just you. When he called her his sun, or his angel, he meant it.

He kissed his way down her ribs, using the towel to catch a few drops of water while his hands shaped her and his mouth worshiped her.

Someday I'm going to buy you a little adornment I can play with. His tongue dipped into her belly button.

Her breath caught in her throat. *I always wanted one so I could get a chain, a really fine gold link chain with little bells on it.*

Instantly he visualized her stark naked, dancing in front of the firelight with only that chain around her hips. His blood thundered in his ears. He crouched low and brought the towel up her ankle to her calf, leaning in to sip at the water on the insides of her thighs. His hair brushed against her legs, and his fingers bit into her hips.

Both of her hands caught at his shoulders for support. She went very still but she didn't protest. He ran his tongue up higher, chasing the drops up toward the vee at the junction of her legs. Her legs quivered and she made a small strangled sound in the back of her throat.

"I think I need dessert tonight, *laskovaya moya*," he murmured. "Do you have any objections?" Before she could answer, he tossed the towel aside and lifted her, carrying her to the bed.

"I don't know what that means," she answered. Her eyes met his and then slid away shyly. "Not exactly."

"It means I want to eat you like candy." He practically growled the explanation. "I could devour you whole and never get enough." He bent his head to hers, brushing coaxing kisses over her trembling lips. "Try this for me. If you don't like it, we'll stop."

He wanted to devour her for real. Touching her soft skin drove him nearly out of his mind. A jackhammer seemed to penetrate his skull and his blood pounded hard in his veins in sheer desperation—but she deserved so much more.

Lexi stared up at Gavriil's face, totally mesmerized. His

features were dark with sensuality, his hooded eyes the color of midnight, filled with so much desire, he took her breath away. She was terrified, truly terrified, but there was no resisting him and the sudden need to learn more about the absolute pleasure she knew he could give her.

She swallowed hard as he tossed the sheet, her only protection, out of his way. His towel came next and she couldn't help glancing down at his manhood. He was intimidating, much thicker and longer than she remembered. Up close he was terrifying, yet his hands slid over her body with such tenderness he disarmed her.

His body moved over hers, covering her like a blanket. Caine had made her face away from him. He hadn't wanted to look at her as he rutted. Gavriil stared into her eyes, and held her gently. His mouth came down on hers and she tasted passion. Aggression. Love.

Tears burned behind her eyes. She couldn't believe a man could act so loving toward her. No one had ever made her feel loved and beautiful and wanted. She gave herself up to his kisses, absorbing the way his body felt against hers. Hard. All muscle. Hot. All over.

She found she liked the difference in the way his body felt against hers. He made her feel feminine and protected. His kisses brought an ache to her breasts and tension between her legs. She held on to her love for him as he kissed his way down to her breasts. Her skin burned, flames licking at her. She felt damp heat gathering between her legs.

Relax, solnyshko moya, *trust me to take good care of you.*

She did trust him, but it was difficult to relax when her body felt heavy and unfamiliar and so . . . desperate. He was setting up a deep craving in her and there was a part of her that feared where it would take her.

I can't breathe. She had no idea a woman could feel this way. Needy. Hungry. Unable to control her body. She tried to stop moving, but her hips couldn't be still and she feared they were taking on a life of their own, desperate for his body. She felt empty and needed him to fill her.

I can't breathe without you.

He whispered the admission into her mind. His voice felt like velvet moving over her hot skin, brushing caresses right along with his tongue and hands. His mouth closed over her breast and just like his kiss, his mouth was more aggressive. He suckled strongly and used the edge of his teeth and the flat of his tongue to drive her up fast.

She heard her own moan, and the sound startled her. It was all happening too fast—her body not her own, but his. He seemed to know exactly where to touch her, to kiss her, even those small stinging bites fed her growing hunger. She really couldn't catch her breath, but she didn't want him to stop.

Her breasts were sensitive and responsive to each tug and pull of his fingers. Jagged lightning sizzled through her bloodstream, connecting her breasts to her feminine core. Her pulse thundered, roaring in her ears. The tension between her legs built unrelentingly.

Lexi buried her fingers in his hair, trying to find a way to steady herself when she felt as if any moment she might fly apart. She really couldn't quite catch her breath.

Gavriil? She needed reassurance. Needed to know that she'd survive. She knew better than to think she'd ever be the same. *Is so much pleasure a sin?* How could it not be?

If so, I'll take sinning over fire and brimstone any day. He pressed a kiss in the valley between her breasts and lifted his head, his eyes meeting hers.

Her heart slammed in her chest. His eyes were dark and sensual, hooded with fierce desire so intense she felt her feminine sheath contract in response.

"I'm loving you, Lexi. My way. The way a man is meant to love his woman. I'm worshiping your body, expressing my feelings for you in the way I'm best at. This is love my way. I can't imagine that we're not meant to love each other."

Before she could reply he bent his head to her body again. His body pinned hers down. The strength in his hands was enormous. He seemed on the edge of his control, his features carved with harsh sensuality. She should have been afraid of him, but she was more afraid of herself. Of the ever-building need growing so strong inside of her.

Gavriil kissed his way to her belly button, dipping his tongue there, while one hand slid between her legs to feel her slick heat. She cried out, the sound shocking her. Just that simple touch had her squirming, her hips bucking. She was embarrassed that she couldn't hold still, her body writhing with need and a hunger she'd never known before.

"Gavriil?" She caught at his hair, the only thing left to her.

He didn't lift his head but stroked his tongue down her belly. *Just relax for me, Lexi. I'll take care of you. Breathe. You'll like this, I promise.*

His voice soothed her as it always did. Soft. Low. So calm, as if nothing ever got to him. *I can't stop moving*, she confessed. She was grateful for the ability to talk to him telepathically. She wasn't certain she could have made the admission aloud.

He kissed his way to the tiny curls guarding treasure and breathed warm air over her. *You can move all you want. There's no right or wrong, just pleasure. If something doesn't feel good, we'll change it up and find the things you do like.*

He would stop if she didn't like whatever he planned. He would stop. She clung to that promise. Gavriil was strong and always in control. He wouldn't take them to a place they couldn't retreat from if necessary. She loved him all the more in that moment.

This is really what you want, Gavriil? She held her breath, needing his answer. Needing to know. He was showing her what love was. She wanted him to take her there with him, to give her the same confidence. She'd been hiding for far too long. She never thought to have love. Until Gavriil.

His head shot up, his hooded eyes fierce with desire, sensual lines carved deep. "I want this more than you could possibly know." His voice was a rough growl. The sound rumbled over her skin like a thousand raspy tongues lapping at her, making her shudder with anticipation. "Let me have this."

How could she deny him? She didn't want to. She wanted to taste the forbidden. His hands already drove her crazy. Her body trembled with need. She wanted to feel his mouth on her. She wanted to know if she could accept what he did and give him whatever he asked for. He didn't make her feel depraved or immoral. He made her feel beautiful and wanted.

"I want to eat every inch of you, Lexi. I need to know you're mine."

His words, his tone of voice, the look on his face, all that dark hunger was impossible for her to resist. She inclined her head because it was impossible to talk, not when he looked at her like that. So hungry, as if he really might devour her.

He spread her thighs with his hands, opening her to the night. To him. She couldn't take her eyes from his face. The fire cast a golden glow over their bodies, moved shadows through the room. Strangely, his face remained in the shadows even when the flames danced over both of them. He looked harsh, his features a mask of sensuality. His eyes were hooded and focused completely on her. He looked at her as if she was really a meal, and he was starving.

Her breath caught in her lungs when he dipped his head and his tongue swiped through her folds. She cried out, shocked. The glittering pleasure was like nothing she had imagined.

Gavriil. She cried out his name, her breath coming in a gasping rush, all at once, her hips bucking under the streak of lightning whipping through her body.

Lexi, you taste like wild honey.

His hands held her thighs apart while he began to lap at her, over and over, a cat licking greedily at cream.

The air left her lungs in a heated rush. He threw her into complete chaos, her mind going numb, her body needing, wanting. Fire raced through her bloodstream, burning her from the inside out. Every muscle tightened. Every nerve ending sent darts of fire racing through her. Tension gathered. Built fast. Her breasts ached. Her stomach lurched and a thousand butterflies took wing. The aching need between her legs grew into a throbbing beat impossible to ignore.

You can't.

I am. He gave a little growl, much like a tiger when someone tried to remove its dinner. *I've waited a lifetime for you—for this. Let me.*

She wasn't certain she would survive. The pleasure was totally unexpected. The fire too hot. The sensations threatening to drown her.

She couldn't take her eyes off of him. His mouth turned aggressive as he dipped his tongue deep to collect spiced honey, drawing it from her body again and again. His tongue plunged into her, stroked her most sensitive button and then his mouth suckled.

She screamed as hot pleasure burst through her, radiating outward like the rays of the sun from his hungry mouth.

I can't. I can't take any more.

It isn't nearly enough. Breathe for me. Relax. This is just the beginning. I want you to feel love, Lexi. Feel it surround you and take you away. My love.

She had to find a way to hold on when the room spun and the walls receded. She couldn't panic, not now when she was so close to achieving her goal and surrendering herself entirely to him. More than anything she wanted him to know she would try to do anything for him.

Lexi dug her fingers into the sheet and bunched the material inside her fists, holding tight and trying to breathe while he lapped and ate and suckled like a wild man. She felt the tension gathering, building. There was no release, no way to stop the shuddering of her body and the fierce need growing out of control.

Gavriil. Fear edged her voice, crept down her spine. That only seemed to add to the desperation between her legs. *I need* . . .

Gavriil lifted his head, his eyes dark with love and desire. "Me. Only me, Lexi. I'm all you need."

17

———

Gavriil knelt between her thighs, keeping her open to him, reluctant to leave his feast, but he was beginning to lose her. The sensations were too much when she'd never experienced them before. He caught her bottom and dragged her to him. Holding his throbbing shaft in one hand, he positioned the weeping head at her slick entrance. She was hot and so damp and ready for him, but he wasn't taking chances.

It was difficult to think with his blood roaring and his pulse pounding in his ears. He was skating on the very edge of his control. Watching her face, he pushed slowly into her scorching-hot sheath. At once her tight muscles surrounded him, silky smooth yet gripping him hard so that the friction of just pushing steadily took his breath. The top of his head threatened to come off. He gritted his teeth to keep from plunging deep and hard in the way his body demanded.

Her eyes widened in shock. Her mouth formed a round *O*. He loved seeing her stretched around him, her body accepting his, taking him inside her where he belonged. He had wanted this moment entirely for her. Never in his life could he remember a time when he'd had to fight for control. Now, when he needed it the most, his training was failing him.

Heat and fire surrounded his shaft. An exquisite burn surrounded him, grasping, tightening, clamping around him like a silken fist. His breath left his lungs in a rush. He threw back his head and closed his eyes just for one moment to absorb the absolute perfection of the sensation.

He moved slowly, fighting the urge in his body to thrust deep and hard, taking him all the way to paradise. Sex had never been like this before. He hadn't used a single gimmick, hadn't tried any technique, he'd simply followed his heart. He felt more alive, more exhilarated than he ever had in his life.

Every nerve ending, damaged or not, sizzled and burned until pleasure overtook pain. His past receded the deeper he plunged into her, the hotter the friction, the more his memories dissipated as if they'd never been. She took him to a place of peace, of love, of absolute passion and pleasure.

His breath hissed out between clenched teeth. *Tell me how you're feeling. Are you hurting? Even a little? You have to let me know.*

He counted his heartbeats, looking down at her face and the passion etched there. Desire in the forest green of her eyes. She panted, little gasping rushes. Flushed skin, dazed eyes, her body writhing beneath his and her hands clutching the sheets told him she was feeling much the same way he was, but he had to be certain.

Terrified. Wonderful. I don't know what I'm feeling but I don't want you to stop.

We won't. We're in this together. I'm going to let go just a little more.

More? Her breath came in a ragged, shocked gasp. *How can there be more?*

There's always more, he assured her.

His hips drew back slowly and then he plunged deep and hard, burying his body inside hers, in her exquisite sheath, the scorching-hot friction sending shock waves through his body, along with a raging firestorm threatening to burn out of control.

Lexi clutched the sheets, her head thrashing wildly on the pillow while Gavriil played her body like a beautiful instrument. Each move he made sent tremors of sheer pleasure racing through every cell in her body. It was impossible to think straight. Each time he plunged into her, he sent a dozen lightning bolts streaking through her, turning her body into an electrical storm.

She expected to see sparks flying all around them. She loved the way he looked with the firelight playing over him. His muscles so clearly defined. His face intense, focused, and utterly sensual. He looked like an ancient warrior come to claim her for his own, determined to share her skin, her body, her heart and mind. That only added to the intensity of her pleasure.

He looped her legs over his shoulders, one arm sliding around her to drag her even closer, and he began to move fast, pummeling into her, a golden jackhammer, going deep and hard so that she felt him driving into her womb. Every intense thrust sent those streaks of lightning sizzling and burning throughout her body, driving her higher, the tension coiling tighter.

Give yourself to me.

She couldn't stop it, that deadly climb, higher, always higher. Everything inside of her wound into a tight coil, the tension ratcheting up notch after notch. She could barely draw a breath. Barely think straight. She wanted. She needed. But she didn't know what. There was only Gavriil and the intensity of their bodies coming together.

A fireball roared through her, setting every nerve ending bursting into flames. She couldn't stop moving, desperate for . . . something.

Let go, Lexi. Just let go. I'm here, angel moy. With you. In you. Trust me. You have to give yourself to me entirely. I need your trust.

She was afraid. Her body really wasn't her own, but his. He surged into her again and again, and the fire roared, scorching hot, until the streaks of lightning threatened to destroy her. She couldn't catch her breath, couldn't think. There was no stopping the sensations swamping her, threatening to overtake her. There was only . . . Gavriil.

His voice gave her the courage to let the sensations take her over. She felt his hands tighten on her. His shaft swelled even more, stretching her impossibly. The friction grew hotter, the pleasure wilder. Her terrified gaze found his dark blue eyes. There was strength there. Love. Tenderness. The emotions were wrapped up in his hunger and desire for her.

Come to me, dusha moya, *all the way.*

His voice caressed her mind so lovingly it brought tears to her eyes. She took a deep breath and let go. The ripples began somewhere deep inside of her body and spread like a tsunami, hard and fast until the sensation was a torrent ripping through her in gigantic swells, down to her thighs, up to her belly and breasts, wave after wave. Her body clamped down like a vise around his, grasping and dragging at his shaft, squeezing and milking, taking him with her.

Thunder roared in her ears. Her blood pumped hot and crazy through her body. Flames licked at her skin. The tsunami seemed endless, wave after wave rocking her, until she heard her own scream, a cry of pure shock and absolute freedom. Gavriil's hoarse cry joined hers.

Lexi watched his face the entire time, wanting—no— needing to know he felt what she was feeling. He had given her a gift beyond all price. Freedom. She had believed herself frigid, ugly, inferior. All of those things. He made her feel beautiful and passionate and equal to him—a partner loved and cherished.

"Are you crying, *solnyshko moya*? There will be no tears. This was too beautiful for tears."

Very slowly Gavriil turned his head and kissed the inside of her legs before placing them gently on the mattress on either side of his body. Every movement sent strong aftershocks rippling through her and around him.

Lexi's hands curled in his hair. Her heart beat hard and fast beneath his own. Tears trickled down her face. He touched one with the pad of his finger, very gently and then leaned forward to sip at more.

"That's making love, Lexi. That's me showing you what you mean to me. That's the way love should be between a man and a woman."

"It's beautiful."

"It's supposed to be beautiful. And earthy. And gritty. And natural. You're beautiful to me, and I'll never be able to have enough of you."

"You're beautiful, Gavriil. Everything about you." She touched his face with trembling fingers. "You have no idea what you've given me."

He was still as hard as a rock. He'd waited a lifetime for her. There was no quick fix for a lifetime of being a mechanical robot. Not human. Without emotion or hope. He stared down into her face. Could any woman be more beautiful? He doubted it. Her hair spilled around her, dark and gleaming red in the firelight, like the finest of wines. Her face was flushed, her mouth swollen from his kisses. Her eyes were shocked and dazed, her gaze moving over his face with an expression he never dreamt he'd see on a woman's face.

To cover the sudden surge of emotion, he leaned down and drew her right breast into his mouth. She was still sensitive and her body shuddered around his, little aftershocks going off so that her sheath rippled around him, gripping tightly. If anything, his cock grew harder and thicker.

"It's impossible to do this again, isn't it? I thought . . ." She trailed off when he moved, a slow, leisurely thrust into her.

He licked at her nipple and then lifted his head, wanting her to understand there was no going back for either of them. "I'll never grow tired of kissing you or holding you or sharing your body with you. Being inside you is my secret haven, a place that can wipe out every bad thing I've ever seen or done."

"I don't think I still have a sane thought in my head," she admitted.

The firelight played over her face. He nuzzled at her breast. "I want to make love to you in every way possible, to give you so much pleasure, Lexi."

"If you give me much more, I might just die. As it was, I was a little afraid we'd go too far."

"There's no such thing as too far or too much. I can always get us back." He kissed her throat and moved his mouth to the side of her neck, just above where her shoulder was. He needed to leave another mark on her. Her breasts had several and there were two on the inside of her thighs, but one more was needed.

"What are you doing?" she asked suspiciously.

"Making certain Benito and Lucia have something to talk about later." He grinned at her, he couldn't help it, not with joy bursting through him. He'd never been so happy or so sated in his life. Sated, but so ready to repeat the experience as soon as possible—as soon as Lexi could without becoming sore. He could stay hard for hours, something he would be forever grateful for.

Holding her tightly, he rolled over, staying inside her, bringing her up on top of him. She gasped, looking more shocked than ever. His hands urged her into a sitting position. His cock stretched her sheath as she drew up her legs, straddling him. The firelight caressed her skin with a soft glow. Her hair tumbled wildly in all directions, falling around her like so much dark silk.

His hands reached up to cup her breasts in his palms. "Look at you, woman. Could you be any more beautiful?"

"You keep saying that."

"Because it's the truth." And it was important to him that she believe him. That she saw herself the way he saw her.

She glanced down at her body—at her breasts resting in his hands. His thumbs had gone straight to her nipples, massaging small caresses back and forth over them. Her eyes widened when she saw the strawberries all over the soft mounds, and a slow blush stole up her body.

"I can't help it if your skin marks easily." He lifted his head to her breasts, using his hands to push them together so he could bury his face in the soft cushion. "Or that you're so beautiful. I can only reap the benefits."

A flick of his tongue brought a fresh flood of hot honey coiling around his cock. Her body tightened around his, a delicious feeling that spread through him like thick molasses. "I get totally lost in your body, *solnyshko moya*. I know I could spend hours worshiping you."

He lay back, his grip dropping to her hips. "Ride me, Lexi. Like this."

His hands guided her, lifting her and bringing her back down. His shaft swelled, grew harder as the friction increased. "That's it, *solnyshko moya*, get that rhythm."

"You really like this, don't you?" There was a smile in her voice. "I might be able to get good at this."

She raised her body slowly, dragging tight muscles over his shaft. Very slowly she sank back down, those same muscles squeezing and gripping hard so that the breath slammed out of his lungs. Through narrowed eyes he watched her take control, her body undulating over his, moving up and down in a slow burn. She seemed lost in the movements, her breasts swaying, her hand stroking his abdomen, just above where their bodies met.

She'd never touched his cock. Not once. He hadn't felt her fingers, or the heat she could give him with her palm and he was ultra aware of her hand so close to his shaft. If she never got that far, he would be okay with it, she was driving him crazy with her body, with that slow, easy ride.

He clenched his teeth against the urge to take control, to increase the speed and friction. Lexi took her time, her head thrown back, intense concentration on her face. He bunched his hands in her hair, dragging it to his face, deliberately tugging on it so that she opened her eyes and looked at him.

Still holding her silky hair in his hands, he pressed his palms to her breasts. "Pick up the pace, woman."

She smiled. Slowly. Teasing. Her green eyes lit up like two sparkling jewels. "Are you going to pretend you don't like this? Because you seem to be stretching me beyond what I thought possible." She lifted her body, her tight muscles sliding over his shaft. She hesitated a heartbeat, just long enough for his cock to jerk. Smiling, she rode him down with equal slowness. "Are you sure? Absolutely certain of what you want?"

He never thought to have a woman of his own, let alone one like Lexi. She seemed delighted having control. Deliberately provocative, tormenting him on purpose with her playfulness. She was fun. She made him laugh. Loving her was the easiest thing he'd ever done in his life, and at the same time, it terrified him.

He couldn't ever lose her. Not ever. The danger was he would hold on too tightly. Lexi needed breathing room. "*Solnyshko moya*, you are going to drive me insane."

"Isn't that the point?" She laughed softly and unexpectedly leaned forward, her hands framing his face, her mouth finding his.

Her kiss turned his heart over. Her sheath clamped down around him, scorching hot, a silken fist gripping him tightly. He lost himself there in her mouth, in her body, his hands coming up to her soft hips. He took control. Of her body. Of her mouth. Thrusting deep with his tongue, with his cock. Love spilled over, until his throat and eyes burned with it, until his body exploded into a million fragments along with hers, soaring, freefalling, coming to rest with her safe in his arms.

He held her tightly, burying his face in her hair, his body shuddering with pleasure, with need, feeling as though he might be in a dream.

"Thank you for finding me," Lexi whispered against his shoulder, her voice muffled, but her lips brushing small kisses over his skin—his scars—as she spoke.

"Thank you for saving me," he whispered back. He held her for a long time, his body locked inside of hers.

A small aftershock rippled around him, and he moved gently inside of her.

Lexi laughed softly. "Seriously, Gavriil. You're going to kill us both. I can't move. I don't think I'm going to be able to walk."

Very reluctantly he pulled out of her and gently set her to one side, on her stomach beside him. "Are you certain, because I'm sure I could go again." He said it more to hear her laughter than seriously. He was going to have to run a hot bath for her to soak away any soreness.

"It's time for me to supplement Lyutyj's feeding. If we keep his strength up, he'll be able to compete for Kiss's milk. Since you have so much energy, you're the one who is going to have to go into the kitchen and get it."

He rolled over and pressed a kiss into the small of her back. "If I leave you and go make his bottle, are you going to be waiting for me? I don't want you disappearing on me."

"I can't move, how can I disappear?" She gave him a half-hearted shove. "I could crawl out the window maybe, but it would be too much trouble."

His smile faded. "Lexi." He pushed back the wild fall of hair so he could see her face. "You aren't going to panic because we made love, are you?"

"I don't feel like panicking, Gavriil," she replied seriously. "But that doesn't mean I won't."

"If I reach for you in the middle of the night, will that make you panic?" He watched her closely, needing to know that she would welcome him—that she trusted him with her body and her heart.

"I can't say," she said, as truthfully as possible. "I don't honestly know what brings on a panic attack, but right now, all I can say is that I love the way you touch me. I love the things you do to me." She started to say something and then stopped herself, biting her lip and turning her head away from him.

Deliberately, Gavriil leaned down and bit her shapely butt.

"Ow." She turned back toward him, glaring. "What was that for?"

"Not talking. Not telling me something important to you. Spill it woman, even if it embarrasses you."

She moistened her lips. "Do you have to be so good at reading me?"

"Yes, because you aren't used to sharing what you're feeling. I'm not either. We both have to work on it." He ran his hand over her bottom, his fingers finding one of the many scars and tracing it gently. He couldn't help himself, he leaned down and pressed kisses along the shiny path.

"Don't you dare bite me again," she cautioned, tensing. "I'll shove you right off this bed."

He laughed. "You could try, *angel moy*, but you're very little and I'm very big, in case you haven't noticed the difference in our sizes." His hand massaged her bottom with slow, sensuous circles. "Talk to me."

She sighed. "I suppose I knew all along you wouldn't get sidetracked. I can only feel what I'm feeling. My body, I mean. I can't tell what you're feeling. When you . . ." She trailed off, blushing.

"What?" He raised an eyebrow. "I did a lot of things to you. Things I plan to do as often as possible. You'll have to be specific."

"You're making this difficult deliberately," she accused.

"I'm trying to show you there's no need to be embarrassed about anything between us. We belong to each other. What we do, what we share, is between us."

She rolled her eyes, and he splayed his fingers over her bottom, over her deliciously beautiful firm muscles.

"I'm growing very fond of your butt." He bent his head and licked along one of the scars. His teeth nipped, and she gave a startled yelp. "Well talk to me. Distract me, because I'm already getting as hard as a rock again."

Her gaze strayed to the growing cock in his lap. He circled it loosely with his hand. "Looking at you does this to me. Thinking about you does this. Watching you sleep. Hearing you laugh." He grinned at her, unrepentant. "Just about anything at all you do, let alone lying here naked with you."

Lexi bit her lip. His slow massage on her bottom had already started a slow burn deep inside. She couldn't very well lie when he was so forthcoming.

"What were you afraid to talk to me about?" He wasn't going to drop it. "I know it was important."

"What if I can never put my mouth on you the way you did me?" She blurted it out, one of her worst fears.

"Never is a long time, Lexi," he said gently.

"I know. I know it is and you told me not to worry, but I know it's a big thing with men. All the women in the compound talked about it. Some of the older ones tried to help me, but it made me sick." She had to confess, bring it out into the open. "He was furious whenever I got sick and he . . ." She stopped herself.

His heart contracted painfully for her. He didn't need to hear what the monster had done to her, he was looking at the evidence. "I told you it didn't matter to me."

"I know what you said, Gavriil, but it matters to me. It matters that I can't give you—everything."

He bent his head again, this time to press kisses into the small of her back and then up her spine. "You have given me everything. Don't you know that yet? What we have is too good to ever consider throwing it away for such a ridiculous reason."

Lexi remained silent, her large green eyes moving over his face.

He sighed. "Do you remember when you asked me questions, right after we first met, and I told you not to ask me unless you wanted the truth?"

She nodded, her expression very solemn.

"I meant what I told you then. I'm not going to lie to you. Too many people have done that. I never will. Sometimes, *solnyshko moya*, you'll wish that I did. I'll tell you when something bothers me."

Her long lashes fanned her cheeks. He went still. He knew she was going to give him something important. He could read her now, that small hesitation, the natural reluctance of sharing her past. She didn't want to open the doors on those memories, but they had shaped her life. Shaped who she was.

"Caine really was a pedophile. You can see that I'm curvy. I started getting breasts and hips around the age of thirteen. He couldn't stand looking at me. He didn't want to even use me for sex after that. Just, you know, me having to do things to him."

She bit her lower lip as if reluctant to continue. He rubbed her bottom again, a slow massage meant to soothe her. He wanted her used to his touch. Wanted her able to lie naked with him like this after they made love. He especially wanted her to share her past with him, to trust him that much. Gavriil remained silent, knowing she struggled to continue, but it had to be her choice.

"He would have gotten rid of me—I know he thought about it a million times—but our farm was a gold mine for the Reverend's church. We practically supported every compound."

"And of course, you were the one, even at such a young age, who made the plants grow for them." He pressed more kisses down her spine and stroked the dark mass of auburn hair spilling down her back.

Lexi nodded. "He tried starving me, to keep me thin. He wouldn't allow me to eat more than one meal a day, but I worked with all the crops so it was easy enough to eat lettuce and tomatoes while I worked."

"And when he found out?"

"He would beat me and then lock me in the box for days. Then he'd be afraid I'd die. It was kind of a vicious circle. That man. Benjamin Frost. The Reverend's right hand. He'd come around and tell Caine he'd take me off his hands. He said Caine wouldn't even have to pay him. I think he suspected I had some kind of gift, but Caine knew if I left, the farm would go downhill. The farm's prosperity gave him power and a certain prestige. He didn't want to lose that."

"And he couldn't break you," Gavriil said, remembering the hatred on Caine's face when he stared at Lexi. He had come looking for her to turn his fortune around again, to punish her for being everything he could never be. Gavriil had seen many men like him over his years in the field.

"I feel broken," Lexi admitted. She frowned. "At least I did. Now that you're here, I don't know what I feel."

"Feel beautiful. Feel feminine. Feel as if you're mine, because you are. And I'm yours. That's our world, Lexi, and those people have no place in it. They don't control you and they can't get to you. I'm standing between you and them and I always will. You can count on that. And you can count on the fact that I'm very, very good at my job."

"Are you going to let Jonas Harrington go after the men threatening me?"

"Sure. He can look for them all he wants and wait until they commit a crime he can lock them up for. Of course they'll get out again in a few years if that happens." Gavriil knew he sounded complacent—too complacent, but prison for men like Benjamin Frost was simply a revolving door. Frost knew how to work the system and when he couldn't, he got others to take care of witnesses.

"Basically it's who finds him first, right? And I told you where to look for him." She rubbed her chin on the sheets, her tone thoughtful.

He shrugged. "You women wanted the chance to clear out the innocents. I'm all for that, and I can wait. I've got eyes and ears on him now. He isn't going to slip through my fingers because you need to wait for a foggy day. He can't sneak up on us. You're safe here on the farm. The fog will come soon enough."

"What if Jonas gets him first? Ilya might tell him where they are."

"Ilya is my brother. He's loyal to Jonas and the Drakes,

there's no doubt about that, but this is a family matter. We keep family safe."

"What does that mean?"

"It means I find anyone who is a threat to our family and I eliminate them. That's what I do, Lexi. I'll make certain I get every last one of them, just to keep you and the others safe." He leaned down again and pressed another kiss into the small of her back. "I'll be right back. I'm going to run you a hot bath. You need to soak for a few minutes or you'll be very sore. You, my little woman, are impossibly tight. And I'm rather . . ."

Her eyes widened with a hint of mischief in them. "Large?"

He laughed and made his way to the bathtub, running the hot water while he found bath salts. Dumping in a generous amount, he added cold, checking the temperature. "You're not falling asleep, are you?"

"Yes. Go away. Feed the pup. I'm exhausted."

"You're taking a bath and then you can fall asleep."

"You're just plain bossy. I thought I was supposed to be the boss, wasn't that the deal we had?"

The drowsy note in her voice drove him crazy. How was he ever supposed to resist her when she sounded sexy and tempting? "As I remember, that was when we were working the farm together. I'm certain I was a perfect helper. I did everything you said. This is my expertise."

She made a disparaging sound. He was fairly certain she'd rolled her eyes. He found her lying exactly as he left her. "If you don't soak in hot water, you'll be too sore for more lovemaking and I've got ideas."

"Go away. I'm too tired for lovemaking, or feeding pups tonight. You're on your own. I'm sleeping right here like this, so leave the fire on."

He rolled her over and lifted her easily into his arms, cradling her against his chest. "Bath time, *solnyshko moya.*"

"You said that meant your sun. Maybe I could be your moon. As in night. Sleep." She wrapped her arms around his neck and laid her head against his heart, her lashes sweeping down.

He put her down into the hot, steaming water.

She gasped and then smiled up at him. "Maybe this was a good idea after all. I didn't realize I was so sore."

He brushed a kiss on top of her head, standing over her, emotion overwhelming him. "I'm going to always take good care of you, Lexi. I haven't ever loved a woman before. It's a new, raw experience. You're my only. The one." Because the wealth of emotion was overpowering, he turned away from her. "I'm going to get the pup his supplement, and you contemplate how much I love you for the next few minutes. Let it sink in."

Lexi stared after him, shocked at his last comment. They danced around the word *love*. It was put out there a few times when Gavriil told her the difference between making love and having sex, but neither one of them was very good at expressing the emotion.

She should have told him she loved him. She hadn't actually said it to him. She wasn't certain she could without crying. After her family had been murdered, her "sisters" had saved her life. She had gone to the group therapy as a last resort, and without the women she loved as her family, she wouldn't have made it through those terrible times. But Gavriil . . .

Gavriil had given her a life, not simply an existence. She didn't know how to feel about his plan to keep them safe. She wasn't exactly happy about it, but she was tired of being afraid. Tired of knowing she didn't dare leave the farm just in case someone spotted her. He was a strong man, a man she could rely on, and there was no doubt in her mind that he would do everything in his power to keep her safe.

Why had Caine come back? Why was Benjamin Frost threatening her? He hadn't liked Caine. Even as a child she could tell he didn't. Caine had been pompous and vain. He believed himself the ultimate authority and didn't like Frost around because he scared everyone. Caine's congregation seemed more respectful and fearful of Frost.

The more prosperous the farm became, the more Caine took credit. He wanted the Reverend's attention. Frost suspected Lexi had something to do with the farm's sudden increase in production, although he couldn't understand why, and when it became apparent Caine no longer wanted her, Frost had come to him with a deal. He'd replace Lexi with a young girl if Caine gave Lexi to him.

She shivered, remembering Frost's vicious stare. He wasn't trying to save her from Caine, that much was certain. She'd learned to get away with a few things and had even begun planning her escape. The last thing she wanted to do was go with Frost. Caine had refused to hand her over, citing the sanctity of marriage. That effectively stopped him from taking another child bride. He'd had to choose between his sexual depravity and his need to be seen by the Reverend as all powerful.

"You're crying."

Lexi's eyes flew open. Gavriil towered over her, looking like an avenging angel—a dark one, but still—her guardian angel. His voice was harsh, his features a stone mask. In his arms he cradled Lyutyj. Her heart gave a little stutter at the sight. She could see him holding a child in his arms just as securely. She knew he would never drop that puppy, no matter what happened. He was a big man, a strong man, but that small living creature was totally safe in his arms.

"I'm not crying because of you. Or us. Never that, Gavriil. Too many memories close. Frost. Caine." She shook her head. "They have no place here in our home. I don't want them to come between us."

She stood up and allowed the water to drain from the tub, taking the towel he handed her as she stepped out. "Do you want children?" The question came out of nowhere. She shocked herself by asking it.

He didn't appear thrown in the least. He didn't even blink. He took her hand and led her back into the bedroom. Sinking down into the chair, he began to feed the puppy with the bottle. Since taking his mother's milk, little Lyutyj could use a regular nipple and greedily took the supplement.

"I had never considered such a thing, Lexi. Me? A father? How could this be when I didn't have a woman of my own? A woman I loved more than life itself? I didn't really think about it until Lucia came over and I saw the two of you with your heads together and you looked so perfectly right."

He reached out his hand, the one with the bottle in it, to run his finger over her abdomen. "Look at you. A woman is such a miracle. Her ability to keep a child safe and secure inside of her amazes me."

His voice made her shiver. His eyes darkened, desire glittering there.

"Once a certain politician, a friend of Sorbacov's, decided he wanted his wife dead. She was pregnant and he had a much younger mistress. I didn't know why Sorbacov ordered the hit, but when I saw her, I knew there was more to it than I'd been told. She was no spy. She was no threat to our country. I did my own investigation. Now, she and her child live somewhere safe, far away from Sorbacov. She has no worries that her husband will ever pursue her or get his friend to send another operative after her again."

Lexi moved behind his chair and circled his neck with her arms, leaning down to hold him close to her. His memories were every bit as horrendous as hers were. She wanted to erase them all for him and replace them with something far different. Laughter. Peace. A home and a woman who loved him.

"I'm glad you stayed with me, Gavriil," she whispered, and brushed his ear with her lips. "I think we're good for each other."

18

"CONDITIONS are perfect tonight," Blythe said, looking back toward the mountainous road. They had parked their vehicles carefully in the trees where they couldn't be seen. "It's definitely a go."

Levi, perched on the tailgate of their pickup beside Rikki, nodded. "We have numerous recordings and we know the main event takes place each evening at eight o'clock. Everyone is inside the building and sitting by precisely eight. If they dare to be late, there's hell to pay."

Lexi shivered. Gavriil didn't change expression or even look at her, but he shifted his weight imperceptibly closer and his palm slid down her arm to her wrist.

We're taking them down, solnyshko moya, *there's no need for bad memories.*

Lexi took a deep breath. "Were there any young brides there?"

"None that we saw," Ilya said. "We were careful to study each of the tapes over and over, Lexi. This compound seems to be operating independently of any others. At least, if there are others, this group doesn't actively interact with them."

The eleven of them—six women and five men—huddled in a circle under cover of the trees. From the road they were impossible to see, even with four vehicles. They were still a distance from the compound where Frost ruled, but they'd have to get closer on foot to avoid detection.

"How many enforcers?" Lissa asked.

"Six," Gavriil answered. "All six men answer to the man by the name of Benjamin Frost, the one who threatened Lexi on the message machine."

Lexi cleared her throat. Her fingers twisted together. Gavriil noted with a silent curse that each of his brothers noticed the sign of nerves. He laid his hand gently over hers, stilling the action.

"Frost worked exclusively with the Reverend," Lexi said, her voice strained. "He went around to each compound and gave the leaders their orders. No one made a decision without his permission. His punishments were extremely brutal. Not even Caine wanted to go against him, although he stood up to him when Frost tried to get him to hand me over. Because Caine was supposedly my husband, Frost couldn't just take me, although several key members believed that Frost was the actual leader of the cult and the Reverend was merely his front man, chosen because he had so much charisma. Whether that's true or not, no one knows for certain."

Max paced under the trees restlessly. "It's clear he's comfortable in the role of leader. He never has to ask twice, and when he enters the meeting hall, there's absolute silence. No one even fidgets."

"Can we see what's happening in the hall where they meet from the entrance to their compound?" Airiana asked.

"You can't be there," Thomas said instantly.

"Anywhere near there," Gavriil added.

Before any of the women could protest, Thomas continued. "Frost has his own security cameras set up. We've marked them on the map surrounding the compound. Frost is smart though. He set up the night vision cameras he did have to give the maximum amount of coverage surrounding his compound."

"Clearly they no longer have the money they had when the Reverend was around, or the manpower," Maxim stated.

"Which is why I think they made the big push to find Lexi," Gavriil said. "I think the cult disintegrated between the arrests, the publicity and the Reverend's death. Their money was gone, and you need money to run the operation. Lexi was a gold mine and they lost her. This wasn't about getting her back to be a wife to someone. They wanted her to turn things around for them again."

Lexi shook her head. "Caine was going to kill me. He told the others to kill me."

"Only after you had trapped him in the ground," Gavriil said. "In the heat of the moment, and the others reacted. They weren't soldiers. They were men out of their element, regardless of how tough they thought they were. And remember, it was Frost and Caine who knew you were the moneymaker, no one else."

"You represented money to them," Levi added. "Frost needs a cover for his operations. We discovered he was running guns and has good connections in the Middle East for his drug business. He had to launder the money and have a good clean operation to present to his congregation and outsiders. Without the Reverend's charismatic nature, and the raids, I'm guessing things went downhill fast."

"He wants Lexi to grow his crops for him," Blythe said. "That's what you're saying. So they call and try to scare her? That's crazy."

"Frost is using intimidation to get his way. Most of his congregation fear him," Maxim said. "I think he's so used to people being afraid of him, he figured we'd hand Lexi over to him, or she'd be so afraid for us that she'd give herself up."

"He's going to get a taste of his own medicine," Lissa said, satisfaction edging her voice. "We need a place we can work from. Somewhere all of us can do our thing together. With both Blythe and Judith here to boost our power, we'll have to make certain we don't overdo it."

Judith laughed. "We want believers. Remember the last time things got away from us? That wasn't pretty."

The women all burst out laughing. Levi and Thomas exchanged sheepish looks.

"I scouted an area I think will work for you," Gavriil said. "We'll be able to protect you and give you a good view of what's happening in the meeting hall. You'll be traipsing through woods though."

"That's not a problem," Rikki said, with a casual swing of her foot. "We dressed in dark clothes, warm and thick, tight around the ankles with good hiking boots. This isn't our first picnic."

Airiana nodded. "We know our way around, Gavriil. We seem like sweet ladies, but we're really not so much that way."

Lissa suddenly turned her head and looked directly at Gavriil. He knew that look. She was warning him to watch over the other women. They might profess to be badasses, but none of them had the killer instinct. He knew that already, but he nodded just the same, just to let her know he understood.

"Did you find out the names of the six enforcers?" Judith asked. "We need to be able to identify them to the congregation as the sinners. As the ones their god is most angry with."

"We've got them," Levi said. "Are you all certain you want to do this?"

The women nodded.

"This will give the opportunity for the ones who want out to make up their minds to really get out," Blythe said. "We don't want any innocents hurt."

Gavriil turned to look out toward the sea where earlier the fog lay in a thick, dark bank far out. The mist had crept in with bony fingers while they were talking, drawing a gray veil over the mountain and shrouding the forest. Moisture hung in the air.

The women had waited for such a night. The storm would come in shortly, hitting just about the time they needed it. He didn't like that they had called in a friend to watch Airiana and Max's four children. He would have much preferred that one of his brothers stay on the farm with them, but it wasn't his business, not really.

Airiana had tried to have Lucia and Benito agree to go to the friend's house, but they had steadfastly refused, not yet ready to venture off their sanctuary. In the end, Gavriil had solved the problem by bringing Drago into the mix. He was on alert in the house with the children and he wouldn't allow anyone else in other than the sitter. Gavriil hoped they took his warning very seriously. He'd made certain to put the responsibility on Lucia. She listened to anything they said about the dogs, and they all knew to go to the safe room should anything happen.

There was minimum risk to the women. He knew that. With his brothers to help protect them, there was even less. Still . . . he didn't want Lexi anywhere near the compound or Benjamin Frost. Watching the tapes of the meetings when Frost spoke, it was obvious that he commanded his congregation through fear alone. His flock didn't like him. They didn't even want to be in the same room with him, yet not a single one dared leave the meeting let alone the compound.

Ilya had found out the man had been an Army Ranger and had been forced out of the service when it was suspected that he was smuggling weapons and drugs out of the Middle East. He was never convicted because the two witnesses were poisoned before they could testify. Frost had been incarcerated at the time and couldn't have committed the crime himself, but there was no doubt in anyone's mind that he'd ordered the hits.

He'd been stripped of his rank and dishonorably discharged. He became a mercenary, and spent time out of the

States. Within three years, the lead investigator, prosecutor and judge all died of poisoning. There was no trail leading back to Frost, but Ilya's source said they all believed he was responsible, they just couldn't prove it.

Frost was not a man to be scared by ghosts or gods. He wouldn't back down. If anything, he would come at Lexi even harder. There was no sense in arguing with any of the women over it. Gavriil knew what he had to do and there was no hesitation on his part. Men like Frost had a reach outside of prison.

The six enforcers were all ex-military as well, men Frost had known in the service or through his mercenary work. They had a cozy little gig, all the women they wanted, men to boss and push around, no real work other than to look scary as well as all the food they could eat. They weren't going to give up so easily either.

Gavriil had tried to talk his brothers out of helping him with his plan to eliminate the threat to Lexi. It was his duty. His problem. He knew he could slip in and out of the compound without detection. He'd already done so numerous times, planning out his every move.

He was no glory hound. He didn't do body counts or notch a piece of wood somewhere. He moved through the shadows and brought death with him. The death reaper was right there, present in the forest, looking out into the gray mist while they spoke in low voices around him.

"We're going in armed," he informed the women, his voice low and devoid of all emotion. "When we tell you to do something, do it without question. If this goes to hell, it will happen fast, and we have to know you'll cooperate with us."

Lissa looked around at her sisters. "Of course we will. Immediately. Without questions, right?"

Blythe nodded. "You're all the experts."

"But Levi and Thomas know we can protect ourselves if we have to," Rikki said. "Don't worry so much."

Gavriil didn't look at Lexi. He'd never gone into a situation with baggage. He worked alone and was used to slipping in and out with no one around. "Lexi, more than anything, you do what I tell you."

He felt her suddenly lift her head. Her sharp glance. She knew. She was very tuned to him. Connected with him. He pressed his thumb deep into the center of his itching palm.

"I have to know you're safe, do you understand me?" He turned his head and let her see the killer in him. That cold reaper of death who should never be set loose on the world. He'd been that phantom too long and he didn't know how to pull back, not in a situation like this one.

Her green gaze collided with his. Held his. The soft forest, the secret place he could fall into where there was only peace. Lexi ignored everyone around her and moved straight to him, to stand directly in front of him. She lifted her hand and stroked a caress down the side of his face. He felt her gentle touch right down to his bones.

"Of course I'll be safe, Gavriil. I'm with you."

Everything in him settled. He took her hand and brought it to his mouth, his teeth biting gently at the pads of her fingers.

"Let's get this done, shall we?" he said. "We've got the vehicles covered just in case. Max, you take the lead. I'll take the rear. We'll need to keep sound from traveling."

"Airiana and Max can muffle sound," Lexi said. "They're not going to let anyone hear us."

The forest was cool and damp, the fog so thick that even walking in a single line, it was difficult to see the person in front of you, yet Lexi moved with complete confidence. He found himself watching her even as he was alert to any danger that might stalk them. Night was falling, making it even harder to see, but she didn't hesitate in the least. Her hands brushed the leaves of the trees and brush as she passed them.

He felt as if the plants reached out toward her, the fronds of ferns, the tall bushes, even the branches on the trees. Her long, thick hair was pulled away from her face and braided into some intricate weave only women seemed to know how to do. He'd watched her earlier braiding her hair, standing in front of the mirror without looking into it. Not once.

Gavriil ran his hand down the long braid. Lexi turned her head to smile at him over her shoulder. Love, he decided, was complicated. Terrifying. Amazing. Love was a woman who could take a man as twisted and broken as he was, and shape him into something far better.

They crowded into the small clearing beneath the circle of trees overlooking the compound. Gavriil had chosen the spot because he could see anyone coming at them from any direction. The weather would prohibit a sniper from finding them with a bullet, even a particularly good one—and he was certain at least one of Frost's enforcers had been a sniper in his military career.

They had several good exits away from the compound, so that if they had to scatter quickly, they could melt into the forest and not be seen. Still . . .

Stay close to me, Lexi.

The women formed a circle while the men moved into positions to protect them. Max brought the screen into the center of the circle, trying to find the best location to pick up the camera's signals. Eventually he heaped dirt and grass into a mound and pressed the screen into it. At once the meeting hall showed.

Members of the congregation wandered around, talking in low voices, difficult to hear.

"Can you clean up the audio?" Gavriil asked. He wanted Frost's reaction to the show.

"Give me a minute," Max said.

"Rikki is really good at that stuff," Blythe said. "She doesn't talk about it, but she can fix just about anything when it comes to electronics."

"The problem could be with the mike or in the receiver," Max said, as he bent over the screen, looking at lines of code.

Rikki looked over his shoulder to peer at the screen.

Airiana lifted her hands into the air and moved them in

a complicated pattern, weaving and binding the fog to her. She began to send it out slowly, long trails within the veil heading down the mountain for the compound. She let it drift, pushing it along with a gentle breeze, so that thin streaks like bony fingers reached toward the building where Frost's congregation was meeting.

"Keep it slow," Blythe cautioned. "We don't want the weather to stop anyone from going."

"It wouldn't stop them. You went to those meetings even if you were sick, or about to give birth. No one ever dared miss them," Lexi said.

A little shiver ran through her, memories crowding close—too close. Lexi knew she needed to do this—to find a way to face her past and defeat it. She was gifted with being bound to earth. She had her sisters who loved and protected her, who had given her a home. She had Gavriil, a man who loved her in spite of her inability to give him everything she would have liked. She needed to feel power-ful and in control of her life again.

She knew Gavriil was giving her this gift despite the fact that he wanted them all as far from Frost as possible. He didn't agree with the idea of scaring the others away. He didn't need them gone. He would hunt down the enforcers and Frost one by one and dispose of the danger to Lexi without all the drama. But for her, he was willing to step back and give her this moment.

Lexi intended to show Gavriil just how powerful the women were. He'd never seen them in action. He had no idea what they could do when they were together, and she wanted to show him so that he wouldn't worry so much about her safety. She knew he saw her as fragile. She couldn't blame him any more than she blamed her sisters. She didn't look that strong when she was always having panic attacks, but she had a core strength that had never failed her.

That strength had allowed her to endure Caine's punish-ments and abuse. It had allowed her to plan her escape knowing he might kill her if he caught her. That same strength had been there when the marshals had told her Caine had murdered her entire family.

Gavriil's palm cupped her face, his thumb sliding over her neck. "We can still go home, Lexi. If this gives you too many bad memories."

She shook her head. "I want to do this, Gavriil. I think it will help. I tried to strike at them using the law. That didn't work. I'm hoping this will at least give the opportunity for those who have become disillusioned to get out while they can. To escape. They need a chance."

He nodded, his jaw tight, eyes cold. She recognized that look for what it was, but he stepped back, giving her room, and she was grateful. She didn't want to have to argue with him. It wasn't really in her nature, and she knew if Gavriil believed in something strongly enough, he would never back down. She absolutely needed to do this.

"We've got audio," Max announced. "Thanks, Rikki. That helped."

"Everyone's taking their seats, Lexi," Judith reported.

Lexi turned back toward the screen and studied the congregation. She could almost feel the tension from where she was. The women sat very close to their men—or very far away, a telling sign she recognized from her days of sitting and waiting for Caine to go in and speak.

She moistened her lips. "He'll walk in after he allows the tension to really stretch out. In about four minutes he'll send in the enforcers. If anyone has grown a little restless, you'll see them stop fidgeting immediately. Those men will walk around and just stare at everyone. Sometimes they'll stop and target someone, but they won't say a word."

"It's all about intimidation," Levi said, disgust in his voice.

Lexi couldn't stop from twisting her fingers together. She knew that would upset Gavriil more than anything else right now. He didn't want her distressed over Frost and his threats. On some level, she knew if she got too upset, Gavriil would sling her over his shoulder and carry her right out of there. She shouldn't have been grateful that she could rely so much on his strength and protection, but she was.

"His enforcers make certain their weapons are visible." She made a major effort to keep her voice from shaking. "They told us it was so we would feel protected from outsiders, but it only made us feel threatened."

Lissa put her hand gently on Lexi's shoulder. "That was the point, right?"

Lexi let her breath out slowly and looked around her at the other women. Each of them had a past—someone they loved murdered and they felt responsible—just as she did. Still, they worked. The six of them just fit together and became something so much more. They empowered one another. Just being with them gave her the courage she needed to see this through.

"Four-minute mark," Levi said. "Just like robots, Lexi, there they are."

Lexi got her first real look at the men Frost surrounded himself with. She didn't recognize any of them. "They have to be from other compounds. The police told me there weren't many left. That they scattered when the arrests began. I'm sure many took the opportunity to disappear, disillusioned by the Reverend's depravity when it came to light."

"The three on the left"—Maxim pointed to them as they walked down the left aisle, definitely appearing intimidating—"all of them served with Frost. They're tight. These three were the suspects in the killings of those who investigated Frost while he was in the service. They left soon after he did and joined the same mercenary company he worked from."

"Judith typed up the notes for all of you with the correct spellings of their names," Thomas added. "Just keep that in front of you, Airiana, when you write their names in the fog. You don't want them to think their god can't spell." He flashed a teasing grin.

"The other three on the right aisle are friends from Frost's mercenary days," Levi explained. "None of them are married, although the one with the beard has been several times."

Thomas nodded. "His last marriage was to a young woman from Afghanistan. They were married about two years but few people ever saw her. The neighbors said they didn't even realize she was no longer with him until the police made inquiries. Her family asked for news of her. Shelton Edwards claimed his wife had gone back to Afghanistan and her family most likely had disposed of her. It seems more likely that he did."

"He was married three times," Levi added. "All three wives were from foreign countries, and all three disappeared without a trace when they supposedly returned home. No marriage lasted more than two years."

"He's a sadistic bastard," Max said. "He had a particular reputation for getting results in interrogation, but there was never a survivor."

Lexi wasn't surprised that Frost surrounded himself with men such as Shelton Edwards. Caine had done the same thing. They were men who thrived on violence and enjoyed seeing others in pain. The congregation was comprised of men and women who followed them, feared them and tried to please them. The men needed those things, enjoyed the power they held over the others and often taunted and tormented them just because they could.

She studied their faces. There were several single men. They had probably loved the idea that women were subservient to men. The men had most likely been promised sweet young innocent brides who would do their bidding at any time.

There were several families, and she could tell which men had joined because they had made honest mistakes and regretted their choices bitterly and those who enjoyed believing their wives were put on earth for the sole purpose of serving their every desire.

That had been a favorite topic of the Reverend and he'd preached it often, using fire and brimstone techniques, taking the roof off the meeting room, pounding his fist on the pulpit and calling up the women to confess the sin of not taking proper care of their husbands.

Husbands gave lists to their leaders. She knew because Caine had happily made up transgression after transgression. She'd been humiliated and punished at nearly every meeting and forced to beg her husband's forgiveness. Lexi wasn't altogether certain she could go through even watching it on camera.

"Okay, he's walking in," Blythe reported. "Lexi, you might want to give them a little foreshadowing. Nothing big. We don't want them running out of the building."

"Rikki, bring in the rain. The larger storm is still a distance out over the ocean, but you've got cloud and moisture to make it work," Judith added. "I'll give you a little boost when you get it going."

"I've got the wind," Airiana said. "I'll drive the rain and fog right at them. The wind is going to do some talking."

"Not too much rain, Rikki," Blythe said hastily when the clouds above the compound burst open. "We need the fog. Airiana, start moving the fog inside the building, but very slowly so no one notices."

Lexi sank onto the ground, brushing aside decades of vegetation. The soil beneath was dark with richness. She pushed her hands deep, feeling the immediate connection, the peace that always stole over her when she touched the soil.

She closed her eyes and concentrated, reaching deep to make that bond even stronger until she could feel the heartbeat of the earth. The heat. The veins of water running beneath the surface. She felt ice and fire. The very pulse of the earth.

Very slowly she closed her fists around the soil, holding it tight in her palm. She moved her hands quickly, forward and back and then down and up. Not far, only a scant quarter of an inch, but at once the ripple began deep below her, stretching out as it ran in a straight line for the meeting hall—for her target.

"Get the fog in there, Airiana," Blythe instructed. "Do you need help?"

"I've got it. I don't want anyone noticing until Lexi's little present arrives. I've got it pouring in through vents, cracks under doors and open windows. I'll have enough."

They all peered at the screen. Lexi kept her hands deep in the earth. She felt the momentum, the gathering of speed, and then the earth buckled beneath the meeting hall floor directly under Benjamin Frost's feet as he stood, his boots planted shoulder-width apart, staring at his flock with a stern countenance and steely eyes.

The floorboards lifted without warning, pitching him forward onto his knees. The ground swelled, rising to meet him, so that he face-planted hard. There was an absolute stunned silence. No one else had felt that well-aimed seismic anomaly, could understand what had happened.

Gavriil dropped his hand on Lexi's shoulder. "I couldn't have placed a more well-aimed charge. Amazing technique."

She couldn't help the sense of pride, but more, the sheer pleasure at seeing Frost on his knees in front of his congregation. Fog poured into the meeting hall from every direction, up from the floor, through windows and vents, even cracks in the wood. The fog swirled around Frost, nearly obscuring him.

A collective gasp was audible as the congregation staring in shocked amazement saw the fog begin spelling out Frost's name. Even the six enforcers didn't move, their mouths open and their jaws slack. Over and over from the ceiling to the floor, the same sentence was written.

Frost does not do God's holy work. Frost does not do God's holy work. Each word was distinctly written, tall, gray block letters, plain for everyone to see.

Frost got one foot under him, and started to rise. The ground shivered, shifted and went out from under him. This time those inside the building felt the tremor, but very slightly. Frost, however, pitched forward once again, facedown, his forehead cracking on the wooden boards.

The writing slid down as if the slate in the air had been wiped clean, yet the letters descended onto the floor to run down both aisles. The letters ran straight toward the six enforcers as if alive, winding around them, ankles and wrists, upward toward their necks until they appeared to be mummies wrapped in gray bands.

Still in shock, none of the enforcers moved. They stared into the air where new letters began to form. The wind wailed Frost's name. The sound was high-pitched and haunting, and the rain began to weep all around the building as if those in heaven were crying for the lost souls.

New sentences appeared in the air. *Frost and his enforcers must be punished. Frost and his enforcers must be punished.* The sentence, like the first, was in block letters and repeated over and over until those letters slipped onto the floor to begin their climb on the enforcers. The next sentence was a list of names.

To be punished. Shelton Edwards. Gene Fielding. Daniel Forest. Trey Bridges. Ronald Howard. James Dawkins. Benjamin Frost. To be punished. Shelton Edwards. Gene Fielding. Daniel Forest. Trey Bridges. Ronald Howard. James Dawkins. Benjamin Frost.

Flames appeared above each name. Red. Orange. Tongues of fire burned in midair over and around each of the condemned names. An eerie glow flickered through the gray mist. Flames shot through the room, danced around the men in the two aisles.

Shelton fired his gun into the wall of fog and flames. A woman screamed. Several wept.

"It's getting dicey in there," Blythe pointed out. "You can't let them shoot into the crowd."

"I've got this," Lexi said. Confidence permeated her voice. She shifted the ground beneath both aisles, hitting her target precisely. The soldiers went down hard in a tangle of arms and legs. "Now, Airiana. Lissa. Rikki. With me."

Get out. Get out. Get out. The fog rolled the letters fast, galvanizing the shocked crowd into action. Rather than risk the aisles where the enforcers were, they shoved their folding chairs out of the way and rushed the back door.

Three of the enforcers managed to gain their feet in

spite of the shaking of the floor beneath them. The last member of the congregation exited the building. The wind instantly picked up, slamming the doors hard and holding them in place.

Now the wind moaned the names of the men inside, rattling the windows while the rain pounded down on the roof in a concentrated deluge. The ground buckled, rising and falling beneath the building, undulating like a snake, cracking the flooring so that boards splintered and rose up and over one another.

The seven men inside crawled toward the exits, dragging themselves while the floor rippled beneath them and the walls began to expand and contract as if breathing.

Gavriil was in awe at the power the women wielded. It was clear they had worked together before. Each move was clear and precise. They executed their attack with precision so that no one else would be harmed. The church members and even Benjamin Frost had to believe the hand of God was somewhere in the mix. What else could it be?

He couldn't help the surge of pride in Lexi. She aimed the seismic attacks perfectly, hitting each target with 100 percent accuracy. Airiana wielded the fog and wind easily, and Lissa somehow managed to pull fire from the electrical charges in the old building. Rikki's rain fell in a pounding attack on the structure, the water hitting with such force that the thin roof began to splinter and leak.

He watched Frost stagger to his feet. He tried gripping the back of a chair for support but the metal glowed red orange. He swore, leapt back, protecting a burned hand, and tripped once again. Every chair in the room began to glow ominously.

The enforcers crawled, dragged themselves or managed to get to their feet in order to get to the exits. When they tried to open the doors, the wind rose in force, howling like a terrible banshee, and refused to allow them out.

Both Edwards and Howard fired multiple shots into a door, the bullets going through the thin wood to leave behind holes. Two of the other enforcers shot out the windows, the glass spiderwebbing and then shattering. Instantly the wind entered, slamming into the men and knocking them back to the rolling floor. The rain found the broken glass and holes in the wood. Water poured inside. More water came up through the floorboards.

"They're leaving," Blythe reported in triumph. "People are flinging suitcases into cars and leaving as fast as possible. You did it. Frost doesn't have any more followers."

"Give them time to get out of there before we let Frost out. He'll be so angry he'll try to kill them," Lissa advised.

Gavriil didn't take his eyes from Lexi's face. Her eyes were glued to the screen, to the man who had helped cause her so much misery. Her hands twisted in the soil and Frost was flung into the air. His body hit several of the chairs before he landed upside down against the wall. The pulpit crashed on top of him.

Water covered the floor, and with every ripple of the earth, it splashed upward and made strong waves. The wind rushed through the room, battering the men, knocking them here and there capriciously. Ropes of sizzling electricity coiled in the air above the men's heads, a dangerous combination with all the water.

Gavriil dropped his hand on Lexi's shoulder. "You're done here. You've accomplished what you wanted. His congregation has left him. He's scared and so are his men. Ease up and then shut it down."

"I'm not finished. No one in my family will be safe as long as Frost or his men are alive. You know that," Lexi said.

Out of the corner of his eye he saw Lissa swing her head around and frown.

"I know this isn't you, Lexi, and you'll never forgive yourself," Gavriil said gently. He crouched down beside her, shackling both wrists. "The rest is my job, not yours. Stand up, *solnyshko moya*, and walk away from this thing."

He kept his voice pitched low, but very firm. He wasn't going to take no for an answer. Lexi could kill in self-defense, she had from what Thomas and Max told him, but it ate at her. This was something else. She would never forget or forgive herself, no matter what she thought now.

He tightened his grip around her wrists and physically pulled her hands from the dirt. At once the ground calmed. The turmoil remained in her, but was no longer reflected in the soil.

"Shut it down, girls," he said over his shoulder.

Lissa obeyed at once. Rikki glanced at Levi, who nodded. Airiana followed suit.

Gavriil rose, pulling Lexi to her feet. He could see she was upset with him, but she didn't say a word. He had the feeling that didn't bode well for him.

"Levi, will you and Thomas take them home and guard them? I've got work to do."

19

LEXI spun around, her green eyes shooting sparks at him. "You? You have work? Do you really think I don't know what that means? You have no right to stop me and then do whatever you want to do."

"Lexi." Gavriil glanced at the screen. The men were recovering fast. They were professionals and they weren't going to be knocked off their stride for long. They'd regroup, try to figure out what happened, and if Frost thought hard enough and looked in a single direction, it would be toward Lexi.

"We'll discuss this at home. I don't have much time. Go with Levi and Thomas."

"If I don't?"

He sighed. "Then I'm going to have to make you really angry at me by putting you over my shoulder, hiking out of here with you, slinging you in the car and sending you home that way. If you tried to get out of the car, I'm not above handcuffing you."

She kicked him hard in the shins. Before he could say or

do anything, she spun around and set off toward the vehicles by herself.

"Whoa, bro," Levi said, not even trying to suppress his grin. "You got yourself in trouble. I don't envy you tonight."

Rikki glared at him. "Macho much?" She stalked after Lexi, hurrying to catch up with her younger sister.

"Thank you," Lissa said, meaning it. She followed the other two women.

Blythe and Judith saluted him and were gone, melting into the forest on the trail leading to their transportation.

Airiana circled Max's neck with her arms, leaning into him, lifting her face for his kiss. "Don't you dare get hurt."

"I won't," Max promised. "You know we have no choice here."

Airiana nodded slowly. "Whatever happens, Jonas is going to be all over it. Watch yourselves."

"Hurry," Max said. "We want to catch them disoriented."

Thomas took her arm and pulled her to his side. "We'll watch over them. No worries. Let's go, Airiana, and leave them to this."

Her gaze clung to Max's for a long moment and then she went with Levi and Thomas in the direction of their vehicles.

"Deal with the cameras before you come down to the compound," Gavriil told his brothers. "Get it done fast. We need to make certain none of them get away and there's no evidence any of us have ever been here. Max, wipe up this site and the path leading to it. We'll get the vehicle tracks when we leave."

"You got it, Gavriil," Max said.

Gavriil started down the trail leading to the compound. A slight noise to his left had him spinning around, gun in his fist.

Lexi rushed out of the trees, knocking the gun away from her and flinging herself into his arms. The force of her rush rocked him. He caught her in a hard hold, making certain his weapon was pointed away from her.

"What is it, *angel moy*?" He brushed kisses over her eyes.

"I'm still very angry with you," she hissed, going up on her toes to put her lips against his ear. "But you stay safe. I don't want one little tiny scratch on you. That will just make me even angrier, and you don't want that."

He caught the sheen of tears in her eyes and his heart did its famous little stutter. Where it bothered him before and made him feel vulnerable, now he simply accepted the fact that she was his world. He caught her chin and lowered his mouth to hers.

She tasted like magic to him. Passion and love. He wrapped himself in her when he lifted his head, his eyes staring down into hers.

"Not a scratch," he echoed. "I'll be right behind you. This won't take long."

Her eyes searched his for a long moment and then she nodded, pulled herself out of his arms and started back down the trail. Levi waited for her just under some trees, and his gaze met his older brother's over her head. He nodded once in understanding of Gavriil's commanding look.

Lexi would have all the protection she needed, and after the display of what the women were capable of when they were together, Gavriil had no doubt that they could protect themselves if necessary.

Once more he moved toward the compound. He went fast, counting on Max and Ilya to destroy the cameras and anything they may have caught on tape. He blurred his image just to be on the safe side, but didn't slow his pace. He wanted this over with once and for all.

Ilya's and Jonas Harrington's research showed that the Reverend's congregation had dwindled down to this last group, held together by Frost and his enforcers. The few remaining members had probably been the diehards, along with one or two new recruits. Frost didn't have the Reverend's charisma. He only knew how to keep people afraid.

He used violence and intimidation, and those tactics weren't going to get him the numbers he wanted.

Gavriil had studied the footage from the tiny cameras he'd installed. There was no evidence that any of the other church members were even aware that Frost had targeted Lexi. Most likely, he was using his scare tactics in the hopes that the women on the farm would be so frightened they would force Lexi out of her sanctuary.

Frost didn't understand true loyalty. His services were paid for, as were his men's. He couldn't possibly understand the bond between the six women inhabiting the farm. He would never understand the decision Levi, Thomas, Max and now Gavriil had made to give up their work and live quietly with those special women.

Shelton Edwards and Ronald Howard emerged cautiously. Both had guns in their fists. The wind hit them hard, nearly driving them back inside. This time it was Max, not Airiana, calling the element to him.

Edwards grabbed the edge of the door and hung on grimly, looking for a target. Howard knelt on one knee, his back against the building, trying to find a buffer against the wind. Mist swirled around them, muffling sound. The rain had ceased, but the cold, wet gray of the fog was a blanket of impending doom.

Gavriil moved in the fog, a phantom, as silent as the hunting leopard in the wild, the soles of his boots gliding through the grass and dirt straight toward Shelton Edwards. He loomed up in front of the man, grasping his head with both hands and giving it a quick jerk before the other knew he was on him. The crack was audible and sharp sounding.

Howard turned his gun toward the sound and pulled the trigger repeatedly. The bullets thumped straight into Shelton Edwards's heart in a tight circle. Gavriil let the body fall to the ground naturally, as if the gunshots were the cause of death and the broken neck happened during the fall. The broken neck and bullets to the heart were so close together, even a coroner would have trouble distinguishing which came first. In his gloved fist was Edwards's gun.

"Shel? Shel, answer me," Howard demanded. He took a step toward his partner, slamming a new magazine into his gun.

Gavriil faded into the background, becoming part of the wall of the building. Howard took two more steps and nearly stumbled over the body.

"Damn it, Shel." Howard wiped the moisture from his face and knelt beside his friend.

"What's going on out there?" James Dawkins emerged with his partner, Gene Fielding. They split the moment they came outside and saw the thick fog. One went left, the other right.

Gavriil crouched low behind several barrels directly behind Howard. From his position he had a clear shot at both men. Using Edwards's gun, he fired three shots rapidly into Dawkins's head, throat and heart.

Fielding returned fire, his bullets slamming into Howard. Howard went down with a shocked, outraged cry that abruptly was cut off by a second and third bullet. Gavriil calmly shot Fielding through the heart and then moved quickly to the building facing the meeting hall. He caught the corner and pulled himself up onto the roof where he flattened himself, his gaze on the broken door of the hall.

A long silence ensued. Gavriil remained absolutely still. The wind shifted, coming from the opposite direction, sliding around the house to bring him the scent of sweat. Daniel Forest approached the front of the building from the left side. He had a narrow alleyway to maneuver through. Trey Bridges and Benjamin Frost moved around the meeting hall from the right side.

Gavriil rolled to his left until he was at the edge of the roof and lay, facing the sky, listening for Forest to come to him. He was very aware of time passing. He needed to make this look as if these men had turned on one another. To do that, he had to keep the time between kills to a minimum.

Max had to retrieve every camera they had planted, no matter how difficult they were to find. The meeting hall was a mess and two had been inside. He couldn't leave any evidence that he'd been there. Jonas Harrington was no fool, and when he saw the compound torn to shreds and dead bodies scattered everywhere, he would come looking at the Prakenskii brothers.

A soft footfall told him Forest was approaching his position. Gavriil allowed him to pass by and then he eased himself over the roof to drop into the dirt just behind the man. The fog wrapped him up in a wet blanket. It was thicker than usual, the kind of fog nightmares were made of.

He waited until Daniel Forest stepped around the corner to face Trey Bridges, who had just emerged from the other side. Standing directly behind Forest, Gavriil fired in Bridges's direction, up high into the forest, and then dropped back into the shadows. Immediately Bridges returned fire, striking Forest several times. Forest managed to squeeze off two shots as he went down. He fell almost at Gavriil's feet, looking up at him, eyes wide with shock as he tried to bring up his gun. Blood bubbled around his mouth and gurgled in his throat.

Gavriil crouched down beside him, not bothering to remove the gun from the dying man's hand. He was already gone, he just didn't know it yet. Bridges had been wounded, he was certain of it. Depending on how badly he was hit, he would do either of two things. He would stay put, unable to drag himself to cover, or he would go up, onto the roof, just as Gavriil had.

Gavriil waited. Unmoving. Utterly still. He blended into his surroundings, a phantom that came and went in absolute silence. His breath barely moved in his lungs. His heart slowed. His mind expanded. He felt movement in the fog, something large displacing the air. The dying man coughed and more blood bubbled around his mouth. He stared at Gavriil with a confused look on his face.

Benjamin Frost had to be the one making his move. His progress was too fluid. He was too sure of himself. Frost inched his way around the front of the building, close to where the other bodies were. He would never, under any circumstances, investigate without cover. Bridges had to have taken to the rooftop.

Gavriil remained still, simply waiting. He'd learned patience in a hard school and knew the first to move often died quickly. Bridges would come to him. So would Frost. They would want to know what had happened to Forest— why Forest had fired on them.

He felt—absolutely nothing. His mind had automatically taken him to that place he'd lived in for so long when he'd hunted his prey. His senses were alive, every one of them on high alert, but he felt nothing at all. There was no hatred. No animosity. Nothing. To him, these weren't men and they never would be. When he looked back on this night, he wouldn't identify them as men. Vermin perhaps, but not human.

A soft scrape above him told him Bridges had made his way to the left side of the roof and was lying flat just above his head.

"I can't see a damn thing, Frost," Bridges hissed into his radio. "Not even Dan's body. It's completely covered by the fog."

"Everyone's dead over here. Everyone. They look like they shot one another. Wait a minute. Shel's neck is broken. It could have happened when he went down. He's shot full of holes, but stay alert."

"I'm bleeding like a stuck pig up here."

"I'm working my way toward you. For God's sake, don't shoot me. Keep your eyes peeled and your mouth shut."

"There's no god here," Bridges muttered, under his breath.

There was no god, but there was the grim reaper and he wasn't satisfied yet. Gavriil eased his body directly under Bridges. The roof was comprised of tar paper and rotted wood. Large cracks had formed from the ground shaking and the pounding rain, leaving gaps Gavriil could see through.

He reached his hand out slowly and inched the knife from Forest's scabbard. Forest had already opened the small safety thong that held the hilt in place so it was easy enough to take it. The knife slid out easily as it was meant to. The blade was a good nine inches long and very sharp. Forest's eyes widened. He opened his mouth to say something, but only bubbles of blood emerged.

Gavriil wasn't overly fond of long blades when a short, less conspicuous one would do, but in this case, the blade would serve him well. Again, using slow motion, he positioned himself in a low crouch. He'd performed the move hundreds of times, but he still took his time, listening, making certain of the exact target. Exploding into action, he leapt into the air, driving the blade of the knife straight through the thin strips of tar paper into the heart of Trey Bridges. He let go and landed softly on the balls of his feet, instantly moving back away from both bodies.

Gavriil listened. There was no sound but Forest's gurgling breath and a rattle in the downed man's throat. A minute went by. Two. Blood began to drip steadily down from the crack in the roof to the ground, landing a few feet from Forest's body.

"I know you're out there," Benjamin called, his tone almost friendly. "Is Bridges dead? Because you sure as hell killed the rest of them."

Frost was fishing. He needed to get Gavriil talking so he would have an idea of where he was. Gavriil had never believed in talking on the job. There just wasn't that much to say. Frost liked preaching. He used his voice to intimidate. He wouldn't be able to stop himself. There was no one left to give orders to.

"You don't have any clue who you're dealing with." Benjamin went from friendly to stern, using his commanding voice.

Gavriil wasn't impressed. He didn't move, but pinpointed Benjamin's position in the fog. He was moving *away* from the meeting hall, not toward it. He was projecting his voice away from his actual position—a tactic that must have served him well in the past.

"I had a real sweet deal here. Whoever you are should be working with me, not against me. There's money and women to be had. Whatever someone paid you is nothing at all compared to what I can show you how to make."

Using the fog to cover his movements, Gavriil eased his body onto the roof and crouching low, ran across the rooftop and leapt to the next one. He landed softly, but his left foot sank beneath the rotted wood, tearing a hole right through it. He immediately stretched out on what was left of the tiles to distribute his weight. It took a moment to extract his foot.

He slipped back to the very edge of the roof and allowed himself to drop to the ground. He knew he'd made noise when his foot had gone through the thin, rotted wood, and even with the fog helping to muffle sound, Benjamin must have heard. He'd been a soldier and a mercenary. The fact that he was still alive was a testimonial that he knew his way around combat situations.

More than anything else, Gavriil was aware of time passing. He didn't want Ilya or Max to join in the actual fight. He'd made that abundantly clear to both of them. They were the cleanup crew, nothing else. But time was his greatest enemy. Jonas Harrington was highly intelligent. He would find out that Airiana and Max had called a trusted friend to come babysit and he would put two and two together—especially if someone happened to report gunfire in the area.

Gavriil slipped around to the back of the building, back toward heavy woods. The forest ran all the way down the mountain almost to the ocean. If Benjamin Frost was making his getaway, he would run this way. There were trails everywhere through the forest, paths Gavriil had found when scouting, that indicated to him they'd been used often to come and go. Frost had to have a vehicle stashed somewhere along the road, down past the compound.

If Frost chose not to run, he would use the forest to circle back in order to try to get behind Gavriil. Gavriil moved at a steady pace, covering ground fast, working out in his mind the best places for Frost to ambush him. Frost knew the area far better than he did, and he would have chosen several places he could defend if he was cornered. The man was far too cunning not to set up his escape.

The forest was thick with fog. Airiana, Max and Rikki had called it from the ocean, so this side of the compound was even more foggy and gray than the other side. Without a wind to disperse it, the mist hung through the trees, heavy with moisture.

He paused, crouching low to feel around him, looking for movement in the heavy mist, or a large spot where the mist had been dispersed. There was no sound at all. No movement. Gavriil looked upward, toward the tops of the trees. Some of the trees were old with thick trunks and wide, gnarled branches, perfect to sit up in and wait for someone to come.

It took three precious minutes to spot Frost, and Gavriil was very aware of each of them. There was no way to make it look like an accident, not with Frost up in the tree, and he'd wanted Harrington to have no concrete evidence that someone else was involved in what had taken place here at the compound.

He swore under his breath as he stretched out in the wet vegetation. He had a clean shot through the foliage, but he'd have to use Bridges's weapon. That meant firing a gun he wasn't familiar with. One hair's breadth off could ruin the shot at this distance. Gavriil went for a body shot, instead of the head, just because he needed to make certain with the distance, the fog and an untried weapon.

He took careful aim and squeezed the trigger. Frost's body jerked and then slowly toppled over, dropping from the branches onto the forest floor. Gavriil waited a couple of heartbeats before he rose and began to make his way toward the spot where Frost had landed. It hadn't been a kill shot. The gun pulled to the left. Still, that fall was going to hurt, if not break bones.

Gavriil heard Frost cursing long before he came up on the drag marks. A steady stream of blood soaked the carpet of leaves where Frost had hit the ground and then tried to pull his body into deeper cover. He was propped up against a tree, his gun in his hand and blood streaming down his chest. He looked as if the fall had broken his arm and an ankle and very possibly his back as well. Frost's skin was gray, and his breathing ragged.

Frost spit blood on the ground as Gavriil walked up to him. "Who the hell are you?" He coughed and spit more blood.

Gavriil didn't answer. Frost was dying and that was good enough for him. He simply wanted the man out of Lexi's life. If Frost had been the brains behind the Reverend's depraved teachings, the world was far better off without him.

Frost swore again and tried to lift his gun. Gavriil shot him through the throat and then through the eye. He left him there, turning away from the man who had caused so much damage to families and young women.

Gavriil felt tired all of a sudden. Weary. He made his way back to the other bodies and put the gun near Bridges's hand. It wasn't a perfect scene, there were a few holes, but it was plausible enough if one didn't have any idea the Prakenskii brothers were around.

He wanted to go home. To her. Lexi. It didn't matter if she was angry with him or not. She was home. He was done with this chapter of his life and looking forward to the next one with her.

He hadn't left tracks, but still, it would be better to dispose of his shoes in the ocean. All the vehicles would have to be thoroughly washed and then driven through the forest surrounding the farm as well as the dirt roads and mud on the farm itself. He believed in being thorough, and since he'd met Jonas Harrington, even more so.

Ilya and Max joined him where they had left the truck. He didn't take the wheel, but slipped into the backseat of the cab and laid his head against the seat.

"We retrieved all of our cameras," Max said, as he slipped into the driver's seat.

Ilya handed back a bottle of water. "You hit anywhere?"

Gavriil shook his head. "No. I'm just plain bone tired."

Ilya nodded, relief creeping into his eyes. "Frost had every single home bugged. We listened to the tapes and were able to leave all of them behind for Jonas to find." There was a touch of distaste in his tone.

Ilya clearly didn't like going behind Harrington's back and Gavriil didn't blame him. They were loyal to the ones they considered family, and to Ilya, Harrington was family.

"Are you going to be able to live with this?" Gavriil asked his youngest brother.

Ilya shrugged. "Why wouldn't I? They were scumbags threatening our family."

"I'm talking about Harrington." Gavriil watched his brother through half-closed eyes. Every nuance. Every tick.

Ilya was as steady as a rock. "Jonas is a good man. My friend. Close enough to call a brother, but this was necessary and he's got a job to do. He might have covered for us if I'd asked him, but it would cost him."

"He'll be suspicious," Max said.

"Yes, but he won't ask me any questions. He won't put me in a position of having to lie to him," Ilya said.

"Stop by one of the cliffs so we can dispose of our shoes," Gavriil instructed.

"These are damn good hiking boots," Max said. "I should have thought of that, although I think Harrington will be more inclined to find a reason to look in your closet than mine."

"I don't know, Max," Ilya said. "Those four kids of yours have him pulling out his hair. He knows they came off that ship and that you're in no way related to them, but he can't prove it. All the paperwork is in order. The moment he recognized you were a Prakenskii he knew you were lying your ass off."

Max turned the truck onto Highway 1, and Gavriil relaxed a little more. He would be very happy once they were home and safe on the farm. Once he was with Lexi.

"There's a cliff just ahead we can use to get rid of the shoes. They'll go deep," Max said. "Levi and Rikki went over several maps with me and told me the places to use when we need them."

Ilya glanced at him sharply. "Use for what? The ocean isn't your personal disposal site."

"Our shoes," Gavriil said without opening his eyes. "What did you think he meant?" There was quiet laughter in his voice.

"Very funny. He didn't mean shoes," Ilya objected. "Since it's only the three of us, have you heard from Viktor or Casimir? Did either of you send them a message telling them we're all here?"

"I sent it," Gavriil admitted. "But neither answered."

"Viktor's been off grid a long time," Max said. "Far too long."

"Casimir as well," Gavriil added. "We would have heard if they were killed. Sorbacov would have made sure of it."

Max pulled their truck into a long drive leading to the cliffs. No one was around and it was easy to change their boots. Max took the dirty ones, filled them full of rocks, hurled them into the sea and watched until they sank. There was no beach to wash up on, not for several miles.

"Did the women know they had to get rid of their shoes as well?" Ilya said, laughter in his voice.

"Who knew that was going to be the one thing they would all object to," Max said. "Well, not all. Lissa didn't object. She was the one who convinced the others that we weren't totally paranoid."

"She's different than the others, not as vulnerable," Ilya said.

"I wouldn't say she isn't vulnerable," Max protested.

"She just covers it better. She's very self-sufficient. And she's damned good with any weapon we've introduced to her. The woman has skills."

Gavriil kept his eyes closed but he felt his brother's stare through the mirror. "Keep your eyes on the road," he reminded mildly.

"You know something about her, don't you?" Max said.

"There isn't much to know," Ilya said. "Jonas did background checks on all the women, and seriously, she comes up clean. She doesn't even have a parking ticket."

"She knows her way around the gym. The other day we were sparring and she nearly took my head off," Max said. "When she didn't, I had the feeling she pulled back. I couldn't prove it, but there's a part of me that thinks she's far more skilled than she's letting on. Levi and Thomas think so as well."

"It's possible," Ilya said. "Anything's possible with these women. It's no wonder they can manage to live with you. Nothing about them is any more real than it is about us."

"They're real," Gavriil replied. "All six of them. They're more real than any other woman or man I've encountered in all my years of being alive."

There was a small silence. Ilya shook his head. "You've got it bad, Gavriil. That woman has you tied up in knots."

Max gave a small snort of derision, quick to defend his older brother. "And Joley Drake doesn't have you wrapped around her little finger?"

Ilya shrugged. "I didn't say there was anything wrong with it, but I'm shocked that Gavriil—or you, Max, for that matter—would have found a woman who could make you want to settle down."

"He's got a point," Gavriil admitted. "I never believed it would happen."

"Has it?" Max asked, suddenly sobering. "Has it really, Gavriil? I can't always tell with you. You're difficult to read, even for me."

Gavriil remained silent for a long moment. These two were his brothers. His family. They'd put their lives on the line for him tonight. Still, he didn't know them as well as he liked, especially Ilya.

He wasn't used to trusting anyone, and Lexi was his one weakness. He had never had anything or anyone in his life he couldn't leave behind in seconds and never look back. That was impossible now. Lexi was . . . his. There would be no leaving her ever.

He let out his breath slowly, loath to admit having an Achilles' heel.

Ilya whistled softly. "Oh, man. He's got it far worse than I imagined."

"Shut up, kid," Gavriil said impolitely. He opened his eyes to mere slits, giving his youngest brother a threatening glare. "The ocean is a huge disposal site."

Ilya and Max both burst out laughing. Gavriil shook his head at their antics, but he couldn't deny that he was secretly happy to hear his brothers' laughter and be the target of their jokes. It made him feel all the more as if he had a family and a home.

"I'm going to drop you off first, Gavriil. Ilya's going to help me with the truck. You can try to worm your way out of trouble with your woman," Max said, as they drove in through the back entrance of the farm.

Gavriil nodded. "Thank you. Both of you. It would have taken me all night to find the cameras and clean the scene. I appreciate it."

Lexi sat in the swing on the front porch, one foot propped against the railing to idly push herself back and forth. As usual, there were no lights on and she sat alone in the dark. Gavriil focused on her immediately. Every cell in his body. Every heartbeat. The rest of the world just seemed to drop away until there was only Lexi.

Her eyes met his as he emerged from the truck and then she was looking him over very carefully for any possible damage. It made him feel loved. Welcomed. She didn't smile, but she stood slowly and walked to the top of the stairs. Gavriil deliberately waited for the truck to leave so they were alone in the dark.

He moved up the stairs until he was on the one just below her. She still wasn't tall enough to be level with him, but it didn't matter. She moved into him, circling his neck with her slender arms and leaning her body against his, melting into him. Gavriil closed his arms around her tightly and just held her there.

"I was worried," she admitted against his shoulder. "Very worried."

"I know, *solnyshko moya*, I'm sorry. It couldn't be helped. I didn't get a scratch on me. Not one."

She pulled her head back, her eyes searching his. "That's good. I would have been so upset, you don't even know. As it is, I'm still very angry with you."

"You kicked me in the shins," he pointed out soberly. He was an intelligent man, and smart men knew one didn't make the mistake of laughing when his woman said she was angry.

"You told me to kick you when I was angry with you, but that isn't near enough of a punishment. You can't just order me around, Gavriil."

"I know you think that, Lexi," he said soberly, framing her face and looking down at her with serious eyes. "But you're wrong."

She opened her mouth to protest but he stopped her with a kiss. He'd needed to kiss her from the moment he'd gotten out of the truck. Lexi might have said she was angry with him, but her mouth tasted of passion. Of love. The magic was there, and he allowed himself a brief respite, basking in the exquisite perfection of her love.

He lifted his head slowly and pressed his forehead to hers, looking into her green eyes. "You order me when it comes to farm work. You know what you're doing and naturally you're the leader because it's your field of expertise. When it comes to threats, violence or danger, I have to take the lead. Isn't that what a partnership is? We both rely on the other's strengths?"

Lexi scowled at him. "You know, when I first met you, you weren't that good at talking. All of a sudden you've got like the silver tongue or something. Once in a while, much to my bitter disappointment, you actually make sense. I think you were sandbagging it."

"Is that a farmer's term? Sandbagging?" He brushed her mouth with his all over again because she really was his sun and she'd just made him light up.

"You know very well what it means," she contradicted.

He caught her by the waist and lifted her out of his way, so he could gain the porch. "Perhaps I do, but with you, I always have to have my best game on, so it doesn't apply. How are the puppies? Is Kiss taking good care of them?"

"Yes, and when I got home, little Lyutyj actually seemed to recognize my voice and scent. He stumbled away from Kiss toward me."

"So of course you held him and gave him more of the supplement." He set her down on the porch and reached past her head to pull open the door. "Have you noticed he's getting a little on the chubby side?"

"He is not," Lexi defended. "I can't believe you would say that."

"Next time you sit outside by yourself in the dark, bring Drago out with you. That's what they're for. Protecting you."

"He'd rather be with Kiss and the puppies."

Drago greeted them both, pressing close, nearly knocking Lexi down. Gavriil gave the large male a soft reprimand and he was much gentler as they made their way down the hall to the laundry room.

"These dogs need to be with people, Lexi. They actually prefer it. In any case, they're working dogs. His job is to protect you. I want him doing his job at all times."

"Drago and Kiss guard you," she countered. "Lyutyj is going to protect me."

"Are you going to argue with every safety rule I give you?" He peeled off his clothes and put them in the washing machine. "You did throw your shoes away, didn't you? And put the clothes you wore tonight in the washer?"

"Yes to all three questions."

He was stark naked and she wasn't running away. Her
eyes moved over his body in a little caress. Her breasts rose
and fell with each breath she dragged into her lungs. He felt
his cock harden, and instantly her gaze dropped down to
his groin.

He held his breath as her fingers opened and she actually
reached a scant two inches toward him, palm out. It was the
slightest gesture, and one she barely seemed aware of, but
his entire body shuddered with the idea that she might
touch him, close her fist around him. Claim that last part of
him for her own.

He turned to face her deliberately, leaning his hip
against the open washing machine, looking as casual as
possible. "It absolutely amazes me how you can make me
want you without even trying, woman." He dropped his
hand just as casually to his rock-hard shaft, closing his fist
around it. "Look at what you do to me, every time."

She smiled and shook her head, but she didn't raise her
gaze to his. She took a step closer. "You always look so
intimidating, Gavriil. When I see you like this, so hard and
long and thick, it doesn't seem possible that you fit inside me."

"You were made for me, Lexi. No one else. I fit perfectly."
He stroked his fist down the shaft and then let go.

Her breath caught in her throat again, and this time she
reached out purposely. Right before her fingers found his
shaft, she looked up at him as if for permission. He didn't
move, didn't say anything at all. She had to make up her
own mind. Her palm closed around him, warm and soft.
Her touch nearly destroyed him. His legs went weak and
his heart pounded in his chest. Blood roared in his ears and
thundered through his veins. With just one tentative touch.

Because she loved him. He held himself very still, fear-
ing to move. His hips, of their own volition, wanted to
thrust upward, to feel that silken glide through her fist, but
he wasn't going to ruin a perfect moment with sex.

"You feel hot." She lifted her gaze to his again. "You

know how people use that term, 'velvet over steel'? That's what you feel like."

She could kill him so easily and she didn't even know it. She had all the power between them. In her soft hands and perfect mouth. In her forest green eyes and her feminine curves. But mostly in the way she saw him. She looked into him and she saw the man he should always have been. The man he was when he was with her.

She swallowed hard and let go of him to smear two pearly droplets over his ultrasensitive head, watching him shudder with the fire racing through his body.

20

___

GAVRIIL reached out and bunched Lexi's hair in his hand. He gave her long ponytail a tug. "You've put it up again, all this glorious hair. It needs to come down." He pulled the little wrap right out of her hair and then used both hands to mess it up, letting the silken mass tumble free.

"What are you doing?"

He grinned at her, his blue eyes alive with sensual mischief. "Maybe we should wash those sweats as well. I think little Lyutyj got a spot of dirt on them. Why don't you strip right here? I can help you."

"How thoughtful of you, Gavriil," Lexi said.

She moistened her lips with the tip of her tongue, hesitating only for a moment. He knew how difficult it was for her to be spontaneous when it came to making love, but she pulled the soft sweatshirt over her head. Her eyes held shy anticipation and raw courage. For him. She was always willing to step out of her comfort zone for him.

He knew few men would understand what it had cost her to wrap her fist around his cock and hold him, just for a moment. To touch him so intimately, but he knew how difficult it was and that she'd done it for him, to show him she loved him and that she would always try for him.

The strange thing was, he knew it really didn't matter to him whether or not she ever got to the point where she could wrap her mouth around him. What mattered was that she loved him enough to try baby steps.

Lexi wasn't wearing a bra and her soft curves thrusting toward him were very tempting. She had high, perfectly formed breasts and a narrow rib cage that went into her tucked-in waist. Her hips flared in a shapely feminine curve that drove him nearly as crazy as her breasts. She had a beautiful body. He couldn't imagine a man forcing her to bind her chest, telling her she was ugly because she'd developed.

He reached out with gentle fingers, shaping her breasts, massaging and cupping them in his palms. He couldn't resist tugging her nipples and rolling them between his fingers just to hear her gasp and see the dazed look come into her eyes.

"I'm pretty crazy about you, Lexi Thompson," he confided.

She smiled up at him, unknowingly pushing closer into his hands. "That's a good thing, Gavriil Prakenskii, because I'm finding that I can't do without you."

He hooked his thumbs in her sweatpants and crouched low to pull them to her ankles. She placed her hands on his arms as she stepped out of them, trembling a little bit. She looked around her helplessly, and he realized that he'd switched on the light when he'd come into the laundry room. She didn't like the brighter lights on when she was naked and about to make love with him. Very casually he stood up, reaching out and flicking the switch off.

The room wasn't totally dark, but she blinked up at him. "Thank you."

"I like looking at you," he said.

"I know you do. I like looking back, it's just that . . ." She trailed off with a little sigh. "I still hate the scars on my back and butt."

He smiled at her. "Silly woman, when I'm facing you I can't see them."

"I know that." She shivered under his focused gaze, little goose-bumps rising on her skin. "But I know they're there, and I want to feel beautiful when I'm standing naked in front of you."

He lifted his palm to cup the side of her face, to rub strands of silky hair between his fingers. "Clearly I'm going to have to do a better job of explaining to you how beautiful and perfect you are to me."

She shook her head, a slow smile stealing into her eyes. "You do a fantastic job. I just have to get to a place where I believe you."

He threw her clothes in the washer with his and started the machine. Water began pouring into the basket. His hand shifted around to the nape of her neck to draw her closer to him, his thumb lifting her face to his.

"I need to kiss you. Sometimes I just *need* to kiss you. I dream about kissing you. Waking or sleeping, I dream about it, but there are times, like now, when kissing you is essential to my well-being."

Her eyebrow shot up and a small smile teased her soft mouth. "Aren't you being just a tiny bit overdramatic? Needing kisses for your well-being?"

"My mental health."

She laughed softly and the music of it played in the pit of his stomach and spread like wildfire to his groin.

"Don't you be laughing at me, woman, when I'm confiding my deepest secrets to you." He bent his head slowly to hers, watching her eyes go wide with desire. For him. There was nothing like the feeling he got, that rush through his bloodstream, when he knew she wanted him the same way he wanted her.

He kissed her gently, tenderly, pouring his heart and soul into it. He'd upset her with his orders, but he'd kept her from doing something she would regret. He wouldn't give the deaths a second thought, but he'd think often on how he'd gotten her angry with him. He knew it was bound to happen, but he would also analyze each time and try to figure out a better way of handling things.

Her mouth was still shy beneath his, but so responsive, kissing him, following his lead, giving him her heart in the way she did. He kissed her over and over until neither could breathe and they had to come up for air.

They smiled at each other like a couple of fools, but he'd never been so happy. He caught her around the waist and lifted her to set her on the very edge of the appliance. "All that work tonight made me hungrier than ever."

Lexi burst out laughing again. "Seriously, Gavriil? On a washing machine?"

"Why not? It might feel good when it starts vibrating."

"Because it's cold on my butt, you crazy man."

Her laughter was contagious. She made his life fun.

"You're such a complainer." He yanked a towel from the dryer, folded it in half and arched an eyebrow at her. "Lift up, this should work."

"You aren't kidding, are you?" Obediently she lifted her bottom so he could slide the towel under her.

"When the machine starts vibrating and the towel starts slipping, don't blame me," he teased.

Lexi stared down at him with her cool green eyes. He knew he would be lost there forever—and he wanted to be. Once, she'd told him he was safe with her. She'd offered to guard him while he slept and she'd meant it. She had given him so much more than she even realized.

Lexi thought she needed him, but it was the other way around. Unrelenting darkness had been his world. He hadn't been able to see the light let alone find his way to it. She had shone the bright light on him and opened him up. She really was his sun.

She stroked her hand down the side of his face. "What is it, Gavriil?"

"I didn't expect to love you so damn much," he said. "I didn't even know this kind of emotion was possible, let alone that I could feel it."

He hadn't known a woman could change a man inside.

She made life worth living. More, she'd made him a believer in humanity.

Her smile was soft, a gentle reflection of who she was inside. He tipped her backward by placing a hand on the flat of her stomach and forcing her to stretch out. Wedging himself between her thighs he bent his head to her breasts, swirling his tongue around her nipples and teasing with the edge of his teeth.

He kissed a trail down to her navel and dipped his tongue, swirling it around and then nipping at her belly. The washing machine suddenly went silent. Her gaze jumped to his. The machine beneath her began to shake. She burst out laughing. That sound was pure music.

Gavriil had seduced women and allowed them to seduce him. The sex act, while enjoyable, had always been sober, a following of a step-by-step manual. Being with Lexi was spontaneous and fun, a magical journey he could never predict.

He found himself laughing along with her, teasing her by blowing raspberries over her skin and nipping his way down her tummy to the vee of curls at the junction of her legs.

Lexi clutched the edges of the washing machine, her laughter stroking at his body like fingers. He loved that sweet music. The joy in her. The joy it brought to him. Who knew sex could be both emotional and fun. Sweet and sexy. Just plain sensual.

He tipped her back farther by pulling both legs over his shoulders. "I have to say, *sladkaya moya*, you look good enough to eat."

"You're so crazy," she said. "On the washing machine? I think we've unbalanced the load or something. It's shaking me all over the place."

Gavriil grinned at her. "That's me shaking you up."

He dipped his head to that hot, sweet center, swiping his tongue through soft folds to get to the honey he knew was waiting there.

Her laughter turned to ragged gasps and little pants. He

feasted, taking his time, enjoying the way her hips bucked and her hands fisted in his hair. He especially enjoyed the cries rising to a crescendo as he used his tongue and mouth and teeth to drive her up hard and fast.

The machine switched cycles again, and he pulled her legs back down, toed a blue plastic crate to him and stood on it. With one arm he dragged her even closer so that he could press the head of his cock into her slick, hot entrance.

"Really? You're really going to do this on the washing machine? I'm going to fall." But her voice was husky and her eyes had that soft dazed look. She was flushed from head to toe.

"You'll never fall, Lexi, because I'm always here to catch you," he said, and thrust deep into her body.

Her eyes went wide with shock. Her mouth formed a perfect *O*. The air rushed from her lungs and her body clamped down around his like a vise. He could feel the vibrations of the machine running through her body to his. It was crazy, just as she'd said. Sexy. Unexpectedly so.

He plunged into her again and again while the washing machine rocked and her body rolled. Her little pants turned to a glorious symphony of chanting his name, gasping and pleading. He didn't want the moment to ever stop. He couldn't quite bring himself to slow down, the friction was too intense, her body tight and scorching hot. As he surged deep and withdrew, her muscles squeezed and dragged at him, sending streaks of fire racing to every cell in his body.

She threw back her head, her long hair flying around them like a cape. A small cry escaped and her body clamped down on his in a vicious orgasm, shocking them both with the intensity of it. There was no ripple of warning, just a series of ferocious waves that seized him and took him along.

There was no holding back for either of them. The tidal wave swept them up, tossing them into a cauldron of tumbling pleasure that had each clutching hard at the other as an anchor.

The ripples went on and on, so that they clung together,

while the washing machine went into its spin cycle, adding to the concoction of sensations pouring through and over their bodies.

"We really might not survive if this gets any better," Lexi whispered, her green eyes drifting over his face.

Gavriil saw the trace of possession there and his cock wanted to come alive all over again while his heart pounded and his mind raced. He loved this woman with every fiber of his being. Every cell in his body.

As if reading his mind, Lexi wrapped her arms around his neck and held him tight. "I'm so in love with you, Gavriil, I don't know what I'd do if I lost you," she confessed in a soft voice—so soft it was barely audible.

Above her head, Gavriil closed his eyes and just held on to her sweet confession. Love really was pain sometimes. Physical. Emotional. Beautiful. His eyes burned and his throat was clogged and the man he'd been for so many long empty years reached for the woman who had changed his life forever. Everything in him belonged to her.

"I love you too, Lexi." Those five words seemed so inadequate to describe the intensity of his feelings for her.

He knew they had a long way to go. They both had been broken and reformed and they would have to find their way, but he'd never been more certain of anything in his life as he was that Lexi and he belonged to each other—belonged together.

"Gavriil?" Lexi lifted her head and looked at him again.

He knew he'd be forever lost in her eyes. "Tell me."

"I've been rethinking the whole marriage thing. Especially if I get pregnant. It's not as if I'm using birth control." She blushed. "I never thought I'd ever have sex, let alone have a chance of getting pregnant. I have to admit, it did occur to me that having your baby would be absolutely a gift. I should have told you I wasn't on birth control."

"It never occurred to me that you were on birth control," Gavriil admitted. "A man like me thinks of these things before he ever touches a woman. It's very necessary in my career to protect myself as well as my partner. I want you to have my baby. I'll admit, when I worried that you would leave me, I hoped you'd be pregnant and not want to go."

Lexi shook her head. "I want *you*, Gavriil. You make me feel alive and happy and very, very safe. I would have been terrified of bringing a child into the world with anyone else, but with you, I know absolutely, no one will ever have the chance to harm us."

He wrapped his arms around her and lifted her from the washing machine. "I don't think I'm ever going to mind washing clothes again," he said.

He kissed her again and again, making a thorough job of it. He had a lifetime, he knew, but still, he didn't think he'd ever get enough.

Keep reading for a special preview of

DARK CRIME

by Christine Feehan

From the Edge of Darkness *anthology,*
available August 2015 from Jove Books

BLAZE McGuire pulled her waist-length red hair into a high ponytail at the back of her head, contemplating the fact that she was going to die tonight—and it was of her own choosing. She was going to war with the Hallahan brothers and their mobster boss. They didn't know it yet, but they would be walking right into hell. They thought they were going to have everything their own way, but they were wrong. *Very* wrong. She was a woman. She was young. They dismissed her as no threat to them. And in that they were making a *very, very* big mistake.

Her hair wasn't just red hair, it was *red*. Her hair had been that vivid, insane color of red since the day she was born. Hence the name her father had given her, staring down at his newborn daughter who was already giving the doctors hell for dragging her out of her safe little world, kicking and screaming into the cold light, her hair blazing along with her lungs—and that should have given them a clue what they were buying when they murdered her father.

Most people didn't know when they were going to die, she mused as she rigged the explosives on the door to blow, the charge precise, sending anyone in front of it outward, a little blowback into her beloved bar, hopefully leaving it intact. Still, if the charge didn't kill them all before they got inside, she would give up the bar's interior in order to take the battle to them. Tonight, the four Hallahan brothers were going to come for her, and she would take as many of them with her as possible.

Sean McGuire had been a good man. A good neighbor. An even better father. The bar was successful because he had a reputation for being honest and he was a good listener; he genuinely cared about his customers, his neighbors and especially his daughter.

He knew everyone by name. He laughed with them. He attended funerals when they lost someone. He got them home at night safe if they drank too much. He cut off the ones who were spending too much and needed to be home with their families. He was just a good man. A good man some mobsters had pulled out of the bar and beaten to death because he wouldn't sign his establishment—the one that had been in the family for two, now three generations— over to them.

Sean had also served in the Marines and he knew his way around weapons, especially the making of bombs. He was a specialist in the field, so much so that he had actually helped out the local bomb squad the three times they'd gotten calls, because what he knew about explosives, few others did. And what he knew, he taught his daughter.

Blaze had been given an unusual education and she'd loved every minute of it. Her father made it clear he loved her and was always proud of her and he'd always been patient with her, but he believed in teaching his daughter everything he would have taught his son. He was patient, but he didn't make it easy because she was a girl. She was required to do everything—and learn everything he knew about defense and offense. She'd soaked up the training.

It had always been the two of them, Sean and Blaze, after her mother left. Truthfully, she remembered her mother as a disconnected woman who was never happy—when she could remember her, and that wasn't often. Her mother left when she was four. They'd never done one single thing together. Not one. She couldn't even recall her mother holding her. It had always been her father.

Sean had been a boxer, a mixed martial arts cage fighter, and he enjoyed the lifestyle. He had always insisted his daughter work out with him. She had—since the time she was two. She grew up boxing with her father. Learning martial arts. Street fighting. She learned to fall properly and she knew all about joints and pressure points. More, Sean hadn't neglected teaching her how to shoot or how to use a knife. He certainly hadn't neglected her training when it came to explosives.

Later, when she was ten, Emeline Masters came into their lives. Emeline lived mostly on the street, shuffled from one home to another, but mostly on the street. Emeline became a family member and spent a great deal of time crawling in Blaze's bedroom window from the fire escape and sleeping inside with her. Sean pretended he didn't know. Emeline, thankfully, was away from all of this and in Europe where Sean had sent her to protect her. Blaze had called her, of course, but told her to stay where no one could harm her.

Blaze smiled grimly to herself as she laid out a grid pattern on the floor of the bar and then paused to glance out the window, looking down the street. This had once been a good, decent neighborhood, a place she had called home for twenty-four years. She'd grown up in the apartment over the bar. It was a big building, right on the corner, prime property. The building and three others on either side had been in their family for generations. Her family had taken good care of them and never sold, not even when property values had soared.

Her eyes narrowed as she returned her attention to the delicate job of setting wires throughout the bar. Low. Midcalf. Thigh. Hip. She crisscrossed them, building a web. Yeah. They should have known all about that redheaded baby when they dragged her father out of his own bar and beat him to death. They'd broken nearly every bone in his body before they killed him. She knew, because the ME had told her.

Rage welled up. Swirled in her belly. Deep. So deep she knew she'd never get it out. She knew why they'd broken his bones. She'd heard about the "persuading" technique from a few of the other business owners. The mobsters wanted properties signed over to them. Her father had already signed his property over to her. *She* owned the bar. They'd gone after the wrong person. And now they were coming for her because she'd sent them an invitation. Not to buy her out, but to war.

She would have signed over the bar to them in a heartbeat if they'd called her and told her they had her father. They thought it was important to teach the neighborhood businesses a lesson—what they wanted, they got. They weren't going to get what they wanted, not even after they killed her. She'd made certain of that. They wouldn't touch Emeline either. They wouldn't get to harm the last person in the world she loved.

Blaze pressed her fingers to her eyes to stop the burning. She hadn't slept, not in days, not since she'd come home to find her father gone, the door to the bar open and blood on the floor. She'd been frantic, running through the streets like a maniac, calling the cops repeatedly only to be told they couldn't do anything for twenty-four hours, but they'd send someone by. They hadn't. She'd sat alone in the apartment over the bar, arms around her knees, rocking herself, trying to tell herself that her father was strong and he knew how to take care of himself, but there was so much blood.

She taped a knife under the table closest to the stairs. If she lived through the initial attack, she would have to have an exit plan. She needed to rig the stairs. If she got to the apartment—and she knew the chances were slim to none— she could go out the escape and up to the window. She did that often. She'd been doing that with Emmy since she was ten years old. Once on the roof, she could choose any direction. She would also stash a couple of weapons up there as well.

Two factions of mobsters had moved into the neighborhood, the first and the most brutal, a year and a half earlier, and they were extremely violent. Four brothers, Irish by the look of them, but Sean hadn't known them and he knew every Irishman in the city, went by the name of Hallahan. The four were always the front men for one of the crime lords, with their grim faces and their ugly demands. All were quick to brutal, extreme violence. And they owned the cops. The police, who had always spent evenings and sometimes days in the bar playing pool, had stopped coming around. She knew they worked for a man by the name of Reginald Coonan. Their boss always stayed in the shadows, but he liked blood and his men liked violence.

A few weeks earlier, a tall, extremely good-looking man in a business suit came by the bar and handed a business card to her father. It had a number printed on it, nothing else. The man was soft-spoken and simply told them if they needed protection, to call that number and someone would come. She found it significant that her father hadn't thrown the card away, even though they both thought this was another crime lord intending to take Coonan's territory from him. Sean had never discussed the incident with her, but he kept the business card safe, right by the phone.

Blaze had never moved the card. But she'd looked at it numerous times. She'd done a little investigating and it hadn't been easy to uncover the identities of any of the mobsters. She knew now the four Irish brothers. Each of them had grown up in Chicago and had moved to her city. They were Hallahans, and all were short, muscular and very scary. They had come to the city because it had gotten a little too hot for them where they'd grown up, and, she suspected, because Reginald Coonan, their boss, had moved from Chicago as well.

She had very little on the other faction. The man that had come so quietly into the bar was named Tariq Asenguard. He owned a dance club—an extremely popular one in the neighborhood. He was quiet, only came out at night, and owned a very kick-ass estate edging the water. The entire place was fenced—and he had multiple acres, a gatehouse and a boat. She didn't know where he'd come from, and every avenue she'd tried to find out more had been shut down.

Everyone knew he had money—lots of it. He was also a very scary man. He could take over a room just by walking into it. She had mixed reviews about him. Half the people who had encounters with him thought he was the devil. The other half were certain he was a saint.

He had a partner, a man by the name of Maksim Volkov, who no one knew anything about. He was the silent partner. He owned the property bordering Tariq Asenguard's estate, but few ever saw him. He was partners with Asenguard in the dance club. Asenguard, who was there often, was clearly the face of the club, but few actually ever saw Volkov. There was something about his name that made Blaze shiver. Tariq Asenguard was definitely a badass, but he was cool about it. Maksim Volkov was a question mark. She knew others worked for them, but it didn't matter now. She didn't care. *They* hadn't murdered her father, so therefore she was throwing in with them. After she was dead.

Methodically, Blaze positioned weapons throughout the room and around the bar, and then practiced getting to them. She didn't want to hesitate. She'd need every second she could get. If nothing else, she wanted to take the Hallahans with her when she went. She felt calm. Nerves would come later. And then the kick of adrenaline.

She glanced at her watch. Outside, light was beginning to fade. The streetlights wouldn't come on. Someone had shattered the old-fashioned gaslights that lent character to the streets. The four brothers almost always came at night. She knew they didn't care if anyone saw their faces and knew who they were. Everyone was far too intimidated by them to come forward.

She just plain wasn't the come-forward-and-testify type, not when she didn't believe for one moment that there would be a conviction. These men had killed her father. They'd tortured him first and then they'd killed him and thrown his broken body out of a moving car, in front of the bar like trash, right at her feet. She hadn't seen them torture or kill Sean, only throw his body at her.

The brothers had timed it just right, coming into the bar at closing when Sean was standing just inside the door. The ME said he found Taser marks, puncture wounds where her father had been taken down, not by one Taser, but by four. The moment they had incapacitated him, they had struck brutally, leaving behind a good amount of blood. It had been Blaze who came home to find the bar unlocked, blood on the floor and her father missing. Even with the blood, the police had done nothing. They promised to send someone around to take a report, but no one showed up. That hadn't surprised her. The cops had all but abandoned her neighborhood and everyone in it.

Blaze looked around the bar. The building—and the bar—were over a hundred years old. She didn't understand why the mobsters spared some of the properties and went after others. Their takeovers seemed random. She'd tried to put together a pattern, but she couldn't find one. It wasn't the businesses they wanted, because after they acquired property, they never opened the business again. The dry cleaner six doors down was closed. The lovely little grocery store on the opposite corner remained closed, forcing all the residents to go out of their neighborhood to get food.

She made her way up the stairs, leaving a trail of weapons. She didn't believe she would ever get to them, but still, she had been taught to plan for every contingency, and living was one of them. The apartment where she'd grown up was large. She loved it. It had been home all her life.

Home. Her father had done that. Given that to her. He laughed a lot. His eyes lit up when he laughed. So many times he'd whirled her around the living room floor, singing at the top of his lungs, making her laugh with him. He lived life large and he'd wanted her to do the same.

She knew her father dated women, but he never brought

them home. She asked a million times why he didn't re-marry, because she was always afraid if she found someone he would be lonely, and she didn't want her father ever to be lonely. Sean simply told her there was no point in set-tling. It was either the right one or no one. He'd learned that lesson the hard way and said he hadn't found the right one, but that he was still looking.

She had always wanted that for him. Wanted someone else to love him the way she did, but he'd never let anyone other than Emeline fully into their lives, and maybe that was what made her the same way. She dated, but she never gave herself to anyone because she knew it wasn't *the* one. Maybe there wasn't really the perfect one. The right one. She'd never know now because she was going to die tonight.

She stashed a go bag with clothes and money on the roof by the fire escape, tucked out of sight. Two more guns and that was it. She was more than ready for war. She stood on the roof for a few minutes just looking out over her neigh-borhood, remembering the sound of laughter. There had always been the murmur of voices and the sound of laugh-ter. Now there was just . . . silence.

Blaze sighed and made her way back down the stairs to the bar. It was a beautiful bar, all curved mahogany. Gleam-ing. Dark wood. The long mirrors and bottles and glasses stacked neatly. She was a good bartender. Fast. Efficient. Flashy. She could flip the bottles and do tricks with the best of them, and some nights her customers called for that. Her father would stand back, shaking his head and laughing, but his eyes were always alive with pride in her.

She'd nudge him out of the way with her hip, tell him, "Let me show you how it's done, old man," and perform a few outrageous tricks, getting the customers fired up. When she did that, they always had a spectacular night. It brought in crowds outside of their neighborhood, so the bar was nearly always full. They didn't lack for money. Still, the mobsters who had murdered her father weren't after the money. They wanted her home. The property. And they were never going to get it, not even after she was dead.

She caught up the phone and dialed the number on the business card, and then idly tapped the edge of the card on the surface of the bar while she waited as the phone rang. Two rings only.

"Talk to me." The voice was soft. Male. Scary beautiful. Just plain scary. Definitely *not* the same man who had come by the bar and left his card. This man had an accent she couldn't place. He sounded dangerous, like a man who didn't have to raise his voice to command a room. Like a man you never—*ever*—wanted to cross.

"I'm Blaze McGuire. Someone with this number came by a couple of weeks ago. The Hallahan brothers killed my father and they're coming for me. An envelope containing the deeds to the properties will be sent to you on my death. Tariq Asenguard and Maksim Volkov will inherit. You can deal with what's left of them after tonight."

There was a small silence and then that voice whispered into her ear. Low. Commanding. "Get. The. *Hell*. Out. Of. There. *Now*."

She froze, her fingers curling around the phone. She felt every single word resonate right through her body. He was good with that voice. Even through the phone she wanted to obey him, and she wasn't all that good at obeying anyone— not even Sean sometimes.

"Can't do that," she said softly. "I'm going to die tonight and they're going to pay. If they don't get inside, and I'm gone, be careful. The entire bar is rigged to blow. One wrong step and you're dead. In the envelope you'll receive, there is a way to disarm everything. Where you can safely step and what to avoid. How to get through the maze."

"Blaze. Get. *Out*."

He said her name as if he knew her. Intimately. As if he had the right to be worried about her. Protect her. As if she belonged to him. Blaze was a name that, to her, didn't sound feminine. He made it that way, his accent caressing the name, making it something altogether different.

Her tongue touched her upper lip. Her breath caught in her lungs. She had to fight the pull of his voice.

"You don't understand," she said softly. "And you don't need to. I have to do this. They aren't going to get away with this."

"No, sweetheart, they are not, but this is not the way to do it. Get out of there and wait for us. We are on the way."

The way his voice moved over her body, stroking like a caress, rasping like a tongue, yet still commanding, sent a chill down her spine. More than anything she wanted to obey. Not because she was afraid of dying, but because the note of command in his voice was affecting her in ways she didn't understand.

"Not going to happen," she whispered, her heart pounding. She had the feeling that he was on the move and that he was moving fast. "They killed my father."

"I know, *draga mea.*" His voice was even softer. More persuasive. Sliding into her mind so she felt warmth where there was darkness and cold. Where there was rage. Where she had to keep a hold of that rage and not allow whatever was in his voice to warm that cold. "We will handle this for you and these men will pay. Get to safety. We are on our way."

She pressed her hand hard to her heart. It was beating far too fast. Pounding. Her mouth had gone dry. Even her head hurt, as if by defying him her physical body protested. It didn't make sense to her. She'd always been her own person, able to stand up to anyone. She didn't want to talk to him anymore, but she couldn't pry her fingers loose from the phone. She just stood there, one hip to the bar because it was holding her up. Her body trembled when she hadn't been trembling faced with certain death.

"I-I . . ." She found herself stammering. All she had to do was put the phone down, but she couldn't. Her fingers were locked around it.

"You do not want your beautiful bar blown all to hell," his voice continued to whisper in her ear. "Our way is so much better. You will continue to have your property. Your home. The neighborhood will be rid of a couple more of the monsters."

So soft. So intimate. As if they were in bed together. Tangled up. Arms and legs. She could almost feel him moving in her. That intimate. And she couldn't drop the phone. She should. But she couldn't. She was mesmerized by his voice. She stared out the large window that took up nearly one entire wall. On the other side of the window were thick iron bars. She'd cried when they'd had to install them. She'd lived there most of her life in complete freedom and then someone somewhere made the decision to ruin their neighborhood.

"People are dying."

"I know, *draga mea*. We will stop them, but giving them your life is giving them another victory."

"They killed my *father*." The words broke from her. She hadn't cried. She'd refused to cry, not even when she'd told Emeline. Not until after. Not until the men who killed him were dead. "They broke him into pieces and then they killed him."

"I know, *inima mea*," he whispered.

She had no idea what language he spoke, only that he spoke it with the most intimate accent possible. She didn't dare look away from the window or she would have closed her eyes to hold his voice to her. Wishing she had known him before she was a stone inside. Before her smoldering fire had grown into a wildfire burning out of control, for vengeance.

"Let us handle this. It is what we do."

"After." She tilted her chin. Straightened her shoulders. "You handle them after." She forced her fingers to loosen their death grip on the phone. His voice was so mesmerizing, so hypnotic, she could almost believe he was a dark sorcerer, bent on controlling her through his voice alone. But she wasn't given to flights of fancy. She had been raised to deal with any issue, and the murder of her father was personal. "After," she whispered again. "You deal with them after."

"Wait, Blaze. Wait for me."

His voice. That voice. It seemed to be inside her. Inside

her head. Stroking her from the inside out. She had always relied on herself or her father. Sean had taught her that. Given her that confidence. But his voice and the way it seemed to be inside her head made her feel as if without him, she wasn't Blaze anymore. She was adrift.

"At least do that for me. Go up into the apartment. I'm about four minutes out. We can deal with them together. You go upstairs. I will come to you from the roof after we get rid of them and we will make a plan. Together."

Blaze closed her eyes and forced her numb fingers to work. She hung up. The moment she did, she felt sick. More, her head hurt. Not a little bit, but pounding, as if by hanging up, something inside her got left behind and set off little jackhammers in her skull. She pressed a hand to her knotted belly and picked up one of the guns lying on the bar. Her hand shook and that shocked her.

She had absolute resolve when it came to bringing justice to her father's murderers. Of course she was afraid. No one wanted to die. But she was confident. And utterly committed to her cause. Still, her hand shook when it never had before. That was how much his voice had shaken her.

A slow heat curled in the pit of her stomach and a small shiver went down her spine. She would have liked to have met the owner of that voice. Yet again, maybe not. She talked with men all the time, the bar separating them. She could laugh and flirt and know there was that boundary no one crossed. His voice had crossed it.

She slammed the magazine into her weapon and turned her attention toward the bar-covered window. She saw the flash of headlights as the car raced down the street toward her property, and she knew instantly it was them—the Hallahans. They had come. Her stomach settled. Adrenaline began to pump. She took a few deep breaths as the big SUV slammed onto the sidewalk and screeched to a halt. All four doors popped open and the men spilled out.

She could see them all clearly, even in the waning light, because she'd changed the lightbulbs outside the bar to illuminate the sidewalk. She'd used a high-wattage bulb, uncaring of what the electricity would cost. She wasn't going to be around to pay it. She studied them, these men—no, monsters—who had beaten her father to death. They'd broken his bones on purpose to torture him. They could have called her, but they hadn't. They enjoyed hurting him.

She didn't take her eyes from the window, watching them come up the sidewalk, moving with confidence, their big, beefy frames rolling from side to side as they moved together to approach the bar.

Everything went silent. Time tunneled, as it often did when a fight was close. Her attention focused on the door. She became aware of her heart beating. Each separate beat. Each pulse. The ebb and flow of her blood as it rushed through her veins. Everything around her went still. Utterly still. She didn't hear insects. She didn't hear traffic. There were no solid footsteps as the men with their steel-toed boots came closer. There was only Blaze and the gun in her hand.

Her hand was rock steady now and she took a slow breath, watching the window, keeping an eye on the door handle of the bar. If they touched that, if they opened the door, it would set off the charge.

Without warning, the Hallahans backed up, moving toward their car, all four of them. Blaze took a step forward, her body hitting the bar. She shook her head. They couldn't leave. She moved quickly around the bar and stopped dead, looking at the web of wiring. The entire room was a trap. She would have to spend an hour dismantling everything. What had tipped them off? They hadn't even gotten close to the entrance. Damn. Damn. *Damn.*

The sisters of Sea Haven are bound by the heart and the magical power of the elements.

FROM #1 *NEW YORK TIMES* BESTSELLING AUTHOR

CHRISTINE FEEHAN

THE SEA HAVEN NOVELS

In the swirling tides of the ocean, she found a handsome stranger...

WATER BOUND

She was the obsession of two men...

SPIRIT BOUND

Her only choice was to trust him...

AIR BOUND

PRAISE FOR CHRISTINE FEEHAN'S SEA HAVEN NOVELS

"The queen of paranormal romance."
—*USA Today*

"Characters as heartwarmingly interesting as those in her Drake Sisters novels and as steamy as those in her Dark novels."
—*Fresh Fiction*

christinefeehan.com
facebook.com/christinefeehanauthor
penguin.com

M1425AS0114